William Enfield

The speaker
Miscellaneous pieces selected from the best English writers

ISBN/EAN: 9783337278304

Printed in Europe, USA, Canada, Australia, Japan

Cover: Foto ©Andreas Hilbeck / pixelio.de

More available books at **www.hansebooks.com**

William Enfield

The speaker

Miscellaneous pieces selected from the best English writers

THE SPEAKER:

OR,

MISCELLANEOUS PIECES,

SELECTED FROM THE

BEST ENGLISH WRITERS,

AND DISPOSED UNDER PROPER HEADS,

WITH A VIEW TO FACILITATE

THE IMPROVEMENT OF YOUTH

IN

READING AND SPEAKING.

TO WHICH IS PREFIXED,

AN ESSAY ON ELOCUTION.

By WILLIAM ENFIELD, L. L. D.

LECTURER ON THE BELLES LETTRES IN
THE ACADEMY AT WARRINGTON.

THE FOURTH EDITION.

——Oculos, paulum tellure moratos
Suftulit ad proceres, expectato querefolvit
Ora. fono; nec abeft facundis *gratia* dictis.

OVID.

DUBLIN:

PRINTED BY JAMES WILLIAMS, NO. 21, SKINNER-ROW,
MDCCLXXXI.

SIR,

THIS work having been undertaken principally with the defign of affifting the Students at *Warrington* in acquiring a juft and graceful Elocution, I feel a peculiar propriety in addreffing it to you, as a public acknowledgment of the fteady fupport which you have given to this Inftitution, and the important fervices which you have rendered it.

IN this Seminary, which was at firft eftablifhed, and has been uniformly conducted, on the extenfive plan of providing a proper courfe of Inftruction for young men in the moft ufeful branches of Science and Literature, you have feen many refpectable characters formed, who are now filling up their ftations in fociety with reputation to themfelves and advantage to the Public. And, while the fame great object continues to be purfued, by faithful endeavours to

A   cultivate

cultivate the underſtanding of youth, and
by a ſteady attention to diſcipline, it is hop-
ed, that you will have the ſatisfaction to obſerve the ſame effects produced, and that the
ſcene will be realized, which OUR POETESS
has ſo beautifully deſcribed:

When this, this little group their country calls
From academic ſhades and learned halls,
To fix her laws, her ſpirit to ſuſtain,
And light up glory thro' her wide domain;
Their various taſtes in different arts diſplay'd,
Like temper'd harmony of light and ſhade,
With friendly union in one maſs ſhall blend,
And this adorn the ſtate, and that defend.

    I am,

        With ſincere Reſpect and Gratitude,

        DEAR SIR,

            Your much obliged,

                and moſt humble Servant,

Warrington Academy,   **WILLIAM ENFIELD.**
October 1ſt, 1774.

E S S A Y

O N

E L O C U T I O N.

MUCH declamation has been employed to convince the world of a very plain truth, that to be able to fpeak well is an ornamental and ufeful accomplifhment. Without the laboured panegyrics of antient or modern orators, the importance of a good elocution is fufficiently obvious. Every one will acknowledge it to be of fome confe-quence, that what a man has hourly occafion to do, fhould be done well. Every private company, and almoft every public affembly affords opportunities of remarking the difference between a juft and graceful, and a faulty and unnatural elocution; and there are few perfons who do not daily experience the advantages of the former, and the inconveniences of the latter. The great difficulty is, not to prove that it is a defirable thing to be able to read and fpeak with propriety, but to point out a practicable and eafy method by which this accomplifhment may be acquired.

FOLLOW

FOLLOW NATURE, is certainly the fundamental law of Oratory, without a regard to which, all other rules will only produce affected declamation, not juſt elocution. And ſome accurate obſervers, judging, perhaps, from a few unlucky ſpecimens of modern eloquence, have concluded that this is the only law which ought to be preſcribed; that all artificial rules are uſeleſs; and that good ſenſe, and a cultivated taſte, are the only requiſites to form a good public ſpeaker. But it is true in the art of ſpeaking, as well as in the art of living, that general precepts are of little uſe till they are unfolded, and applied to particular caſes. To obſerve the various ways by which nature expreſſes the ſeveral perceptions, emotions and paſſions of the human mind, and to diſtinguiſh theſe from the mere effect of arbitrary cuſtom or falſe taſte; to diſcover and correct thoſe tones, and habits of ſpeaking, which are groſs deviations from nature, and as far as they prevail muſt deſtroy all propriety and grace of utterance; and to make choice of ſuch a courſe of practical leſſons, as ſhall give the Speaker an opportunity of exerciſing himſelf in each breach of elocution; all this muſt be the effect of attention and labour; and in all this much aſſiſtance may certainly be derived from inſtruction. What are rules or leſſons for acquiring this or any other art, but the obſervations of others, collected into a narrow compaſs, and digeſted in a natural order, for the direction of the unexperienced and unpractiſed learner? And what is there in the art of ſpeaking, which ſhould render it incapable of receiving aid from precepts?

PRESUMING then, that the acquiſition of the art of ſpeaking, like all other practical arts, may be facilitated by rules, I proceed to lay before my readers, in a plain didactic form, ſuch Rules reſpecting elocution, as appear beſt adapted to form a correct and graceful Speaker.

RURE

RULE I.

Let your Articulation be diſtinct and deliberate.

A GOOD Articulation confiſts in giving a clear and full utterance to the ſeveral ſimple and complex ſounds. The nature of theſe ſounds, therefore, ought to be well underſtood; and much pains ſhould be taken to diſcover and correct thoſe faults in articulation, which, though often aſcribed to ſome defect in the organs of ſpeech, are generally the conſequence of inattention or bad example. Many of theſe reſpect the founding of the conſonants. Some cannot pronounce the letter *l*, and others the ſimple ſounds *r, s, th, ſh*; others generally omit the aſpirate *h*. Theſe faults may be corrected, by reading ſentences, ſo contrived as often to repeat the faulty ſounds; and by guarding againſt them in familiar converſation.

OTHER defects in articulation regard the complex ſounds, and conſiſt in a confuſed and cluttering pronunciation of words. The moſt effectual methods of conquering this habit, are, to read aloud paſſages choſen for the purpoſe (ſuch for inſtance as abounds with long and unuſual words, or in which many ſhort ſyllables come together) and to read, at certain ſtated times, much ſlower than the ſenſe and juſt ſpeaking would require. Almoſt all perſons, who have not ſtudied the art of ſpeaking, have a habit of uttering their words ſo rapidly, that this latter exerciſe ought generally to be made uſe of for a conſiderable time at firſt: for where there is a uniformly rapid utterance, it is abſolutely impoſſible that there ſhould be ſtrong emphaſis, natural tones, or any juſt elocution.

AIM at nothing higher, till you can read diſtinctly and deliberately.

A 3

Lᴇᴀʀɴ to fpeak flow, all other graces
Will follow in their proper places.

R U L E   II.

Let your pronunciation be bold and forcible.

AN infipid flatnefs and languor is almoft the univerfal fault in reading; and even public fpeakers often fuffer their words to drop from their lips
with fuch a faint and feeble utterance, that they appear neither to underftand or feel what they fay
themfelves, nor to have any defire that it fhould be
underftood or felt by their audience.   This is a fundamental fault: a fpeaker without energy, is a lifelefs ftatue.

Iɴ order to acquire a forcible manner of pronouncing your words, inure yourfelf while reading to draw
in as much air as your lungs can contain with eafe,
and to expel it with vehemence, in uttering thofe
founds which require an emphatical pronunciation;
read aloud in the open air, and with all the exertion
you can command; preferve your body in an erect
attitude while you are fpeaking; let all the confo-
nant founds be expreffed with a full impulfe or per-
cuffion of the breath, and a forcible action of the
organs employed in forming them; and let all the
vowel founds have a full and bold utterance. Practife thefe rules with perfeverance, till you have acquired ftrength and energy of fpeech.

Bᴜᴛ in obferving this rule, beware of running into the extreme of vociferation. We find this fault
chiefly among thofe, who, in contempt and defpite
of all rule and propriety, are determined to command
the attention of the vulgar. Thefe are the fpeakers,
who, in Shakefpear's phrafe, " offend the judicious
hearer to the foul, by tearing a paffion to rags, to
                                                very

very tatters, to split the ears of the groundlings."
Cicero compares such speakers to cripples who get
on horse-back because they cannot walk: they bel-
low, because they cannot speak.

R U L E III.

*Acquire a compass and variety in the height of your
voice.*

THE monotony so much complained of in public speakers, is chiefly owing to the neglect of
this rule. They generally content themselves with
one certain key, which they employ on all occasions,
and on every subject: or if they attempt variety, it
is only in proportion to the number of their hearers,
and the extent of the places in which they speak;
imagining, that speaking in a high key is the same
thing as speaking loud; and not observing, that
whether a speaker shall be heard or not, depends
more upon the distinctness and force with which he
utters his words, than upon the height at which he
pitches his voice.

But it is an essential qualification of a good
speaker, to be able to alter the height, as well as
the strength and the tone of his voice, as occasion
requires. Different species of speaking require different heights of voice. Nature instructs us to relate
a story, to support an argument, to command a servant, to utter exclamations of anger or rage, and to
pour forth lamentations and sorrows, not only with
different tones, but different elevations of voice.
Men at different ages of life, and in different situati-
ons, speak in very different keys. The vagrant
when he begs; the soldier, when he gives the word
of command; the watchman, when he announces
the hour of the night; the sovereign, when he issues
his edict; the senator, when he harangues; the
lover, when he whispers his tender tale; do not dif-

fer

fer more in the tones which they ufe, than in the key
in which they fpeak. Reading and fpeaking, therefore, in which all the variations of expreffion in real
life are copied, muft have continual variations in the
height of the voice.

To acquire the power of changing the key on
which you fpeak at pleafure, accuftom yourfelf to
pitch your voice in different keys, from the loweft
to the higheft notes you can command. Many of
thefe would neither be proper nor agreeable in fpeaking; but the exercife will give you fuch a command
of voice, as is fcarcely to be acquired by any other
method. Having repeated this experiment till you
can fpeak with eafe at feveral heights of the voice;
read, as exercifes on this rule, fuch compofitions as
have a variety of fpeakers, or fuch as relate dia-
logues, obferving the height of voice which is proper to each, and endeavouring to change them as
nature directs.

In the fame compofition there may be frequent occafion to alter the height of the voice, in paffing
from one part to another, without any change of
perfon. Shakefpear's " All the world's a ftage," &c.
and his defcription of the Queen of the Fairies, afford examples of this. Indeed every fentence which
is read or fpoken will admit of different elevations of
the voice in different parts of it; and on this chiefly,
perhaps entirely, depends the *melody* of pronunciation.

R U L E   IV.

Pronounce your words with propriety and elegance.

IT is not eafy indeed to fix upon any ftandard, by
which the propriety of pronunciation is to be determined. Mere men of learning, in attempting to
make the etymology of words the rule of pronunciation,

ation, often pronounce words in a manner, which brings upon them the charge of affectation and pedantry. Mere men of the world, notwithstanding all their politenefs, often retain fo much of their provincial dialect, or commit fuch errors both in fpeaking and writing, as to exclude them from the honour of being the ftandard of accurate pronunciation. We fhould perhaps look for this ftandard only among thofe who unite' thefe two characters, and with the correctnefs and precifion of true learning combine the eafe and elegance of genteel life. An attention to fuch models, and a free intercourfe with the polite world, are the beft guards againft the peculiarities and vulgarifms of provincial dialects. Thofe which refpect the pronunciation of words are innumerable. Some of the principal of them are; omitting the afpirate *h* where it ought to be ufed, and inferting it where there fhould be none; confounding and interchanging the *v* and *w*; pronouncing the diphthong *ou* like *au* or like *oo*, and the vowel *i* like *oi* or *e*; and cluttering many confonants together without regarding the vowels. Thefe faults, and all others of the fame nature, muft be corrected in the pronunciation of a gentleman, who is fuppofed to have feen too much of the world, to retain the peculiarities of the diftrict in which he was born.

R U L E   V.

Pronounce every word confifting of more than one fylla-
ble with its proper ACCENT.

THERE is a neceffity for this direction, becaufe many fpeakers have affected an unufual and pedantic mode of accenting words, laying it down as a rule, that the accent fhould be caft as far backwards as poffible; a rule which has no foundation in the conftruction of the Englifh language, or in the laws of harmony. In accenting words, the general cuftom and a good ear are the beft guides:

A 5

only

only it may be obferved that accent fhould be regu-
lated, not by any arbitrary rules of quantity, or by
the falfe idea that there are only two lengths in fyllables, and that two fhort fyllables are always e-
qual to one long, but by the number and nature of
the fimple founds.

RULE VI.

*In every fentence, diftinguifh the more fignificant words
by a natural, forcible, and varied* EMPHASIS.

EMPHASIS points out the precife meaning of a
fentence, fhows in what manner one idea is connected with, and rifes out of another, marks the feveral claufes of a fentence, gives to every part its
proper found, and thus conveys to the mind of the
reader the full import of the whole. It is in the
power of emphafis to make long and complex fentences appear intelligible and perfpicuous. But for this
purpofe it is neceffary, that the reader fhould be perfectly acquainted with the exact conftruction and
full meaning of every fentence which he recites.
Without this it is impoffible to give thofe inflexions
and variations to the voice, which nature requires:
and it is for want of this previous ftudy, more perhaps than from any other caufe, that we fo often
hear perfons read with an improper emphafis, or
with no emphafis at all, that is, with a ftupid monotony. Much ftudy and pains are neceffary in acquiring the habit of juft and forcible pronunciation;
and it can only be the effect of clofe attention and
long practice, to be able, with a mere glance of the
eye, to read any piece with *good emphafis and good
difcretion.*

It is another office of Emphafis to exprefs the oppofition between the feveral parts of a fentence
where the ftyle is pointed and antithetical. Pope's
Effay on Man, and his Moral Effays, and the Pro-
verbs

verbs of Solomon, will furnifh many proper exercifes in this fpecies of fpeaking. In fome fentences the antithefis is double, and even treble; thefe muft be expreffed in reading, by a very diftinct emphafis on each part of the oppofition. The following inftances are of this kind:

ANGER may glance into the breaft of a wife man; but refts only in the bofom of fools.

AN angry man who fuppreffes his paffion, thinks worfe than he fpeaks; and an angry man that will chide, fpeaks worfe than he thinks.

BETTER to reign in hell, than ferve in heaven.

HE rais'd a mortal to the fkies;
She brought an angel down.

EMPHASIS likewife ferves to exprefs fome particular meaning not immediately arifing from the words, but depending upon the intention of the fpeaker, or fome incidental circumftance. The following fhort fentence may have three different meanings, according to the different place of the Emphafis: Do *you* intend to go to *London, this fummer?*

IN order to acquire a habit of fpeaking with a juft, and forcible emphafis, nothing more is neceffary than previoufly to ftudy the conftruction, meaning, and fpirit of every fentence, and to adhere as nearly as poffible to the manner in which we diftinguifh one word from another in converfation; for in familiar difcourfe we fcarcely ever fail to exprefs ourfelves emphatically, or place the emphafis improperly. With refpect to artificial helps, fuch as diftinguifhing words or claufes of fentences by particular characters or marks; I believe it will always be found, upon trial, that they miflead inftead of affifting the reader, by not leaving him at full liberty to follow his own underftanding and feelings

THE

THE most common faults respecting emphasis are, laying so strong an emphasis on one word as to leave no power of giving a particular force to other words, which, though not equally, are in a certain degree emphatical; and placing the greatest stress on conjunctive particles, and other words of secondary importance. These faults are strongly characterised in Churchill's censure of Mossop.

> With studied improprieties of speech
> He soars beyond the hackney critic's reach,
> To epithets allots emphatic state,
> Whilst principals, ungrac'd, like lacquies wait;
> In ways first trodden by himself excels,
> And stands alone in indeclinables;
> Conjunction, preposition, adverb, join
> To stamp new vigour on the nervous line.
> In monosyllables his thunders roll,
> HE, SHE, IT, AND, WE, YE; THEY, fright the soul.

EMPHASIS is often destroyed by an injudicious attempt to read melodiously. Agreeable inflexions and easy variations of the voice, as far as they arise from, or are consistent with just speaking, are worthy of attention. But to substitute one unmeaning tune, in the room of all the proprieties and graces of good elocution, and then to applaud this manner, under the appellation of *musical* speaking, can only be the effect of great ignorance and inattention, or of a depraved taste. If public speaking must be musical, let the words be set to music in recitative, that these melodious speakers may no longer lie open to the sarcasm; *Do you read or sing? if you sing, you sing very ill.* Seriously, it is much to be wondered at, that this kind of reading, which has so little merit considered as music, and none at all considered as speaking, should be so studiously practised by many speakers, and so much admired by many hearers. Can a method of reading, which is so entirely different from the usual manner of conversation, be natural and right? Is it possible that all the varieties

of

of sentiment which a public speaker has occasion to introduce, should be properly expressed by one melodious tone and cadence, employed alike on all occasions and for all purposes?

R U L E   VII.

Acquire a just variety of Pause and Cadence.

ONE of the worst faults a speaker can have, is to make no other pauses than what he finds barely necessary for breathing. I know of nothing that such a speaker can so properly be compared to, as an alarum-bell, which, when once set a-going, clatters on till the weight that moves it, is run down. Without pauses, the sense must always appear confused and obscure, and often be misunderstood; and the spirit and energy of the piece must be wholly lost.

In executing this part of the office of a speaker, it will by no means be sufficient to attend to the points used in printing; for these are far from marking all the pauses which ought to be made in speaking. A mechanical attention to these resting places has perhaps been one chief cause of monotony, by leading the reader to a uniform cadence at every full period. The use of points is to assist the reader in discerning the grammatical construction, not to direct his pronunciation. In reading, it may often be proper to make a pause where the printer has made none. Nay, it is very allowable for the sake of pointing out the sense more strongly, preparing the audience for what is to follow, or enabling the speaker to alter the tone or height of the voice, sometimes to make a very considerable pause, where the grammatical construction requires none at all. In doing this, however, it is necessary that in the word immediately preceding the pause, the voice be kept up in such a manner as to intimate to the

hearer

hearer that the sense is not compleated. Mr. GAR-RICK, the first of speakers, often observes this rule, with great success. This particular excellence Mr. Sterne has described in his usual sprightly manner. See the following Work, Book VI. Chap. III.

BEFORE a full pause it has been customary in reading to drop the voice in a uniform manner ; and this has been called the *cadence*. But surely nothing can be more destructive of all propriety and energy than this habit. The tones and heights at the close of a sentence ought to be infinitely diversified, according to the general nature of the discourse, and the particular construction and meaning of the sentence. In plain narrative,. and especially in argumentation, the least attention to the manner in which we relate a story, or support an argument in conversation will show, that it is more frequently proper to raise the voice than to fall it at the end of a sentence. Interrogatives, where the speaker seems to expect an answer, should almost always be elevated at the close, with a particular tone, to indicate that a question is asked. Some sentences are so constructed, that the last words require a stronger emphasis than any of the preceding ; while others admit of being closed with a soft and gentle sound. Where there is nothing in the sense which requires the last found to be elevated or emphatical, an easy fall, sufficient to show that the sense is finished, will be proper. And in pathetic pieces, especially those of the plaintive, tender or solemn kind, the tone of the passion will often require a still greater cadence of the voice. But before a speaker can be able to fall his voice with propriety and judgment at the close of a sentence, he must be able to keep it from falling, and to rise it with all the variation which the sense requires. The best method of correcting a uniform cadence is frequently to read *select sentences*, in which the style is pointed and frequent *antitheses* are introduced, and argumentative pieces, or such as abound with interrogatives.

R U L E   VIIII.

Accompany the Emotions and Passions which your words express, by correspondent tones, looks, and gestures.

THERE is the language of emotions and passi-ons, as well as of ideas. To express the for-mer is the peculiar province of words ; to express the latter, nature teaches us to make use of tones, looks, and gestures. When anger, fear, joy, grief, love, or any other active passion arises in our minds, we naturally discover it by the particular manner in which we utter our words ; by the features of the countenance, and by other well known signs. And even when we speak without any of the more violent emotions, some kind of feeling usually accompanies our words, and this, whatever it be, hath its proper external expression. Expression indeed hath been so little studied in public speaking, that we seem almost to have forgotten the language of nature, and are ready to consider every attempt to recover it, as the laboured and affected effort of art. But nature is al-ways the same ; and every judicious imitation of it will always be pleasing. Nor can any one deserve the appellation of a good speaker, much less of a complete orator, till to distinct articulation, a good command of voice, and just emphasis, he is able to add the various expressions of emotion and passion.

To enumerate these expressions, and describe them in all their variations, is impracticable. Attempts have been made with some success to analize the language of ideas ; but the language of sentiment and emotion has never yet been analized ; and per-haps it is not within the reach of human ability, to write a Philosophical Grammar of the passions. Or, if it were possible in any degree to execute this de-sign, I cannot think, that from such a grammar it

would

would be poffible for any one to inftruct himfelf in the ufe of the language. All endeavours therefore to make men Orators by defcribing to them in words the manner in which their voice, countenance, and hands are to be employed, in expreffing the paffions, muft, in my apprehenfion, be weak and ineffectual. And, perhaps, the only inftruction which can be given with advantage on this head, is this general one : Obferve what manner the feveral emotions or paffions are expreffed in real life, or by thofe who have with great labour and tafte acquired a power of imitating nature ; and accuftom yourfelf either to follow the great original itfelf, or the beft copies you meet with, always however, "with this fpecial obfervance, that you o'erstep not the modesty of nature".

In the application of thefe rules to practice, in order to acquire a juft and graceful elocution, it will be neceffary to go through a regular courfe of exercifes ; beginning with fuch as are moft eafy, and proceeding by flow fteps to fuch as are moft difficult. In the choice of thefe, the practitioner fhould pay a particular attention to his prevailing defects, whether they regard articulation, command of voice, emphafis, or cadence : and he fhould content himfelf with reading and fpeaking with an immediate view to the correcting of his fundamental faults, before he aims at any thing higher. This may be irkfome and difagreeable ; it may require much patience and refolution; but it is the only way to fucceed. For if a man cannot read fimple fentences, or plain narrative or didactic pieces, with diftinct articulation, juft emphafis, and proper tones, how can he expect to do juftice to the fublime defcriptions of poetry, or the animated language of the paffions ?

In performing thefe exercifes, the learner fhould daily read aloud by himfelf, and as often as he has opportunity, under the correction of an inftructor

or friend. He fhould alfo frequently recite compofitions *memoriter*. This method has feveral advantages : it obliges the fpeaker, to dwell upon the
ideas which he is to exprefs, and hereby enables him
to difcern their particular meaning and force, and
gives him a previous knowledge of the feveral inflexions, *emphafes*, and tones which the words require. And by taking off his eye from the book, it
in part relieves him from the influence of the fchool-
boy habit of reading in a different key and tone from
that of converfation ; and gives him greater liberty
to attempt the expreffion of the countenance and
gefture.

I⊤ were much to be wifhed, that all public fpeakers would deliver their thoughts and fentiments,
either from memory or immediate conception : for,
befides that there is an artificial uniformity which almoft always diftinguifhes reading from fpeaking, the
fixed pofture, and the bending of the head which
reading requires, are inconfiftent with the freedom,
eafe, and variety of juft elocution. But, if this is
too much to be expected, efpecially from Preachers,
who have fo much to compofe, and are fo often
called upon to fpeak in public ; it is however extremely defirable, that they fhould make themfelves
fo well acquainted with their difcourfe as to be able
with a fingle glance of the eye, to take in feveral
claufes, or the whole, of a fentence. *

I ʜᴀᴠᴇ only to add, that after the utmoft pains
have been taken to acquire a juft elocution, and this
with the greateft fuccefs ; there is fome difficulty in
carrying the art of fpeaking out of the fchool, or
chamber, to the bar, the fenate, or the pulpit. A
young man, who has been accuftomed to perform
frequent exercifes in this art in private, cannot eafily
perfuade himfelf, when he appears before the public,

* See Dean Swift's advice on this head in his Letter to a
young Clergyman.

lic, to confider the bufinefs he has to perform in any other light, than as a trial of fkill, and a difplay of oratory. Hence it is, that the character of an Orator has of late often been treated with ridicule, fometimes with contempt. We are pleafed with the eafy and graceful movements which the true gentleman has acquired by having learned to dance ; but we are offended by the coxcomb, who is always exhibiting his formal dancing-bow, and minuet-ftep. So, we admire the manly eloquence and noble ardour of a British Legiflator, rifing up in defence of the rights of his country ; the quick recollection, the forcible reafoning, and the ready utterance of the accomplifhed Barrifter; and the fublime devotion, genuine dignity, and unaffected earneftnefs of the facred Orator : but when a man in either of thefe capacities, fo far forgets the ends and degrades the confequence of his profeffion, as to fet himfelf forth to public view under the character of a Spouter, and to parade it in the ears of the vulgar with all the pomp of artificial eloquence, though the unfkilful may gaze and applaud, the judicious cannot but be grieved and difgufted. Avail yourfelf, then, of your fkill in the Art of Speaking, but always employ your powers of elocution with caution and modefty ; remembering, that though it be defirable to be admired as an eminent Orator, it is of much more importance to be refpected, as a wife Statefman, an able Lawyer, or a ufeful Preacher.

THE CONTENTS.

BOOK I.

SELECT SENTENCES.

Page 1 to 16,

BOOK II.

NARRATIVE PIECES.

BOOK III.

DIDACTIC PIECES.

B O O K   IV.

ARGUMENTATIVE PIECES.

B O O K   V.

ORATIONS and HARANGUES.

B O O K   VI.

D I A L O G U E S.

BOOK VII.

BOOK

B O O K VIII.

PATHETIC PIECES.

B O O K

B O O K I.

SELECT SENTENCES.

C H A P. I.

TO be ever active in laudable purfuits, is the diftinguifhing characteriftic of a man of merit.

THERE is an heroic innocence, as well as an heroic courage.

THERE is a mean in all things. Even virtue it-felf hath its ftated limits; which not being ftrictly obferved, ceafes to be virtue.

IT is wifer to prevent a quarrel before hand, than to revenge it afterwards.

IT is much better to reprove, than to be angry fecretly.

No revenge is more heroic, than that which tor-ments envy by doing good.

THE defcretion of a man deferreth his anger, and it is his glory to pafs over a tranfgreffion.

MONEY, like manure, does no good till it is fpread. There is no real ufe of riches, except in the diftribution; the reft is all conceit.

A WISE man will defire no more than what he may get juftly, ufe foberly, diftribute chearfully, and live upon contentedly.

A CONTENTED mind, and a good confcience, will make a man happy in all conditions. He knows not how to fear, who dares to die.

B

THERE

THERE is but one way of fortifying the foul againſt all gloomy preſages and terrors of mind ; and that is, by ſecuring to ourſelves the friendſhip and protection of that Being who difpofes of events, and governs futurity.

PHILOSOPHY is then only valuable, when it ſerves for the law of life, and not for the oſtentation of ſcience.

C H A P. II.

WITHOUT a friend the world is but a wilder-neſs.

A MAN may have a thouſand intimate acquaintances, and not a friend among them all. If you have one friend think yourſelf happy.

WHEN once you profeſs yourſelf a friend, endeavour to be always ſuch. He can never have any true friends, that will be often changing them.

PROSPERITY gains friends, and adverſity tries them.

NOTHING more engages the affection of men, than a handſome addreſs, and graceful converſation.

COMPLAISANCE renders a ſuperior amiable, an equal agreeable, and an inferior acceptable.

EXCESS of ceremony ſhews want of breeding. That civility is beſt, which excludes all ſuperfluous formality.

INGRATITUDE is a crime ſo ſhameful, that the man was never yet found, who would acknowledge himſelf guilty of it.

TRUTH is born with us; and we muſt do violence to nature, to ſhake off our veracity.

THERE cannot be a greater treachery, than firſt to raiſe a confidence, and then deceive it.

BY others faults, wiſe men correct their own.

No man hath a thorough taſte of profperity, to whom adverſity never happened.

WHEN

When our vices leave us, we flatter ourselves that we leave them.

It is as great point of wisdom to hide ignorance, as to discover knowledge.

Pitch upon that course of life which is the most excellent; and habit will render it the most delightful.

C H A P.   III.

CUSTOM is the plague of wise men, and the idol of fools.

As to be perfectly just, is an attribute of the divine nature ; to be so to the utmost of our abilities, is the glory of man.

No man was ever cast down with the injuries of fortune, unless he had before suffered himself to be deceived by her favours.

Anger may glance in the breast of a wise man, but rests only in the bosom of fools.

None more impatiently suffer injuries, than those that are most forward in doing them.

By taking revenge, a man is but even with his enemy ; but in passing it over, he is superior.

To err is human ; to forgive, divine.

A more glorious victory cannot be gained over another man, than this, that when the injury began on his part, the kindness should begin on ours.

The prodigal robs his heir, the miser robs himself.

We should take a prudent care for the future, but so as to enjoy the present. It is no part of wisdom, to be miserable to-day, because we may happen to be so to-morrow.

To mourn without measure is folly; not to mourn at all, insensibility.

Some would be thought to do great things, who are but tools and instruments ; like the fool who fancied he played upon the organ, when he only blew the bellows.

THOUGH a man may become learned by another's learning, he can never be wife but by his own wifdom.

HE who wants good fenfe is unhappy in having learning ; for he has thereby more ways of expofing himfelf.

IT is ungenerous to give a man occafion to blufh at his own ignorance, in one thing, who perhaps may excel us in many.

No object is more pleafing to the eye, than the fight of the man whom you have obliged ; nor any mufic fo agreeable to the ear, as the voice of one that owns you for his benefactor.

THE coin that is moft current among mankind is flattery ; the only benefit of which is, that by hearing what we are not, we may be inftructed what we ought to be.

THE character of the perfon who commends you, is to be confidered before you fet a value on his efteem. The wife man applauds him whom he thinks moft virtuous, the reft of the world him who is moft wealthy.

THE temperate man's pleafures are durable, becaufe they are regular ; and all his life is calm and ferene, becaufe it is innocent.

A GOOD man will love himfelf too well to lofe, and his neighbour too well to win, an eftate by gaming. The love of gaming will corrupt the beft principles in the world.

C H A P. IV.

AN angry man who fuppreffes his paffions, thinks worfe than he fpeaks : and an angry man that will chide, fpeaks worfe than he thinks.

A GOOD word is an eafy obligation ; but not to fpeak ill requires only our filence, which cofts us nothing.

IT is to affectation the world owes its whole race of coxcombs. Nature in her whole drama never

drew

drew such a part; she has sometimes made a fool, but a coxcomb is always of his own making.

It is the infirmity of little minds, to be taken with every appearance, and dazzled with every thing that sparkles; but great minds have but little admiration, because few things appear new to them.

It happens to men of learning, as to ears of corn; they shoot up, and raise their heads high, while they are empty; but when full, and swelled with grain, they begin to flag and droop.

He that is truly politic knows how to contradict with respect, and to please without adulation; and is equally remote from an insipid complaisance, and a low familiarity.

The failings of good men are commonly more published in the world than their good deeds; and one fault of a deserving man, shall meet with more reproaches, than all his virtues, praise: such is the force of ill-will, and ill-nature.

It is harder to avoid censure, than to gain applause; for this may be done by one great or wise action in an age; but to escape censure, a man must pass his whole life without saying or doing one ill or foolish thing.

When Darius offered Alexander ten thousand talents to divide Asia equally with him, he answered, the earth cannot bear two suns, nor Asia two kings. Parmenio, a friend to Alexander, hearing the great offers Darius had made, said, were I Alexander I would accept them. So would I, replied Alexander, were I Parmenio.

Nobility is to be considered only as an imaginary distinction, unless accompanied with the practice of those generous virtues by which it ought to be obtained. Titles of honour conferred upon such as have no personal merit, are at best but the royal stamp set upon base metal.

Though an honourable title may be conveyed to posterity, yet the ennobling qualities, which are the

foul

foul of greatnefs, are a fort of incommunicable perfections, and cannot be transferred. If a man could
bequeath his virtues by will, and fettle his fenfe and
learning upon his heirs, as certainly as he can his
lands, a noble defcent would then indeed be a valuable privilege.

Truth is always confiftent with itfelf, and needs
nothing to help it out. It is always near at hand,
and fits upon our lips, and is ready to drop out before
we are aware: whereas a lie is troublefome, and
fets a man's invention upon the rack; and one trick
needs a great many more to make it good.

The pleafure which affects the human mind with
the moft lively and tranfporting touches, is the fenfe
that we act in the eye of infinite wifdom, power,
and goodnefs, that will crown our virtuous endeavours here with a happinefs hereafter, large as our
defires, and lafting as our immortal fouls; without
this the higheft ftate of life is infipid, and with it
the loweft is a paradife.

C H A P. V.

HONOURABLE age is not that which ftandeth
in length of time, nor that is meafured by
number of years; but wifdom is the grey hair unto
man, and unfpotted life is old age.

Wickedness, condemned by her own witnefs,
is very timorous, and being preffed with confcience,
always forecafteth evil things; for fear is nothing
elfe, but a betraying of the fuccours which reafon
offereth.

A wise man will fear in every thing. He that
contemneth fmall things fhall fall by little and little.

A rich man beginning to fall is held up of his
friends; but a poor man being down is thruft away
by his friends: when a rich man is fallen he hath
many helpers; he fpeaketh things not to be fpoken,
and yet men juftify him; the poor man flipt and
they rebuked him; he fpoke wifely, and could have
no

no place. When a rich man speaketh, every man holdeth his tongue, and, look, what he saith they extol it to the clouds; but if a poor man speak, they say, what fellow is this?

MANY have fallen by the edge of the sword, but not so many as have fallen by the tongue. Well is he that is defended from it, and hath not passed through the venom thereof; who hath not drawn the yoke thereof, nor been bound in her bonds; for the yoke thereof is a yoke of iron, and the bands thereof are bands of brass; the death thereof is an evil death.

MY son, blemish not thy good deeds, neither use uncomfortable words, when thou givest any thing. Shall not the dew assuage the heat? so is a word better than a gift. Lo, is not a word better than a gift? but both are with a gracious man.

BLAME not, before thou hast examined the truth; understand first, and then rebuke.

IF thou wouldest get a friend, prove him first, and be not hasty to credit him; for some men are friends for their own occasions, and will not abide in the day of thy trouble.

FORSAKE not an old friend, for the new is not comparable to him: a new friend is as new wine; when it is old thou shalt drink it with pleasure.

A FRIEND cannot be known in prosperity; and an enemy cannot be hidden in adversity.

ADMONISH thy friend; it may be, he hath not done it; and if he have, that he do it no more. Admonish thy friend; it may be, he hath not said it, or if he have, that he speak it not again. Admonish a friend; for many times it is a slander; and believe not every tale. There is one that slippeth in his speech, but not from his heart; and who is he that hath not offended with his tongue?

WHOSO discovereth secrets loseth his credit, and shall never find a friend to his mind.

HONOUR thy father with thy whole heart, and
B 4

forget

forget not the forrows of thy mother: how canſt thou recompenſe them the things that they have done for thee?

THERE is nothing ſo much worth as a mind well inſtructed.

THE lips of talkers will be telling ſuch things as pertain not to them; but the words of ſuch as have underſtanding are weighed in the ballance. The heart of fools is in their mouth, but the tongue of the wiſe is in their heart.

To labour, and to be content with that a man hath, is a ſweet life.

BE in peace with many; neverthelefs, have but one counſellor of a thouſand.

BE not confident in a plain way.

LET reaſon go before every enterprize, and counſel before every action.

C H A P.   VI.

THE latter part of a wiſe man's life is taking up in curing the follies, prejudices, and falſe opinions he had contracted in the former.

CENSURE is the tax a man pays to the public for being eminent.

VERY few men properly ſpeaking live at preſent, but are providing to live another time.

PARTY is the madneſs of many, for the gain of a few.

To endeavour to work upon the vulgar with fine ſenſe, is like attempting to hew blocks of marble with a razor.

SUPERSTITION is the ſpleen of the ſoul.

HE who tells a lie is not ſenſible how great a taſk he undertakes; for he muſt be forced to invent twenty more to maintain that one.

SOME people will never learn any thing, for this reaſon, becauſe they underſtand every thing too ſoon.

THERE is nothing wanting to make all rational and difintereſted people in the world of one religion, but that they ſhould talk together every day.

MEN

MEN are grateful, in the fame degree that they are refentful.

YOUNG men are fubtle arguers ; the cloak of honour covers all their faults, as that of paffion, all their follies.

OECONOMY is no difgrace ; it is better living on a little, than out-living a great deal.

NEXT to the fatisfaction I receive in the profperity of an honeft man, I am beft pleafed with the confufion of a rafcal.

WHAT is often termed fhynefs, is nothing more than refined fenfe, and an indifference to common obfervations.

THE higher character a perfon fupports, the more he fhould regard his minuteft actions.

EVERY perfon infenfibly fixes upon fome degree of refinement in his difcourfe, fome meafure of thought which he thinks worth exhibiting. It is wife to fix this pretty high, although it occafions one to talk the lefs.

To endeavour all one's days to fortify our minds with learning and philofophy, is to fpend fo much in armour, that one has nothing left to defend.

DEFERENCE often fhrinks and withers as much upon the approach of intimacy, as the fenfitive plant does upon the touch of one's finger.

MEN are fometimes accufed of pride, merely becaufe their accufers would be proud themfelves if they were in their places.

PEOPLE frequently ufe this expreffion, I am inclined to think fo and fo, not confidering that they are then fpeaking the moft literal of all truths.

MODESTY makes large amends for the pain it gives the perfons who labour under it, by the prejudice it affords every worthy perfon in their favour.

THE difference there is betwixt honour and honefty feems to be chiefly in the motive. The honeft man does that from duty, which the man of honour does for the fake of character.

B 5

A LIAR

A LIAR begins with making falſehood appear like truth, and ends with making truth itſelf appear like falſehood.

VIRTUE ſhould be conſidered as a part of taſte ; and we ſhould as much avoid deceit, or ſiniſter meaning in diſcourſe, as we would puns, bad language, or falſe grammar.

CHAP. VII.

DEFERENCE is the moſt complicate, the moſt indirect, and the moſt elegant of all compliments.

HE that lies in bed all a ſummer's morning, loſes the chief pleaſure of the day : he that gives up his youth to indolence, undergoes a loſs of the ſame kind.

SHINING characters are not always the moſt agreeable ones. The mild radiance of an emerald, is by no means leſs pleaſing than the glare of the ruby.

To be at once a rake and to glory in the character, diſcovers at the ſame time a bad diſpoſition, and a bad taſte.

How is it poſſible to expect that mankind will take advice, when they will not ſo much as take warning ?

ALTHOUGH men are accuſed for not knowing their own weakneſs, yet perhaps as few know their own ſtrength. It is in men as in ſoils, where ſometimes there is a vein of gold which the owner knows not of.

FINE ſenſe and exalted ſenſe are not half ſo valuable as common ſenſe. There are forty men of wit for one man of ſenſe ; and he that will carry nothing about him but gold, will be every day at a loſs for want of ready change.

LEARNING is like mercury, one of the moſt powerful and excellent things in the world in ſkilful hands ; in unſkilful, moſt miſchievous.

A MAN ſhould never be aſhamed to own he has
been

been in the wrong ; which is but faying, in other words, that he is wifer to day than he was yefterday.

Wherever I find a great deal of gratitude in a poor man, I take it for granted there would be as much generofity if he were a rich man.

Flowers of rhetoric in fermons or ferious difcourfes, are like the blue and red flowers in corn, pleafing to thofe who come only for amufement, but prejudicial to him who would reap the profit.

It often happens that thofe are the beft people, whofe characters have been moft injured by flanderers ; as we ufually find that to be the fweeteft fruit, which the birds have been pecking at.

The eye of a critic is often like a microfcope, made fo very fine and nice, that it difcovers the atoms, grains and minuteft articles, without ever comprehending the whole, comparing the parts, or feeing all at once the harmony.

Men's zeal for religion is much of the fame kind as that which they fhew for a foot-ball ; whenever it is contefted for, every one is ready to venture their lives and limbs in the difpute ; but when that is once at an end, it is no more thought on, but fleeps in oblivion, buried in rubbifh, which no one thinks it worth his pains to rake into, much lefs to remove.

Honour is but a fictitious kind of honefty ; a mean but neceffary fubftitute for it, in focieties who have none : it is a fort of paper credit, with which men are obliged to trade, who are deficient in the fterling cafh of true morality and religion.

Persons of great delicacy fhould know the certainty of the following truth : there are abundance of cafes which occafion fufpence, in which whatever they determine they will repent of their determination ; and this through a propenfity of human nature to fancy happinefs in thofe fchemes which it does not purfue.

The chief advantage that ancient writers can

boaft

boaſt over modern ones ſeems owing to ſimplicity. Every noble truth and ſentiment was expreſſed by the former in a natural manner, in word and phraſe ſimple, perſpicuous, and incapable of improvements. What then remained for latter writers, but affectation, witticiſm, and conceit?

C H A P.   VIII.

WHAT a piece of work is man! how noble in reaſon! how infinite in faculties! in form and moving how expreſs and admirable! in action how like an angel! in apprehenſion how like a God.

If to do, were as eaſy as to know what were good to do, chapels had beenchurches, and poor men's cottages princes palaces. He is a good divine that follows his own inſtructions: I can eaſier teach twenty what were good to be done, than to be one of the twenty to follow my own teaching.

Men's evil manners live in braſs; their virtues we write in water.

The web of our life is of a mingled yarn, good and ill together; our virtues would be proud, if our faults whipped them not; and our crimes would deſpair, if they were not cheriſhed by our virtues.

The ſenſe of death is moſt in apprehenſion;
And the poor beetle that we tread upon,
In corporal ſuffrance feels a pang as great
As when a giant dies.

How far the little candle throws his beams!
So ſhines a good deed in a naughty world.

————————Love all, truſt a few,
Do wrong to none: be able for thine enemy
Rather

Rather in power, than in ufe : keep thy friend
Under thine own life's key : be check'd for filence,
But never tax'd for fpeech.

THE cloud-capt towers, the gorgeous palaces,
The folemn temples, the great globe itfelf,
Yea, all which it inherit, fhall diffolve;
And, like the bafelefs fabric of a vifion,
Leave not a wreck behind! we are fuch ftuff
As dreams are made on, and our little life
Is rounded with a fleep.

OUR indifcretion fometimes ferves us well,
When our deep plots do fall; and that fhould teach
      us,
There's a divinity that fhapes our ends,
Rough-hew them how we will.

THE poet's-eye in a fine frenzy rolling,
Doth glance from heaven to earth, from earth to
      heaven;
And as imagination bodies forth
The form of things unknown, the poet's pen
Turns them to fhape, and gives to airy nothing,
A local habitation and a name.

HEAVEN doth with us, as we with torches do,
Not light them for ourfelves : for if our virtues
Did not go forth of us, 'twere all alike
As if we had them not. Spirits are not finely touch'd,
But to fine iffues : nor nature never lends
The fmalleft fcruple of her excellence,
But, like a thrifty goddefs, fhe determines
Herfelf the glory of a creditor,
Both thanks and ufe.

WHAT ftronger breaft-plate than a heart untainted?
Thrice is he armed that hath his quarrel juft;
And he but naked (tho' lock'd up in fteel)
Whofe confcience with injuftice is corrupted.

C H A P. IX.

OH, world, thy flippery turns! friends now faſt
       ſworn,
Whoſe double boſoms ſeem to wear one heart,
Whoſe hours, whoſe bed, whoſe meal and exerciſe
Are ſtill together; who twine (as 'twere) in love
Inſeparable; ſhall within this hour,
On a diſſention of a doit, break out
To bittereſt enmity. So felleſt foes,
Whoſe paſſions and whoſe plots have broke their
      ſleep,
To take the one the other, by ſome chance,
Some trick not worth an egg, ſhall grow dear friends,
And interjoin their iſſues.

————————So it falls out,
That what we have we prize not to the worth,
While we enjoy it; but being lack'd and loſt,
Why then we rate the value; then we find
The virtue that poſſeſſion would not ſhew us
Whilſt it was ours.

Cowards die many times before their deaths;
The valiant never taſte of death but once.
Of all the wonders that I yet have heard,
It ſeems to me moſt ſtrange that men ſhould fear;
Seeing that death, a neceſſary end,
Will come, when it will come.

There is ſome ſoul of goodneſs in things evil,
Would men obſervingly diſtil it out.
For our bad neighbour makes us early ſtirrers;
Which is both healthful, and good huſbandry.
Beſides, they are our outward conſciences,
And preachers to us all; admoniſhing,
That we ſhould dreſs us fairly for our end.

O MOMEN-

O momentary grace of mortal men,
Which we more hunt for than the grace of God!
Who builds his hope in th' air of men's fair looks,
Lives like a drunken sailor on a maft,
Ready with every nod to tumble down,
Into the fatal bowels of the deep.

—— Who shall go about
To cozen fortune, and be honourable
Without the stamp of merit? Let none presume
To wear an undeserved dignity.
O that estates, degrees, and offices,
Were not derived corruptly, that clear honour
Were purchased by the merit of the wearer!
How many then should cover that stand bare!
How many be commanded, that command!

Oh, who can hold a fire in his hand,
By thinking on the frosty Caucasus?
Or cloy the hungry edge of appetite,
By bare imagination of a feast!
Or wallow naked in December snow,
By thinking on fantastic summer's heat?
Oh, no! the apprehension of the good,
Gives but the greater feeling to the worse;
Fell sorrow's tooth doth never rankle more,
Than when it bites, but lanceth not the fore.

———— 'Tis slander,
Whose edge is sharper than the sword; whose tongue
Outvenoms all the worms of Nile; whose breath
Rides on the posting winds, and doth belie
All corners of the world. Kings, queens, and states,
Maids, matrons, nay the secrets of the grave,
This viperous slander enters.

There is a tide in the affairs of men,
Which, taken at the flood, leads on to fortune;
Omitted, all the voyage of their life
Is bound in shallows, and in miseries.

To

To morrow, and to morrow, and to morrow,
Creeps in this petty space from day to day,
To the last syllable of recorded time,
And all our yesterdays have lighted fools
The way to dusky death.   Out, out, brief candle!
Life's but a walking shadow, a poor player,
That struts and frets his hour upon the stage,
And then is heard no more! It is a tale
Told by an idiot, full of sound and fury,
Signifying nothing.

BOOK

BOOK II.

NARRATIVE PIECES.

CHAP. I.

THE DERVISE.

A DERVISE, travelling through Tartary, being arrived at the town of Balk, went into the king's palace by miftake, as thinking it to be a publick inn or caravanfary. Having looked about him for fome time, he entered into a long gallery, where he laid down his wallet, and fpread his carpet, in order to repofe himfelf upon it after the manner of the eaftern nations. He had not been long in this pofture before he was difcovered by fome of the guards, who afked him what was his bufinefs in that place? The Dervife told them he intended to take up his night's lodging in that caravanfary. The guards let him know, in a very angry manner, that the houfe he was in was not a caravanfary, but the king's palace. It happened that the king himfelf paffed through the gallery during this debate, and fmiling at the miftake of the Dervife, afked him how he could poffibly be fo dull as not to diftinguifh a palace from a caravanfary? Sir, fays the Dervife, give me leave to afk your majefty a queftion or two. Who were the perfons that lodged in this houfe when it was firft built? The king replied, His anceftors. And who, fays the Dervife, was the laft perfon that lodged here? The king replied,

plied, His father. And who is it, says the Dervise, that lodges here at present? The king told him, That it was himself. And who, says the Dervise, will be here after you? The king answered, The young prince his son. ' Ah sir, said the Dervise, a ' house that changes its inhabitants so often, and ' receives such a perpetual succession of guests, is ' not a palace but a caravansary.'

Spectator.

C H A P. II.

A T U R K I S H T A L E.

WE are told that the Sultan Mahmoud, by his perpetual wars abroad, and his tyranny at home, had filled his dominions with ruin and desolation, and half unpeopled the Persian Empire. The Visier to this great Sultan (whether an humourist or an enthusiast, we are not informed) pretended to have learned of a certain Dervise to understand the language of birds, so that there was not a bird that could open his mouth, but the Visier knew what it was he said. As he was one evening with the emperor, in their return from hunting, they saw a couple of owls upon a tree that grew near an old wall out of a heap of rubbish. I would fain know, says the Sultan, what those two owls are saying to one another; listen to their discourse and give me an account of it. The Visier approached the tree, pretending to be very attentive to the two owls. Upon his return to the Sultan, Sir, says he, I have heard part of their conversation, but dare not tell you what it is. The Sultan would not be satisfied with such an answer, but forced him to repeat word for word every thing the owls had said. You must know then, said the Visier, that one of these owls has a son, and the other a daughter, between whom they are now upon a treaty of marriage. The father of the son said to the father of the daughter,

in

in my hearing, brother, I confent to this marriage, provided you will fettle upon your daughter fifty ruined villages for her portion. To which the father of the daughter replied, inftead of fifty I will give her five hundred if you pleafe. God grant a long life to Sultan Mahmoud; whilft he reigns over us, we fhall never want ruined villages.

The ftory fays, the Sultan was fo touched with the fable, that he rebuilt the towns and villages which had been deftroyed, and from that time forward confulted the good of his people.

SPECTATOR.

C H A P.   III.

AVARICE AND LUXURY.

THERE were two very powerful tyrants engaged in a perpetual war againft each other: the name of the firft was Luxury, and of the fecond Avarice. The aim of each of them was no lefs than univerfal monarchy over the hearts of mankind. Luxury had many generals under him, who did him great fervice, as Pleafure, Mirth, Pomp, and Fafhion. Avarice was likewife very ftrong in his officers, being faithfully ferved by Hunger, Induftry, Care and Watchfulnefs: he had likewife a privy-counfellor who was always at his elbow, and whifpering fomething or other in his ear: the name of this privy-counfellor was Poverty. As Avarice conducted himfelf by the counfels of Poverty, his antagonift was entirely guided by the dictates and advice of Plenty, who was his firft counfellor and minifter of ftate, that concerted all his meafures for him, and never departed out of his fight. While thefe two great rivals were thus contending for empire, their conquefts were very various, Luxury got poffeffion of one heart, and Avarice of another. The father of a family would often range himfelf under the banners of Avarice, and the fon under thofe of Luxury.

ry.   The wife and hufband would often declare themfelves on the two different parties; nay, the fame perfon would very often fide with one in his youth, and revolt to the other in his old age. Indeed the wife men of the world ftood neuter; but, alas, their numbers were not confiderable. At length when thefe two potentates had wearied themfelves with waging war upon one another, they agreed upon an interview, at which neither of their counfellors were to be prefent. It is faid that Luxury began the parley, and after having reprefented the endlefs ftate of war in which they were engaged, told his enemy, with a franknefs of heart which is natural to him, that he believed they two fhould be very good friends, were it not for the inftigations of Poverty, that pernicious counfellor, who made an ill ufe of his ear, and filled him with groundlefs apprehenfions and prejudices. To this Avarice replied, that he looked upon Plenty (the firft minifter of his antagonift) to be a much more deftructive counfellor than Poverty, for that he was perpetually fuggefting pleafures, banifhing all the neceffary cautions againft want, and confequently undermining thofe principles on which the government of Avarice was founded. At laft, in order to an accommodation, they agreed upon this preliminary; that each of them fhould immediately difmifs his privy-counfellor. When things were thus far adjufted towards a peace, all other differences were foon accommodated, infomuch that for the future they refolved to live as good friends and confederates, and to fhare between them whatever conquefts were made on either fide. For this reafon we now find Luxury and Avarice taking poffeffion of the fame heart, and dividing the fame perfon between them. To which I fhall only add, that fince the difcarding of the counfellors above-mentioned, Avarice fupplies Luxury in the room of Plenty, as Luxury prompts Avarice in the place of Poverty.

SPECTATOR.

C H A P.

C H A P. IV.

PLEASURE and PAIN.

THERE were two families which from the beginning of the world were as oppofite to each other as light and darknefs. The one of them lived in heaven, and the other in hell. The youngeft defcendant of the firft family was Pleafure, who was the daughter of Happinefs, who was the child of Virtue, who was the off-fpring of the Gods. Thefe, as I faid before, had their habitation in heaven. The youngeft of the oppofite family was Pain, who was the fon of Mifery, who was the child of Vice, who was the off-fpring of the Furies. The habitation of this race of beings was in hell.

THE middle ftation of nature between thefe two oppofite extremes was the earth, which was inhabited by creatures of a middle kind, neither fo virtuous as the one, nor fo vicious as the other, but partaking of the good and bad qualities of thefe two oppofite families. Jupiter confidering that this fpecies commonly called man, was too virtuous to be miferable, and too vicious to be happy; that he might make a diftinction between the good and the bad, ordered the two youngeft of the above-mentioned families, Pleafure who was the daughter of Happinefs, and Pain who was the fon of Mifery, to meet one another upon this part of nature which lay in the half-way between them, having promifed to fettle it upon them both, provided they could agree upon the divifion of it, fo as to fhare mankind between them.

PLEASURE and Pain were no fooner met in their new habitation, but they immediately agreed upon this point, that Pleafure fhould take poffeffion of the virtuous, and Pain of the vicious part of that fpecies which was given up to them. But upon examining to which of them any individual they met with belonged, they found each of them had a right to him;

for

for that, contrary to what they had feen in their old places of refidence, there was no perfon fo vicious who had not fome good in him, nor any perfon fo virtuous who had not in him fome evil. The truth of it is, they generally found upon fearch, that in the moft vicious man Pleafure might lay a claim to an hundredth part, and that in the moft virtuous man Pain might come in for at leaft two thirds. This they faw would occafion endlefs difputes between them, unlefs they could come to fome accommodation. To this end there was a marriage propofed between them, and at length concluded: by this means it is that we find Pleafure and Pain are fuch conftant yoke-fellows, and that they either make their vifits together, or are never far afunder. If Pain comes into a heart, he is quickly followed by Pleafure; and if Pleafure enters, you may be fure Pain is not far off.

But notwithftanding this marriage was very convenient for the two parties, it did not feem to anfwer the intention of Jupiter in fending them among mankind. To remedy therefore this inconvenience, it was ftipulated between them by article, and confirmed by the confent of each family, that notwithftanding they here poffeffed the fpecies indifferently; upon the death of every fingle perfon, if he was found to have in him a certain proportion of evil, he fhould be difpatched into the infernal regions by a paffport from Pain, there to dwell with Mifery, Vice, and the Furies. Or on the contrary, if he had in him a certain proportion of good, he fhould be difpatched into heaven by a paffport from Pleafure, there to dwell with Happinefs, Virtue, and the Gods.

Spectator.

C H A P.

C H A P. V.

L A B O U R.

LABOUR, the off-fpring of Want, and the mother of Health and Contentment, lived with her two daughters in a little cottage, by the fide of a hill, at a great diftance from town. They were totally unacquainted with the great, and had kept no better company than the neighbouring villagers; but having a defire of feeing the world, they forfook their companions and habitation, and determined to travel. Labour went foberly along the road with Health on her right hand, who by the fprightlinefs of her converfation 'and fongs of chearfulnefs and joy, foftened the toils of the way; while Contentment went fmiling on the left, fupporting the fteps of her mother, and by her perpetual good-humour increafing the vivacity of her fifter.

IN this manner they travelled over forefts and through towns and villages, till at laft they arrived at the capital of the kingdom. At their entrance into the great city, the mother conjured her daughters never to lofe fight of her; for it was the will of Jupiter, fhe faid, that their feparation fhould be attended with the utter ruin of all three. But Health was of too gay a difpofition to regard the counfels of Labour: fhe fuffered herfelf to be debauched by Intemperance, and at laft died in child-birth of Difcafe. Contentment, in the abfence of her fifter, gave herfelf up to the enticement of Sloth, and was never heard of after: while Labour, who could have no enjoyment without her daughters, went every where in fearch of them, till fhe was at laft feized by Laffitude in her way, and died in mifery.

WORLD.

AN old man and a little boy were driving an afs to the next market to fell. What a fool is this fellow (fays a man upon the road) to be trudging it on foot with his fon, that his afs may go light! The old man, hearing this, fet his boy upon the afs, and went whiftling by the fide of him. Why, firrah! (cries a fecond man to the boy) is it fit for you to be riding, while your poor old father is walking on foot? The father, upon this rebuke, took down his boy from the afs, and mounted himfelf. Do you fee (fays a third) how the lazy old knave rides along upon his beaft, while his poor little boy is almoft crippled with walking? The old man no fooner heard this, than he took up his fon behind him. Pray, honeft friend (fays a fourth) is that afs your own? Yes, fays the man. One would not have thought fo, replied the other, by your loading him fo unmercifully. You and your fon are better able to carry the poor beaft than he you. Any thing to pleafe, fays the owner; and alighting with his fon, they tied the legs of the afs together, and by the help of a pole endeavoured to carry him upon their fhoulders over the bridge that led to the town. This was fo entertaining a fight, that the people ran in crowds to laugh at it; till the afs, conceiving a diflike to the over complai-fance of his mafter, burft afunder the cords that tied him, flipt from the pole, and tumbled into the river. The poor old man made the beft of his way home, afhamed and vexed that by endeavouring to pleafe every body, he had pleafed nobody, and loft his afs into the bargain.

WORLD.

H E R C U L E S's   C H O I C E.

WHEN Hercules was in that part of his youth, in which it was natural for him to confider what courfe of life he ought to purfue, he one day retired into a defert, where the filence and folitude of the place very much favoured his meditations.   As he was mufing on his prefent condition, and very much perplexed in himfelf on the ftate of life he fhould chufe, he faw two women of a larger ftature than ordinary approaching towards him.   One of them had a very noble air, and graceful deportment; her beauty was natural and eafy, her perfon clean and unfpotted, her eyes caft towards the ground with an agreeable referve, her motion and behaviour full of modefty, and her raiment as white as fnow. The other had a great deal of health and floridnefs in her countenance, which fhe had helped with an artificial white and red; and endeavoured to appear more graceful than ordinary in her mein, by a mix- ture of affectation in all her geftures.   She had a wonderful confidence and affurance in her looks, and all the variety of colours in her drefs that fhe thought were the moft proper to fhew her complex- ion to advantage.   She caft her eyes upon herfelf, then turned them on thofe that were prefent, to fee how they liked her, and often looked on the figure fhe made in her own fhadow.   Upon her nearer ap- proach to Hercules, fhe ftepped before the other lady, who came forward with a regular compofed carriage, and running up to him, accofted him after the following manner.

My dear Hercules, fays fhe, I find you are very much divided in your own thoughts upon the way of life that you ought to chufe: be my friend, and fol- low me; I will lead you into the poffeffion of plea- fure, and out of the reach of pain, and remove you

C

from

from all the noise and disquietude of business. The affairs of either war or peace shall have no power to disturb you. Your whole employment shall be to make your life easy, and to entertain every sense with its proper gratification. Sumptuous tables, beds of roses, clouds of perfumes, concerts of music, crouds of beauties, are all in readiness to receive you. Come along with me into this region of delights, this world of pleasure, and bid farewel for ever to care, to pain, to business: _

HERCULES hearing the lady talk after this manner, desired to know her name; to which she answered, my friends, and those who are well acquainted with me, call me Happiness; but my enemies and those who would injure my reputation, have given me the name of Pleasure.

BY this time the other lady was come up, who addressed herself to the young hero in a very different manner.

HERCULES, says she, I offer myself to you, because I know you are descended from the Gods, and give proofs of that descent by your love to virtue, and application to the studies proper for your age. This makes me hope you will gain both for yourself and me an immortal reputation. But, before I invite you into my society and friendship, I will be open and sincere with you, and must lay down this as an established truth, that there is nothing truly valuable which can be purchased without pains and labour. The Gods have set a price upon every real and noble pleasure. If you would gain the favour of the Deity, you must be at the pains of worshipping him; if the friendship of good men, you must study to oblige them; if you would be honoured by your country, you must take care to serve it In short, if you would be eminent in war or peace, you must become master of all the qualifications that can make you so. These are the only terms and conditions upon which I can propose happiness. The Goddess of pleasure here broke in upon her discourse: you
see,

fee, faid fhe, Hercules, by her own confeffion, the way to her pleafures is long and difficult, whereas that which I propofe is fhort and eafy. Alas! faid the other lady, whofe vifage glowed with paffion, made up of fcorn and pity, what are the pleafures you propofe? To eat before you are hungry, drink before you are athirft, fleep before you are tired, to gratify appetites before they are raifed, and raife fuch appetites as nature never planted. You never heard the moft delicious mufic, which is the praife of one's felf; nor faw the moft beautiful object, which is the work of one's own hands. Your votaries pafs away their youth is a dream of miftaken pleafures, while they are hoarding up anguifh, torment, and remorfe, for old age.

As for me, I am the friend of Gods and of good men, an agreeable companion to the artizan, an houfhold guardian to the fathers of families, a patron and protector of fervants, an affociate in all true and generous friendfhips. The banquets of my votaries are never coftly, but always delicious; for none eat or drink at them who are not invited by hunger and thirft. Their flumbers are found, and their wakings chearful. My young men have the pleafure of hearing themfelves praifed by thofe who are in years; and thofe who are in years, of being honoured by thofe who are young. In a word, my followers are favoured by the Gods, beloved by their acquaintance, efteemed by their country, and after the clofe of their labours honoured by pofterity.

We know by the life of this memorable hero, to which of thefe two ladies he gave up his heart: and I believe, every one who reads this will do him the juftice to approve his choice.

Tatler.

C H A P.   VIII.

P I T Y.

IN the happy period of the golden age, when all the celeſtial inhabitants deſcended to the earth, and converſed familiarly with mortals, among the moſt cheriſhed of the heavenly powers were twins, the off-ſpring of Jupiter, LOVE and JOY. Where-ever they appeared, the flowers ſprang up beneath their feet, the ſun ſhone with a brighter radiance, and all nature ſeemed embelliſhed by their preſence. They were inſeparable companions, and their grow-ing attachment was favoured by Jupiter, who had decreed that a laſting union ſhould be ſolemnized be-tween them ſo ſoon as they were arrived at maturer years.   But in the mean time the ſons of men devi-ated from their native innocence; vice and ruin over-ran the earth with giant ſtrides; and Aſtrea with her train of celeſtial viſitants forſook their pol-luted abodes.   Love alone remained, having been ſtolen away by Hope, who was his nurſe, and con-veyed by her to the foreſts of Arcadia, where he was brought up among the ſhepherds.   But Jupiter aſſigned him a different partner, and commanded him to eſpouſe SORROW, the daughter of Atè.   He com-plied with reluctance; for her features were harſh and diſagreeable, her eyes ſunk, her forehead con-tracted into perpetual wrinkles, and her temples were covered with a wreath of cypreſs and worm-wood.   From this union ſprang a virgin, in whom might be traced a ſtrong reſemblance to both her parents; but the ſullen and unamiable features of her mother were ſo mixed and blended with the ſweet-neſs of her father, that her countenance, though mournful, was highly pleaſing.   The maids and ſhepherds of the neighbouring plains gathered round and called her PITY.   A redbreaſt was obſerved to build in the cabin where ſhe was born; and while ſhe

was

was yet an infant, a dove purfued by a hawk flew
into her bofom. This nymph had a dejected appearance, but fo foft and gentle a mein that fhe was beloved to a degree of enthufiafm. Her voice was low
and plaintive, but inexpreffibly fweet; and fhe loved
to lie four hours together on the banks of fome wild
and melancholy ftream, finging to her lute. She
taught men to weep, for fhe took a ftrange delight
in tears; and often, when the virgins of the hamlet
were affembled at their evening fports, fhe would
fteal in amongft them, and captivate their hearts by
her tales full of a charming fadnefs. She wore on
her head a garland compofed of her father's myr-
tles twifted with her mother's cyprefs.

One day, as fhe fat mufing by the waters of He-
licon, her tears by chance fell into the fountain; and
ever fince, the Mufes' fpring has obtained a ftrong
tafte of the infufion. Pity was commanded by Jupiter to follow the fteps of her mother through the
world, dropping balm into the wounds fhe made,
and binding up the hearts fhe had broken. She follows with her hair loofe, her bofom bare and throbbing, her garments torn by the briars, and her feet
bleeding with the roughnefs of the path. The
nymph is mortal, for her mother is fo; and when fhe
has fulfilled her deftined courfe upon the earth, they
fhall both expire together, and LOVE be again united to JOY, his immortal and long betrothed bride.

MRS. BARBAULD.

C H A P.   IX.

THE DEAD ASS.

AND this, faid he, putting the remains of a
cruft into his wallet—and this fhould have
been thy portion, faid he, hadft thou been alive to
have fhared with me. I thought by the accent,
it had been an apoftrophe to his child; but it was
to his afs, and to the very afs we had feen dead in

C 3

the

the road, which had occasioned La Fleur's misad-venture.   The man seemed to lament it much; and it instantly brought into my mind Sancho's lamentation for his; but he did it with more true touches of nature.

The mourner was sitting upon a stone bench at the door, with the afs's pannel and its bridle on one side, which he took up from time to time—then laid them down—looked at them, and shook his head.   He then took his cruft of bread out of his wallet again, as if to eat it; held it some time in his hand—then laid it upon the bit of his afs's bridle—looked wistfully at the little arrangement he had made—and gave a sigh.

The simplicity of his grief drew. numbers about him, and La Fleur among the reft, whilft the horses were getting ready; as I continued fitting in the poft-chaife, I could fee and hear over their heads.

He faid he had come laft from Spain, where he had been from the furtheft borders of Franconia? and had got fo far on his return home, when his afs died.   Every one feemed defirous to know what bufinefs could have taken fo old and a poor a man fo far a journey from his own home.

It had pleafed heaven, he faid, to blefs him with three fons, the fineft lads in all Germany; but ha-ving in one week loft two of them by the fmall-pox, and the youngeft falling ill of the fame diftemper, he was afraid of being bereft of them all; and made a vow, if Heaven would not take him from him al-fo he would go in gratitude to St. Iago in Spain.

When the mourner got thus far in his ftory, he ftopp'd to pay nature her tribute—and wept bitterly.

He faid Heaven had accepted the conditions; and that he had fet out from his cottage with this poor creature, who had been a patient partner of his journey—that it had eat the fame bread with him all the way, and was unto him as a friend.

Every body who ftood about him, heard the poor fellow with concern—La Fleur offered him money.
—The

—The mourner said he did not want it—it was not the value of the ass—but the loss of him—The ass, he said, he was assured, loved him—and upon this told them a long story of a mischance upon their passage over the Pyrenean mountains which had separated them from each other three days: during which time the ass had sought him as much as he had sought the ass, and that they had neither scarce eat or drank till they met.

Tʜᴏᴜ haft one comfort, friend, said I, at least in the loss of thy poor beast: I am sure thou haft been a merciful master to him.—Alas! said the mourner, I thought so, when he was alive—but now he is dead I think otherwise.—I fear the weight of myself and my afflictions together have been too much for him—they have shortened the poor creature's days, and I fear I have them to answer for. —Shame on the world! said I to myself—Did we love each other, as this poor soul but loved his ass —t'would be something.—

Sᴛᴇʀɴᴇ.

C H A P.   X.

Tʜᴇ   S W O R D.

WHEN states and empires have their periods of declension, and feel in their turns what distress and poverty is—I stop not to tell the causes which gradually brought the house d'E**** in Britany into decay. The Marquis dE**** had fought up against his condition with great firmness : wishing to preserve and still shew to the world some little fragments of what his ancestors had been—their indiscretions had put it out of his power. There was enough left for the little exigencies of obscurity— But he had two boys who looked up to him for light —he thought they deserved it. He had tried his sword—it could not open the way—the mounting was too expensive—and simple œconomy was not a match for it—there was no resource but commerce.

C 4

Iɴ

In any other province in France, save Britany, this was smiting the root for ever of the little tree his pride and affection wished to see re-blossom—But in Britany, there being provision for this, he availed himself of it, and taking an occasion when the states were assembled at Rennes, the Marquis, attending with his two sons, entered the court: and having pleaded the right of an antient law of the duchy, which, though seldom claimed, he said, was no less in force: he took his sword from his side—Here—said he—take it; and be trusty Guardians of it, till better times put me in condition to reclaim it.

THE president accepted the Marquis's sword—he stayed a few minutes to see it deposited in the archives of his house—and departed.

THE Marquis and his whole family embarked on the next day for Martinico, and in about nineteen or twenty years of successful application to business, with some unlooked for bequest from distant branches of this house—returned home to reclaim his nobility, and to support it.

IT was an incident of good fortune which will never happen to any traveller, but a sentimental one, that I should be at Rennes at the very time of this solemn requisition : I call it solemn—it was so to me.

THE Marquis entered the court with his whole family ; he supported his lady—his eldest son supported his sister, and his youngest was at the other extreme of the line next his mother—he put his handkerchief to his face twice—

—THERE was a dead silence. When the Marquis had approached within six paces of the tribunal, he gave the Marchioness to his youngest son, and advancing three steps before his family—he reclaimed his sword—His sword was given him, and the moment he got it into his hand he drew it almost out of the scabbard—it was the shining face of a friend he had once given up. He looked attentively a long time at it, beginning at the hilt, as if to see whether

it

it was the fame—when obferving a little ruft which
it had contracted near the point, he brought it near
his eye, and bending his head down over it—I think
I faw a tear fall upon the place : I could not be deceived by what followed.

" I SHALL find, faid he, fome other way, to get
" it off."

WHEN the Marquis had faid this, he returned
his fword into his fcabbard, made a bow to the guardian of it—and with his wife and daughter and his
two fons following him, walked out.

O HOW I envied him his feelings !

STERNE.

CHAP. XI.

MARIA.

FIRST PART.

THEY were the fweeteft notes I ever heard ;
and I inftantly let down the foreglafs to
hear them more diftinctly——'Tis Maria, faid the
poftilion, obferving I was liftening——Poor Maria,
continued he, (leaning his body on one fide to let
me fee her, for he was in a line betwixt us) is fitting
upon a bank playing her vefpers upon her pipe, with
her little goat befide her.

THE young fellow uttered this with an accent and
a look fo perfectly in tune to a feeling heart, that I
inftantly made a vow, I would give him a four and
twenty fous piece, when I got to Moulines——

——AND who is poor Maria ? faid I.

THE love and pity of all the villages around us;
faid the poftilion——it is but three years ago, that
the fun did not fhine upon fo fair, fo quick-witted
and amiable a maid ; a better fate did Maria deferve,
than to have her bands forbid by the intrigues of the
curate of the parifh who publifhed them——

HE was going on, when Maria, who had made a
fhort paufe, put the pipe to her mouth and began the
air again—they were the fame notes ;—yet were ten

C 5

times

times fweeter : It is the evening fervice to the Virgin, faid the young man——but who has taught her to play it —or how fhe came by her pipe, no one knows; we think that Heaven has affifted her in both ; for ever fince fhe has been unfettled in her mind, it feems her only confolation—fhe has never once had the pipe out of her hand, but plays that fervice upon it almoft night and day.

The poftilion delivered this with fo much difcretion and natural eloquence, that I could not help decyphering fomething in his face above his condition, and fhould have fifted out his hiftory, had not poor Maria's taken fuch full poffeffion of me.

We had got up by this time almoft to the bank where Maria was fitting : fhe was in a thin white jacket, with her hair, all but two treffes, drawn up into a filk net, with a few olive leaves twifted a little fantaftically on one fide——fhe was beautiful ; and if ever I felt the full force of an honeft heart-ach, it was the moment I faw her——

—God help her ! poor damfel ! above a hundred maffes, faid the poftilion, have been faid in the feveral parifh churches and convents around, for her, ——but without effect ; we have ftill hopes, as fhe is fenfible for fhort intervals, that the Virgin at laft will reftore her to herfelf ; but her parents, who know her beft, are hopelefs upon that fcore, and think her fenfes are loft for ever.

As the poftilion fpoke this, Maria made a cadence fo melancholy, fo tender and querulous, that I fprung out of the chaife to help her, and found myfelf fitting betwixt her and her goat before I relapfed from my enthufiafm.

Maria looked wifhfully for fome time at me, and then at her goat—and then at me—and then at her goat again, and fo on, alternately——

——Well, Maria, faid I foftly—What refemblance do you find ?

I do intreat the candid reader to believe me, that it was from the humbleft conviction of what a beaft

man

man is——that I afked the queftion; and that I would
not have let fallen an unfeafonable pleafantry in the
venerable prefence of Mifery, to be entitled to all
the wit that ever Rabelais fcattered.

Adieu, Maria !——adieu, poor haplefs damfel !——
——fome time, but not now, I may hear thy forrows
from thy own lips——but I was deceived ; for that
moment fhe took her pipe, and told me fuch a tale
of woe with it, that I rofe up, and with broken and
irregular fteps walked foftly to my chaife.

SECOND PART.

WHEN we had got within half a league of
Moulines, at a little opening in the road leading to a thicket, I difcovered poor Maria fitting under a poplar——fhe was fitting with her elbow in her
lap, and her head leaning on one fide within her hand
——a fmall brook ran at the foot of the tree.

I bid the poftilion go on with the chaife to
Moulines——and La Fleur to befpeak my fupper——and
that I would walk after him.

She was dreffed in white, and much as my friend
defcribed her, except that her hair hung loofe, which
before was twifted within a filk net. She had, fuper-
added likewife to her jacket, a pale green ribband
which fell acrofs her fhoulder to the waift ; at the
end of which hung her pipe. Her goat had been as
faithlefs as her lover; and fhe had got a little dog
in lieu of him, which fhe had kept tied by a ftring to
her girdle ; as looking at her dog, fhe drew him towards her with the ftring——" Thou fhalt not leave
" me, Sylvio," faid fhe. I looked in Maria's eyes,
and faw fhe was thinking more of her father than
of her lover or her little goat ; for as fhe uttered
them the tears trickled down her cheeks.

I sat down clofe by her ; and Maria let me wipe
them away as they fell, with my handkerchief. I
then fteeped it in my own——and then in hers——and
then in mine——and then I wiped hers again——and as
I did it, I felt undefcribable emotions within me,

as I am fure could not be accounted for from any combinations of matter and motion.

I am pofitive I have a foul : nor can all the books with which materialifts have peftered the world ever convince me of the contrary.

When Maria had come a little to herfelf, I afked her if fhe remembered a pale thin perfon of a man, who had fat down betwixt her and her goat about two years before ? She faid fhe was unfettled much at that time, but remembered it upon two accounts ——that ill as fhe was fhe faw the perfon pitied her ; and next, that her goat had ftolen his handkerchief, and fhe had beat him for the theft—fhe had wafhed it, fhe faid, in the brook, and kept it ever fince in her poket, to reftore it to him in cafe fhe fhould ever fee him again, which fhe added, he had half promifed her. As fhe told me this, fhe took the handkerchief out of her pocket to let me fee it ; fhe had folded it up neatly in a couple of vine leaves, tied round with a tendril—on opening it I faw an S marked in one of the corners.

She had fince that, fhe told me, ftrayed as far as Rome, and walked round St. Peter's once—and returned back—that fhe found her way alone acrofs the Apennines—had travelled over all Lombardy without money—and through the flinty roads of Savoy without fhoes—how fhe had borne it, and how fhe had got fupported, fhe could not tell—but God tempers the wind, faid Maria, to the fhorn lamb.

Shorn indeed ! and to the quick, faid I :andwaft thou in my own land, where I have a cottage, I would take thee to it and fhelter thee ; thou fhouldft eat of my own bread, and drink of my own cup. I would be kind to thy Sylvio—in all thy weakneffes and wanderings I would feek after thee and bring thee back——when the fun went down I would fay my prayers, and when I had done, thou fhouldft play thy evening fong upon thy pipe, nor would the incenfe of my facrifice be worfe accepted for entering heaven along with that of a broken heart.

Nature.

Nature melted within me as I uttered this ; and Maria obfervirg, as I took out my handkerchief, that it was fteeped too much already to be of ufe, would needs go wafh it in the ftream. And where will you dry it, Maria ? faid I—I will dry it in my bofom, faid fhe—it will do me good.

And is your heart ftill fo warm, Maria ? faid I.

I touched upon the ftring on which hung all her forrows—fhe looked with wiftful diforder for fome time in my face ; and then, without faying any thing, took her pipe, and played her fervice to the Virgin—The ftring I had touched ceafed to vibrate—in a moment or two Maria returned to herfelf—let her pipe fall—and rofe up.

And where are you going, Maria ? faid I.—She faid, to Moulines.—Let us go, faid I, together.—Maria put her arm within mine, and lengthening the ftring, to let the dog follow—in that order we entered Moulines.

Though I hate falutations and greetings in the market place, yet when we got into the middle of this, I ftopped to take my laft look and laft farewel of Maria.

Maria, though not tall, was neverthelefs of the firft order of fine forms——affliction had touched her looks with fomething that was fcarce earthly—ftill fhe was feminine—and fo much was there about her of all that the heart wifhes, or the eye looks for in woman, that could the traces be ever worn out of her brain, and thofe of Eliza's out of mine, fhe fhould not only eat of my bread and drink of my own cup, but Maria fhould lie in my bofom, and be unto me as a daughter.

Adieu, poor lucklefs maiden ! — imbibe the oil and wine which the compaffion of a ftranger, as he journieth on his way, now pours into thy wounds—the Being who has twice bruifed thee can only bind them up for ever.

STERNE.

CHAP.

C H A P. XII.

THE CAMELION.

OFT has it been my lot to mark
A proud, conceited, talking fpark,
With eyes, that hardly ferv'd at moft
To guard their mafter 'gainft a poft,
Yet round the world the blade has been
To fee whatever could be feen,
Returning from his finifh'd tour,
Grown ten times perter than before ;
Whatever word you chance to drop,
The travell'd fool your mouth will ftop,
" Sir, if my judgment you'll allow—
" I've feen—and fure I ought to know"—
So begs you'd pay a due fubmiffion,
And acquiefce in his decifion.

Two travellers of fuch a caft,
As o'er Arabia's wilds they paft,
And on their way in friendly chat
Now talk'd of this and then of that,
Difcours'd awhile, mongft other matter,
Of the Camelion's form and nature,
" A ftranger animal cries one,
" Sure never liv'd beneath the fun :
" A lizard's body lean and long,
" A fifh's head, a ferpent's tongue,
" Its tooth with triple claw disjoin'd ;
" And what a length of tail behind !
" How flow its pace ! and then its hue—
" Who ever faw fo fine a blue ?"
 " Hold there, the other quick replies,
" 'Tis green—I faw it with thefe eyes,
" As late with open mouth it lay,
" And warm'd it in the funny ray ;
" Stretch'd at its eafe the beaft I view'd,
" And faw it eat the air for food."
 " I've feen it, Sir, as well as you,
" And muft again affirm it blue.

" At

" At leifure I the beaft furvey'd ,
" Extended in the cooling fhade."
 ' Tis green, 'tis green, Sir, I affure ye"————
" Green ! cries the other in a fury———
" Why, Sir———d'ye think I've loft my eyes ?"
" 'Twere no great lofs, the friend replies,
" For, if they always ferve you thus,
" You'll find 'em but of little ufe,"
So high at laft the conteft rofe,
From words they almoft came to blows :
When luckily came by a third——
To him the queftion they referr'd ;
And begg'd he'd tell him, if he knew,
Whether the thing was green or blue,
 " Sirs, cries the umpire, ceafe your pother——
" The creature's neither one nor t'other.
" I caught the animal laft night,
" And view'd it o'er by candle-light :
" I mark'd it well—'twas black as jet——
" You ftare—but Sirs, I've got it yet,
" And can produce it." " Pray, Sir, do,
" I'll lay my life, the thing is blue,"
" And I'll be fworn, that when you've feen
" The reptile, you'll pronounce him green."
 " Well then, at once to eafe the doubt,
" Replies the man, I'll turn him out :
" And when before your eyes I've fet him,
" If you don't find him black, I'll eat him."
He faid ; then full before their fight
Produc'd the beaft, and lo !———'twas white.——
Both ftar'd, the man look'd wond'rous wife——
" My children," the Camelion cries,
(Then firft the creature found a tongue):
" You all are right, and all are wrong
" When next you talk of what you view,
" Think others fee as well as you :
" Nor wonder, if you find that none
" Prefers your eye-fight to his own."

MERRICK.

C H A P.

C H A P.   XIII.

The YOUTH and the PHILOSOPHER.

A GRECIAN Youth, of talents rare,
  Whom Plato's philofophic care
Had form'd for virtue's nobler view,
By precept and example too,
Wou'd often boaft his matchlefs fkill,
To curb the fteed, and guide the wheel,
And as he pafs'd the gazing throng,
With graceful eafe, and fmack'd the thong,
The idiot wonder they exprefs'd
Was praife and tranfport to his breaft.

  At length quite vain, he needs would fhew
His mafter what his art could do ;
And bade his flave the chariot lead
To Academus facred fhade.
The trembling groves confefs'd its fright,
The wood-nymphs ftarted at the fight :
The Mufes drop the learned lyre,
And to their inmoft fhades retire !
Howe'er the youth with forward air,
Bows to the fage, and mounts the car,
The lafh refounds, the courfers fpring,
The chariot marks the rolling ring,
And gath'ring crowds with eager eyes,
And fhouts, purfue him as he flies.

  Triumphant to the goal return'd,
With nobler thirft his bofom burn'd ;
And now along th' indented plain,
The felf-fame track he marks again,
Purfues with care the nice defign,
Nor ever deviates from the line.

  Amazement feiz'd the circling crcwd ;
The youths with emulation glow'd ;
Ev'n bearded fages hail'd the boy,
And all, but Plato, gaz'd with joy,
For he, deep-judging fage, beheld
With pain the triumphs of the field :

Ard

And when the charioteer drew nigh,
And, flush'd with hope, had caught his eye,
Alas ! unhappy youth. he cry'd,
Expect no praise from me, (and sigh'd)
With indignation I survey
Such skill and judgment thrown away.
The time profusely squander'd there,
On vulgar arts beneath thy care,
If well employed, at less expence,
Had taught thee honour, virtue, sense,
And rais'd thee from a coachman's fate
To govern men, and guide the state.

WHITEHEAD.

C H A P. XIV.

Sir B A L A A M,

WHERE London's column, pointing at the skies,
  Like a tall bully, lifts the head, and lies;
There dwelt a Citizen of sober fame,
A plain good man, and Balaam was his name ;
Religious, punctual, frugal, and so forth ;
His word would pass for more than he was worth.
One solid dish his week-day meal affords,
An added pudding solemniz'd the Lord's :
Constant at Church, and Change; his gains were sure,
His giving rare, save farthings to the poor.
  The Devil was piqu'd such saintship to behold,
And long'd to tempt him, like good Job of old :
But Satan now is wiser than of yore,
And tempts by making rich, not making poor.
  Rouz'd by the Prince of Air, the whirlwinds sweep
The surge, and plunge his Father in the deep ;
Then full against his Cornish lands they roar.
And two rich shipwrecks bless the lucky shore.
  Sir Balaam now, he lives like other folks,
He takes his chirping pint, and cracks his jokes :
" Live yourself," was soon my Lady's word;
And lo! two puddings smoak'd upon the board.

Asleep

Afleep and naked as an Indian lay,
An honeft factor ftole a Gem away :
He pledg'd it to the knight ; the knight had wit,
So kept the Di'mond, and the rogue was bit.
Some fcruple rofe, but thus he eas'd his thought,
" I'll now give fix-pence where I gave a groat ;
" Where once I went to church, I'll now go twice—
" And am fo clear too of all other vice."
    The tempter faw his time ; the work he ply'd;
Stocks and fubfcriptions pour on ev'ry fide,
'Till all the Dæmon makes his full defcent
In one abundant fhow'r of Cent *per* Cent,
Sinks deep within him, and poffeffes whole,
Then dubs Director, and fecures his foul.
    Behold Sir Balaam now a man of fpirit,
Afcribes his gettings to his parts and merit ;
What late he called a Bleffing, now was Wit,
And God's good Providence, a lucky Hit.
Things change their titles, as our manners turn :
His Compting-houfe employ'd the Sunday morn :
Seldom at Church ('twas fuch a bufy life)
But duly fent his family and wife.
There (fo the Devil ordain'd) one Chriftmas-tide
My good old Lady catch'd a cold, and dy'd.
    A nymph of Quality admires our Knight ;
He marries, bows at Court, and grows polite :
Leaves the dull Cits, and joins (to pleafe the Fair)
The well-bred cuckolds in St. James's air :
In Britain's Senate he a feat obtains,
And one more Penfioner St. Stephen gains,
My Lady falls to play ; fo bad her chance,
He muft repair it ; takes a bribe from France,
The Houfe impeach him ; Coningfby harangues ;
The court forfake him, and Sir Balaam hangs.
Wife, fon, and daughter, Satan ! are thy own,
His wealth, yet dearer, forfeit to the Crown :
The Devil and the King divide the prize,
And fad Sir Balaam curfes God and dies.

Pope.

C H A P.

C H A P. XV.

E D W I N AND E M M A.

FAR in the windings of a vale,
    Faſt by a ſheltering wood,
The ſafe retreat of health and peace,
    A humble cottage ſtood.

There beauteous EMMA flouriſh'd fair
    Beneath a mother's eye,
Whoſe only wiſh on earth was now
    To ſee her bleſt, and die.

The ſofteſt bluſh that nature ſpreads
    Gave colour to her cheek ;
Such orient colour ſmiles thro' heav'n
    When May's ſweet mornings break.

Nor let the pride of great ones ſcorn
    This charmer of the plains ;
That ſun which bids their diamond blaze,
    To deck our lily deigns.

Long had ſhe fir'd each youth with love,
    Each maiden with deſpair;
And tho' by all a wonder own'd,
    Yet knew not ſhe was fair.

Till EDWIN came, the pride of ſwains,
    A ſoul that knew no art,
And from whoſe eyes ſerenely mild,
    Shone forth the feeling heart.

A mutual flame was quickly caught,
    Was quickly too reveal'd ;
For neither boſom lodg'd a wiſh,
    Which virtue keeps conceal'd.

What

What happy hours of heartfelt blifs,
   Did love on both beſtow !
But blifs too mighty long to laſt,
   Where fortune proves a foe.

His ſiſter, wh6 like envy form'd,
   Like her in miſchief joy'd,
To work them harm, with wicked ſkill
   Each darker art employ'd.

The father too, a ſordid man,
   Who love nor pity knew,
Was all unfeeling as the rock
   From whence his riches grew.

Long had he ſeen their mutual flame,
   And ſeen it long unmov'd ;
Then with a father's frown at laſt,
   He ſternly diſapprov'd.

In EDWIN's gentle heart a war
   Of differing paſſions ſtrove ;
His heart which durſt not diſobey,
   Yet could not ceaſe to love.

Deny'd her ſight, he oft behind
   The ſpreading hawthorn crept,
To ſnatch . a glance, to mark the ſpot
   Where EMMA walk'd and wept.

Oft too in Stanemore's wintry waſte,
   Beneath the moonlight ſhade;
In ſighs to pour his ſoften'd ſoul
   The midnight mourner ſtray'd.

His cheeks, where love with beauty glow'd,
   A deadly pale oercaſt ;
So fades the freſh roſe in his prime,
   Before the northern blaſt.

The

The parents now, with late remorſe,
   Hung o'er his dying bed,
And weary'd heav'n with fruitleſs pray'rs,
   And fruitleſs ſorrows ſhed.

'Tis paſt, he cry'd, but if your ſouls
   Sweet mercy yet can move,
Let theſe dim eyes once more behold
   What they muſt ever love.

She came ; his cold hand ſoftly touch'd,
   And bath'd with many a tear ;
Faſt falling o'er the primroſe pale
   So mourning dews appear.

But oh ! his ſiſter's jealous care
   (A cruel ſiſter ſhe !)
Forbad what EMMA came to ſay,
   My EDWIN, live for me.

Now homeward as ſhe hopeleſs went,
   The church-yard path along,
The blaſt blew cold, the dark owl ſcream'd
   Her lover's fun'ral ſong.

Amid the gloom of night,
   Her ſtarting fancy found
In ev'ry buſh his hovering ſhade,
   His groan in every found

Alone, appall'd, thus had ſhe paſs'd
   The viſionary vale,
When lo ! the death-bell ſmote her ear,
   Sad ſounding in the gale.

Juſt then ſhe reach'd, with trembling ſteps,
   Her aged mother's door ;
He's gone, ſhe cry'd, and I ſhall ſee
   That angel face no more.

I fell,

I feel, I feel this breaking heart
  Beat high against my side :
From her white arm down sunk her head,
  She shiver'd, sigh'd, and died.

C H A P.   XVI.

CELADON and AMELIA.

'TIS listening fear, and dumb amazement all :
    When to the startled eye the sudden glance
Appears far south, eruptive thro' the cloud ;
And following slower in explosion vast,
The Thunder raises his tremendous voice.
At first, heard solemn o'er the verge of heaven,
The tempest growls ; but as it nearer comes,
And rolls its awful burden on the wind
The lightnings flash a larger curve, and more ;
The noise astounds : till over head a sheet
Of livid flame discloses wide ; then shuts,
And opens wider ; shuts and opens still
Expansive, wrapping either in a blaze.
Follows the loosen'd aggravated roar,
Enlarging, deepening, mingling ; peal on peal
Crush'd horrible, convulsing heaven and earth.
  Guilt hears appall'd, with deeply troubled thought.
And yet not always on the guilty head
Descends the fated flash. Young CELADON
And his AMELIA were a matchless pair ;
With equal Virtue form'd and equal grace,
The same, distinguish'd by their sex alone :
Hers the mild lustre of the blooming morn,
And his the radiance of the risen day.
  They lov'd : but such their guiltless passion was,
As in the dawn of time inform'd the heart
Of innocence, and undissembling truth.
'Twas friendship heighten'd by the mutual wish,
Th' enchanting hope, and sympathetic glow,
Beam'd from the mutual eye. Devoting all
To love, each was to each a dearer self ;
                              Supremely

Supremely happy in th' awaken'd power
Of giving joy. Alone, amid the shades,
Still in harmonious intercourse they liv'd
The rural day, and talk'd the flowing heart,
Or figh'd, and look'd unutterable things.
   So pass'd their life, a clear united stream,
By care unruffled : till, in evil hour,
The tempest caught them on the tender walk,
Heedless how far, and where its mazes stray'd,
While, with each other bless, creative love
Still bade eternal Eden smile around.
Heavy with instant fate her bosom heav'd
Unwonted sighs, and stealing oft a look
Tow'rds the big gloom, on CELADON her eye
Fell tearful, wetting her disordered cheek.
In vain affuring love, and confidence
In HEAVEN, reprefs'd her fear ; it grew, and shook
Her frame near diffolution. He perceiv'd
Th' unequal conflict, and as angels look
On dying faints, his eyes compaffion shed,
With love illumin'd high. " Fear not, he said,
" Sweet innocence ! thou ftranger to offence;
" And inward ftorm ! HE, who yon skies involves
" In frowns of darkness, ever smiles on thee
" With kind regard. O'er thee the fecret shaft
" That wastes at midnight, or th' undreaded hour
" Of noon, flies harmlefs : and that very voice,
" Which thunders terror thro' the guilty heart,
" With tongues of feraphs whispers peace to thine.
" 'Tis fafety to be near thee, fure and thus
" To clafp perfection !) From his void embrace,
(Myfterious Heaven ?) that moment, to the ground,
A blacken'd corfe, was ftruck the beauteous maid.
But who can paint the lover as he ftood,
Pierc'd by fevere amazement, hating life,
Speechlefs, and fix'd in all the depth of woe !
So, faint refemblance ! on the marble tomb,
The well-diffembled mourner ftooping ftands,
For ever filent, and for ever fad.
THOMSON.
C H A P.

C H A P. XVII.

J U N I O and T H E A N A.

SOON as young reason dawn'd in Junio's breast,
  His father sent him from these genial isles,
To where old Thames with conscious pride surveys
Green Eton, soft abode of every Muse.
Each classic beauty soon he made his own ;
And soon fam'd Isis saw him woo the Nine,
On her inspiring banks ; Love tun'd his song;
For fair Theana was his only theme,
Acasto's daughter, whom, in early youth,
He oft distinguish'd ; and for whom he oft
Had clim'd the bending cocoa's airy height,
To rob it of its nectar ; which the maid,
When he presented, more nectareous deem'd.——
The sweetest sappadillas oft he brought ;
From him more sweet ripe sappadillas seem'd.——
Nor had long absence yet effac'd her form ;
Her charms still triumph'd o'er Britannia's fair.
One morn he met her in Sheen's royal walks :
Nor knew, till then, sweet Sheen contain'd his all.
His taste mature approv'd his infant choice.
In colour, form, expression, and in grace,
She shone all perfect ; while each pleasing art,
And each soft virtue that the sex adorns,
Adorn'd the woman. My imperfect strain
Can ill describe the transports Junio felt
At this discovery. He declar'd his love ;
She own'd his merit, nor refus'd his hand.

  And shall not Hymen light his brightest torch,
For this delighted pair ? Ah, Junio knew,
His sire detested his Theana's house !——
Thus duty, reverence, gratitude, conspir'd
To check their happy union. He resolv'd
(And many a sigh that resolution cost)
To pass the time, till death his sire remov'd,
in visiting old Europe's letter'd climes :

While

While she (and many a tear that parting drew)
Embark'd, reluctant, for her native isle.
   Tho' learned, curious, and tho' nobly bent
With each rare talent to adorn his mind,
His native land to serve; no joys he found.—
Yet sprightly Gaul, yet Belgium, Saturn's reign ;
Yet Greece, of old the seat of every Muse,
Of freedom, courage; yet Ausonia's clime,
His steps explor'd : where painting, music's strains,
Where arts, where laws (philosophy's best child)
With rival beauties, his attention claim'd.
To his just-judging, his instructed eye,
The all-perfect Medicean Venus seem'd
A perfect semblance of his Indian fair :
But, when she spoke of love, her voice surpass'd
The harmonious warblings of Italian song.
   Twice one long year elaps'd, when letters came,
Which briefly told him of his father's death.
Afflicted, filial, yet to Heaven resign'd,
Soon he reach'd Albion, and as soon embark'd,
Eager to clasp the object of his love.
   Blow, prosperous breezes; swiftly sail, thou Po :
Swift sail'd the Po, and happy breezes blew.
   In Biscay's stormy seas an armed ship,
Of force superior, from loud Charente's wave
Clapt them on board.   The frighted flying crew
Their colours strike; when dauntless Junio, fir'd
With noble indignation, kill'd the chief,
Who on the bloody deck dealt slaughter round.
The Gauls retreat : the Britons loud huzza ;
And touch'd with shame, with emulation stung,
So plied their cannon, plied their missile fires,
That soon in air the hapless Thunderer blew.
   Blow, prosperous breezes; swiftly sail, thou Po :
May no more dangerous fights retard thy way !
   Soon Porto Santo's rocky heights they 'spy,
Like clouds dim rising in the distant sky.
Glad Eurus whistles; laugh the sportive crew;
Each sail is set to catch the favouring gale,
While on the yard-arm the harpooner sits.
Strikes the boneta, or the shark insnares.
D

The

The little nautilus with purple pride
Expands his fails, and dances o'er the waves:
Small winged fifhes on the fhrouds alight;
And beauteous dolphins gently play'd around.

    Tho' faster then the tropic-bird they flew,
Oft Junio cried, ah! when fhall we fee land?
Soon land they made: and now in thought he clafp'd
His Indian bride, and deem'd his toils o'er paid.

    She, no lefs anxious, every evening walk'd
On the cool margin of the purple main,
Intent her Junio's veffel to defcry.

    On eve, (faint calms for many a day had rag'd)
The winged Dæmons of the tempeft rofe;
Thunder, and rain, the lightning's awful power.
She fled: could innocence, could beauty claim
Exemption from the grave; the ethereal bolt,
'That ftretch'd her fpeechlefs, o'er her lovely head
Had innocently roll'd.

    Mean while, impatient Junio leap'd afhore,
Regardlefs of the Dæmons of the ftorm.
Ah! youth! what woes, too great for man to bear,
Are ready to burft on thee? Urge not fo
Thy flying courfer. Soon Theana's porch
Receiv'd him: at his fight, the ancient flaves
Affrighted fhriek, and to the chamber point:——
Confounded, yet unknowing what they meant,
He entered hafty——

    Ah! what a fight for one who lov'd fo well!
All pale and cold, in every feature death,
Theana lay; and yet a glimpfe of joy
Played on her face, while with faint, faultering voice,
She thus addrefs'd the youth, whom yet fhe knew,

    " Welcome, my Junio, to thy native fhore!
" Thy fight repays this fummons of my fate:
" Live, and live happy; fometimes think of me:
" By night, by day, you ftill engag'd my care;
" And next to God, you now my thoughts employ:
" Accept of this——My little all I give;
" Would it were larger"——Nature could no more:
She look'd, embrac'd him, with a groan expir'd.

But

But fay, what ftrains, what language can exprefs
The thoufand pangs, which tore the lover's breaft?
Upon the breathlefs corfe himfelf he threw,
And to her clay-cold lips, with trembling hafte,
Ten thoufand kiffes gave.   He ftrove to fpeak;
Nor words he found : he clafp'd her in his arms;
He figh'd, he fwoon'd, look'd up and died away.

One grave contains this haplefs, faithful pair;
And ftill the Cane-ifles tell their matchlefs love !
GRAINGER.

C H A P.   XVIII.

DOUGLAS to Lord RANDOLPH.

MY name is NORVAL : on the Grampian hills
My father feeds his flock ; a frugal fwain,
Whofe conftant cares were to encreafe his ftore,
And keep his only fon, myfelf at home.
For I had heard of battles, and I long'd
To follow to the field fome warlike lord ;
And heaven foon granted what my fire denied.
This moon which rofe laft night, round as my fhield,
Had not yet fill'd her horns, when, by her light,
A band of fierce barbarians, from the hills,
Rufh'd like a torrent down upon the vale,
Sweeping our flocks and herds. The fhepherds fled,
For fafety, and for fuccour.   I alone,
With bended bow, and quiver full of arrows,
Hover'd about the enemy, and mark'd
The road he took, then hafted to my friends :
Whom, with a troop of fifty chofen men,
I met advancing.   The purfuit I led,
Till we o'ertook the fpoil-encumbered foe.
We fought and conquer'd. Ere a fword was drawn,
An arrow from my bow had pierc'd their chief,
Who wore that day the arms which now I wear.
Returning home in triumph, I difdain'd
The fhepherd's flothful life; and having heard
That our good king had fummon'd his bold peers,

D 2
To

To lead their warriors to the Carron side,
I left my father's houfe, and took with me
A chofen fervant to conduct my fteps :——
Yon trembling coward who forfook his mafter.
Journying with this intent, I paft thefe towers,
And, heaven-directed, came this day to do
The happy deed that gilds my humble name.

HOME.

C H A P. XIX.

OTHELLO's APOLOGY.

MOST potent, grave, and reverend Signiors,
  My very noble and approved good mafters;
That I have ta'en away this old man's daughter,
It is moft true; true, I have married her;
The very head and front of my offending
Hath this extent; no more. Rude am I in fpeech,
And little blefs'd with the foft phrafe of peace ;
For fince thefe arms of mine had feven years' pith,
Till now fome nine moons wafted, they have us'd
Their deareft action in the tented field ;
And little of this great world can I fpeak,
More than pertains to feats of broils and battle ;
And therefore little fhall I grace my caufe,
In fpeaking for myfelf.   Yet, by your patience,
I will a round unvarnifh'd tale deliver,
Of my whole courfe of love; what drugs, what
        charms,
What conjuration, and what mighty magic,
(For fuch proceeding I am charg'd withal)
I won his daughter with.——————
    Her father lov'd me, oft invited me ;
Still queftioned me the ftory of my life,
From year to year; the battles, fieges, fortunes,
That I have paft.
I ran it through, ev'n from my boyifh days,
To th' very moment that he bade me tell it.
Wherein I fpoke of moft difaftrous chances,

Of

Of moving accidents by flood and field :
Of hair-breadth 'scapes in th' imminent deadly
          breach :
Of being taken by the infolent foe,
And fold to flavery ; of my redemption thence,
And with it all my travel's hiftory :
Wherein of antres vaft, and defarts idle,
Rough quarries, rocks, and hills, whofe heads touch
          heav'n,
It was my bent to fpeak.—All thefe to hear
Would Defdemona ferioufly incline.
But ftill the houfe-affairs would draw her thence,
Which ever as fhe could with hafte difpatch,
She'd come again, and with a greedy ear
Devour up my difcourfe : which I obferving,
Took once a pliant hour, and found good means
To draw from her a prayer of earneft heart,
That I would all my pilgrimage dilate ;
Whereof by parcels fhe had fomething heard,
But not diftinctively.   I did confent,
And often did beguile her of her tears,
When I did fpeak of fome diftrefsful ftroke
That my youth fuffer'd.   My ftory being done,
She gave me for my pains a world of fighs.
She fwore, in faith, 'twas ftrange, 'twas paffing
          ftrange,
'Twas pitiful, 'twas wond'rous pitiful——
She wifh'd fhe had not heard it ;——yet fhe wifh'd
That Heav'n had made her fuch a man :—fhe thank'd
          me,
And bade me, if I had a friend that lov'd her,
I fhould but teach him how to tell my ftory,
And that would woo her.   On this hint I fpake ;
She lov'd me for the dangers I had paft ;
And I lov'd her, that fhe did pity them.
This only is the witchcraft I have us'd.

SHAKESPEAR.

D 3   B O O K

B O O K III.

DIDACTIC PIECES.

C H A P. I.

On M O D E S T Y.

I KNOW no two words that have been more abuf-
ed by the different and wrong interpretations
which are put upon them, than thefe two, Modefty
and Affurance. To fay, fuch a one is a modeft man,
fometimes indeed paffes for a good character; but
at prefent is very often ufed to fignify a fheepifh
aukward fellow, who has neither good breeding,
politenefs, nor any knowledge of the world.

AGAIN, A man of affurance, though at firft it
only denoted a perfon of a free and open carriage,
is now very ufually applied to a profligate wretch,
who can break through all the rules of decency and
morality without a blufh.

I SHALL endeavour therefore in this effay to reftore thefe words to their true meaning, to prevent
the idea of Modefty from being confounded with that
of Sheepifhnefs, and to hinder impudence from paffing for Affurance.

IF I was put to define Modefty, I would call it,
The reflection of an ingenuous mind, either when a
man has committed an action for which he cenfures
himfelf, or fancies that he is expofed to the cenfure
of others.

FOR this reafon a man truly modeft is as much
fo when he is alone as in company, and as fubject to
a blufh

a blush in his closet, as when the eyes of multitudes are upon him.

I do not remember to have met with any instance of modesty with which I am so well pleased, as that celebrated one of the young Prince, whose father, being a tributary king to the Romans, had several complaints laid against him before the senate, as a tyrant and oppressor of his subjects. The Prince went to Rome to defend his father, but coming into the senate, and hearing a multitude of crimes proved upon him, was so oppressed when it came to his turn to speak, that he was unable to utter a word. The story tells us, that the fathers were more moved at this instance of modesty and ingenuity, than they could have been by the most pathetic oration; and, in short, pardoned the guilty father for this early promise of virtue in the son.

I take Assurance to be, The faculty of possessing a man's self, or of saying and doing indifferent things without any uneasiness or emotion in the mind. That which generally gives a man assurance, is a moderate knowledge of the world, but above all, a mind fixed and determined in itself to do nothing against the rules of honour and decency. An open and assured behaviour is the natural consequence of such a resolution. A man thus armed, if his words or actions are at any time misinterpreted, retires within himself, and from a consciousness of his own integrity, assumes force enough to despise the little censures of ignorance or malice.

Every one ought to cherish and encourage in himself the modesty and assurance I have here mentioned.

A man without assurance is liable to be made uneasy by the folly or ill-nature of every one he converses with. A man without modesty is lost to all sense of honour and virtue.

It is more than probable, that the Prince abovementioned possessed both these qualifications in a

very

very eminent degree. Without affurance he would never have undertaken to fpeak before the moft auguft affembly in the world; without modefty he would have pleaded the caufe he had taken upon him, though it had appeared ever fo fcandalous.

FROM what has been faid, it is plain, that modefty and affurance are both amiable, and may very well meet in the fame perfon. When they are thus mixed and blended together, they compofe what we endeavour to exprefs when we fay, a modeft affurance; by which we underftand the juft mean between bafhfulnefs and impudence.

I SHALL conclude with obferving that as the fame man may be both modeft and affured, fo it is alfo poffible for the fame perfon to be both impudent and bafhful.

WE have frequent inftances of this odd kind of mixture in people of depraved minds and mean education; who, though they are not able to meet a man's eyes, or pronounce a fentence without confufion, can voluntarily commit the greateft villanies, or moft indecent actions.

SUCH a perfon feems to have made a refolution to do ill even in fpite of himfelf, and in defiance of all thofe checks and reftraints his temper and complexion feem to have laid in his way.

UPON the whole, I would endeavour to eftablifh this maxim, That the practice of virtue is the moft proper method to give a man a becoming affurance in his words and actions. Guilt always feeks to fhelter itfelf in one of the extremes, and is fometimes attended with both.

SPECTATOR.

CHAP.

I HAVE always preferred Chearfulnefs to Mirth. The latter I confider as an act, the former as a habit of the mind. Mirth is fhort and tranfient, chearfulnefs fixed and permanent. Thofe are often raifed into the greateft tranfports of mirth, who are fubject to the greateft depreffions of melancholy: on the contrary, chearfulnefs, though it does not give the mind fuch an exquifite gladnefs, prevents us from falling into any depths of forrow. Mirth is like a flafh of lightning, that breaks through a gloom of clouds, and glitters for a moment; chearfulnefs keeps up a kind of day-light in the mind, and fills it with a fteady and perpetual ferenity.

Men of auftere principles look upon mirth as too wanton and diffolute for a ftate of probation, and as filled with a certain triumph and infolence of heart that is inconfiftent with a life which is every moment obnoxious to the greateft dangers. Writers of this complexion have obferved, that the facred Perfon who was the greateft pattern of perfection was never feen to laugh.

Chearfulness of mind is not liable to any of thefe exceptions; it is of a ferious and compofed nature; it does not throw the mind into a condition improper for the prefent ftate of humanity, and is very confpicuous in the characters of thofe who are looked upon as the greateft Philofophers among the Heathens, as well as among thofe who have been defervedly efteemed as faints and holy men among Chriftians.

If we confider chearfulnefs in three lights, with regard to ourfelves, to thofe we converfe with, and to the great Author of our being, it will not a little recommend itfelf on each of thefe accounts. The man who is poffeffed of this excellent frame of mind,

is

is not only eafy in h[is] thoughts, but a perfect mafter of all the powers and faculties of his foul : his imagination is always clear, and his judgment undifturbed : his temper is even and unruffled, whether in action or in folitude. He comes with a relifh to all thofe goods whic' nature has provided for him, taftes all the pleafures of the creation which are poured upon him, and does not feel the full weight of thofe accidental evils which may befall him.

IF we confider him in relation to the perfons whom he converfes with, it naturally produces love and good-will towards him. A chearful mind is not only difpofed to be affable and obliging; but raifes the fame good-humour in thofe who come within its influence. A man finds himfelf pleafed, he does not know why, with the chearfulnefs of his companion : it is like a fudden funfhine that awakens a fecret delight in the mind, without her attending to it. The heart rejoices of its own accord, and naturally flows out into friendfhip and benevolence towards the perfon who has fo kindly an effect upon it.

WHEN I confider this chearful ftate of mind in its third relation, I cannot but look upon it as a conftant habitual gratitude to the Author of nature. An inward chearfulnefs is an implicit praife and thankfgiving to Providence under all its difpenfations. It is a kind of acquiefcence in the ftate wherein we are placed, and a fecret approbation of the Divine will in his conduct towards men.

A MAN, who ufes his beft endeavours to live according to the dictates of virtue and right reafon, has two perpetual fources of chearfulnefs, in the confideration of his own nature, and of that Being on whom he has a dependence. If he looks into himfelf, he cannot but rejoice in that exiftence, which is fo lately beftowed upon him, and which, after millions of ages, will be ftill new, and ftill in its beginning. How many felf-congratulations naturally rife in the mind, when it reflects on this its entrance into eternity, when it takes a view of thofe

improveable

all, with regard to thofe who have a right notion of it. Secondly, with regard to thofe who have a miftaken notion of it. And thirdly, with regard to thofe who treat it as chimerical, and turn it into ridicule.

IN the firft place, true honour, though it be a different principle from religion, is that which produces the fame effects. The lines of action, though drawn from different parts, terminate in the fame point. Religion embraces virtue, and it is enjoined by the laws of God; honour, as it is graceful and ornamental to human nature. The religious man fears, the man of honour fcorns to do an ill action. The latter confiders vice as fomething that is beneath him, the other as fomething that is offenfive to the Divine Being. The one as what is unbecoming, the other as what is forbidden. Thus Seneca fpeaks in the natural and genuine language of a man of honour, when he declares that were there no God to fee or punifh vice, he would not commit it, becaufe it is of fo mean, fo bafe, and fo vile a nature.

I SHALL conclude this head with the defcription of honour in the part of young Juba.

Honour's facred tie, the law of kings,
The noble mind's diftinguifhing perfection,
That aids and ftrengthens virtue when it meets her,
And imitates her actions where fhe is not.
It ought not to be fported with.——

CATO.

IN the fecond place, we are to confider thofe who have miftaken notions of honour. And thefe are fuch as eftablifh any thing to themfelves for a point of honour which is contrary either to the laws of God, or of their country; who think it more honourable to revenge than to forgive an injury; who make no fcruple of telling a lie, but would put any man to death that accufes them of it; who are more careful to guard their reputation by their courage than

than by their virtue. True fortitude is indeed so becoming in human nature, that he who wants it scarce deserves the name of a man; but we find several who so much abuse this notion, that they place the whole idea of honour in a kind of brutal courage; by which means we have had many among us who have called themselves men of honour, that would have been a disgrace to a gibbet. In a word, the man who sacrifices any duty of a reasonable creature to a prevailing mode or fashion, who looks upon any thing as honourable that is displeasing to his Maker, or destructive to society, who thinks himself obliged by this principle to the practice of some virtues and not of others, is by no means to be reckoned among true men of honour.

TIMOGENES was a lively instance of one actuated by false honour. Timogenes would smile at a man's jest who ridiculed his Maker, and at the same time, run a man through the body that spoke ill of his friend. Timogenes would have scorned to have betrayed a secret, that was intrusted with him, though the fate of his country depended upon the discovery of it. Timogenes took away the life of a young fellow in a duel, for having spoken ill of Belinda, a lady whom he himself had seduced in her youth, and betrayed into want and ignominy. To close his character, Timogenes, after having ruined several poor tradesmen's families, who had trusted him, sold his estate to satisfy his creditors; but like a man of honour, disposed of all the money he could make of it, in the paying off his play debts, or to speak in his own language, his debts of honour.

IN the third place we are to consider those persons who treat this principle as chimerical, and turn it into ridicule. Men who are professedly of no honour, are of a more profligate and abandoned nature than even those who are actuated by false notions of it, as there is more hope of a heretic than of an atheist. These sons of infamy consider honour with old Syphax, in the play before-mentioned, as a fine imaginary

ginary

ginary notion that leads aftray youn unexperienced men, and draws them into real mifchefs, while they are engaged in the purfuits of a fhadow. Thefe are generally perfons who, in Shakefpear's phrafe, " are worn and hackneyed in the ways of men ;" whofe imaginations are grown callous, and have loft all thofe delicate fentiments which are natural to minds that are innocent and undepraved. Such old battered mifcreants ridicule every thing as romantic that comes in competition with their prefent intereft, and treat thofe perfons as vifionaries, who dare ftand up in a corrupt age, for what has not its immediate reward joined to it. The talents, intereft, or experience of fuch men, make them very often ufeful in all parties, and at all times. But whatever wealth and dignities they may arrive at, they ought to confider, that every one ftands as a blot in the annals of his country, who arrives at the temple of honour by any other way than through that of virtue.

Guardian.

C H A P.   V.

On GOOD HUMOUR.

GOOD humour may be defined a habit of being pleafed; a conftant and perennial foftnefs of manner, eafinefs of approach, and fuavity of difpofition ; like that which every man perceives in himfelf, when the firft tranfports of new felicity have fubfided, and his thoughts are only kept in motion by a flow fucceffion of foft impulfes. Good humour is a ftate between gaiety and unconcern ; the act or emanation of a mind at leifure, to regard the gratification of another.

It is imagined by many, that whenever they afpire to pleafe, they are required to be merry, and to fhew the gladnefs of their fouls by flights of pleafantry, and burfts of laughter. But though thefe men may be for a time heard with applaufe and admiration,

miration, they seldom delight us long. We enjoy them a little, and then retire to easiness and good humour, as the eye gazes a while on eminences glittering with the sun, but soon turns aching away to verdure and to flowers.

GAIETY is to good humour as animal perfumes to vegetable fragrance; the one overpowers weak spirits, and the other recreates and revives them. Gaiety seldom fails to give some pain; the hearers either strain their faculties to accompany its towerings, or are left behind in envy and despair. Good humour boast no faculties which every one does not believe in his power, and pleases principally by not offending.

IT is well known that the most certain way to give any man pleasure, is to persuade him that you receive pleasure from him, to encourage him to freedom and confidence, and to avoid any such appearance of superiority as may overbear and depress him. We see many that by this art only, spend their days in the midst of caresses, invitations, and civilities; and without any extraordinary qualities or attainments, are the universal favourites of both sexes, and certainly find a friend in every place. The darlings of the world will, indeed, be generally found such as excite neither jealousy nor fear, and are not considered as candidates for any eminent degree of reputation, but content themselves with common accomplishments, and endeavour rather to solicit kindness than to raise esteem. Therefore in assemblies and places of resort it seldom fails to happen, that though at the entrance of some particular person every face brightens with gladness, and every hand is extended in salutation, yet if you pursue him beyond the first exchange of civilities, you will find him of very small importance; whereas the good-natured man is welcome to the whole company, and looked upon as one by whom all conceive themselves admired, one with whom any one is at liberty to amuse himself when he can find no other auditor or companion, as one with whom all are at ease,

who

who will hear a jeſt without criticiſm, and a narrative without contradiction, who laughs at every wit,
and yields to every diſputer.

There are many whoſe vanity always inclines
them to aſſociate with thoſe from whom they have
no reaſon to fear mortification ; and there are times
in which the wiſe and the knowing are willing to
receive praiſe without the labour of deſerving it, in
which the moſt elevated mind is willing to deſcend,
and the moſt active to be at reſt.   All therefore are
at ſome hour or another fond of companions whom
they can entertain upon eaſy terms, and who will
relieve them from ſolitude, without condemning
them to vigilance and caution. We are moſt inclined to love when we have nothing to fear, and he
that encourages us to pleaſe ourſelves, will not be
long without preference in our affection to thoſe
whoſe learning holds us at the ſame diſtance of pu-
pils, or whoſe wit calls all attention from us, and
leaves us without importance, and without regard.

It is remarked by prince Henry, when he ſees
Falſtaff lying on the ground. " that he could have
" better ſpared a better man.". He was well acquainted with the vices and follies of him whom he
lamented, but while his conviction compelled him
to do juſtice to ſuperior qualities, his tenderneſs ſtill
broke out at the remembrance of Falſtaff, of the
chearful companion, the loud buffoon, with whom he
had paſſed his time in all the luxury of idleneſs, who
had gladdened him with unenvied merriment, and
whom he could at once enjoy and deſpiſe.

You may perhaps think this account of thoſe
who are diſtinguiſhed for their good humour, not
very conſiſtent with the praiſes which I have be-
ſtowed upon it. But ſurely nothing can more evi-
dently ſhew the value of this quality, than that it
recommends thoſe who are deſtitute of all other excellencies, and procures regard to the trifling, friendſhip to the worthleſs, and affection to the dull.

Good

Good humour is indeed generally degraded by the characters in which it is found ; for being considered as a cheap and vulgar quality, we find it often neglected by those that having excellencies of higher reputation and greater splendor, perhaps imagine that they have some right to gratify themselves at the expence of others, and are to demand compliance, rather than to practife it. It is by some unfortunate mistake that almost all those who have any claim to esteem or love, prefs their pretensions with too little consideration of others. This mistake my own interest as well as my zeal for general happiness makes me desirous to rectify ; for I have a friend, who because he knows his own fidelity, and usefulness, is never willing to sink into a companion. I have a wife whose beauty first subdued me, and whose wit confirmed her conquest ; but whose beauty now serves no other purpose than to entitle her to tyranny, and whose wit is only used to justify perverfeness.

Surely nothing can be more unreasonable than to lofe the will to please, when we are conscious of the power, or shew more cruelty than to chufe any kind of influence before that of kindness. He that regards the welfare of others, should make his virtue approachable, that it may be loved and copied ; and he that considers the wants which every man feels, or will feel of external assistance, must rather wish to be surrounded by those that love him, than by those that admire his excellencies, or folicit his favours ; for admiration ceases with novelty, and interest gains its end and retires. A man whose great qualities want the ornament of superficial attractions, is like a naked mountain with mines of gold, which will be frequented only till the treasure is exhausted.

RAMBLER.

CHAP.

NOTHING has fo much expofed men of learning to contempt and ridicule, as their ignorance of things which are known to all but themfelves. Thofe who have been taught to confider the inftitutions of the fchools, as giving the laft perfection to human abilities, are furprized to fee men wrinkled with ftudy, yet wanting to be inftructed in the minute circumftances of propriety, or the neceffary forms of daily tranfaction ; and quickly fhake off their reverence for modes of education, which they find to produce no ability above the reft of mankind.

Books, fays Bacon, can never teach the ufe of books. The ftudent muft learn by commerce with mankind to reduce his fpeculations to practice, and accommodate his knowledge to the purpofes of life.

It is too common for thofe who have been bred to fcholaftic profeffions, and paffed much of their time in academies where nothing but learning confers honours, to difregard every other qualification, and to imagine that they fhall find mankind ready to pay homage to their knowledge, and to crowd about them for inftruction. They therefore ftep out from their cells into the open world, with all the confidence of authority and dignity of importance ; they look round about them at once with ignorance and fcorn on a race of beings to whom they are equally unknown and equally contemptible, but whofe manners they muft imitate, and with whofe opinions they muft comply, if they defire to pafs their time happily among them.

To leffen that difdain with which fcholars are inclined to look on the common bufinefs of the world, and the unwillingnefs with which they condefcend

to learn what is not to be found in any fyftem of philofophy, it may be neceffary to confider that though
admiration is excited by abftrufe refearches and remote difcoveries, yet pleafure is not given, nor affection conciliated, but by fofter accomplifhments,
and qualities more eafily communicable to thofe
about us. He that can only converfe upon quefti-
ons, about which only a fmall part of mankind has
knowledge fufficient to make them curious, muft
lofe his days in unfocial filence, and live in the crowd
of life without a companion. He that can only be
ufeful on great occafions, may die without exerting
his abilities, and ftand a helplefs fpectator of a
thoufand vexations which fret away happinefs,
and which nothing is required to remove but
a little dexterity of conduct and readinefs of expedients.

No degrees of knowledge attainable by man is able
to fet him above the want of hourly affiftance, or to
extinguifh the defire of fond endearments, and tender officioufnefs ; and therefore, no one fhould think
it unneceffary to learn thofe arts by which friendfhip
may be gained. Kindnefs is preferved by a conftant
reciprocation of benefits or interchange of pleafures;
but fuch benefits only can be beftowed, as others are
capable of receiving, and fuch pleafures only impart-
ed, as others are qualified to enjoy.

By this defcent from the pinnacles of art no honour will be loft; for the condefcenfions of learning
are always overpaid by gratitude. An elevated genius employed in little things, appears, to ufe the
fimile of Longinus, like the fun in his evening
declination, he remits his fplendor but retains
his magnitude, and pleafes more though he dazzles
lefs.

RAMBLER.

C H A P.

C H A P. VI.

ON THE ADVANTAGES OF UNITING GENTLENESS OF MANNERS WITH FIRMNESS OF MIND.

I Mentioned to you, fome time ago, a fentence, which I would moft earneftly wifh you always to retain in your thoughts, and obferve in your conduct. It is *fuaviter in modo, fortiter in re.* I do not know any one rule fo unexceptionably ufeful and neceffary in every part of life.

The *fuaviter in modo* alone would degenerate and fink into a mean, timid complaifance, and paffivenefs, if not fupported and dignified by the *fortiter in re;* which would alfo run into impetuofity and brutality, if not tempered and foftened by the *fuaviter in modo:* however, they are feldom united. The warm, choleric man, with ftrong annimal fpirits, defpifes the *fuaviter in modo,* and thinks to carry all before him by the *fortiter in re.* He may poffibly by great accident, now and then fucceed, when he has only weak and timid people to deal with ; but his general fate will be, to fhock, offend, be hated and fail. On the other hand, the cunning crafty man, thinks to gain all his ends by the *fuaviter in modo* only : he becomes all things to all men ; he feems to have no opinion of his own, and fervilely adopts the prefent opinion of the prefent perfon ; he infinuates himfelf only into the efteem of fools, but is foon detected, and furely defpifed by every body elfe. The wife man (who differs as much from the cunning, as from the choleric man) alone joins the *fuaviter in modo* with the *fortiter in re.*

IF you are in authority, and have a right to command, your commands, delivered *fuaviter in modo* will be willingly, chearfully, and confequently well obeyed ; whereas, if given only *fortiter,* that is brutally, they will rather, as Tacitus fays, be interpret-
ed

ed than executed. For my own part, if I bid my footman bring me a glaſs of wine, in a rough, inſulting manner, I ſhould expect, that in obeying me, he would contrive to ſpill ſome of it upon me ; and I am ſure I ſhould deſerve it. A cool ſteady reſolution would ſhew, that where you have a right to command, you will be obeyed ; but, at the ſame time, a gentleneſs in the manner of enforcing that obedience, ſhould make it a chearful one, and ſoften, as much as poſſible, the mortifying conſciouſneſs of inferiority. If you are to aſk a favour, or even to ſolicit your due, you muſt do it *ſuaviter in modo,* or you will give thoſe, who have a mind to refuſe you either, a pretence to do it, by reſenting the manner ; but, on the other hand, you muſt, by a ſteady perſeverance and decent tenaciouſneſs, ſhow the *fortiter in re.* In ſhort, This precept is the only way I know in the world, of being loved without being deſpiſed, and feared without being hated. It conſtitutes the dignity of character, which every wiſe man muſt endeavour to eſtabliſh.

If therefore you find that you have a haſtineſs in your temper, which unguardedly breaks out into indiſcreet ſallies, or rough expreſſions, to either your ſuperiors, your equals, or your inferiors, watch it narrowly, check it carefully, and call the *ſuaviter in modo* to your aſſiſtance : at the firſt impulſe of paſſion be ſilent, till you can be ſoft. Labour even to get the command of your countenance ſo well, that thoſe emotions may not be read in it : a moſt unſpeakable advantage in buſineſs ! On the other hand, let no complaiſance, no gentleneſs of temper, no weak deſire of pleaſing on your part, no wheedling, coaxing, nor flattery, on other people's, make you recede one jot from any point that reaſon and prudence have bid you purſue ; but return to the charge, perſiſt, perſevere, and you will find moſt things attainable that are poſſible. A yielding, timid meekneſs is always abuſed and inſulted by the unjuſt and the unfeeling ; but meekneſs when ſuſtained by the *fortiter*

in

in re, is always refpected, commonly fuccefsful. In your friendfhips and connections, as well as in your enmities, this rule is particularly ufeful ; let your firmnefs and vigour preferve and invite attachments to you ; but, at the fame time, let your manner hinder the enemies of your friends and dependants from becoming yours : let your enemies be difarmed by the gentlenefs of your manner, but let them feel at the fame time, the fteadinefs of your juft refentment; for there is great difference between bearing malice, which is always ungenerous, and a refolute felf defence, which is always prudent and juftifiable.

I conclude with this obfervation, That gentlenefs of manners, with firmnefs of mind, is a fhort, but full defcription of human perfection, on this fide of religious and moral duties.

Lord Chesterfield.

C H A P.   VIII.

On GOOD SENSE.

WERE I to explain what I underftand by good fenfe, I fhould call it right reafon ; but right reafon that arifes, not from formal and logical deductions, but from a fort of intuitive faculty in the foul, which diftinguifhes by immediate perception : a kind of innate fagacity, that in many of its properties feems very much to refemble inftinct. It would be improper, therefore, to fay, that Sir Ifaac Newton fhewed his good fenfe, by thofe amazing difcoveries which he made in natural philofophy : the operations of this gift of heaven are rather inftantaneous, than the refult of any tedious procefs. Like Diamed, after Minerva had endued him with the power of difcerning gods from mortals, the man difcovers at once the truth of thofe objects he is moft concerned to diftinguifh ; and conducts himfelf with fuitable caution and fecurity.

It is for this reafon, poffibly, that this quality of the mind is not fo often found united with learning as

E

one

one could wish : for good sense being accustomed to receive her discoveries without labour or study, she cannot so easily wait for those truths, which being traced at a distance, and lying concealed under numberless covers, require much pains and application to unfold.

But though good sense is not in the number, nor always, it must be owned, in the company of the sciences ; yet is it (as the most sensible of poets has justly observed)

> fairly worth the seven.

Rectitude of understanding is indeed the most useful, as well as the most noble of human endowments, as it is the sovereign guide and director in every branch of civil and social intercourse.

Upon whatever occasion this enlightening faculty is exerted, it is always sure to act with distinguished eminence; but its chief and peculiar province seems to lie in the commerce of the world. Accordingly we may observe, that those who have conversed more with men than with books ; whose wisdom is derived rather from experience than contemplation ; generally possess this happy talent with superior perfection, For good sense, though it cannot be acquired, may be improved ; and the world, I believe, will ever be found to afford the most kindly soil for its cultivation.

C H A P.   IX.

On S T U D Y.

STUDIES serve for delight, for ornament, and for ability. Their chief use for delight is in privateness and retiring ; for ornament, is in discourse ; and for ability, is in the judgment and disposition of business. For expert men can execute, and perhaps judge of particulars one by one ; but the general counsels, and the plots, and marshalling of affairs, come best from those that are learned. To spend too much time in studies is sloth ; to use them too much

for

for ornament is affectation; to make judgment wholly by their rules is the humour of a scholar. They perfect nature, and are perfected by experience; for natural abilities are like natural plants, that need pruning by study, and studies themselves do give forth directions too much at large, except they be bounded in by experience. Crafty men contemn studies, simple men admire them, and wise men use them: for they teach not their own use, but that is a wisdom without them, won by observation. Read not to contradict and confute, not to believe and take for granted, nor to find talk and discourse, but to weigh and consider. Some books are to be tasted, others to be swallowed, and some few to be chewed and digested; that is, some books are to be read only in parts; others to be read, but not curiously; and some few to be read wholly, and with diligence and attention. Some books also may be read by deputy, and extracts made of them by others; but that should be only in the less important arguments, and the meaner sort of books; else distilled books are like common distilled waters, flashy things. Reading maketh a full man; conference a ready man; and writing an exact man. And therefore, if a man write little, he had need have a present wit; and if he read little, he had need have much cunning to seem to know that he doth not.

Bacon.

CHAP. X.
On SATIRICAL WIT.

—TRUST me, this unwary pleasantry of thine will sooner or later bring thee into scrapes and difficulties, which no after wit can extricate thee out of. In these sallies, too oft, I see, it happens, that the person laughed at, considers himself in the light of a person injured, with all the rights of such a situation belonging to him; and when thou viewest him in that light too, and reckon'st upon his friends, his family, his kindred and allies, and mustereth up with them the many recruits which will list under him from a sense of common danger; 'tis no extravagant arithmetic to say, that for every ten jokes, thou hast got an hundred enemies; and till thou hast gone on, and raised a swarm of wasps about thine ears, and art half stung to death by them, thou wilt never be convinced it is so.

I cannot suspect it in the man whom I esteem, that there is the least spur from spleen or malevolence of intent in these sallies. I believe and know them to be truly honest and sportive: but consider that fools cannot distinguish this, and that knaves will not; and thou knowest not what it is, either to provoke the one, or to make merry the other: whenever they associate for mutual defence, depend upon it, they will carry on the war in such a manner against thee, my dear friend, as to make thee heartily sick of it, and of thy life too.

Revenge from some baneful corner shall level a tale of dishonour at thee, which no innocence of heart or integrity of conduct shall set right. The fortunes of thy house shall totter,——thy character, which led the way to them, shall bleed on every side of it—thy faith be questioned--thy works belied—thy wit forgotten—thy learning trampled on. To wind up the last scene of thy tragedy, Cruelty and Cowardice, twin ruffians, hired and set on by Malice in the dark, shall strike together at all thy infirmities and mistakes: the best of us, my friend, lie open there, and trust me—when to gratify a private appetite, it is once resolved upon, that an innocent and an helpless creature shall be sacrificed, it is an easy matter to pick up sticks enough from any thicket where it has strayed, to make a fire to offer it up with.

Sterne.

CHAP. XI.

HAMLET's INSTRUCTIONS
TO THE PLAYERS.

SPEAK the speech, I pray you, as I pronounced it to you, trippingly on the tongue. But if you mouth it, as many of our players do, I had as lieve the town-crier had spoke my lines. And do not saw the air too much with your hand thus ; but use all gently ; for in the very torrent, tempest, and, as I may say, whirlwind of your passion, you must acquire and beget a temperance that may give it smoothnefs. Oh ! it offends me to the soul, to hear a robustuous periwig-pated fellow tear a passion to tatters, to very rags, to split the ears of the ground-lings ; who (for the moft part) are capable of nothing, but inexplicable dumb shews and noise :. I would have such a fellow whipp'd for o'erdoing termagant ; it out-herods Herod. Pray you, avoid it.

Be not too tame neither; but let your own discretion be your tutor. Suit the action to the word, the word to the action, with this special observance, that you o'erstep not the modesty of nature : for any thing so overdone is from the purpose of playing ; whose end, both at the first and now, was and is, to hold, as 'twere, the mirror up to nature ; to shew virtue her own feature, scorn her own image, and the very age and body of the time, his form and pressure. Now, this overdone, or come tardy of, though it make the unskilful laugh, cannot but make the judicious grieve : the censure of one of which must in allowance o'erweigh a whole theatre of others. Oh ! there be players that I have seen play, and heard others praise, and that highly (not to speak it profanely) that, neither having the accent of Christian, nor the gait of Christian, Pagan, nor man, have so strutted and bellowed, that I have thought some of nature's journeymen had made men,

E 3   and

and not made them well ; they imitated humanity
fo abominably. (

AND let thofe that play your clowns, fpeak no
more than is fet down for them : for there be of
them that will themfelves laugh, to fet on fome
quantity of barren fpectators to laugh too ; though,
in the mean time, fome neceffary queftion of the
play be then to be confidered—that's villainous,
and fhews a moft pitiful ambition in the fool that
ufes it.

SHAKESPEAR.

C H A P.   XII.

THE PRESENT CONDITION OF MAN
VINDICATED.

HEAV'N from all creatures hides the book of
Fate,
All but the Page prefcrib'd their prefent ftate :
From brutes what men, from men what fpirits know:
Or who could fuffer Being here below ?
The lamb thy riot dooms to bleed to-day,
Had he thy Reafon, would he fkip and play ?
Pleas'd to the laft he crops the flow'ry food,
And licks the hand juft raifed to fhed his blood.
Oh blindnefs to the future ! kindly given,
That each may fill the circle mark'd by Heav'n,
Who fees with equal eye, as God of all,
A hero perifh, or a fparrow fall,
Atoms and fyftems into ruin hurl'd,
And now a bubble burft, and now a world.
    Hope humbly then ; with trembling pinions foar;
Wait the great teacher death ; and God adore.
What future blifs, he gives not thee to know,
But gives that Hope to be thy bleffing now.
Hope fprings eternal in the human breaft ;
Man never is, but always to be bleft :
The foul uneafy, and confin'd from home,
Refts and expatiates in a life to come.

Lo,

Lo, the poor Indian! whofe untutor'd mind
Sees God in clouds, or hears him in the wind ;
His foul proud Science never taught to ftray
Far as the folar walk, or milky way;
Yet fimple Nature to his hope has given,
Behind the cloud-topt hill, an humbler heav'n;
Some fafer world in depth of woods embrac'd,
Some happier ifland in the wat'ry wafte,
Where flaves once more their native land behold,
No fiends torment, no Chriftians thirft for gold.
To Be, contents his natural defire,
He afks no Angel's wing, no Seraph's fire;
But thinks, admitted to that equal fky,
His faithful dog fhall bear him company.

Go, wifer thou ! and in thy fcale of fenfe,
Weigh thy Opinion againft Providence;
Call imperfection what thou fancieft fuch,
Say, here he gives too little, there too much :
Deftroy all creatures for thy fport or guft,
Yet cry, If Man's unhappy, God's unjuft;
If Man alone ingrofs not Heav'n's high care,
Alone made perfect here, immortal there :
Snatch from his hand the balance and the rod,
Re-judge his juftice, be the God of God.
In Pride, in reas'ning Pride, our error lies ;
All quit their fphere, and rufh into the fkies.
Pride ftill is aiming at the bleft abodes,
Men would be Angels, Angels would be Gods.
Afpiring to be Gods, if Angels fell,
Afpiring to be Angels, Men rebel :
And who but wifhes to invert the laws
Of Order, fins againft th' Eternal Caufe.

Pope.

C H A P. XIII.

ON THE ORDER OF NATURE.

SEE, thro' this air, this ocean, and this earth,
  All matter quick, and bursting into birth.
Above, how high progressive life may go!
Around, how wide! how deep extend below!
Vast chain of Being! which from God began,
Nature's ethereal, human, angel, man;
Beast, bird, fish, insect, what no eye can see,
No glass can reach; from Infinite to thee,
From thee to Nothing.—On superior pow'rs
Were we to press, inferior might on ours:
Or in the full creation leave a void,
Where, one step broken, the great scale's destroy'd.
From Nature's chain whatever link you strike,
'Tenth or ten thousandth, breaks the chain alike.
  And, if each system in gradation roll,
Alike essential to th' amazing Whole,
The least confusion but in one, not all
That system only, but the whole must fall.
Let earth, unbalanc'd from her orbit fly,
Planets and suns rush lawless thro' the sky;
Let ruling Angels from their spheres be hurl'd,
Being on Being wreck'd, and world on world;
Heav'n's whole foundations to their centre nod,
And Nature tremble to the throne of God.
All this dread ORDER break----for whom? for thee?
Vile worm?----oh Madness! Pride! Impiety!
  What if the foot, ordain'd the dust to tread,
Or hand, to toil, aspir'd to be the head?
What if the head, the eye, or ear repin'd
To serve mere engines to the Ruling Mind?
Just as absurd for any part to claim
'To be another, in this gen'ral frame:
Just as absurd, to mourn the tasks or pains,
The great directing MIND of ALL ordains.

All

All are but parts of one ftupendous whole;
Whofe body Nature is, and God the foul :
That, chang'd thro' all, and yet in all the fame,
Great in the earth, as in th' ethereal frame,
Warms in the fun, refrefhes in the breeze,
Glows in the ftars, and bloffoms in the trees,
Lives thro' all life, extends thro' all extent,
Spreads undivided, operates unfpent;
Breathes in our foul, informs our mortal part,
As full, as perfect, in a hair as heart;
As full, as perfect, in vile Man that mourns,
As the rapt Seraph that adores and burns :
To him no high, no low, no great, no fmall;
He fills, he bounds, connects and equals all.

 Ceafe then, nor ORDER Imperfection name :
Our proper blifs depends on what we blame.
Know thy own point : This kind, this due degree
Of blindnefs, weaknefs, Heav'n beftows on thee.
Submit.—In this, or any other fphere,
Secure to be as bleft as thou canft bear :
Safe in the hand of one difpofing Pow'r,
Or in the natal, or the mortal hour.
All Nature is but Art, unknown to thee ;
All Chance, Direction, which thou canft not fee;
All Difcord, Harmony not underftood ;
All partial Evil, univerfal Good :
And, fpite of Pride, in erring Reafon's fpite,
One truth is clear, WHATEVER IS, IS RIGHT.

POPE.

CHAP.   XIV.

THE ORIGIN OF SUPERSTITION AND TYRANNY.

WHO firft taught fouls enflav'd and realms un-
        done ?
Th' enormous faith of many made for one ;
That proud exception to all Nature's laws,
T'invert the world, and counter-work its Caufe ?

E 5 Force

Force firſt made Conqueſt, and that conqueſt, Law
'Till Superſtition taught the tyrant awe,
Then ſhar'd the Tyranny, then lent it aid,
And Gods of Conq'u'rors, Slaves of ſubjects made :
She 'midſt the lightning's blaze, and thunder's
    ſound,
When rock'd the mountains, and when groan'd the
    ground,
She taught the weak to bend, the proud to pray
To Pow'r unſeen, and mightier far than they :
She, from the rending earth and burſting ſkies,
Saw Gods deſcend, and fiends infernal riſe :
Here fix'd the dreadful, there the bleſt abodes ;
Fear made her Devils, and weak hope her Gods;
Gods partial, changeful, paſſionate, unjuſt,
Whoſe attributes were Rage, Revenge, or Luſt ;
Such as the ſouls of cowards might conceive,
And form'd like tyrants, tyrants would believe.
Zeal then, not charity, became the guide;
And hell was built on ſpite, and heav'n on pride.
Then ſacred ſeem'd th' ethereal vault no more;
Altars grew marble then, and reek'd with gore :
Then firſt the Flamen taſted living food;
Next his grim idol ſmear'd with human blood;
With Heav'n's own thunders ſhook the world below,
And play'd the God an engine on his foe.
   So drives Self love, thro' juſt and thro' unjuſt,
To one man's pow'r ambition, lucre, luſt :
The ſame Self-love, in all, becomes the cauſe
Of what reſtrains him, Government and Laws.
For, what one likes, if others like as well,
What ſerves one will, when many wills rebel ?
How ſhall he keep, what, ſleeping or awake,
A weaker may ſurprize, a ſtronger take ?
His ſafety muſt his liberty reſtrain :
All join to guard what each deſires to gain.
Forc'd into virtue thus by ſelf-defence,
Ev'n Kings learn'd juſtice and benevolence :
Self-love forſook the path it firſt purſu'd,
And found the private in the public good.

'Twas

'Twas then, the ftudious head or gen'rous mind,
Follow'r of God, or friend of human kind,
Poet or patriot, rofe but to reftore
The Faith and Moral, Nature gave before ;
Re-lum'd her ancient light, not kindled new;
If not God's image, yet his fhadow drew :
Taught Pow'r's due ufe to People and to Kings,
'Taught not to flack, nor ftrain its tender ftrings,
The lefs, or greater, fet fo juftly true,
That touching one muft ftrike the other too;
'Till jarring int'refts, of themfelves create
Th' according mufic of a well-mix'd State.
Such is the world's great harmony, that fprings
From Order, Union, full Confent of things :
Where fmall and great, where weak and mighty,
       made
To ferve, not fuffer, ftrengthen, not invade :
More pow'rful each as needful to the reft,
And, in proportion as it blefses, bleft ;
Draw to one point, and to one centre bring
Beaft, Man, or Angel, Servant, Lord, or King,
  For Forms of Government let fools conteft ;
Whate'er is beft adminifter'd is beft :
For modes of Faith let graceful zealots fight ;
His can't be wrong whole life is in the right :
In Faith and Hope the world will difagree,
But all Mankind's concern is Charity :
All muft be falfe that thwart this one Great End;
And all of God, that blefs Mankind or mend.
  Man, like the gen'rous vine, fupported lives,
The ftrength he gains is from th' embrace he gives;
On their own Axis as the Planets run,
Yet make at once their circle round the Sun;
So two confiftent motions act the Soul ;
And one regards itfelf, and one the Whole.
  Thus God and Nature link'd the gen'ral frame,
And bade Self-love and Social be the fame.
                   Pope.

CHAP. XV.

On HAPPINESS.

OH Happiness ! our being's end and aim !
  Good, Pleasure, Ease, Content ! whate'er
    thy name :
That something still which prompts th' eternal
    sigh,
For which we bear to live, nor fear to die,
Which still so near us, yet beyond us lies,
O'erlook'd, seen double, by the fool, and wise.
Plant of celestial seed ! if dropt below,
Say, in what mortal soil thou deign'st to grow ?
Fair op'ning to some Court's propiteous shine,
Or deep with diamonds in the flaming mine ?
Twin'd with the wreaths Parnassian laurels yield,
Or reap'd in iron harvests of the field ?
Where grows ?——where grows it not ? If vain our
    toil,
We ought to blame the culture, not the soil :
Fix'd to no spot is Happiness sincere,
'Tis no where to be found, or ev'ry where ;
'Tis never to be bought, but always free,
And, fled from monarchs, St. John ! dwells with
    thee.
    Ask of the Learn'd the way ? The Learn'd are
    blind ;
This bids to serve, and that to shun mankind ;
Some place their bliss in action, some in ease,
Those call it Pleasure, and Contentment these ;
Some sunk to beasts, find pleasure end in pain ;
Some swell'd to Gods, confess ev'n Virtue vain ;
Or indolent, to each extreme they fall,
To trust in ev'ry thing, or doubt of all.
   Who thus define it, say they more or less
Than this, that Happiness is Happiness ?
    Take Nature's path, and mad opinions leave ;
All states can reach it, and all heads conceive ;
Obvious

Obvious her goods, in no extreme they dwell;
There needs but thinking right, and meaning well;
And mourn our various portions as we please,
Equal is Common Sense, and Common Ease.
   Remember, Man, " the Universal Cause
" Acts not by partial, but by gen'ral laws;"
And makes what happiness we justly call
Subsist not in the good of one, but all.
There's not a blessing Individuals find,
But some way leans and hearkens to the kind:
No Bandit fierce, no Tyrant mad with pride,
No cavern'd Hermit, rests self satisfy'd:
Who most to shun or hate Mankind pretend,
Seek an admirer, or would fix a friend:
Abstract what others feel, what others think,
All pleasures sicken, and all glories sink:
Each has his share: and who would more obtain,
Shall find, the pleasure pays not half the pain.
   Order is Heav'n's first law; and this confest,
Some are, and must be, greater than the rest,
More rich, more wise; but who infers from hence
That such are happier, shocks all common sense.
Heav'n to Mankind impartial we confess,
If all are equal in their Happiness:
But mutual wants this Happiness increase;
All Nature's diff'rence keeps all Nature's peace.
Condition, circumstance is not the thing;
Bliss is the same in subject or in king,
In who obtain defence, or who defend,
In him who is, or him who finds a friend:
Heav'n breathes thro' ev'ry member of the whole
One common blessing, as one common soul.
But Fortune's gifts if each alike possest,
And each were equal, must not all contest?
If then to all men Happiness was meant,
God in Externals could not place Content.
   Fortune her gifts may variously dispose,
And these be happy call'd, unhappy those;
But Heav'n's just balance equal will appear,
While those are plac'd in Hope, and these in Fear:

Not

Not prefent good or ill, the joy or curfe,
But future views of better, or of worfe.
Oh fons of earth! attempt ye ftill to rife,
By mountains pil'd on mountains, to the fkies?
Heav'n ftill with laughter the vain toil furveys,
And buries madmen in the heaps they raife.
　Know, all the good that individuals find,
Or God and Nature meant to mere Mankind,
Reafon's whole pleafure, all the joys of Senfe,
Lie in three words, Health, Peace, and Compe-
　　　tence.

Pope.

C H A P.　XVI.

O N　V I R T U E.

KNOW then this truth (enough for man to
　　　know)
" Virtue alone is Happinefs below."
The only point where human blifs ftands ftill,
And taftes the good without the fall to ill;
Where only Merit conftant pay receives,
Is bleft in what it takes, and what it gives;
The joy unequal'd, if its end it gain,
And if it lofe, attended with no pain:
Without fatiety, tho' e'er fo blefs'd,
And but more relifh'd as the more diftrefs'd:
The broadeft mirth unfeeling Folly wears,
Lefs pleafing far than Virtue's very tears:
Good, from each object, from each place acquir'd,
For ever exercis'd, yet never tir'd;
Never elated, while one man's opprefs'd;
Never dejected, while another's blefs'd;
And where no wants, no wifhes can remain,
Since but to wifh more Virtue, is to gain.
　See the fole blifs Heav'n could on all beftow!
Which who but feels can tafte, but thinks can know:
Yet poor with fortune, and with learning blind,
The bad muft mifs; the good, untaught, will find;

Slave.

Slave to no feɛt, who takes no private road,
But looks thro' Nature, up to Nature's God;
Purfues that Chain, which links th' immenfe defign,
Joins heav'n and earth, and mortal and divine;
Sees, that no Being any blifs can know,
But touches fome above, and fome below;
Learns from this union of the rifing Whole,
The firft, laft purpofe of the human foul;
And knows where Faith, Law, Morals, all began,
All end, in LOVE OF GOD, and LOVE OF MAN.

   For him alone, Hope leads from goal to goal,
And opens ftill, and opens on his foul;
"Till lengthen'd on to Faith, and unconfin'd,
It pours the blifs that fills up all the mind.
He fees, why Nature plants in Man alone
Hope of known blifs, and Faith in blifs unknown:
(Nature, whofe diɛtates to no other kind
Are giv'n in vain, but what they feek they find)
Wife is her prefent; fhe conneɛts in this
His greateft Virtue with his greateft Blifs;
At once his own bright profpeɛt to be bleft,
And ftrongeft motive to affift the reft.

   Self-love thus pufh'd to focial, to divine,
Gives thee to make thy neighbour's bleffing thine.
Is this too little for thy boundlefs heart?
Extend it, let thy enemies have part:
Grafp the whole world of Reafon, Life, and Senfe,
In one clofe fyftem of Benevolence:
Happier as kinder, in whate'er degree,
And height of Blifs but height of Charity.

   God loves from Whole to Parts: But human
          foul
Muft rife from Individuals to the Whole.
Self-love but ferves the virtuous mind to wake,
As the fmall pebble ftirs the peaceful lake;
The centre mov'd, a circle ftrait fucceeds,
Another ftill, and ftill another fpreads;
Friend, parent, neighbour, firft it will embrace;
His country next; and next all human race;

Wide

Wide and more wide, th' o'erflowings of the mind
Take ev'ry creature in, of ev'ry kind ;
Earth smiles around, with boundless bounty blest,
And Heav'n beholds its image in his breast.

Pope.

C H A P.   XVII.

On VERSIFICATION

MANY by Numbers judge a Poet's song;
  And smooth or rough, with them, is right
    or wrong :
In the bright Muse tho' thousand charms conspire,
Her voice is all these tuneful fools admire ;
Who haunt Parnassus but to please their ear,
Not mend their minds; as some to Church repair,
Not for the Doctrine, but the music there.
These equal syllables alone require,
Tho' oft the ear the open vowels tire ;
While expletives their feeble aid do join ;
And ten low words oft creep in one dull line :
While they ring round the same unvary'd chimes,
With sure returns of still expected rhymes ;
Where-e'er you find " the cooling western breeze,"
In the next line, it " whispers thro' the trees :"
If crystal streams " with pleasing murmurs creep,"
The reader's threaten'd (not in vain) with " sleep:"
Then, at the last and only couplet fraught
With some unmeaning thing they call a thought,
A needless Alexandrine ends the song,
That, like a wounded snake, drags its slow length
   along.
  Leave such to tune their own dull rhymes, and
    know
What's roundly smooth, or languishingly slow ;
And praise the easy vigour of a line,
Where Denham's strength, and Waller's sweetness
   join.
True ease in writing comes from art, not chance,
As those move easiest who have learn'd to dance.

'Tis

'Tis not enough no harſhneſs gives offence,
The ſound muſt ſeem an Echo to the ſenſe :
Soft is the ſtrain when Zephyr gently blows,
And the ſmooth ſtream in ſmoother numbers flows :
But when loud ſurges laſh the ſounding ſhoar,
The hoarſe, rough verſe ſhould like the torrent
    roar :
When Ajax ſtrives ſome rock's vaſt weight to
    throw,
The line too labours, and the words move ſlow ;
Not ſo, when ſwift Camilla ſcours the plain,
Flies o'er th' unbending corn, and ſkims along the
    main.
Hear how Timotheus' vary'd lays ſurpriſe,
And bid alternate paſſions fall and riſe !
While, at each change, the ſon of Libyan Jove
Now burns with glory, and then melts with love :
Now his fierce eyes with ſparkling fury glow,
Now ſighs ſteal out, and tears begin to flow ;
Perſians and Greeks like turns of nature found,
And the World's victor ſtood ſubdu'd by Sound !
                           POPE.

C H A P. XVIII.

L E S S O N S OF W I S D O M.

HOW to live happieſt ; how avoid the pains;
    The diſappointments, and diſguſts of thoſe
Who would in pleaſure all their hours employ ;
The precepts here of a divine old man
I could recite. Tho' old, he ſtill retain'd
His manly ſenſe, and energy of mind.
Virtuous and wiſe he was, but not ſevere ;
He ſtill remembered that he once was young ;
His eaſy preſence check'd no decent joy.
Him even the diſſolute admir'd : for he
A graceful looſeneſs when he pleas'd put on,
And laughing could inſtruct. Much had he read,
                           Much

Much more had feen ; he ftudied from the life,
And in th' original perus'd mankind.
    Vers'd in th' woes and vanities of life
He pitied man ; and much he pitied thofe
Whom falfely-fmiling fate has curs'd with means
To diffipate their days in queft of joy.
Our aim is Happinefs ; 'tis yours, 'tis mine,
He faid, 'tis the purfuit of all that live ;
Yet few attain it, if 'twas e'er attain'd.
But they the wideft wander from the mark,
Who thro' the flow'ry paths of faunt'ring Joy
Seek this coy Goddefs ; that from ftage to ftage
Invites us ftill, but fhifts as we purfue.
For not to name the pains that pleafure brings
To counterpoife itfelf, relentlefs Fate
Forbids that we thro' gay voluptuous wilds
Should ever roam : And were the Fates more kind,
Our narrow luxuries would foon be ftale.
Were thefe exhauftlefs, Nature would grow fick,
And cloy'd with pleafure, fqueamifhly complain
That all was vanity, and life a dream.
Let nature reft ; Be bufy for yourfelf,
And for your friend ; be bufy even in vain
Rather than teize her fated appetites.
Who never fafts, no banquet e'er enjoys ;
Who never toils or watches, never fleeps.
Let nature reft : And when the tafte of joy
Grows keen, indulge ; but fhun fatiety.
    'Tis not for mortals always to be bleft.
But him the leaft the dull or painful hours
Of life opprefs, whom fober Senfe conducts,
And Virtue thro' this labyrinth we tread.
Virtue and Senfe I mean not to disjoin ;
Virtue and Senfe are one : and truft me, he
Who has not virtue is not truly wife.
Virtue (for mere good-nature is a fool)
Is fenfe and fpirit, with humanity :
'Tis fometimes angry, and its frown confounds ;
'Tis even vindictive, but in vengeance juft.
Knaves

Knaves fain would laugh at it; some great ones
    dare;
But at his heart the most undaunted son
Of fortune dreads its name and awful charms.
To noblest uses this determines wealth:
This is the solid pomp of prosperous days:
The peace and shelter of adversity.
And if you pant for glory, build your fame
On this foundation, which the secret shock
Defies of Envy and all-sapping Time.
The gaudy gloss of Fortune only strikes
The vulgar eye: The suffrage of the wise,
The praise that's worth ambition, is attain'd
By Sense alone, and dignity of mind.
   Virtue the strength and beauty of the soul,
Is the best gift of heaven: a happiness
That even above the smiles and frowns of fate
Exalts great Nature's favourites: a wealth
That ne'er encumbers, nor to baser hands
Can be transferr'd: it is the only good
Man justly boasts of, or can call his own.
Riches are oft by guilt and baseness earn'd;
Or dealt by chance, to shield a lucky knave,
Or throw a cruel sun-shine on a fool.
But for one end, one much-neglected use,
Are riches worth your care (for Nature's wants
Are few, and without opulence supplied)
This noble end is to produce the Soul:
To show the virtues in their fairest light;
To make Humanity the Minister
Of bounteous Providence; and teach the breast
That generous luxury the Gods enjoy.
   Thus, in his graver vein, the friendly Sage
Sometimes declaim'd. Of Right and Wrong, he
    taught
Truths as refin'd as ever Athens heard;
And (strange to tell) he practis'd what he preach'd.
Armstrong.

C H A P.

C H A P.   XIX.

Against INDOLENCE;

A N   E P I S T L E.

IN frolick's hour, ere serious thought had birth,
There was a time, my dear CORNWALLIS, when
The muse would take me on her airy wing
And waft to views romantic; there present
Some motly vision, shade and sun : the cliff
O'erhanging, sparkling brooks, and ruins grey;
Bade me meanders trace, and catch the form
Of varying clouds, and rainbows learn to paint.
  Sometimes ambition, brushing by, wou'd twitch
My mantle, and with winning look sublime
Allure to follow.   What tho' steep the track,
Her mountain's top would over pay when climb'd·
The scaler's toil; her temple there was fine,
And lovely thence the prospects.   She could tell
Where laurels grew, whence many a wreath anti-
      que;
But more advis'd to shun the barren twig,
(What is immortal verdure without fruit ?)
And woo some thriving art : her num'rous mines
Were open to the searcher's skill and pains.
  Caught by th' harangue, heart beat, and flutt'ring
      pulse
Sounded irregular marches to be gone——
What, pause a moment when Ambition calls ?
No, the blood gallops to the distant goal,
And throbs to reach it.   Let the lame sit still.
When Fortune gentle, at the hill's verge extreme,
Array'd in decent garb, but somewhat thin,
Smiling approach'd; and what occasion ask'd,
Of climbing ? She already provident
Had cater'd well, if stomach cou'd digest
Her viand, and a palate not too nice.
Unfit she said, for perilous attempt,
That manly limb requir'd, and sinew tough.

She

She took, and laid me in a vale remote,
Amid the gloomy scene of fir and yew,
On poppy beds, where Morpheus strew'd the ground:
Obscurity her curtain round me drew,
And syren Sloth a dull quietus sung:
  Sithence no fairy lights, no quick'ning ray,
Nor stir of pulse, nor objects to entice
Abroad the spirits; but the cloyster'd heart
Sits squat at home, like pagod in a nitch
Obscure, or grandees with nod-watching eye,
And folded arms, in presence of the throne,
Turk, or Indostan.—Cities, forums, courts
And prating sanhedrims, and drumming wars,
Affect no more than stories told to bed
Lethargic, which at intervals the sick
Hears and forgets, and wakes to doze again.
Instead of converse and variety,
The same trite round, the same stale silent scene:
Such are thy comforts, blessed Solitude!
But Innocence is there, but Peace all kind,
And simple Quiet with her downy couch,
Meads lowing, tune of birds, and lapse of streams,
And Saunter with a book, and warbling Muse,
In praise of hawthorns—Life's whole business this?
Is it to bask i' th' sun? if so a snail
Were happy crawling on the southern wall.
  Why sits Content upon a cottage-sill
At even tide, and blesseth the coarse meal
In footy corner? why sweet slumbers wait
Th' hard pallat? not because from haunt remote
Sequester'd in a dingle's bushy lap.
'Tis labour makes the peasant's sav'ry fare,
And works out his repose: for ease must ask,
The leave of diligence to be enjoy'd.
  Oh! listen not to that enchantress Ease,
With seeming smile; her palatable cup
By standing grows insipid; and beware
The bottom, for there's poison in the lees.
What health impair'd, and crowds inactive maim'd!
What daily martyrs to her sluggish cause!

Less

Lefs ſtrict devoir the Rufs and Perſian claim
Defpotic ; and, as fubjects long inur'd
To fervile burthen, grow fupine and tame,
So fares it with our Sov'reign and her train.

    What tho' with lure fallacious ſhe pretend
From worldly bondage to fet free, what gain
Her votaries ? What avails from iron chains
Exempt, if rofy fetters bind as faſt ?

    Beſtir, and anfwer your creation's end.
Think we that man with vig'rous pow'r endow'd,
And room to ſtretch, was deſtin'd to fit ſtill ?
Sluggards are Nature's rebels, ſlight her laws,
Nor live up to the terms on which they hold
Their vital leafe.   Laborious terms and hard ;
But fuch the tenure of our earthly ſtate !
Riches and fame are Induſtry's reward ;
The nimble runner courfes Fortune down,
And then he banquets, for ſhe feeds the bold.
` Think what you owe your country, what yourfelf.
If fplendor charm not, yet avoid the fcorn
That treads on lowly ſtations.   Think of fome
Aſſiduous booby mounting o'er your head,
And thence with faucy grandeur looking down :
Think of (Reflection's ſtab !) the pitying friend
With ſhoulder ſhrug'd and forry. Think that Time
Has golden minutes, if difcreetly feiz'd :
And if fome fad example, indolent,
To warn and fcare be wanting——think of me.

C H A P.   XX.

ELEGY to a YOUNG NOBLEMAN
LEAVING THE UNIVERSITY.

ERE yet, ingenuous Youth, thy ſteps retire
    From Cam's fmooth margin, and the peaceful
        vale,
Where fcience call'd thee to her ſtudious quire,
    And met thee mufing in her cloyſters pale ;
O ! let thy friend (and may he boaſt the name)
    Breathe from his artlefs reed one parting lay ;

A lay like this thy early Virtues claim,
　　And this let voluntary Friendſhip pay.
Yet know the time arrives, the dang'rous time,
　　When all thoſe Virtues, opening now ſo fair,
Tranſplanted to the world's tempeſtuous clime,
　　Muſt learn each Paſſion's boiſt'rous breath to bear.
There if Ambition peſtilent and pale,
　　Or Luxury ſhould taint their vernal glow;
If cold Self-intereſt, with her chilling gale,
　　Shou'd blaſt th' unfolding bloſſoms ere they blow;
If mimic hues, by Art, or Faſhion ſpread,
　　Their genuine, ſimple colouring ſhould ſupply;
O! with them may theſe laureate honours fade;
　　And with them (if it can) my Friendſhip die.
——And do not blame, if tho' thyſelf inſpire,
　　Cautious I ſtrike the panegyric ſtring:
The muſe full oft purſues a meteor fire,
　　And, vainly ventrous, ſoars on waxen wing.
Too actively awake at Friendſhip's voice,
　　The Poet's boſom pours the fervent ſtrain,
Till ſad Reflection blames the haſty choice,
　　And oft invokes Oblivion's aid in vain.
Go then, my Friend, nor let thy candid breaſt
　　Condemn me, if I check the plauſive ſtring;
Go to the wayward world; compleat the reſt;
　　Be, what the pureſt Muſe would wiſh to ſing.
Be ſtill thyſelf; that open path of Truth,
　　Which led thee here, let Manhood firm purſue;
Retain the ſweet ſimplicity of Youth,
　　And, all thy virtue dictates, dare to do.
Still ſcorn, with conſcious pride, the maſk of Art;
　　On Vice's front let fearful caution lour,
And teach the diffident, diſcreeter part
　　Of Knaves that plot, and fools that fawn for Power.
So, round thy brow when Age's honours ſpread,
　　When Death's cold hand unſtrings thy Mason's
　　　　lyre,
When the green turf lies lightly on his head,
　　Thy worth ſhall ſome ſuperior bard inſpire:
He, to the ampleſt bounds of Time's domain,
　　On Rapture's plume ſhall give thy name to fly;

For

For truft, with rev'rence truft this Sabine ftrain :
   " The Mufe forbids the virtuous Man to die."

                                        MASON.

C H A P.   XXI.

ON THE MISERIES OF HUMAN LIFE.

AH little think the gay licentious proud,
      Whom pleafure, power, and affluence fur-
            round ;
They who their thoughtlefs hours in giddy mirth,
And wanton, often cruel, riot wafte :
Ah little think they, while they dance along,
How many feel, this very moment death,
And all the fad variety of pain ;
How many fink in the devouring flood,
Or more devouring flame : how many bleed,
By fhameful variance betwixt Man and Man :
How many pine in want, and dungeon glooms ;
Shut from the common air, and common ufe
Of their own limbs : how many drink the cup
Of baleful grief, or eat the bitter bread
Of mifery : fore pierc'd by wintry winds,
How many fhrink into the fordid hut
Of chearlefs poverty : how many fhake
With all the fiercer tortures of the mind,
Unbounded paffion, madnefs, guilt, remorfe ;
Whence tumbled headlong from the height of life
They furnifh matter for the tragic mufe :
Even in the vale, where wifdom loves to dwell,
With friendfhip, peace, and contemplation join'd,
How many rack'd with honeft paffions, droop
In deep retir'd diftrefs : how many ftand
Around the death-bed of their deareft friends,
And point the parting anguifh.——Thought fond
      Man
Of thefe, and all the thoufand namelefs ills,
That one inceffant ftruggle render life,

                                        One

One fcene of toil, of fuffering, and of fate,
Vice in his high career would ftand appall'd,
And heedlefs rambling Impulfe lea to think;
The confcious heart of charity wou'd warm,
And her wide wifh benevolence dili e;
The focial tear would rife, the focial figh;
And into clear perfection, gradual blifs,
Refining ftill, the focial paffions work.

Thomson.

C H A P. XXII.

REFLECTIONS on a FUTURE STATE.

'TIS done!—dread Winter fpreads his la
       glooms,
An dreigns tremendous o'er the conquer'd ye
How dead the vegetable kingdom lies!
How dumb the tuneful! horror wide extends
His defolate domain. Behold, fond Man!
See here thy pictur'd life, pafs fome few yea
Thy flowering Spring, thy Summer's ardent it
The fober Autumn fading into age,
And pale concluding Winter comes at laft,
And fhuts the fcene. Ah! whither now are fi
Thofe dreams of goodnefs? thofe unfolid hope
Of happinefs? thofe longings after fame?
Thofe reftlefs cares? thofe bufy buftling days
Thofe gay-fpent feftive nights? thofe vec
     thoughts
Loft between good and ill, that fhar'd thy l
All now are vanifh'd! Virtue fole furvive
Immortal, never-failing friend of Man,
His guide to happinefs on high.—And fee!
'Tis come, the glorious morn! the fecond
Of heaven, and earth! awakening Nature hear
The new creating word, and ftarts to life,
In every heightened form, from pain and dea
For ever free. The great eternal fcheme
Involving all, and in a perfect whole

F   U.

Uniting, as the profpect wider fpreads,
To reafon's eye refin'd clear up apace,
Ye vainly wife, ye blind prefumptuous! now,
Confounded in the duft, adore that POWER,
And WISDOM oft arraign'd : fee now the caufe,
Why unaffuming worth in fecret liv'd,
And dy'd, neglected : why the good Man's fhare
In life was gall and bitternefs of foul :
Why the lone widow, and, her orphans pin'd,
In ftarving folitude ; while luxury,
In palaces, lay ftraining her low thought,
To form unreal wants : why heaven-born truth,
And moderation fair, wore the red marks
Of fuperftition's fcourge : why licens'd pain,
That cruel fpoiler, that embofom'd foe,
Imbitter'd all our blifs.   Ye good diftreft !
Ye noble few ! who here unbending ftand
Beneath life's preffure, yet bear up a while,
And what your bounded view, which only faw
A little part, deem'd Evil is no more :
The ftorms of WINTRY TIME will quickly pafs,
And one unbecoming SPRING incircle all.

THOMSON.

CHAP. XXIII.

ON PROCRASTINATION.

BE wife to-day ; 'tis madnefs to defer ;
  Next day the fatal precedent will plead ;
Thus on, till wifdom is pufh'd out of life.
Procraftination is the thief of time ;
Year after year it fteals, till all are fled,
And to the mercies of a moment leaves
The vaft concerns of an eternal fcene.
  Of man's miraculous miftakes, this bears
The palm, " That all men are about to live,"
For ever on the brink of being born.
All pay themfelves the compliment to think

They,

They, one day, shall not drivel; and their pride
On this reversion takes up ready praise;
At least, their own; their future selves applauds;
How excellent that life they ne'er will lead!
Time lodg'd in their own hands is Folly's vails;
That lodg'd in Fate's, to Wisdom they consign;
The thing they can't but purpose, they postpone;
'Tis not in Folly, not to scorn a fool:
And scarce in human Wisdom to do more.
All promise is poor dilatory man,
And that thro' ev'ry stage. When young, indeed,
In full content we, sometimes, nobly rest,
Unanxious for ourselves; and only wish,
As duteous sons, our fathers were more wise.
At thirty man suspects himself a fool;
Knows it at forty, and reforms his plan;
At fifty chides his infamous delay,
Pushes his prudent purpose to Resolve;
In all the magnanimity of thought
Resolves, and re-resolves; then dies the same.

 And why? Because he thinks himself immortal.
All men think all men mortal, but themselves;
Themselves, when some alarming shock of fate
Strikes thro' their wounded hearts the sudden dread;
But their hearts wounded, like the wounded air,
Soon close; where past the shaft, no trace is found.
As from the wing no scar the sky retains;
The parted wave no furrow from the keel;
So dies in human hearts the thought of death.
Ev'n with the tender tear which nature sheds
O'er those we love, we drop it in the grave.
Young.

C(HAP. XXIV.

THE PAIN ARISING FROM VIRTUOUS EMOTIONS ATTENDED WITH PLEASURE.

———— BEHOLD the ways
Of Heav'ns eternal deftiny to man,
For ever juft, benevolent and wife :
That VIRTUE's awful fteps, howe'er purfued
By vexing fortune and intrufive PAIN,
Should never be divided from her chafte,
Her fair attendant, PLEASURE. Need I urge
'Thy tardy thought through all the various round
Of this exiftence, that thy foft'ning foul
At length may learn what energy the hand
Of virtue mingles in the bitter tide
Of paffion fwelling with diftrefs and pain,
To mitigate the fharp with gracious drops
Of cordial pleafure ? Afk the faithful youth,
While the cold urn of her whom long he lov'd
So often fills his arms ; fo often draws
His lonely footfteps at the filent hour,
To pay the mournful tribute of his tears ?
O ! he will tell thee, that the wealth of worlds
Should ne'er feduce his bofom to forego
That facred hour, when ftealing from the noife
Of care and envy, fweet remembrance fooths
With virtue's kindeft looks his aching breaft,
And turns his tears to rapture ?—Afk the crowd
Which flies impatient from the village-walk
To climb the neigh'bring cliffs, when far below
The cruel winds have hurl'd upon the coaft
Some helplefs bark ; while facred pity melts
The gen'ral eye, or terror's icy hand
Smites their diftorted limbs and horrent hair ;
While every mother clofer to her breaft
Catches her child, and pointing where the waves
Foam thro' the fhatter'd veffel, fhrieks aloud,

As

As one poor wretch that fpreads his piteous arms
For fuccour, fwallow'd by the roaring furge,
As now another, dafh'd againft the rock,
Drops lifelefs down : O deemeft thou indeed
No kind endearment here by nature giv'n
To mutual terror and compaffion's tears ?
To fweetly-melting foftnefs which attracts,
O'er all the edge of pain, the focial pow'rs
To this their proper action and their end ?
Afk thy own heart ; when at the midnight hour,
Slow thro' that ftudious gloom thy paufing eye
Led by the glimm'ring taper moves around
The facred volumes of the dead, the fongs
Of Grecian bards, and records writ by fame
For Grecian heroes, where the prefent pow'r
Of heaven and earth furveys th' immortal page,
E'en as a father bleffing, while he reads
The praifes of his fon ; if then thy foul,
Spurning the yoke of thefe ingloriou days,
Mix in their deeds and kindle with their flame ;
Say, when the profpect blackens on thy view,
When rooted from the bafe, heroic ftates
Mourn in the duft and tremble at the frown
Of curft ambition ;—when the pious band
Of youths that fought for freedom and their fires
Lie fide by fide in gore ;—when ruffian-pride
Ufurps the throne of juftice, turns the pomp
Of public pow'r, the majefty of rule,
The fword, the laurel, and the purple robe,
To flavifh empty pageants, to adorn
A tyrant's walk, and glitter in the eyes
Of fuch as bow the knee ;—when honour'd urns
Of patriots and of chiefs, the awful buft
And ftoried arch, to glut the coward-rage
Of regal envy, ftrew the public way
With hallow'd ruins ;—when the mufe's haunt,
The marble porch where wifdom wont to talk
With Socrates or Tully, hears no more,
Save the hoarfe jargon of contentious monks,
Or female fuperftition's midnight pray'r ;——
When ruthlefs rapine from the hand of time

F 3

Tears

Tears the deftroying fcythe, with furer blow
To fweep the works of glory from their bafe ;
Till defolation o'er the grafs-grown ftreet
Expands his raven-wings, and up the wall,
Where fenates once the pride of monarchs doom'd,
Hiffes the gliding fnake thro' hoary weeds
That clafp the mould'ring column ;—thus defac'd,
Thus widely mournful when the profpect thrills
Thy beating bofom, when the patriot's tear
Starts from thine eye, and thy extended arm
In fancy hurls the thunderbolt of Jove
To fire the impious wreath on Philip's brow,
Or dafh Octavius from the trophied car ;—
Say, does thy fecret foul repine to tafte
The big diftrefs ? Or would'ft thou then exchange
Thofe heart ennobling forrows, for the lot
Of him who fits amid the gaudy herd
Of mute barbarians bending to his nod, .
And bears aloft his gold-invefted front,
And fays within himfelf, " I am a king,
" And wherefore fhould the clam'rous voice of
       woe
" Intrude upon mine ear ?"—The baleful dregs
Of thefe late ages, this inglorious draught
Of fervitude and folly, have not yet,
Bleft be th' Eternal Ruler of the world !
Defil'd to fuch a depth of fordid fhame
The native honours of the human foul,
Nor fo effac'd the image of its fire.

AKENSIDE.

C H A P. XXV.

On T A S T E.

SAY, what is tafte, but the internal pow'rs
    Active, and ftrong, and feelingly alive
To each fine impulfe ? a difcerning fenfe
Of decent and fublime, with quick difguft
From things deform'd or difarrang'd, or grofs

In

In fpecies ? This nor gems, nor ftores of gold,
Nor purple ftate, nor culture can beftow ;
But God alone, when firft his active hand
Imprints the facred bias of the foul,
He, mighty Parent ! wife and juft in all,
Free as the vital breeze or light of heav'n,
Reveals the charms of nature.   Afk the fwain
Who journeys homeward from a fummer day's
Long labour, why, forgotten of his toils
And due repofe, he loiters to behold
The funfhine gleaming as thro' amber clouds
O'er all the weftern fky ; full foon, I ween,
His rude expreffions and untutor'd airs,
Beyond the pow'r of language, will unfold
The form of beauty fmiling at his heart,
How lovely ! how commanding ! But tho' heav'n
In every breaft hath fown thefe early feeds
Of love and admiration, yet in vain,
Without fair culture's kind parental aid,
Without enlivening funs, and genial fhow'rs
And fhelter from the blaft, in vain we hope
The tender plant fhould rear its blooming head,
Or yield the harveft promis'd in its fpring.
Nor yet will every foil with equal ftores
Repay the tiller's labour ; or attend
His will, obfequious, whether to produce
The olive or the laurel,   Diff'rent minds
Incline to diff'rent objects ; one purfues
The vaft alone, the wonderful, the wild ;
Another fighs for harmony, and grace,
And gentleft beauty.   Hence when lightning fires
The arch of heav'n, and thunders rock the ground ;
When furious whirlwinds rend the howling air,
And ocean, groaning from his loweft bed,
Heaves his tempeftuous billows to the fky ;
Amid the mighty uproar, while below
The nations tremble, Shakefpear looks abroad
From fome high cliff, fuperior, and enjoys
The elemental war.   But Waller longs,
All on the margin of fome flow'ry ftream,
To fpread his carelefs limbs amid the cool

Or

Of plantane shades, and to the list'ning deer,
The tale of slighted vows and love's disdain
Resounds soft-warbling all the live-long day :
Confenting Zephyr sighs ; the weeping rill
Joins in his plaint, melodious ; mute the groves ;
And hill and dale with all their echoes mourn.
Such and so various are the tastes of men.

AKENSIDE.

C H A P.   XXIV.

The PLEASURES arising from a CULTIVATED IMAGINATION.

O BLEST of heav'n, whom not the languid songs
  Of luxury, the Siren ! not the bribes
Of fordid wealth, nor all the gaudy spoils
Of pageant honour, can feduce to leave
Those ever-blooming sweets, which from the store
Of nature fair imagination culls
To charm th' enliven'd soul ! What tho' not all
Of mortal offspring can attain the height
Of envied life ; tho' only few possess
Patrician treasures or imperial state ;
Yet nature's care, to all her children just,
With richer treasures and an ampler state
Endows at large whatever happy man
Will deign to use them.   His the city's pomp,
The rural honour his.   Whate'er adorns
The princely dome, the column and the arch,
The breathing marbles and ,the sculptur'd gold
Beyond the proud possessor s narrow claim,
His tuneful breast enjoys.   For him, the spring
Distils her dews, and from the silken gem
Its lucid leaves unfolds : for him, the hand
Of autumn tinges every fertile branch
With blooming gold, and blushes like the morn.
Each passing hour sheds tribute from her wing ;
And still new beauties meet his lonely walk,
And loves unfelt attract him.   Not a breeze

Flies

Flies o'er the meadow, not a cloud imbibes
The setting sun's effugence, not a strain
From all the tenants of the warbling shado
Ascends, but whence his bosom can partake
Fresh pleasure, unreprov'd.   Nor thence partakes
Fresh pleasure only : for th' attentive mind,
By this harmonious action on her pow'rs,
Becomes herself harmonious : wont so oft
In outward things to meditate the charm
Of sacred order, soon she seeks at home
To find a kindred order to exert
Within herself this elegance of love,
This fair-inspir'd delight : her temper'd pow'rs
Refine at length, and every passion wears
A chaster, milder, more attractive mein.
But if to ample prospects, if to gaze
On nature's form, where negligent of all
These lesser graces, she assumes the port
Of that eternal majesty that weigh'd
The world's foundations, if to these the mind
Exalts her daring eye; then mightier far
Will be the change, and nobler.   Would the forms
Of servile custom cramp her gen'rous pow'rs ?
Would sordid policies, the barb'rous growth
Of ignorance and rapine, bow her down
To tame pursuits, to indolence and fear ?
Lo ! she appeals to nature, to the winds
And rolling waves, the sun's unwearied course,
The elements and seasons : all declare
For what th' eternal Maker has ordain'd
The pow'rs of man : we feel within ourselves
His energy divine : he tells the heart,
He meant, he made us to behold and love
What he beholds and loves, the general orb
Of life and being ; to be great like him,
Beneficent and active.   Thus the men
Whom nature's works can charm, with God himself
Hold converse : grow familiar, day by day,
With his conceptions, act upon his plan ;
And form to his, the relish of their souls.

AKENSIDE.

F 5

BOOK

BOOK IV.

ARGUMENTATIVE PIECES.

CHAP. I.

On ANGER.

QUESTION. *WHETHER Anger ought to be suppressed entirely, or only to be confined within the bounds of moderation?*

THOSE who maintain that resentment is blameable only in the excess, support their opinion with such arguments as these :

SINCE Anger is natural and useful to man, entirely to banish it from our breast, would be an equally foolish and vain attempt : for as it is difficult, and next to impossible to oppose nature with success; so it were imprudent, if we had it in our power, to cast away the weapons, with which she has furnished us for our defence. The best armour against injustice is a proper degree of spirit, to repel the wrongs that are done, or designed against us : but if we divest ourselves of all resentment, we shall perhaps prove too irresolute and languid, both in resisting the attacks of injustice, and inflicting punishment upon those, who have committed it. We shall therefore sink into contempt, and by the tameness of our spirit, shall invite the malicious to abuse and affront us. Nor will others fail to deny us the regard, which is due from them, if once they think us incapable of resentment. To remain unmoved at gross injuries, has the appearance of stupidity, and will

make

make us defpicable and mean, in the eyes of many who are not to be influenced by any thing but their fears.

AND as a moderate fhare of refentment is ufeful in its effects, fo it is innocent in itfelf, nay often commendable. The virtue of mildnefs is no lefs remote from infenfibility, on the one hand, than from fury, on the other. It implies, that we are angry only upon proper occafions, and in a due degree; that we are never tranfported beyond the bounds of decency, or indulge a deep and lafting refentment; that we do not follow, but lead our paffion, governing it as our fervant; not fubmitting ourfelves to it as our mafter. Under thefe regulations it is certainly excufable, when moved only by private wrongs: and being excited by the injuries, which others fuffer, it befpeaks a generous mind and deferves commendation. Shall a good man feel no indignation againft injuftice and barbarity? not even when he is witnefs to fhocking inftances of them? when he fees a friend bafely and cruelly treated; when he obferves,

 Th' oppreffor's wrong, the proud man's contumely,
 The infolence of office, and the fpurns
 That patient merit of th' unworthy takes;

SHALL he ftill enjoy himfelf in perfect tranquillity? Will it be a crime, if he conceives the leaft refentment? Will it not rather be fomewhat criminal, if he is deftitute of it? in fuch cafes we are commonly fo far from being afhamed of our anger, as fomething mean, that we are proud of it, and confefs it openly, as what we count laudable and meritorious.

THE truth is, there feems to be fomething manly, and we are bold to fay, fomething virtuous in a juft and well conducted refentment. In the mean time, let us not be fufpected of endeavouring to vindicate rage, and peevifhnefs, and implacable refentment. No; fuch is their deformity, fo horrid and manifeft are their evils they produce, that they do not admit of any defence or juftification. We condemn, we deteft them, as unnatural, brutifh, unmanly and
monftrous.

monftrous. All we contend for, is, that it is better to be modrate in our refentment, than to fupprefs it altogether. Let us therefore keep it under a ftrict difcipline, and carefully reftrain it within the bounds which reafon prefcribes, with regard to the occafion, degree and continuance of it. But let us not prefume to extirpate any of thofe affections, which the wifdom of God has implanted in us, which are fo nicely balanced, and fo well adjufted to each other, that by deftroying one of them, we may perhaps diforder and blemifh the whole frame of our nature.

TO thefe arguments, thofe who adopt the opinion that Anger fhould be entirely fuppreffed, reply:

You tell us, anger is natural to man; but nothing is more natural to man, than reafon, mildnefs and benevolence. Now with what propriety can we call that natural to any creature, which impairs and oppofes the moft effential and diftinguifhing parts of its conftitution? Sometimes indeed we may call that natural to a fpecies, which being found in moft of them is not produced by art or cuftom. That anger is in this fenfe natural, we readily grant; but deny that we therefore cannot, or may not lawfully extinguifh it. Nature has committed to our management the faculties of the mind, as well as the members of the body; and, as when any of the latter become pernicious to the whole, we cut them off and caft them away; in like manner, when any of our affections are become hurtful and ufelefs in our frame, by cutting them off, we do not in the leaft counteract the intention of nature. Now fuch is anger to a wife man. To fools and cowards it is a neceffary evil; but to a perfon of moderate fenfe and virtue, it is an evil, which has no advantage attending it. The harm it muft do him is very apparent. It muft ruffle his temper; make him lefs agreeable to his friends, difturb his reafon, and unfit him for difcharging the duties of life in a becoming manner. By only diminifhing his paffion, he may leffen, but cannot remove the evil,

for

for the only way to get clear of the one, is by entirely difmiffing the other.

How then will anger be fo ufefig to him, as to make it worth his while to retain it in any degree ? He may defend his own rights ; affift an injured friend; profecute and punifh a villain ; I fay his prudence and friendfhip, his public fpirit and calm refolution will enable him to do all this, and to do it in a much more fafe, proper and effectual manner, without the affiftance of anger, than with it. He will be defpifed and neglected, you fay, if he appears to have no refentment. You fhould rather fay, if he appears to have no fedate wifdom and courage ; for thefe qualities will be fufficient of themfelves to fecure him from contempt, and maintain him in the poffeffion of his juft authority. Nor does any thing commonly leffen us more in the eyes of others, than our own paffion. It often expofeth us to the contempt and derifion of thofe, who are not in our power ; and if it makes us fear'd, it alfo makes us proportionably hated, by our inferiors and dependants. Let the influence it gives us be ever fo great, that man muft pay very dear for his power, who procures it at the expence of his own tranquility and peace.

Besides, the imitation of anger, which is eafily formed, will produce the fame effect upon others, as if the paffion was real. If therefore to quicken the flow, to roufe the inattentive, and reftrain the fierce, it is fometimes expedient, that they believe you are moved, you may put on the outward appearance of refentment. Thus you may obtain the end of anger, without the danger and vexation that attend it ; and preferve your authority, without forfeiting the peace of your mind.

However manly and vigorous anger may be thought, it is in fact, but a weak principle, compared with the fedate refolution of a wife and virtuous man. The one is uniform and permanent, like the ftrength of a perfon in perfect health ; the other like a force, which proceedeth from a fever, is violent

for

for a time, but it soon leaves the mind more feeble than before. To him therefore who is armed with a proper firmness of soul, no degree of passion can be useful in any respect. And to say it can ever be laudable and virtuous, is indeed a sufficiently bold assertion. For the most part we blame it in others, and though we are apt to be indulgent enough to our own faults, we are often ashamed of it in ourselves. Hence it is common to hear men excusing themselves, and seriously declaring, they were not angry, when they have given unquestionable proofs to the contrary. But do we not commend him, who resents the injuries done to a friend or innocent person? Yes, we commend him; yet not for his passion, but for that generosity and friendship, of which it is the evidence. For let any one impartially consider, which of these characters he esteems the better; his, who interests himself in the injuries of his friend, and zealously defends him with perfect calmness and serenity of temper; or his, who pursues the same conduct under the influence of resentment.

If anger then is neither useful nor commendable, it is certainly the part of wisdom, to suppress it entirely. We should rather confine it, you tell us, within certain bounds. But how shall we ascertain the limits, to which it may, and beyond which it ought not to pass! When we receive a manifest injury, it seems we may resent it, provided we do it with moderation. When we suffer a worse abuse, our anger. I suppose, may rise somewhat higher, Now, as the degrees of injustice are infinite, if our anger must always be proportioned to the occasion, it may possibly proceed to the utmost extravagance. Shall we set bounds to our resentment, while we are yet calm? how can we be assured, that being once yet loose, it will not carry us beyond them; or shall we give passion the reins, imagining we can resume them at pleasure, or trusting it will tire or stop itself, as soon as it has run to its proper length; as well might

might we think of giving laws to a tempeſt; as well might we endeavour to run mad by rule and method.

In reality, it is much eaſier to keep ourſelves void of reſentment, than to reſtrain it from exceſs, when it has gained admiſſion; for if reaſon, while her ſtrength is yet entire, is not able to preſerve her dominion, what can ſhe do when her enemy has in part prevailed and weakened her force? To uſe the illuſtration of an excellent author, we can prevent the beginnings of ſome things, whoſe progreſs afterwards we cannot hinder. We can fear to caſt ourſelves down from a precipice, but if once we have taken the fatal leap, we muſt deſcend, whether we will, or no. Thus the mind, if duly cautious, may ſtand firm upon the rock of tranquility; but if ſhe raſhly forſakes the ſummit, ſhe can ſcarce recover herſelf, but is hurried away downwards by her own paſſion, with increaſing violence.

Do not ſay, that we exhort you to attempt that which is impoſſible. Nature has put it in our power to reſiſt the motions of anger. We only plead inability, when we want an excuſe for our own negligence. Was a paſſionate man to forfeit a hundred pounds, as often as he was angry, or was he ſure he muſt die the next moment after the firſt ſally of his paſſion, we ſhould find, he had a great command of his temper, whenever he could prevail upon himſelf to exerciſe a proper attention about it. And ſhall we not eſteem it worthy of equal attention; worthy of our utmoſt care and pains to obtain that immoveable tranquility of mind, without which we cannot reliſh, either life itſelf, or any one of its employments?——Upon the whole then, we both may and ought, not merely to reſtrain, but extirpate anger. It is impatient of rule; in proportion as it prevails, it will diſquiet our minds; it has nothing commendable in itſelf, nor will it anſwer any valuable purpoſe in life.

HOLLAND.

C H A P.

CHAP. II.

VIRTUE our HIGHEST INTEREST.

I FIND myfelf exifting upon a little fpot, furrounded every way by an immenfe unknown ex-
panfion.—Where am I ? What fort of a place do I
inhabit ? It is exactly accommodated, in every in-
ftance to my convenience ? Is there no excefs of
cold, none of heat, to offend me ? Am I never
annoyed by animals, either of my own kind, or a
different ? Is every thing fubfervient to me, as
though I had ordered all myfelf ?—No—nothing
like it—the fartheft from it poffible——The world
appears not then originally made for the private
convenience of me alone ?—It does not.—But is it
not poffible fo to accommodate it, by my own particular induftry ?——If to accommodate man and
beaft, heaven and earth ; if this be beyond me, 'tis
not poffible—What confequence then follows ? Or
can there be any other than this—If I feek an intereft of my own, detached from that of others; I
feek an intereft which is chimerical, and can never
have exiftence ?

How then muft I determine ? Have I no intereft
at all ?—If I have not, I am a fool for ftaying here.
'Tis a fmoaky houfe, and the fooner out of it, the
better.—But why no intereft ?—Can I be contented
with none, but one feparate and detached ?—Is a
focial intereft joined with others fuch an abfurdity, as
not to be admitted ? The bee, the beaver, and the
tribes of herding animals, are enough to convince me,
that the thing is, fomewhere at leaft, poffible. How
then am I affured, that 'tis not equally true of man ?
——Admit it ; and what follows ?—If fo, then Honour and Juftice are my intereft—then the whole
train of Moral Virtues are my intereft ; without
fome portion of which, not even thieves can maintain fociety.

BUT

But farther still—I stop not here—I pursue this social interest, as far as I can trace my several relations. I pass from my own stock, my own neighbourhood, my own nation, to the whole race of mankind, as dispersed thoughout the earth—Am I not related to them all, by the mutual aids of commerce ; by the general intercourse of arts and letters ; by that common nature, of which we all participate ?—— Again—I must have food and cloathing.—Without a proper genial warmth, I instantly perish.— Am I not related, in this view, to the very earth itself ? To the distant sun, from whose beams I derive vigour ? To that stupendous course and order of the infinite host of heaven, by which the times and seasons uniformly pass on ?—Were this order once confounded, I could not probably survive a moment; so absolutely do I depend on this common general welfare.

What then have I to do, but to enlarge Virtue into Piety ? Not only honour and justice, and what I owe to man, is my interest ; but gratitude also, acquiescence, resignation, adoration, and all I owe to this great polity, and its greater Governor, our common Parent.

But if all these moral and divine habits be my interest, I need not surely seek for a better. I have an interest compatible with the spot on which I live —I have an interest which may exist, without alteing the plan of Providence ; without mending or marring the general order of events.—I can bear whatever happens with manlike magnanimity ; can be contented, and fully happy in the good, which I possess ; and can pass through this turbid, this fickle, fleeting period, without bewailings, or envyings, or murmurings, or complaints.

Harris.

CHAP. III.

THE SAME SUBJECT.

ALL men purfue Good, and would be happy, if they knew how ; not happy for minutes, and miferable for hours, but happy, if poffible, through every part of their exiflence. Either therefore there is a good of this fteady durable kind, or there is none. If none, then all good muft be tranfient and uncertain ; and if fo, an object of loweft value, which can little deferve either our attention, or inquiry. But if there be a better good, fuch a good as we are feeking ; like every other thing, it muft be derived from fome caufe; and that caufe muft be either external, internal, or mixed, in as much as except thefe three, there is no other poffible. Now a fteady, durable good, cannot be derived from an external caufe, by reafon all derived from externals muft fluctuate, as they fluctuate. By the fame rule, not from a mixture of the two; becaufe the part which is external will proportionally deftroy its effence. What then remains but the caufe internal ; the very caufe which we have fuppofed, when we place the Sovereign Good in Mind—in Rectitude of Conduct ?

HARRIS.

CHAP. IV.

ON THE IMMORTALITY OF THE SOUL,

AMONG other excellent arguments for the Immortality of the Soul, there is one drawn from the perpetual progrefs of the foul to its perfection without a poffibility of ever arriving at it; which is a hint that I do not remember to have feen opened and improved by others who have written on this
subject,

subject, though it seems to me to carry a great weight with it. How can it enter into the thoughts of man, that the soul, which is capable of such immense perfections, and of receiving new improvements to all eternity, shall fall away into nothing almost as soon as it is created ? Are such abilities made for no purpose ? A brute arrives at a point of perfection that he can never pass : in a few years he has all the endowments he is capable of; and were he to live ten thousand more, would be the same thing he is at present. Were a human soul thus at a stand in her accomplishments, were her faculties to be full blown, and incapable of farther enlargements, I could imagine it might fall away infensibly, and drop at once into a state of annihilation. But can we believe a thinking being that is in a perpetual progress of improvements, and travelling on from perfection to perfection, after having just looked abroad into the works of its Creator, and made a few discoveries of his infinite goodness, wisdom, and power, must perish at her first setting out, and in the very beginning of her enquiries ?

Man, considered as in his present state, seems only sent into the world to propagate his kind. He provides himself with a successor, and immediately quits his post to make room for him.

He does not seem born to enjoy life, but to deliver it down to others. This is not surprising to consider in animals, which are formed for our use, and can finish their business in a short life. The silk-worm, after having spun her task, lays her eggs and dies. But in this life man can never take in his full measure of knowledge ; nor has he time to subdue his passions, establish his soul in virtue, and come up to the perfection of his nature, before he is hurried off the stage. Would an infinitely wise Being make such glorious creatures for so mean a purpose? Can he delight in the production of such abortive intelligences, such short-lived reasonable beings ? Would he give us talents that are not to be exerted ? Capacities that are never to be gratified ? How can we

find

find that wisdom which shines through all his works, in the formation of man, without looking on this world as only a nursery for the next, and believing that the several generations of rational creatures, which rise up and disappear in such quick successions, are only to receive their first rudiments of existence here, and afterwards to be transplanted into a more friendly climate, where they may spread and flourish to all eternity?

There is not, in my opinion, a more pleasing and triumphant consideration in religion than this of the perpetual progress which the soul makes towards the perfection of its nature, without ever arriving at a period in it. To look upon the soul as going on from strength to strength, to consider that she is to shine for ever with new accessions of glory, and brighten to all eternity; that she will be still adding virtue to virtue, and knowledge to knowledge; carries in it something wonderfully agreeable to that ambition which is natural to the mind of man. Nay, it must be a prospect pleasing to God himself, to see his creation for ever beautifying in his eyes, and drawing nearer to him, by greater degrees of resemblance.

Methinks this single consideration, of the progress of a finite spirit to perfection, will be sufficient to extinguish all envy in inferior nature, and all contempt in superior. That cherubim, which now appears as a God to a human soul, knows very well that the period will come about in eternity, when the human soul shall be as perfect as he himself now is: nay, when she shall look down upon that degree of perfection, as much as she now falls short of it. It is true the higher nature still advances, and by that means preserves his distance and superiority in the scale of being; but he knows that, how high soever the station is of which he stands possessed at present, the inferior nature will at length mount up to it, and shine forth in the same degree of glory.

With what astonishment and veneration may we look into our souls, where there are such hidden
stores

ftores of virtue and knowledge, fuch inexhaufted fources of perfection ! We know not yet what we fhall be, nor will it ever enter into the heart of man to conceive the glory that will be always in referve for him. The foul, confidered in relation to its Creator, is like one of thofe mathematical lines that may draw nearer to another to all eternity, without a poffibility of touching it : and can there be a thought fo tranfporting, as to confider ourfelves in thefe perpetual approaches to Him, who is not only the ftandard of perfection, but of happinefs !

Spectator.

C H A P.   V.

On the BEING of a GOD.

RETIRE ;——The world fhut out ;——Thy
   thoughts call home;
Imagination's airy wing reprefs;——
Lock up thy fenfes ;—Let no paffion ftir ;
Wake all to Reafon;—Let her reign alone—
Then, in thy Soul's deep filence, and the depth
Of Nature's filence, midnight, thus inquire,
As I have done——
 WHAT am I ? and from whence?——I nothing
  know,
But that I am; and, fince I am, conclude
Something eternal; had there e'er been nought,
Nought ftill had been ; Eternal there muft be.—
But what eternal ?—Why not human race ?
And ADAM's anceftors without an end ?—
That's hard to be conceiv'd; fince ev'ry link
Of that long chain'd fucceffion is fo frail ;
Can ev'ry part depend, and not the whole ?
Yet grant it true ; new difficulties rife;
I'm ftill quite out at fea ; nor fee the fhore.
Whence earth, and thefe bright orbs ? — Eternal
  too ?—
Grant matter was eternal ; ftill thefe orbs

Would

Would want fome other Father;—Much defign
Is feen in all their motions, all their makes;
Defign implies intelligence, and art:
That can't be from themfelves—or man; that art
Man fcarce can comprehend, could man beftow?
And nothing greater, yet allow'd, than man.—
Who, motion, foreign to the fmalleft grain,
Shot thro' vaft maffes of enormous weight?
Who bid brute matter's reftive lump affume
Such various forms, and give it wings to fly?
Has matter innate motion? Then each atom,
Afferting its indifputable right
To dance, would form an univerfe of duft:
Has matter none? Then whence thefe glorious
    forms,
And boundlefs flights, from fhapelefs, and repos'd?
Has matter more than motion? Has it thought,
Judgment, and genius? Is it deeply learn'd
In Mathematics? Has it fram'd fuch laws,
Which, but to guefs, a NEWTON made immortal?—
If art, to form; and counfel, to conduct;
And that with greater far, than human fkill,
Refides not in each block;—a GODHEAD
    reigns.—
And, if a GOD there is, that GOD how great?

YOUNG.

BOOK

B O O K V.

ORATIONS and HARANGUES.

C H A P. I.

JUNIUS BRUTUS over the dead body of LUCRETIA.

YES, noble lady, I fwear by this blood, which was once fo pure, and which nothing but royal villainy could have polluted, that I will purfue Lucius Tarquinius the proud, his wicked wife, and their children, with fire and fword ; nor will I ever fuffer any of that family, or of any other whatfoever, to be King in Rome : Ye Gods, I call you to witnefs this my oath !—There, Romans, turn your eyes to that fad fpectacle—the daughter of Lucretius, Collatinus's wife—fhe died by her own hand. See there a noble lady, whom the luft of a Tarquin reduced to the neceffity of being her own executioner, to atteft her innocence. Hofpitably entertained by her as a kinfman of her hufband's, Sextus, the perfidious gueft, became her brutal ravifher. The chafte, the generous Lucretia could not furvive the infult. Glorious woman ! But once only treated as a flave, fhe thought life no longer to be endured. Lucretia, a woman, difdained a life that depended on a tyrant's will; and fhall we, fhall men with fuch an example before our eyes, and after five-and twenty years of ignominious fervitude, fhall we, through a fear of dying, defer one fingle inftant to affert our liberty ? No, Romans, now is the time ;

the

the favourable moment we have so long waited for is come. Tarquin is not at Rome. The Patricians are at the head of the enterprize. The city is abundantly provided with men, and arms, and all things necessary. There is nothing wanting to secure the success, if our own courage does not fail us. And shall those warriors, who have ever been so brave when foreign enemies were to be subdued, or when conquests were to be made to gratify the ambition and avarice of Tarquin, be then only cowards, when they are to deliver themselves from slavery ? Some of you are perhaps intimidated by the army which Tarquin now commands. The soldiers, you imagine, will take the part of their general. Banish so groundless a fear. The love of liberty is natural to all men. Your fellow citizens in the camp feel the weight of oppression with as quick a sense as you that are in Rome : they will as eagerly seize the occasion of throwing off the yoke. But let us grant there may be some among them, who, through baseness of spirit or a bad education, will be disposed to favour the tyrant : The number of these can be but small, and we have means sufficient in our hands to reduce them to reason. They have left us hostages more dear to them than life. Their lives, their children, their fathers, their mothers, are here in the city. Courage, Romans, the Gods are for us ; those Gods, whose Temples and altars the impious Tarquin has profaned by sacrifices and libations made with polluted hands, polluted with blood, and with numberless unexpiated crimes committed against his subjects. Ye Gods, who protected our forefathers, ye Genii, who watch for the preservation and glory of Rome, do you inspire us with courage and unanimity in this glorious cause, and we will to our last breath defend your worship from all profanation.

Livy.

CHAP. II.

HANNIBAL ᴛᴏ ʜɪs SOLDIERS.

I KNOW not, foldiers, whether you or your prifoners be encompaffed by fortune with the ftrict-
er bonds and neceffities. Two feas inclofe you on
the right and left;—not a fhip to fly to for efcaping.
Before you is the Po, a river broader and more rapid
than the Rhone, behind you are the Alps, over
which, even when your numbers were undiminifhed,
you were hardly able to force a paffage. Here then,
foldiers, you muft either conquer or die, the very
firft hour you meet the enemy. But the fame fortune which has thus laid you under the neceffity of
fighting, has fet before your eyes thofe rewards of
victory, than which no men are ever wont to wifh
for greater from the immortal Gods. Should we by
our valour recover only Sicily and Sardinia, which
were ravifhed from our fathers, thofe would be no
inconfiderable prizes. Yet, what are thefe? The
wealth of Rome, whatever riches fhe has heaped
together in the fpoils of nations, all thefe, with the
mafters of them, will be yours. You have been
long enough employed in driving the cattle upon the
vaft mountains of Lufitania and Celtiberia; you
have hitherto met with no reward worthy of the
labours and dangers you have undergone. The
time is now come to reap the full recompenfe of your
toilfome marches over fo many mountains and rivers, and through fo many nations, all of them in
arms. This is the place which fortune has appointed to be the limits of your labours; it is here that
you will finifh your glorious warfare, and receive an
ample recompenfe of your compleated fervice. For
I would not have you imagine, that victory will be
as difficult as the name of a Roman war is great and
founding. It has often happened that a defpifed
enemy has given a bloody battle, and the moft re-

G

nowned

nowned kings and nations have by a small force been overthrown. And if you but take away the glitter of the Roman name, what is there, wherein they may stand in competition with you? For (to say nothing of your service in war for twenty years together with so much valour and success) from the very pillars of Hercules, from the ocean, from the utmost bounds of the earth, through so many war-like nations of Spain and Gaul, are you not come hither victorious? And with whom are you now to fight? With raw soldiers, an undisciplined army, beaten, vanquished, besieged by the Gauls the very last summer, an army unknown to their leader, and unacquainted with him.

Or shall I, who was born, I might almost say, but certainly brought up, in the tent of my father, that most excellent general, shall I, the conqueror of Spain and Gaul, and not only of the Alpine nations, but, which is greater yet, of the Alps themselves, shall I compare myself with this half-year captain? A captain before whom should one place the two armies without their ensigns, I am persuaded he would not know to which of them he is consul? I esteem it no small advantage, soldiers, that there is not one among you, who has not often been an eye-witness of my exploits in war; not one of whose valour I myself have not been a spectator, so as to be able to name the times and places of his noble atchievements; that with soldiers, whom I have a thousand times praised and rewarded, and whose pupil I was, before I became their general, I shall march against an army of men, strangers to one another.

On what side soever I turn my eyes, I behold all full of courage and strength; a veteran infantry, a most gallant cavalry; you, my allies, most faithful and valiant; you, Carthaginians, whom not only your country's cause, but the justest anger impels to battle. The hope, the courage of assailants, is always greater than of those who act upon the defensive. With hostile banners displayed, you are come down upon Italy; you bring the war. Grief,
injuries,

injuries, indignities fire your minds, and fpur you forward to revenge.—Firft they demanded me; that I, your general, fhould be deliver'd up to them; next, all of you, who had fought at the fiege of Saguntum; and we were to be put to death by the extremeft tortures. Proud and cruel nation! Every thing muft be yours, and at your difpofal! You are to prefcribe to us with whom we fhall make war, with whom we fhall make peace! You are to fet us bounds; to fhut us up within hills and rivers; but you, you are not to obferve the limits which yourfelves have fixed! Pafs not the Iberus. What next? Touch not the Saguntines; Saguntum is upon the Iberus, move not a ftep towards that city. Is it a fmall matter then, that you have deprived us of our ancient poffeffions, Sicily and Sardinia; you would have Spain too? Well, we fhall yield Spain; and then—you will pafs into Africa. Will pafs, did I fay?—This very year they ordered one of their confuls into Africa, the other into Spain. No, foldiers, there is nothing left for us but what we can vindicate with our fwords. Come on then. Be men. The Romans may with more fafety be cowards; they have their own country behind them, have places of refuge to fly to, and are fecure from danger in the roads thither; but for you there is no middle fortune between death and victory. Let this be but well fixed in your mind, and once again, I fay, you are conquerors.

LIVY.

C H A P.   III.

C. MARIUS to the ROMANS, on their hesitating to appoint him GENERAL in the EXPEDITION against JUGURTHA, merely on account of his extraction.

IT is but too common, my countrymen, to obſerve a material difference between the behaviour of thoſe, who ſtand candidates for places of power and truſt, before, and after their obtaining them. They ſolicit them in one manner, and execute them in another. They ſet out with a great appearance of activity, humility, and moderation; and they quickly fall into ſloth, pride, and avarice. It is undoubtedly, no eaſy matter to diſcharge, to the general ſatisfaction, the duty of a ſupreme commander in troubleſome times. I am, I hope, duly ſenſible of the importance of the office I propoſe to take upon me, for the ſervice of my country. To carry on, with effect, an expenſive war, and yet be frugal of the public money; to oblige thoſe to ſerve, whom it may be delicate to offend; to conduct, at the ſame time, a complicated variety of operations; to concert meaſures at home anſwerable to the ſtate of things abroad; and to gain every valuable end, in ſpite of oppoſition from the envious, the factious, and the diſaffected; to do all this, my countrymen, is more difficult, than is generally thought. And, beſides the diſadvantages, which are common to me with all others in eminent ſtations, my caſe is in this reſpect, peculiarly hard; that, whereas a commander of patrician rank, if he is guilty of a neglect, or breach of duty, has his great connections, the antiquity of his family, the important ſervices of his anceſtors, and the multitudes he has by power engaged in his intereſt, to ſcreen him from condign puniſhment: my whole ſafety depends upon myſelf; which renders it the more indiſpenſably neceſſary

for

for me to take care, that my conduct be clear and unexceptionable. Befides, I am well aware, my countrymen, that the eye of the public is upon me; and that, though the impartial, who prefer the real advantage of the common wealth to all other confiderations, favour my pretenfions, the patricians want nothing fo much, as an occafion againft me. It is, therefore, my fixed refolution; to ufe my beft endeavours, that you be not difappointed in me, and that their indirect defigns againft me may be defeated. I have, from my youth, been familiar with toils, and with dangers. I was faithful to your intereft, my countrymen, when I ferved you for no reward, but that of honour. It is not my defign to betray you, now that you have conferred upon me a place of profit. You have committed to my conduct the war againft Jugurtha. The Patricians are offended at this. But where would be the wifdom of giving fuch a command to one of their honourable body, a perfon of illuftrious birth, of antient family, of innumerable ftatues, but—of no experience? What fervice would his long line of dead anceftors, or his multitude of motionlefs ftatues, do his country in the day of battle? What could fuch a general do, but, in his trepidation and inexperience, have recourfe to fome inferior commander, for direction in difficulties, to which he was not himfelf equal? Thus, your Patrician general would, in fact, have a general over him; fo that, the acting commander would ftill be a Plebeian. So true is this, my countrymen, that I have myfelf known thofe, who have been chofen confuls, begin then to read the hiftory of their own country, of which till that time, they were totally ignorant; that is, they firft obtained the employment, and then bethought themfelves of the qualifications neceffary for the proper difcharge of it. I fubmit to your judgment, Romans, on which fide the advantage lies, when the comparifon is made between Patrician haughtinefs, and Plebeian experience. The very actions, which they have only read, I have partly feen, and partly myfelf atchieved.

G 3　　　　　What

What they know by reading, I know by action. They are pleafed to flight my mean birth: I defpife their mean characters. Want of birth and fortune is the objection againft me: want of perfonal worth againft them. But are not all men of the fame fpecies? What can make a difference between one man and another, but the endowments of the mind? For my part, I fhall always look upon the braveft man as the nobleft man. Suppofe it were enquired of the fathers of fuch Patricians as Albinus and Beftia, whether, if they had their choice, they would defire fons of their character, or of mine; what would they anfwer, but that they would wifh the worthieft to be their fons? If the Patricians have reafon to defpife me, let them likewife defpife their anceftors, whofe nobility was the fruit of their virtue. Do they envy the honours beftowed upon me? Let them envy likewife my labours, my abftinence, and the dangers I have undergone for my country; by which I have acquired them. But thofe worthlefs men lead fuch a life of inactivity, as if they defpifed any honours you can beftow; whilft they afpire to honours, as if they had deferved them by the moft induftrious virtue. They arrogate the rewards of activity for their having enjoyed the pleafures of luxury. Yet none can be more lavifh than they are, in praife of their anceftors. And they imagine they honour themfelves by celebrating their forefathers. Whereas they do the very contrary. For, as much as their anceftors were diftinguifhed for their virtues, fo much are they difgraced by their vices. The glory of anceftors cafts a light, indeed, upon their pofterity; but it only ferves to fhew what the defcendants are. It alike exhibits to public view their degeneracy, and their worth. I own, I cannot boaft of the deeds of my forefathers; but I hope I may anfwer the cavils of the Patricians by ftanding up in defence of what I have myfelf done. Obferve, now, my countrymen, the injuftice of the Patricians. They arrogate to themfelves honours on account of the exploits done by their forefathers, whilft they

will

will not allow me the due praife for performing the very fame fort of actions in my own perfon. He has no ftatues, they cry, of his family. He can trace no venerable line of anceftors.—What then? Is it matter of more praife to difgrace ones illuftrious anceftors, than to become illuftrious by one's own good behaviour? What if I can fhew no ftatues of my family? I can fhew the ftandards, the armour, and the trappings, which I myfelf have taken from the vanquifhed: I can fhew the fcars of thofe wounds, which I have received by facing the enemies of my country. Thefe are my ftatues. Thefe are the honours I boaft of; not left me by inheritance, as theirs; but earned by toil, by abftinence, by valour, amidft clouds of duft, and feas of blood; fcenes of action, where thofe effeminate Patricians, who endeavour, by indirect means, to depreciate me in your efteem, have never dared to fhew their faces.

Sallust.

C H A P.   IV.

CALISTHENES's REPROOF of CLEON's FLATTERY to ALEXANDER.

IF the king were prefent, Cleon, there would be no need of my anfwering to what you have juft propofed. He would himfelf reprove you for endeavouring to draw him into an imitation of foreign abfurdities, and for bringing envy upon him by fuch unmanly flattery. As he is abfent, I take upon me to tell you in his name, that no praife is lafting, but what is rational; and that you do what you can to leffen his glory, inftead of adding to it. Heroes have never among us been deified till after their death. And, whatever may be your way of thinking, Cleon, for my part, I wifh the king may not, for many years to come, obtain that honour. You have mentioned, as precedents of what you propofe, Hercules, and Bacchus. Do you imagine, Cleon, that they

G 4

were

were deified over a cup of wine? And are you and I qualified to make gods? Is the king, our sovereign, to receive his divinity from you and me, who are his subjects? First try your power, whether you can make a king. It is, surely, easier to make a king, than a god; to give an earthly dominion, than a throne in heaven. I only wish, that the gods may have heard, without offence, the arrogant proposal you have made, of adding one to their number; and that they may still be so propitious to us, as to grant the continuance of that success to our affairs, with which they have hitherto favoured us. For my part, I am not ashamed of my country; nor do I approve of our adopting the rites of foreign nations, or learning from them how we ought to reverence our kings. To receive laws, or rules of conduct, from them, what is it, but to confess ourselves inferior to them?

Quintus Curtius.

C H A P. V.

The SCYTHIAN AMBASSADORS to ALEXANDER.

IF your person were as gigantic as your desires, the world would not contain you. Your right hand would touch the east, and your left the west, at the same time. You grasp at more than you are equal to. From Europe you reach Asia: from Asia you lay hold on Europe. And if you should conquer all mankind, you seem disposed to wage war with woods and snows, with rivers and wild beasts, and to attempt to subdue nature. But have you considered the usual course of things? Have you reflected, that great trees are many years in growing to their height, and are cut down in an hour? It is foolish to think of the fruit only, without considering the height you have to climb, to come at it. Take care lest, while you strive to reach the top, you fall to the ground

with

with the branches, you have laid hold on. The
lion when dead is devoured by ravens; and ruſt
conſumes the hardneſs of iron. There is nothing ſo
ſtrong, but it is in danger from what is weak. It
will, therefore, be your wiſdom, to take care how
you venture beyond your reach. Beſides, what have
you to do with the Scythians, or the Scythians with
you? We have never invaded Macedon: why ſhould
you attack Scythia? We inhabit vaſt deſerts, and
pathleſs woods, where we do not want to hear of the
name of Alexander. We are not diſpoſed to ſubmit
to ſlavery; and we have no ambition to tyrannize
over any nation. That you may underſtand the genius of the Scythians, we preſent you with a yoke of
oxen, an arrow, and a goblet. We uſe theſe reſpec-
tively in our commerce with friends, and with foes.
We give to our friends the corn, which we raiſe by
the labour of our oxen. With the goblet we join
with them in pouring drink-offerings to the gods:
and with arrows we attack our enemies. We have
conquered thoſe, who have attempted to tyrannize
over us in our own country, and likewiſe the kings
of the Medes and Perſians, when they made unjuſt
war upon us; and we have opened to ourſelves a
way into Egypt. You pretend to be the puniſher of
robbers; and are yourſelf the general robber of mankind. You have taken Lydia: you have ſeized
Syria: you are maſter of Perſia: you have ſubdued
the Bactrians; and attacked India. All this will not
ſatisfy you, unleſs you lay your greedy and inſatiable
hands upon our flocks and our herds. How imprudent is your conduct! You graſp at riches, the poſſeſſion of which only encreaſes your avarice. You
increaſe your hunger by what ſhould produce ſatie-
ty; ſo that the more you have the more you deſire.
But have you forgot how long the corqueſt of the
Bactrians detained you? While you were ſubduing
them, the Sogdians revolted. Your victories ſerve
no other purpoſe, than to find you employment by
producing new wars. For the buſineſs of every conqueſt is twofold; to win, and to preſerve. And

G 5

though

though you may be the greatest of warriors, you must expect, that the nations you conquer will endeavour to shake off the yoke as fast as possible. For what people chooses to be under foreign dominion? If you will cross the Tanais, you may travel over Scythia, and observe how extensive a territory we inhabit. But to conquer us is quite another business. Your army is loaded with cumbrous spoils of many nations. You will find the poverty of the Scythians, at one time, too nimble for your pursuit; and, at another time, when you think we are fled far enough from you, you will have us surprize you in your camp. For the Scythians attack with no less vigour than they fly. Why should we put you in mind of the vastness of the country you will have to conquer! The deserts of Scythia are commonly talked of in Greece; and all the world knows, that our delight is to dwell at large, and not in towns, or plantations. It will therefore be your wisdom to keep, with strict attention, what you have gained. Catching at more, you may lose what you have. We have a proverbial saying in Scythia, That Fortune has no feet, and is furnished only with hands, to distribute her capricious favours, and with fins to elude the grasp of those, to whom she has been bountiful. You give yourself out to be a god, the son of Jupiter Ammon. It suits the character of a god, to bestow favours on mortals; not to deprive them of what they have. But if you are no god: reflect on the precarious condition of humanity. You will thus shew more wisdom, than by dwelling on those subjects, which have puffed up your pride, and made you forget yourself. You see how little you are likely to gain by attempting the conquest of Scythia. On the other hand, you may, if you please, have in us a valuable alliance. We command the borders of both Europe and Asia. There is nothing between us and Bactria, but the river Tanais; and our territory extends to Thrace, which, as we have heard, borders on Macedon. If you decline attacking us in a hostile manner you may have

our

our friendſhip. Nations, which have never been at war, are on an equal footing. But it is in vain, that confidence is repoſed in a conquered people. There can be no ſincere friendſhip between the oppreſſors and the oppreſſed. Even in peace, the latter think themſelves entitled to the rights of war againſt the former. We will, if you think good, enter into a treaty with you, according to our manner, which is, not by ſigning, ſealing, and taking the gods to witneſs, as is the Grecian cuſtom; but by doing actual ſervices. The Scythians are not uſed to promiſe; but to perform without promiſing. And they think an appeal to the gods ſuperfluous; for that thoſe, who have no regard for the eſteem of men, will not heſitate to offend the gods, by perjury. You may therefore conſider with yourſelf, whether you had better have a people of ſuch a character, and ſo ſituated as to have it in their power either to ſerve you, or to annoy you, according as you treat them; for allies, or for enemies.

QUINTUS CURTIUS.

C H A P. VI.

GALGACUS, the GENERAL OF THE CALEDONII, TO HIS ARMY, TO INCITE THEM TO ACTION AGAINST THE ROMANS.

COUNTRYMEN, and FELLOW-SOLDIERS!

WHEN I conſider the cauſe, for which we have drawn our ſwords, and the neceſſity of ſtriking an effectual blow, before we ſheath them again, I feel joyful hopes ariſing in my mind, that this day an opening will be made for the reſtoration of Britiſh liberty, and for ſhaking off the infamous yoke of Roman ſlavery. Caledonia is yet free. The all-graſping power of Rome has not yet been able to ſeize our liberty. But it is only to be preſerved by
valour.

valour. You are not to expect, that you should escape the ravage of the general plunderers of mankind, by any sentiment of moderation in them. When the countries, which are more accessible, come to be subdued, they will then force their way into those, which are harder to be overcome. And if they should conquer the dry land, over the whole world, they will then think of carrying their arms beyond the ocean, to see whether there be not certain unknown regions, which they may attack, and reduce under subjection to the Roman Empire. For we see, that if a country is thought to be powerful in arms, the Romans attack it, because the conquest will be glorious; if inconsiderable in the military art, because the victory will be easy; if rich, they are drawn thither by the hope of plunder; if poor, by the desire of fame. The east and the west, the south and the north, the face of the whole earth, is the scene of their military atchievements; the world is too little for their ambition, and their avarice. They are the only nation ever known to be equally desirous of conquering a poor kingdom as a rich one. Their supreme joy seems to be ravaging, fighting, and shedding of blood; and when they have unpeopled a region, so that there are none left alive to bear arms, they say, they have given peace to that country.

Nature itself has peculiarly endeared, to all men, their wives, and their children. But it is known to you, my countrymen, that the conquered youth are daily draughted off to supply the deficiencies in the Roman army. The wives, the sisters, and the daughters of the conquered are either exposed to the violence, or at least corrupted by the arts, of these cruel spoilers. The fruits of our industry are plundered, to make up the tributes imposed on us by oppressive avarice. Britons sow their fields; and the greedy Romans reap them. Our very bodies are worn out in carrying on their military works; and our toils are rewarded by them with abuse and stripes. Those, who are born to slavery, are bought and maintained by their master. But this unhappy coun-

try

try pays for being enflaved, and feeds thofe who enflave it. And our portion of difgrace is the bittereft, as the inhabitants of this ifland are the laft who have fallen under the galling yoke. Our native bent againft tyranny, is the offence which moft fenfibly irritates thofe lordly ufurpers. Our diftance from the feat of government, and our natural defence by the furrounding ocean, renders us obnoxious to their fufpicions: for they know, that Britons are born with an inftinctive love of liberty; and they conclude, that we muft be naturally led to think of taking the advantage of our detached fituation, to difengage ourfelves, one time or other, from their oppreffion.

Thus, my countrymen, and fellow-foldiers, fufpected and hated, as we ever muft be by the Romans, there is no profpect of our enjoying even a tolerable ftate of bondage under them. Let us then, in the name of all that is facred, and in defence of all that is dear to us, refolve to exert ourfelves, if not for glory, at leaft for fafety; if not in vindication of Britifh honour, at leaft in defence of our lives. How near were the Brigantines to fhake off the yoke—led on too by a woman! They burnt a Roman fettlement: they attacked the dreaded Roman legions in their camp. Had not their partial fuccefs drawn them into a fatal fecurity, the bufinefs had been completed. And fhall not we, of the Caledonian region, whofe territories are yet free, and whofe ftrength is entire, fhall we not, my fellow-foldiers, attempt fomewhat, which may fhew thefe foreign ravagers, that they have more to do, than they think of, before they be mafters of the whole ifland?

But, after all, who are thefe mighty Romans? Are they gods; or mortal men, like ourfelves? Do we not fee, that they fall into the fame errors, and weakneffes, as others? Does not peace effeminate them? Does not abundance debauch them? Does not wantonnefs enervate them? Do they not even go to excefs in the moft unmanly vices? And can you imagine, that they, who are remarkable for their vices,

ces, are likewife remarkable for their valour? What, then, do we dread?—Shall I tell you the truth, my fellow-foldiers? It is by means of our inteftine divifions, that the Romans have gained fuch great advantage over us. They turn the mifconduct of their enemies to their own praife. They boaft of what they have done, and fay nothing of what they might have done, had we been fo wife, as to unite againft them.

What is this formidable Roman army? Is it not compofed of a mixture of people from different countries; fome more, fome lefs, difpofed to military atchievements; fome more, fome lefs, capable of bearing fatigue and hardfhip. They keep together, while they are fuccefsful. Attack them with vigour: diftrefs them: you will fee them more difunited among themfelves, than we are now. Can any one imagine, that Gauls, Germans, and,—with fhame I muft add, Britons, who bafely lend, for a time, their limbs, and their lives, to build up a foreign tyranny; can one imagine, that thefe will be longer enemies, than flaves? or that fuch an army is held together by fentiments of fidelity, or affection? No: the only bond of union among them is fear. And, whenever terror ceafes to work upon the minds of that mixed multitude, they who now fear, will then hate, their tyrannical mafters. On our fide there is every poffible incitement to valour. The Roman courage is not, as ours, inflamed by the thoughts of wives and children in danger of falling into the hands of the enemy. The Romans have not parents, as we have, to reproach them, if they fhould defert their infirm old age. They have no country here to fight for. They are a motley collection of foreigners, in a land wholly unknown to them, cut off from their native country, hemmed in by the furrounding ocean, and given, I hope, a prey into our hands, without all poffibility of efcape. Let not the found of the Roman name affright your ears. Nor let the glare of gold or filver, upon their armour, dazzle your eyes. It is not by gold or filver, that

men

men are either wounded, or defended; though they are rendered a richer prey to the conquerors. Let us boldly attack this difunited rabble. We fhall find among themfelves a reinforcement to our army. The degenerate Britons, who are incorporated into their forces, will through fhame of their country's caufe deferted by them, quickly leave the Romans, and come over to us. The Gauls, remembering their former liberty, and that it was the Romans who deprived them of it, will forfake their tyrants, and join the affertors of freedom. The Germans who remain in their army, will follow the example of their countrymen, the Ufipii, who fo lately deferted. And what will there be then, to fear? A few half-garrifoned forts; a few municipal towns, inhabited by worn-out old men; difcord univerfally prevailing, occafioned by tyranny in thofe who command, and obftinacy in thofe who fhould obey. On our fide, an army united in the caufe of their country, their wives, their children, their aged parents, their liberties, their lives. At the head of this army, I hope I do not offend againft modefty in faying there is a General ready to exert all his abilities, fuch as they are, and to hazard his life in leading you to victory, and to freedom.

I conclude, my countrymen, and fellow-foldiers, with putting you in mind, that on your behaviour this day depends your future enjoyment of peace and liberty, or your fubjection to a tyrannical enemy, with all its grievous confequences. When therefore, you come to engage—think of your anceftors—and think of your pofterity.

Tacitus.

C H A P.   VII.

The EARL of ARUNDEL's SPEECH,
PROPOSING AN ACCOMMODATION BETWEEN
HENRY II. AND STEPHEN.

IN the midst of a wide and open plain, Henry found Stephen encamped, and pitched his own tents within a quarter of a mile of him, preparing for a battle with all the eagerness, that the desire of empire and glory could excite, in a brave and youthful heart, elate with success. Stephen also much wished to bring the contest between them to a speedy decision: but, while he and Eustace were consulting with William of Ipres, in whose affection they most confided, and by whose private advice they took all their measures, the earl of Arundel, having assembled the English nobility, and principal officers, spoke to this effect.

IT is now above sixteen years, that on a doubtful and disputed claim to the crown, the rage of civil war has almost continually infested this kingdom. During this melancholy period how much blood has been shed! What devastations and misery have been brought on the people! The laws have lost their force, the crown its authority: licentiousness and impunity have shaken all the foundations of public security. This great and noble nation has been delivered a prey to the basest of foreigners, the abominable scum of Flanders, Brabant, and Bretagne, robbers, rather than soldiers, restrained by no laws, divine or human, tied to no country, subject to no prince, instruments of all tyranny, violence, and oppression. At the same time, our cruel neighbours, the Welsh and the Scotch, calling themselves allies or auxiliaries to the Empress, but in reality enemies and destroyers of England, have broken their bounds, ravaged our borders, and taken from us whole provinces, which we can never hope to recover, while,

instead

inftead of employing our united force againft them, we continue thus madly, without any care of our public fafety or national honour, to turn our fwords againft our own bofoms. What benefits have we gained to compenfate all thefe loffes, or what do we expect ? When Matilda was miftrefs of the kingdom, though her power was not yet confirmed, in what manner did fhe govern ? Did fhe not make even thofe of her own faction, and court, regret the king ? Was not her pride more intolerable ftill than his levity, her rapine than his profufenefs ? Were any years of his reign fo grievous to the people, fo offenfive to the nobles, as the firft days of hers ? When fhe was driven out, did Stephen correct his former bad conduct ? Did he difmifs his odious foreign favourite.? Did he difcharge his lawlefs foreign hirelings, who had fo long been the fcourge and the reproach of England ? Have they not lived ever fince upon free quarter, by plundering our houfes and burning our cities ? And now to compleat our miferies, a new army of foreigners, Angevins, Gafcons, Poictevins, I know not who, are come over with Henry Plantagenet, the fon of Matilda ; and many more, no doubt, will be called to affift him, as foon as ever his affairs abroad will permit ; by whofe help, if he be victorious, England muft pay the price of their fervices : our lands, our honours, muft be the hire of thefe rapacious invaders. But fuppofe we fhould have the fortune to conquer for Stephen, what will be the confequence ? Will victory teach him moderation ? Will he learn from fecurity that regard to our liberties, which he could not learn from danger ? Alas ! the only fruit of our good fuccefs, will be this ; the eftates of the earl of Leicefter and others of our countrymen, who have now quitted the party of the king, will be forfeited ; and new confifcations will accrue to William of Ipres.

But let us not hope, that, be our victory ever fo complete, it will give any lafting peace to this kingdom. Should Henry fall in this battle, there are two other brothers, to succeed to his claim, and support his faction, perhaps with less merit, but certainly with as much ambition as he. What shall we do then to free ourselves from all these misfortunes ?—Let us prefer the interest of our country to that of our party, and to all those passions, which are apt, in civil dissentions, to inflame zeal into madness, and render men the blind instruments of those very evils, which they fight to avoid. Let us prevent all the crimes and all the horrors that attend a war of this kind, in which conquest itself is full of calamity, and our most happy victories deserve to be celebrated only by tears. Nature herself is dismayed, and shrinks back from a combat, where every blow that we strike may murder a friend, a relation, a parent. Let us hearken to her voice, which commands us to refrain from that guilt. Is there one of us here, who would not think it a happy and glorious act, to save the life of one of his country-men ? What a felicity then, and what a glory, must it be to us all, if we save the lives of thousands of Englishmen, that must otherwise fall in this battle, and in many other battles, which hereafter, may be fought in this quarrel ? It is in our power to do so — It is in our power to end the controversy, both safely and honourably; by an amicable agreement ; not by the sword. Stephen may enjoy the royal dignity for his life, and the succession may be secured to the young duke of Normandy with such a present rank in the state, as befits the heir of the crown. Even the bitterest enemies, of the king must acknowledge, that he is valiant, generous, and good-natured : his warmest friends cannot deny, that he has a great deal of rashness and indiscretion. Both may therefore conclude, that he should not be deprived of the royal authority, but that he ought to be restrained from a further abuse of it ; which can be done by no means, so certain and effectual, as what I propose : for thus his power will be tempered, by the presence, the counsels, and influence of Prince Henry ; who from his own interest in the weal of the kingdom, which he is to

inherit,

inherit, will always have a right to interpose his advice, and even his authority, if it be neceſſary, againſt any future violation of our liberties ; and to procure an effectual redreſs of our grievances, which we have hitherto fought in vain. If all the Engliſh in both armies unite, as I hope that they may, in this plan of pacification, they will be able to give the law to the foreigners, and oblige both the king and the duke to conſent to it. This will ſecure the public tranquility, and leave no ſecret ſtings of reſentment, to rankle in the hearts of a ſuffering party, and produce future diſturbances. As there will be no triumph, no inſolence, no excluſive right to favour on either ſide, there can be no ſhame, no anger, no uneaſy deſire of change. It will be the work of the whole nation; and all muſt wiſh to ſupport what all have eſtabliſhed. The ſons of Stephen indeed may endeavour to oppoſe it : but their efforts will be fruitleſs, and muſt end very ſoon, either in their ſubmiſſion or their ruin. Nor have they any reaſonable cauſe to complain. Their father himſelf did not come to the crown by hereditary right. He was elected in preference to a woman and an infant, who were deemed not to be capable of ruling a kingdom. By that election our allegiance is bound to him during his life : but neither that bond, nor the reaſon for which we choſe him, will hold, as to the choice of a ſucceſſor. Henry Plantagenet is now grown up to an age of maturity, and every way qualified to ſucceed to the crown. He is the grandſon of a king whoſe memory is dear to us, and the neareſt heir male to him in the courſe of deſcent : he appears to reſemble him in all his good qualities, and to be worthy to reign over the Normans and Engliſh, whoſe nobleſt blood, united, enriches his veins. Normandy has already ſubmitted to him with pleaſure. Why ſhould we now divide that duchy from England, when it is ſo greatly the intereſt of our nobility to keep them always connected ? If we had no other inducement to make us deſire a reconciliation between him and Stephen, this would be ſufficient.

Our

Our eſtates in both countries, will, by that means, be ſecured, which otherwiſe we muſt forfeit, in the one, or the other, while Henry remains poſſeſſed of Normandy : and it will not be an eaſy matter to drive them from thence, even though we ſhould compel him to retire from England. But by amicably compounding his quarrel with Stephen, we ſhall maintain all our intereſts, private and public. His greatneſs abroad will increaſe the power of this kingdom : it will make us reſpectable and formidable to France : England will be the head of all thoſe ample dominions, which extend from the Britiſh ocean to the Pyrenean mountains. By governing, in his youth ſo many different ſtates, he will learn to govern us, and come to the crown, after the deceaſe of king Stephen, accompanied in all the arts of good policy. His mother has willingly reſigned to him her pretenſions, or rather ſhe acknowledges that his are ſuperior : we therefore can have nothing to apprehend on that ſide. In every view, our peace, our ſafety, the repoſe of our conſciences, the quiet and happineſs of our poſterity will be firmly eſtabliſhed by the means I propoſe. Let Stephen continue to wear the crown that we give him, as long as he lives ; but after his death let it deſcend to that prince, who alone can put an end to our unhappy diviſions. If you approve my advice, and will empower me to treat in your names, I will immediately convey your deſires to the king and the duke.

LORD LYTTLETON.

C H A P.   VIII.

Mr. PULTENEY's SPEECH on the motion
for reducing the ARMY.

S I R,

WE have heard a great deal about parliamentary armies, and about an army continued from year to year ; I have always been, Sir, and always ſhall be againſt a ſtanding army of any kind : to me

it

it is a terrible thing, whether under that of parliamentary or any other defignation ; a ftanding army is ftill a ftanding army, whatever name it be called by ; they are a body of men diftinct from the body of the people : they are governed by different laws, and blind obedience and an entire fubmiffion to the orders of their commanding officer is their only principle. The nations around us, Sir, are already enflaved, and have been enflaved by thofe very means ; by means of their ftanding armies they have every one loft their liberties ; it is indeed impoffible that the liberties of the people can be preferved in any country where a numerous ftanding army is kept up. Shall we then taken any of our meafures from the example of our neighbours ? No, Sir, on the contrary, from their misfortunes we ought to learn to avoid thofe rocks upon which they have fplit.

It fignifies nothing to tell me, that our army is commanded by fuch gentlemen as cannot be fuppofed to join in any meafure for enflaving their country; it may be fo ; I hope it is fo ; I have a very good opinion of many gentlemen now in the army ; I believe they would not join in any fuch meafures ; but their lives are uncertain, nor can we be fure how long they may be continued in command ; they may be all difmiffed in a moment, and proper tools of power put in their room. Befides, Sir, we know the paffions of men, we know how dangerous it is to truft the beft of men with too much power. Where was there a braver army than that under Julius Cæfar ? Where was there ever an army that had ferved their country more faithfully ? That army was commanded generally by the beft citizens of Rome, by men of great fortune and figure in their country ; yet that army enflaved their country. The affections of the foldiers towards their country, the honour and integrity of the under officers, are not to be depended on ; by the military law, the adminiftration of juftice is fo quick, and the punifhments fo fevere, that neither officer nor foldier dares offer to difpute the orders of his fupreme commander ; he

muft

muſt not conſult his own inclinations : If an officer were commanded to pull his own father out of this houſe, he muſt do it ; he dares not diſobey ; immediate death would be the ſure conſequence of the leaſt grumbling. And if an officer were ſent into the court of requeſts, accompanied by a body of muſketeers with ſcrewed bayonets, and with orders to tell us what we ought to do, and how we were to vote, I know what would be the duty of this houſe ; I know it would be our duty to order the officer to be taken and hanged up at the door of the lobby : but Sir, I doubt much if ſuch a ſpirit could be found in the houſe, or in any houſe of Commons that will ever be in England.

SIR, I talk not of imaginary things ; I talk of what has happened to an Engliſh houſe of Commons, and from an Engliſh army; not only from an Engliſh army, but an army that was raiſed by that very houſe of Commons, an army that was paid by them, and an army that was commanded by generals appointed by them. Therefore do not let us vainly imagine, that an army raiſed and maintained by authority of Parliament, will always be ſubmiſſive to them : if an army be ſo numerous as to have it in their power to over-awe the Parliament, they will be ſubmiſſive as long as the Parliament does nothing to diſoblige their favourite general ; but when that caſe happens, I am afraid that in place of the Parliament's diſmiſſing the army, the army will diſmiſs the Parliament, as they have done heretofore. Nor does the legality or illegality of that Parliament, or of that army, alter the caſe ; for with reſpect to that army, and according to their way of thinking, the Parliament diſmiſſed by them was a legal Parliament ; they were an army raiſed and maintained according to law, and at firſt they were raiſed as they imagined, for the preſervation of thoſe liberties which they afterwards deſtroyed.

IT has been urged, Sir, that whoever is for the Proteſtant ſucceſſion muſt be for continuing the army : for that very reaſon, Sir, I am againſt continuing

ing the army. I know that neither the Proteftant fucceffion in his Majefty's moft illuftrious houfe, nor any fucceffion, can ever be fafe as long as there is a ftanding army in the country. Armies, Sir, have no regard to hereditary fucceffion. The firft two Cæfars at Rome did pretty well, and found means to keep their armies in tolerable fubjection, becaufe the generals and officers were all their own creatures. But how did it fare with their fucceffors ? Was not every one of them named by the army, without any regard to hereditary right, or to any right ? A cobler, a gardener, or any man who happened to raife himfelf in the army, and could gain their affections, was made emperor of the world : was not every fucceeding emperor raifed to the throne, or tumbled headlong into the duft, according to the mere whim or mad frenzy of the foldiers ?

WE are told this army is defired to be continued but for one year longer, or for a limited term of years. How abfurd is this diftinction ? Is there any army in the world continued for any term of years ? Does the moft abfolute monarch tell his army, that he is to continue them for any number of years, or any number of months ? How long have we already continued our army from year to year ? And if it thus continues, wherein will it differ from the ftanding armies of thofe countries which have already fubmitted their necks to the yoke ? We are now come to the Rubicon ; our army is now to be reduced, or it never will ; from his Majefty's own mouth we are affured of a profound tranquility abroad, we know there is one at home ; if this is not a proper time, if thefe circumftances do not afford us a fafe opportunity for reducing at leaft a part of our regular forces, we never can expect to fee any reduction ; and this nation, already overloaded with debts and taxes, muft be loaded with the heavy charge of perpetually fupporting a numerous ftanding army ; and remain for ever expofed to the danger of, having its liberties and privileges trampled upon by any future King or miniftry, who fhall take it in their heads to

do

do fo, and fhall take a proper care to model the army for that purpofe.

C H A P.   IX.

Sir JOHN St. AUBIN's SPEECH for repeal-ing the SEPTENNIAL ACT.

Mr. Speaker,

THE fubject matter of this debate is of fuch importance, that I fhould be afhamed to return to my electors, without endeavouring, in the beft manner I am able, to declare publicly the reafons which induced me to give my moft ready affent to this queftion.

The people have an unqueftionable right to frequent new Parliaments by ancient ufage ; and this ufage has been confirmed by feveral laws, which have been progreffively made by our anceftors, as often as they found it neceffary to infift on this effential privilege.

Parliaments were generally annual, but never continued longer than three years, till the remarkable reign of Henry VIII. He, Sir, was a Prince of unruly appetites, and of an arbitrary will : he was impatient of every reftraint ; the laws of God and man fell equally a facrifice, as they ftood in the way of his avarice, or difappointed his ambition ; he therefore introduced long Parliaments, becaufe he very well knew, that they would become the proper inftruments of both ; and what a flavifh obedience they paid to all his meafures is fufficiently known.

If we come to the reign of King Charles the Firft, we muft acknowledge him to be a prince of a contrary temper ; he had certainly an innate love for religion and virtue. But here lay the misfortune—he was led from his natural difpofition by fycophants and flatterers ; they advifed him to neglect the calling of frequent new Parliaments, and therefore, by not taking the conftant fenfe of his people in

what

what he did, he was worked up into so high a notion of prerogative, that the Commons (in order to restrain it) obtained that independant fatal power, which at last unhappily brought him to his most tragical end, and at the same time subverted the whole constitution. And I hope we shall learn this lesson from it, never to compliment the crown, with any new or extravagant powers, nor to deny the people those rights, which by ancient usage they are entitled to; but to preserve the just and equal balance, from which they will both derive mutual security, and which, if duly observed, will render our constitution the envy and admiration of all the world.

King Charles the Second naturally took a surfeit of Parliaments in his father's time, and was therefore extremely desirous to lay them aside. But this was a scheme impracticable. However, in effect, he did so: for he obtained a Parliament, which, by its long duration, like an army of veterans, became so exactly disciplined to his own measures, that they knew no other command but from that person who gave them their pay.

This was a safe and most ingenious way of enslaving a nation. It was very well known, that arbitrary power, if it was open and avowed, would never prevail here. The people were therefore amused with the specious form of their ancient constitution: it existed, indeed, in their fancy; but like a mere phantom, had no substance nor reality in it, for the power, the authority, the dignity of Parliaments were wholly lost. This was that remarkable Parliament which so justly obtained the opprobrious name of Pension Parliament; and was the model from which I believe, some later Parliaments have been exactly copied.

At the time of the revolution, the people made a fresh claim of their ancient privileges; and as they had so lately experienced the misfortune of long and servile Parliaments, it was then declared, that they should be held frequently. But, it seems, their full meaning was not understood by this declaration; and

H

there-

therefore, as in every new settlement the intention of all parties should be specifically manifested, the Parliament never ceased struggling with the crown, till the triennial law was obtained : the preamble of it is extremely full and strong ; and in the body of the bill you will find the word *declared* before *enacted*, by which I apprehend, that though this law did not immediately take place at the time of the revolution, it was certainly intended as declaratory of their first meaning, and therefore stands a part of that original contract under which the constitution was then settled. His majesty's title to the crown, is primarily derived from that contract ; and if, upon a review, there shall appear to be any deviations from it, we ought to treat them as so many injuries done to that title. And I dare say, that this house, which has gone through so long a series of services to his Majesty, will at last be willing to revert to those original stated measures of government, to renew and strengthen that title.

But, Sir, I think the manner in which the septennial law was first introduced, is a very strong reason why it should be repealed. People, in their fears, have very often recourse to desperate expedients, which, if not cancelled in season, will themselves, prove fatal to that constitution, which they were meant to secure. Such is the nature of the septennial law ; it was intended only as a preservative against a temporary inconvenience : the inconvenience is removed, but the mischievous effects still continue ; for it not only altered the constitution of Parliaments, but it extended the same Parliament beyond its natural duration ; and therefore carries the most unjust implication with it, That you may at any time usurp the most indubitable, the most essential privilege of the people——I mean that of chusing their own representatives. A precedent of such a dangerous consequence, of so fatal a tendency, that I think it would be a reproach to our statute-book, if that law was any longer to subsist, which might record it to posterity.

This

This is a season of virtue and public spirit. Let us take advantage of it to repeal those laws which infringe our liberties, and introduce such as may restore the vigour of our ancient constitution.

Human nature is so very corrupt, that all obligations lose their force, unless they are frequently renewed.——Long Parliaments become therefore independent of the people, and when they do so, there always happens a most dangerous dependence elsewhere.

Long Parliaments give the ministers an opportunity of getting acquaintance with members, of practising his several arts to win them into his schemes.—— This must be the work of time——Corruption is of so base a nature, that at first sight it is extremely shocking——Hardly any one has submitted to it all at once.——His disposition must be previously understood, the particular bait must be found out with which he is to be allured, and after all, it is not without many struggles that he surrenders his virtue.—— Indeed, there are some, who will at once plunge themselves into any base action; but the generality of mankind are of a more cautious nature, and will proceed only by leisurely degrees.——One or two perhaps have deserted their colours the first campaign, some have done it a second.——But a great many, who have not that eager disposition to vice, will wait till a third.

For this reason, short parliaments have been less corrupt than long ones; they are observed, like streams of water, always to grow more impure the greater distance they run from the fountain-head.

I am aware, it may be said, that frequent new Parliaments will produce frequent new expences, but I think quite the contrary; I am really of opinion, that it will be a proper remedy against the evil of liberty at elections; especially as you have provided so wholesome a law to co operate upon these occasions.

H 2 II. BRIBERY

Bribery at elections, whence did it arise? Not from country gentlemen, for they are sure of being chosen without it; it was, Sir, the invention of wicked and corrupt ministers, who have from time to time, led weak Princes into such destructive measures, that they did not dare to rely upon the natural representation of the people.——Long Parliaments, Sir, first introduced Bribery, because they were worth purchasing at any rate :——Country gentlemen, who have only their private fortunes to rely upon, and have no mercenary ends to serve, are unable to oppose it, especially if at any time the public treasure shall be unfaithfully squandered away to corrupt their boroughs.——Country gentlemen, indeed, may make some weak efforts ; but as they generally prove unsuccessful, and the time of a fresh struggle is at so great a distance, they at last grow faint in the dispute, give up their country for lost, and retire in despair.——Despair naturally produces indolence, and that is the proper disposition for slavery. Ministers of state understand this very well, and are therefore unwilling to awaken the nation out of its lethargy, by frequent elections——They know that the spirit of liberty, like every other virtue of the mind, is to be kept alive only by constant action; that it is impossible to enslave this nation, while it is perpetually upon its guard ——Let country gentlemen then, by having frequent opportunities of exerting themselves, be kept warm and active in their contention for the public good : this will raise that zeal and spirit, which will at last get the better of those undue influences, by which the officers of the crown, though unknown to the several boroughs, have been able to supplant country gentlemen of great characters and fortune, who live in their neighbourhood.——I do not say this upon idle speculation only.—— I live in a country where it is too well known, and I appeal to many gentlemen in the house, to more out of it (and who are so for this very reason) for the truth of my assertion. Sir, it is a sore which has been long eating into the most vital part of the constitution, and I hope the
time

time will come when you will probe it to the bottom——For if a minifter fhould ever gain a corrupt familiarity with our boroughs, if he fhould keep a regifter of them in his clofet, and, by fending down his treafury-mandates fhould procure a fpurious reprefentative of the people, the off-fpring of his corruption, who will be at all times ready to reconcile and juftify the moft contradictory meafures of his adminiftration, and even to vote every crude indigefted dream of their patron into a law; if the maintenance of his power fhould become the fole object of their attention, and that they fhould be guilty of the moft violent breach of Parliamentary truft, by giving the King a difcretionary liberty of taxing the people without limitation or controul; the laft fatal compliment they can pay to the crown:——if this fhould ever be the unhappy condition of this nation, the people indeed may complain; but the doors of that place where their complaints fhould be heard, will for ever be fhut againft them.

Our difeafe, I fear, is of a complicated nature, and I think that this motion is wifely intended to remove the firft and principal diforder.——Give the people their ancient right of frequent new elections; they will reftore the decayed authority of Parliaments, and will put our conftitution into a natural condition of working out her own cure.

Sir, upon the whole, I am of opinion, that I cannot exprefs a greater zeal for his Majefty, for the liberties of the people, or the honour and dignity of this houfe, than by feconding the motion which the honourable gentleman has made you.

H 3

CHAP.

C H A P. X.

Sir ROBERT WALPOLE's REPLY.

Mr. Chancellor of the Exchequer,

THOUGH the queſtion has been already ſo fully oppoſed, that there is no great occaſion to ſay any thing farther againſt it, yet I hope, the houſe will indulge me the liberty of giving ſome of thoſe reaſons, which induce me to be againſt the motion. In general I muſt take notice, that the nature of our conſtitution ſeems to be very much miſtaken by the gentlemen who have ſpoken in favour of this motion. It is certain, that ours is a mixt government, and the perfection of our conſtitution conſiſts in this, that the monarchical, ariſtocratical, and democratical form of government, are mixt and interwoven in ours, ſo as to give us all the advantages of each, without ſubjecting us to the dangers and inconveniences of either. The democratical form of government, which is the only one I have now occaſion to take notice of, is liable to theſe inconveniencies. That they are generally too tedious in their coming to any reſolution, and ſeldom briſk and expeditious enough in carrying their reſolutions into execution: that they are always wavering in their reſolutions, and never ſteady in any of the meaſures they reſolve to purſue; and that they are often involved in factions, ſeditions and inſurrections, which expoſes them to be made the tools, if not the prey of their neighbours: therefore in all the regulation we make, with reſpect to our conſtitution, we are to guard againſt running too much into that form of government which is properly called democratical: this was, in my opinion, the effect of the triennial law, and will again be the effect, if ever it ſhould be reſtored.

THAT triennial elections would make our government too tedious in all their reſolves, is evident; becaufe, in fuch cafe, no prudent adminiftration would ever refolve upon any meafure of confequence, till they had felt not only the pulfe of the parliament, but the pulfe of the people; and the minifters of ftate would always labour under this difadvantage, that, as fecrets of ftate muft not be immediately divulged, their enemies, (and enemies they will always have) would have a handle for expofing their meafures, and rendering them difagreeable to the people, and thereby carrying perhaps a new election againft them, before they could have an opportunity of juftifying their meafures, by divulging thofe facts and circumftances, from whence the juftice and the wifdom of their meafures would clearly appear.

THEN, Sir, it is by experience well known, that what is called the populace of every country, are apt to be too much elated with fuccefs, and too much dejected with every misfortune; this makes them wavering in their opinions about affairs of ftate, and never long of the fame mind; and as this houfe is chofen by the free and unbiaffed voice of the people in general, if this choice were fo often renewed, we might expect, that this houfe would be as wavering, and as unfteady as the people ufually are; and it being impoffible to carry on the public affairs of the nation, without the concurrence of this houfe, the minifters would always be obliged to comply, and confequently would be obliged to change their meafures, as often as the people changed their minds.

WITH feptennial Parliaments, Sir, we are not expofed to either of thefe misfortunes, becaufe, if the minifters, after having felt the pulfe of the parliament, which they can always foon do, refolve upon any meafures, they have generally time enough before the new elections come on, to give the people a proper information, in order to fhew them the juftice and the wifdom of the meafures they have purfued; and if the people fhould be at any time too much elated, or too much dejected, or fhould without a caufe change their mind, thofe at the helm of

H 4

affairs

affairs have time to set them right, before a new election comes on.

As to faction and sedition, Sir, I will grant, that in monarchical and aristocratical governments, it generally arises from violence and oppression; but in democratical governments, it always arises from the people's having too great a share in the government; for in all countries, and in all governments, there always will be many factious and unquiet spirits, who can never be at rest either in power or out of power: when in power, they are never easy, unless every man submits entirely to their direction, and when out of power, they are always working and intriguing against those that are in, without any regard to justice, or to the interest of their country: in popular governments such men have too much game, they have too many opportunities for working upon and corrupting the minds of the people, in order to give them a bad impression of, and to raise discontents against those that have the management of the public affairs for the time; and these discontents often break out into seditions and insurrections. This, Sir, would in my opinion be our misfortune if our Parliaments were either annual or triennial; by such frequent elections, there would be so much power thrown into the hands of the people as would destroy that equal mixture, which is the beauty of our constitution: in short, our government would really become a democratical government, and might from thence very probably diverge into a tyrannical. Therefore, in order to preserve our constitution, in order to prevent our falling under tyranny and arbitrary power, we ought to preserve that law, which I really think has brought our constitution to a more equal mixture, and consequently to a greater perfection than it was ever in, before the law took place.

As to bribery and corruption, Sir, if it be possible to influence, by such base means, the majority of the electors of Great Britain, to chuse such men as
would

would probably give up their liberti
poffible to influence, by fuch means,
the members of this houfe, to confen
blifhment of arbitrary power, I would r
that the calculations, made by the gen
other fide were juft, and their inferen
I am perfuaded, that neither of the
As the members of this houfe generally
always be gentlemen of fortune and t
country; is it poffible to fuppofe, tha
could, by a penfion, or a poft, be influ
fent to the overthrow of our conftituti
the enjoyment, not only of what he
what he before had, would be render
precarious? I will allow, Sir, that w
bribery, the price muft be higher or lo
-ly in proportion to the virtue of the n
be bribed; but it muft likewife, be gra
humour he happens to be in at the ti
he happens to be endowed with, adds
his virtue. When no encroachments a
the rights of the people; when the
think themfelves in any danger, there
of the electors, who by a bribe of ten g
be induced to vote for one candidate r
nother; but if the court were making
ments upon the rights of the people,
would without doubt, arife in the n
fuch a cafe, I am perfuaded, that none
even of fuch electors, could be induc
a court candidate; no, not for ten t
THERE may, Sir, be fome bribery
on in the nation: I am afraid there v
fome; but it is no proof of it, that ftran
times chofen; for a gentleman may hav
tural influence over a borough in his ne
as to be able to prevail with them to ch
he pleafes to recommend; and if upo
-mendation they chufe one or two of hi
are perhaps ftrangers to them, it is not t

be inferred that the two ftrangers were chofen their re-
prefentatives by the means of bribery and corruption.

To infinuate, Sir, that money may be iffued from
the public treafury for bribing at elections; is really
fomething very extraordinary, efpecially in thofe
gentlemen who know how many checks are upon e-
very fhilling that can be iffued from thence ; and how
regularly the money granted in one year for the public fervice of the nation, muft always be accounted
for, the very next feffion, in this houfe, and likewife
in the other, if they have a mind to call for any fuch
account. And as to the gentlemen in offices, if they
have any advantage over country gentlemen, in having fomething elfe to depend on befides their own
private fortunes, they have likewife many difadvan-
tages : they are obliged to live here at London with
their families, by which they are put to a much greater expence, than gentlemen of equal fortunes who
live in the country : this lays them under a very great
difadvantage, with refpect to the fupporting their
intereft in the country. The country gentleman, by
living among the electors, and purchafing the necef-
faries for his family from them, keeps up an acquaintance and correfpondence with them, without putting himfelf to any extraordinary charge ; whereas a
gentleman who lives in London, has no other way
of keeping up an acquaintance or correfpondence
among his friends in the country, but by going down
once or twice a year at a very extraordinary charge,
and often without any other bufinefs ; fo that we
may conclude, a gentleman in office cannot, even in
feven years, fave much for diftributing in ready money at the time of an election ; and I really believe,
if the fact were narrowly inquired into, it would appear, that the gentlemen in office are as little guilty
of bribing their electors with ready money, as any
other fet of gentlemen in the kingdom.

THAT there are ferments often rifing among the
people without any juft caufe, is what I am furpri-
fed to hear controvertd, fince very late experience
may convince us of the contrary : do not we know

what

what a ferment was raifed in the nation, towards the latter end of the late Queen's reign ? And it is well known, what a fatal change in the affairs of this nation was introduced, or at leaft confirmed, by an election's coming on while the nation was in that ferment : do not we know what a ferment was raifed in the nation, foon after his late majefty's acceffion ? And if an election had then been allowed to come on, while the nation was in that ferment, it might perhaps have had as fatal effects as the former ; but thank God, this was wifely provided againft by the very law which is now wanted to be repealed.

As fuch ferments may hereafter often happen, I muft think that frequent elections will always be dangerous ; for which reafon, as far as I can fee at prefent, I fhall, I believe, at all times, think it a very dangerous experiment to repeal the feptennial bill.

C H A P. XI.

Lord LYTTLETON's SPEECH on the REPEAL OF THE ACT CALLED THE JEW BILL, in the year 1753.

Mr. Speaker,

I SEE no occafion to enter at prefent into the merits of the bill we paft the laft feffion for the naturalization of Jews ; becaufe I am convinced, that in the prefent temper of the nation, not a fingle foreign Jew will think it expedient to take any benefit of that act ; and therefore the repealing of it is giving up nothing. I affented to it laft year in hopes it might induce fome wealthy Jews to come and fettle among us : in that light I faw enough utility in it, to make me incline rather to approve than diflike it ; but, that any man alive could be zealous, either for or againft it, I confefs I had no idea. What affects our religion, is indeed of the higheft and moft ferious importance. God forbid we fhould be ever indif-

ferent

ferent about that! but, I thought this had no more to do with religion than any turnpike act we past in that seffion; and, after all the divinity that has been preached on the subject, I think so still.

Resolution and steadiness are excellent qualities; but it is the the application of them upon which their value depends. A wise government, Mr. Speaker, will know where to yield, as well as where to resist: and, there is no surer mark of littleness of mind in an administration, than obstinacy in trifles. Public wisdom on some occasions must condescend to give way to popular folly, especially in a free country, where the humour of the people must be considered as attentively. as the humour of a king in an absolute monarchy. Under both forms of government a prudent and honest ministry will indulge a small folly, and will resist a great one. Not to vouchsafe now and then a kind indulgence to the former, would discover an ignorance of human nature: not to resist the latter at all times, would be meanness and servility.

Sir, I look on the bill we are at present debating, not as a sacrifice made to popularity (for it sacrifices nothing) but as a prudent regard to some consequences arising from the nature of the clamour raised against the late act for naturalizing Jews, which seem to require a particular consideration.

It has been hitherto the rare and envied felicity of his Majesty's reign, that his subjects have enjoyed such a settled tranquility, such a freedom from angry religious disputes, as is not to be paralleled in any former times. The true Christian spirit of moderation, of charity, of universal benevolence, has prevailed in the people, has prevailed in the clergy of all ranks and degrees, instead of those narrow principles, those bigotted prejudices, that furious, that implacable, that ignorant zeal, which had often done so much hurt both to the church and state. But from the ill-understood, insignificant act of parliament you are now moved to repeal, occasion has been taken to deprive us of this inestimable advantage. It is a pretence to disturb the peace of the church, to infuse

idle

idle fears into the minds of the people, and make religion itself an engine of sedition. It behoves the piety, as well as the wisdom of Parliament, to disappoint those endeavours. Sir, the very worst mischief that can be done to religion, is to pervert it to the purposes of faction. Heaven and hell are not more distant than the benevolent spirit of the gospel, and the malignant spirit of party. The most impious wars ever made were those called holy wars. He, who hates another man for being a Christian, is himself not a Christian. Christianity, Sir, breathes love, and peace, and good will to man. A temper conformable to the dictates of that holy religion has lately distinguished this nation; and a glorious distinction it was! But there is latent, at all times, in the minds of the vulgar, a spark of enthusiasm; which, if blown by the breath of a party, may, even when it seems quite extinguished, be suddenly revived and raised to a flame. The act of last session for naturalizing Jews, has very unexpectedly administered fuel to feed that flame. To what a height it may rise, if it should continue much longer, one cannot easily tell; but, take away the fuel, and it will die of itself.

It is the misfortune of all the Roman Catholic countries, that there the church and the state, the civil power and the hierarchy, have separate interests; and are continually at variance with the other. It is our happiness, that here they form but one system. While this harmony lasts, whatever hurts the church, hurts the state: whatever weakens the credit of the governors of the church, takes away from the civil power a part of its strength, and shakes the whole constitution.

Sir, I trust and believe, that by speedily passing this bill, we shall silence that obloquy, which has so unjustly been cast upon our reverend prelates (some of the most respectable that ever adorned our church) for the part they took in the act which this repeals. And it greatly concerns the whole community, that they should not lose that respect, which is so justly

due

due to them, by a popular clamour kept up in op-
position to a measure of no importance in itself.
But if the departing from that measure should not
remove the prejudice so maliciously raised, I am
certain that no further step you can take will be
able to remove it; and therefore I hope you will
stop here. This appears to be a reasonable and safe
condescension, by which no body will be hurt; but
all beyond this, would be dangerous weakness in government. It might open a door to the wildest enthusiasm, and to the most mischievous attacks of
political disaffection working upon that enthusiasm.
If you encourage and authorise it to fall on the sy-
nagogue, it will go from thence to the meeting-
house, and in the end to the palace. But let us be
careful to check its further progress. The more
zealous we are to support Christianity, the more vi-
gilant should we be in maintaining toleration. If we
bring back persecution, we bring back the anti-
christian spirit of popery; and when the spirit is
here, the whole system will soon follow. Toleration is the basis of all public quiet. Is is a character
of freedom given to the mind, more valuable, I
think, than that which secures our persons and estates. Indeed, they are inseparably connected together: for, where the mind is not free, where the
conscience is enthralled, there is no freedom. Spi-
ritual tyranny puts on the galling chains: but civil
tyranny is called in, to rivet and fix them. We see
it in Spain, and many other countries; we have for-
merly both seen and felt it in England. By the
blessings of God, we are now delivered from all
kinds of oppression. Let us take care, that they may
never return.

CHAP. XII.

IN PRAISE OF VIRTUE.

VIRTUE is of intrinsic value and good desert, and of indispensable obligation; not the creature of will, but necessary and immutable; not local or temporary, but of equal extent and antiquity with the DIVINE MIND! not a mode of sensation, but everlasting TRUTH; not dependant on power, but the guide of all power. VIRTUE is the foundation of honour and esteem, and the source of all beauty, order, and happiness in nature. It is what confers value on all the other endowments and qualities of a reasonable being, to which they ought to be absolutely subservient, and without which the more eminent they are, the more hideous deformities and the greater curses they become. The use of it is not confined to any one stage of our existence, or to any particular situation we can be in, but reaches through all the periods and circumstances of our beings.—Many of the endowments and talents we now possess, and of which we are too apt to be proud, will cease entirely with the present state; but this will be our ornament and dignity in every future state to which we may be removed. Beauty and wit will die, learning will vanish away, and all the arts of life be soon forgot; but virtue will remain for ever. This unites us to the whole rational creation, and fits us for conversing with any order of superior natures, and for a place in any part of God's works. It procures us the approbation and love of all wise and good beings, and renders them our allies and friends.—But what is of unspeakably greater consequence is, that it makes God our friend, assimilates and unites our minds to his, and engages his almighty power in our defence.—Superior beings of all ranks are bound by it no less than ourselves. It has the same authority in all worlds that it has in this.

this. The further any being is advanced in excellence and perfection, the greater is his attachment to it, and the more is he under its influence.—To say no more; 'Tis the LAW of the whole universe; it stands first in the estimation of the Deity; its original is His nature; and it is the very object that makes Him lovely.

SUCH is the importance of Virtue.—Of what consequence, therefore, is it that we practise it?—There is no argument or motive which is at all fitted to influence a reasonable mind, which does not call us to this. One virtuous disposition of soul is perferable to the greatest natural accomplishments and abilities, and of more value than all the treasures of the world.—If you are wise, then, study virtue, and contemn every thing that can come in competition with it. Remember, that nothing else deserves one anxious thought or wish. Remember, that this alone is honour, glory, wealth, and happiness. Secure this, and you secure every thing. Lose this, and all is lost.

PRICE.

CHAP. XIII.

THE SPEECH OF BRUTUS ON THE DEATH OF CÆSAR.

ROMANS, countrymen, and lovers! hear me for my cause; and be silent, that you may hear. Believe me for mine honour, and have respect to mine honour, that you may believe. Censure me in your wisdom, and awake your senses, that you may the better judge. If there be any in this assembly, any dear friend of Cæsar's, to him I say, that Brutus's love to Cæsar was no less than his. If then that friend demand, why Brutus rose against Cæsar? this is my answer: Not that I loved Cæsar less, but that I loved Rome more. Had you rather Cæsar were living, and die all slaves; than that Cæ-

sar

far were dead to live all freemen? As Cæfar loved me, I weep for him; as he was fortunate, I rejoice at it; as he was valiant I honour him; but as he was ambitious, I flew him. There are tears for his love, joy for his fortune, honour for his valour, and death for his ambition. Who's here fo bafe, that would be a bond-man? If any, fpeak; for him have I offended. Who's here fo rude, that would not be a Roman? If any, fpeak; for him have I offended. Who's here fo vile, that will not love his country? If any, fpeak; for him have I offended.——I paufe for a reply——

None?——then none have I offended.——I have done no more to Cæfar than you fhall do to Brutus. The queftion of his death is enrolled in the Capitol; his glory not extenuated, wherein he was worthy; nor his offences inforced, for which he fuffered death.——

Here comes his body, mourned by Mark Antony; who, though he had no hand in his death, fhall receive the benefit of his dying, a place in the common wealth: as which of you fhall not? With this I depart, that as I flew my beft lover for the good of Rome, I have the fame dagger for myfelf, when it fhall pleafe my country to need my death.

Shakespear.

C H A P. XIV.

GLOUCESTER's SPEECH to the NOBLES.

BRAVE Peers of England, pillars of the ftate,
To you Duke Humphry muft unload his grief,
Your grief, the common grief of all the land.
What! did my brother Henry fpend his youth,
His valour, coin, and people in the wars?
Did he fo often lodge in open field,
In winter's cold, and fummer's parching heat,
To conquer France, his true inheritance?
And did my brother Bedford toil his wits

To

To keep by policy what Henry got?
Have you yourfelves, Somerfet, Buckingham,
Brave York, and Salifbury, victorious Warwick,
Receiv'd deep fcars in France and Normandy?
Or hath mine uncle Beaufort, and myfelf,
With all the learned council of the Realm,
Studied fo long, fat in the council-houfe,
Early and late, debating to and fro,
How France and Frenchmen might be kept in awe?
And was his Highnefs in his infancy
Crowned in Paris, in defpight of foes?
And fhall thefe labours and thefe honours die?
Shall Henry's conqueft, Bedford's vigilance,
Your deeds of war, and all our counfel, die?
O Peers of England, fhameful in this league,
Fatal this marriage; cancelling your fame,
Blotting your names from books of memory;
Razing the characters of your renown,
Defacing monuments of conquer'd France,
Undoing all, as all had never been.

SHAKESPEAR.

BOOK

BOOK VI.

DIALOGUES.

CHAP. I.

ON HAPPINESS.

IT was at a time, when a certain Friend, whom I highly value, was my gueſt. We had been ſitting together, entertaining ourſelves with Shakeſpear. Among many of his characters, we had looked into that of Wolſey. How ſoon, ſays my friend, does the cardinal in diſgrace abjure that happineſs, which he was lately ſo fond of? Scarcely out of office, but he begins to exclaim.

Vain pomp and glory of the world! I hate ye. So true it is, that our ſentiments ever vary with the ſeaſon; and that, in adverſity we are of one mind, in proſperity of another. As for his mean opinion, ſaid I, of human happineſs, it is a truth, which ſmall reflection might have taught him long before. There ſeems little need of diſtreſs to inform us of this. I rather commend the ſeeming wiſdom of that eaſtern monarch, who in the affluence of proſperity, when he was proving every pleaſure, was yet ſo ſenſible of their emptineſs, their inſufficiency to make him happy, that he proclaimed a reward to the man, who ſhould invent a new delight. The reward indeed was proclaimed, but the delight was not to be found. If by delight, ſaid he, you mean ſome good; ſomething conducing to real happineſs; it might have been found, perhaps, and yet not fit the monarch's
fancy.

fancy. Is that, said I, poffible? It is poffible, replied he, though it had been the fovereign good itfelf. And indeed what wonder? Is it probable
that fuch a mortal as. an Eaftern monarch; fuch a
pampered, flattered, idle mortal, fhould have attention, or capacity for a fubject fo delicate? A fubject
enough to exercife the fubtleft and moft acute?

WHAT then is it you efteem, said I, the fovereign good to be? It fhould feem by your repre-
fentation, to be fomething very uncommon. Afk
me not the queftion, faid he, you know not where it
will carry us. Its general idea indeed is eafy and
plain; but the detail of particulars is perplexed and
long; paffions and opinions for ever thwart us; a
paradox appears in almoft every advance. Befides,
did our inquiries fucceed ever fo happily, the very
fubject itfelf is always enough to give me pain.
That, replied I, feems a paradox indeed. It is not,
faid he, from any prejudice, which I have conceiv-
ed againft it; for to man I efteem it the nobleft in
the world. Nor is it fit for being a fubject, to which
my genius will not lead me; for no fubject at all
times has more employed my attention. But the
truth is, I can fcarce ever think of it, but an unfortunate ftory occurs to my mind. "A certain
" ftar-gazer, with his telefcope was once viewing
" the moon; and defcribing her feas, her moun-
" tains, and her territories. Says a clown to his
" companion, Let him fpy what he pleafes; we are
" as near to the moon, as he and all his brethren."
So fares it alas! with thefe our moral fpeculations.
Practice too often creeps, where theory can foar.
The philofopher proves as weak, as thofe whom he
moft contemns. A mortifying thought to fuch as
well attend it. Too mortifying replied I, to be
long dwelt on. Give us rather, your general idea
of the fovereign good. This is eafy from your own
account, however intricate the detail.

THUS then, faid he, fince you are fo urgent, it is
thus that I conceive it. The Sovereign Good, is
that,

that, the poſſeſſion of which renders us happy.
And how, ſaid I, do we poſſeſs it? Is it ſenſual, or
intellectual? There you are entering, ſaid he, upon
the detail. This is beyond your queſtion. Not a
ſmall advance, ſaid I, to indulge poor curioſity?
Will you raiſe me a thirſt, and be ſo cruel not to al-
lay it? It is not, replied he, of my raiſing, but your
own. Beſides I am not certain, ſhould I attempt to
proceed, whether you will admit ſuch authorities as
it is poſſible I may vouch. That, ſaid I, muſt be determined by their weight and character. Suppoſe,
ſaid he, it ſhould be mankind; the whole human
race. Would you not think it ſomething ſtrange, to
ſeek of thoſe concerning Good, who purſue it a
thouſand ways, and many of them contradictory? I
confeſs, ſaid I, it ſeems ſo. And yet continued he,
were there a point, in which diſſentients ever agreed,
this agreement would be no mean argument in favour of its truth and juſtneſs. But where, replied
I, is this agreement to be found?

He anſwered me by aſking, what if it ſhould appear, that there were certain original characteriſtics
and preconceptions of Good, which were natural,
uniform and common to all men; which all recog-
nized in their various purſuits; and that the difference lay only in the applying them to particulars?
This requires, ſaid I, to be illuſtrated. As if, continued he, a company of travellers, in ſome wide
foreſt, were all intending for one city, but each by a
route peculiar to himſelf. The roads indeed would
be various, and many perhaps falſe; but all who
travelled, would have one end in view. It is evident, ſaid I, they would. So fares it then, added
he, with mankind in the purſuit of good. The
ways indeed are many, but what they ſeek is One.

For inſtance: Did you ever hear of any, who in
purſuit of their good were for living the life of a bird,
an inſect, or a fiſh. None. And why not? It would
be inconſiſtent, anſwered I, with their nature. You
ſee then, ſaid he, they all agree in this; that what
they purſue, ought to be conſiſtent, and agreeable to

their

their proper nature. So ought it, said I, undoubtedly. It so, continued he, one pre-conception is discovered, which is common to good in general: It is, that all good is supposed something agreeable to nature. This indeed, replied I, seems to be agreed on all hands.

But again, said he, Is there a man scarcely to be found of a temper so truly mortified, as to acquiesce in the lowest, and shortest necessaries of life? Who aims not, if he be able, at something farther, something better? I replied, scarcely one. Do not multitudes pursue, said he, infinite objects of desire, acknowledged, every one of them, to be in no respect necessaries? Exquisite viands, delicious wines, splendid apparel, curious gardens; magnificent apartments adorned with pictures and sculpture; music and poetry, and the whole tribe of elegant arts? It is evident, said I. If it be, continued he, it should seem that they all considered the chief or Sovereign Good, not to be that, which conduces to bare existence or mere being; for to this the necessaries alone are adequate. I replied they were. But if not this, it must be somewhat conducive to that, which is superior to mere being. It must. And what, continued he, can this be, but well-being, under the various shapes, in which differing opinions paint it? Or can you suggest any thing else? I replied, I could not. Mark here, then, continued he, another pre-conception, in which they all agree; the Sovereign Good is somewhat conducive, not to mere being, but to well-being. I replied, it had so appeared.

Again, continued he. What labour, what expence, to procure those rarities, which our own poor country is unable to afford us! How is the world ransacked to its utmost verges, and luxury and arts imported from every quarter! Nay more: How do we baffle nature herself; invert her order; seek the vegetables of spring in the rigours of winter, and winter's ice during the heats of summer! I replied, we did. And what disappointment, what remorse,

when

when endeavours fail ? It is true. If this then be evident, faid he, it fhould feem, that whatever we defire as our Chief and Sovereign Good, is fomething which, as far as poffible, we would accommodate to all places and times. I anfwered, So it appeared. See then, faid he, another of its characteriftics, another pre-conception.

But farther ftill; What contefts for wealth! What fcrambling for property! What perils in the purfuit; what follicitude in the maintenance! And why all this? To what purpofe, what end ? Or is not the reafon plain ? Is it not that wealth may continually procure us, whatever we fancy good; and make that perpetual, which would otherwife be tranfient? I replied, it feemed fo. It is not farther defired, as fupplying us from ourfelves; when without it, we muft be beholden to the benevolence of others, and depend on their caprice for all that we enjoy? It is true, faid I, this feems a reafon.

Again; Is not power of every degree as much contefted for, as wealth ? Are not the magiftracies, honours, principalities, and empire, the fubjects of ftrife, and everlafting contention? I replied, They were. And why, faid he, this? To obtain what end ? Is it not to help us, like wealth, to the poffeffion of what we defire? It is not farther to afcertain, to fecure our enjoyments; that when others would deprive us, we may be ftrong enough to refift them ? I replied it was.

Or to invert the whole; Why are there, who feek receffes the moft diftant and retired ? Flee courts and power, and fubmit to parfimony and obfcurity ? Why all this, but from the fame intention ? From an opinion that fmall poffeffions, ufed moderately, are permanent; that larger poffeffions, raife envy, and are more frequently invaded; that the fafety of power and dignity is more precarious, than that of retreat; and that therefore they have chofen, what is moft eligible upon the whole?

It

It is not, said I, improbable, that they act by some such motive.

Do you not see then, continued he, two or three more pre-conceptions of the Sovereign Good, which are sought for by all, as essential to constitute it? And what, said I, are these? That it should not be transient, nor derived from the will of others, nor in their power to take away; but the durable, self-derived, and (if I may use the expression) in-deprivable. I confess, said I, it appears so. But we have already found it to be considered, as something agreeable to our nature; conducive, not to mere being, but to well-being; and what we aim to have accommodated to all places and times. We have.

THERE may be other characteristics, said he, but these I think sufficient. See then its idea; behold it, as collected from the original, natural, and universal pre-conceptions of all mankind. The Sovereign Good, they have taught us, ought to be something *agreeable to our nature ; conducive to well-being ; accommodated to all places and times ; durable, self-derived,* and *indeprivable.* Your account, said I, appears just.

HARRIS.

C H A P.   II.

THE SAME SUBJECT.

BRUTUS perished untimely, and Cæsar did no more.—These words I was repeating the next day to myself, when my friend appeared, and chearfully bade me good-morrow. I could not return his compliment with an equal gaiety, being intent, somewhat more than usual, on what had passed the day before. Seeing this, he proposed a walk into the fields. The face of nature, said he, will perhaps dispel these glooms. No assistance, on my part, shall be wanting, you may be assured. I accepted his

proposal;

proposal; the walk began; and our former conversation insensibly renewed.

Brutus, said he, perished untimely, and Cæsar did no more.—It was thus, as I remember, not long since you were expressing yourself. And yet suppose their fortunes to have been exactly parallel. —Which would you have preferred? Would you have been Cæsar, or Brutus? Brutus, replied I, beyond all controversy. He asked me, why? Where was the difference, when their fortunes, as we now supposed them, were considered as the same? There seems, said I, abstract from their fortunes, something, I know not what, intrinsically preferable in the life and character of Brutus. If that, said he, be true, then must we derive it, not from the success of his endeavours, but from their truth and rectitude. He had the comfort to be conscious, that his cause was a just one. It was impossible the other should have any such feeling. I believe, said I, you have explained it.

Suppose then, continued he, (it is but merely an hypothesis) suppose, I say, we were to place the Sovereign Good in such a rectitude of Conduct merely, and not in the Event. Suppose we were to fix our Happiness, not in the actual attainment of that health, that perfection of a social state, that fortunate concurrence of externals, which is congruous to our nature, and which all have a right to pursue; but solely fix it in the mere doing whatever is correspondent to such an end, even though we never attain, or are near attaining it. In fewer words; What to make our natural state the standard only to determine our conduct: and place our happiness in the rectitude of this conduct alone? On such an hypothesis (and we consider it as nothing farther) we should not want a good, perhaps, to correspond to our pre-conceptions; for this, it is evident, would be correspondent to them all. Your doctrine, replied I, is so new and strange, that though you have been copious in explaining, I can hardly yet comprehend you.

I

It

It amounts all, said he, but to this: Place your happiness, where your praise is. I asked, Where he supposed that? Not, replied he, in the pleasures which you feel, more than your disgrace lies in the pain; not in the casual prosperity of fortune, more than your disgrace in the casual adversity; but in just complete action throughout every part of life, whatever be the face of things, whether favourable, or the contrary.

But why then, said I, such accuracy about externals? So much pains to be informed, what are pursuable, what avoidable? It behoves the Pilot, replied he, to know the seas and the winds; the nature of tempests, calms and tides. They are the subjects, about which his art is conversant. Without a just experience of them, he can never prove himself an artist. You know we look not for his reputation either in fair gales, or in adverse; but in the skilfulness of his conduct, be these events as they happen. In like manner fares it with the moral artist. He, for a subject, has the whole of human life: health and sickness; pleasure and pain; with every other possible incident, which can befal him during his existence. If his knowledge of all these be accurate and exact, so too must his conduct, in which we place his happiness. But if this knowledge be defective, must not his conduct be defective also? I replied, So it should seem. And if his conduct, then his happiness? It is true.

You see then, continued he, even though externals were as nothing; though it was true, in their own nature, they were neither good nor evil; yet an accurate knowledge of them is, from our hypothesis, absolutely necessary. Indeed, said I, you have proved it.

He continued—Inferior artists may be at a stand, because they want materials. From their stubbornness and intractability, they may often be disappointed. But as long as life is passing, and nature continues to operate, the moral artist of life has at all times all he desires. He can never want a subject fit to exercife him in his proper calling; and that, with this happy motive to the conftancy of his endeavours, that the croffer, the harfher, the more untoward the events, the greater his praife, the more illuftrious his reputation.

All this, faid I, is true, and cannot be denied. But one circumftance there appears, where your fimilies feem to fail. The praife indeed of the *Pilot* we allow to be in his conduct; but *it is in* the fuccefs of that conduct, where we look *for his* happinefs. If a ftorm arife, and the fhip be loft, we call him not happy, how well foever he may have conducted. It is then only we congratulate him, when he has reached the defired haven. Your diftinction, faid he, is juft. And it is here lies the noble prerogative of moral artifts, above all others. But yet I know not how to explain myfelf, I fear my doctrine will appear fo ftrange. You may proceed, faid I, fafely, fince you advance it but as an hypothefis.

Thus then, continued he—The end in other arts is ever diftant and removed. It confifts not in the mere conduct, much lefs in a fingle energy; but is the juft refult of many energies, each of which are effential to it. Hence, by obftacles unavoidable, it may often be retarded: nay more, may be fo embarraffed, as never poffibly to be attained. But in the moral of life, the very Conduct is the End; the very conduct, I fay, itfelf, throughout every its minuteft energy; becaufe each of thefe, however minute, partake as truly of rectitude, as the largeft combination of them, when confidered collectively. Hence of all arts is this the only one perpetually complete in every inftant, becaufe it needs not, like other arts, time to arrive at that perfection, at which in every inftant it is arrived already. Hence by duration it is not rendered either more or lefs perfect; completion, like truth, admitting no degrees, and being in no fenfe capable of either intenfion or remiffion. And hence too by neceffary connection (which is a greater paradox than all) even that Happinefs or Sovereign Good, the end of this moral art,

is

is itfelf too, in every inftant, confummate and complete; is neither heightened nor diminifhed by the quantity of its duration, but is the fame to its enjoyers, for a moment or a century.

UPON this I fmiled. He afked me the reafon; It is only to obferve, faid I, the courfe of our inquiries. A new hypothefis has been advanced: appearing fomewhat ftrange, it is defired to be explained. You comply with the requeft, and in purfuit of the explanation, make it ten times more obfcure and unintelligible, than before. It is but too often the fate, faid he, of us commentators. But you know in fuch cafes what is ufually done. When the comment will not explain the text, we try whether the text will not explain itfelf. This method, it is poffible, may affift us here. The hypothefis, which we would have illuftrated, was no more than this: That the Sovereign Good lay in Rectitude of Conduct; and that this Good correfponded to all our pre-conceptions. Let us examine then, whether, upon trial, this correfpondence will appear to hold; and for all that we have advanced fince, fuffer it to pafs, and not perplex us. Agreed, faid I willingly, for now I hope to comprehend you.

RECOLLECT then, faid he. Do you not remember that one pre-conception of the Sovereign Good was, to be accommodated to all times and places? I remember it. And is there any time, or any places, whence Rectitude of Conduct may be excluded? Is there no right action in profperity, a right action in adverfity? May there not be a decent, generous, and laudable behaviour, not only in peace, in power, and in health; but in war, in oppreffion, in fickness, and in death? There may.

AND what fhall we fay to thofe other pre-conceptions; to being durable, felf-derived, and indeprivable? Can there be any Good fo durable, as the power of always doing right? Is there any Good conceivable, fo entirely beyond the power of others? Or if you hefitate, and are doubtful, I would willingly be informed, into what circumftances may

fortune

fortune throw a brave honeſt man, where it ſhall not be in his power to act bravely and honeſtly? If there are no ſuch, then Rectitude of Conduct, if a Good, is a good indeprivable. I confeſs, ſaid I, it appears ſo.

But farther, ſaid he; Another pre-conception of the Sovereign good was, to be agreeable to nature. It was. And can any thing be more agreeable to a rational and ſocial animal, than rational and ſocial conduct? Nothing. But Rectitude of conduct is with us Rational and Social Conduct. It is.

Once more, continued he; Another pre-conception of this Good was, to be conducive not to mere-being, but to well-being. Admit it. And can any thing, believe you, conduce ſo probably to the well-being of a rational ſocial animal, as the right exercife of that reaſon, and of thoſe ſocial affections? Nothing. And what is this ſame exercife, but the higheſt Rectitude of conduct? Certainly.

HARRIS.

CHAP. III.

ON CRITICISM.

—— AND how did Garrick ſpeak the ſoliloquy laſt night? Oh, againſt all rules, my lord, moſt ungrammatically? betwixt the ſubſtantive and the adjective, which ſhould agree together in number, caſe and gender, he made a breach thus,——ſtopping as if the point wanted ſettling;——and betwixt the nominative caſe, which your lordſhip knows ſhould govern the verb, he ſuſpended his voice in the epilogue a dozen times, three ſeconds and three fifths by a ſtop-watch, my lord, each time—Admirable grammarian!—But in ſuſpending his voice—was the ſenſe ſuſpended likewiſe? did no expreſſion of attitude or countenance fill up the chaſm?—Was the eye ſilent? Did you narrowly look?—I look'd only at the ſtop-watch, my lord,—Excellent obſerver!

AND what of this new book the whole world makes such a rout about?—Oh! 'tis out of all plumb, my lord,—quite an irregular thing! not one of the angles at the four corners was a right angle.—I had my rule and compasses, &c. my lord, in my pocket.—Excellent critic!

—AND for the epic poem your lordship bid me look at;—upon taking the length, breadth, height, and depth of it, and trying them at home upon an exact scale of Bossu's——'tis out, my lord, in every one of its dimensions.—Admirable connoisseur!

——AND did you step in, to take a look at the grand picture in your way back?—Tis a melancholy daub! my lord; not one principle of the pyramid in any one group!————and what a price!————for there is nothing of the colouring of Titian————the expression of Rubens———— the grace of Raphael————the purity of Dominichino————the correigiefcity of Corregio————the learning of Pouffin————the airs of Guido———— the tafte of the Carrachi's————or the grand contour of Angelo.

GRANT me patience, just Heaven!—Of all the cants which are canted in this canting world ————though the cant of hypocrites may be the worft————the cant of criticifm is the moft tormenting!

I WOULD go fifty miles on foot, to kifs the hand of that man, whofe generous heart will give up the reins of his imagination into his author's hands————be pleafed he knows not why, and cares not wherefore.

STERNE.

C H A P.

C H A P. IV.

On N E G R O E S.

WHEN Tom, an' pleaſe your honour, got to the ſhop there was nobody in it, but a poor negro girl, with a bunch of white feathers ſlightly tied to the end of a long cane, flapping away flies——not killing them——'Tis a pretty picture ! ſaid my uncle Toby——ſhe had ſuffered perſecution, Trim, and had learnt mercy.——

——She was good, an' pleaſe your honour, from nature as well as from hardſhips; and there are circumſtances in the ſtory of that poor friendleſs ſlut that would melt a heart of ſtone, ſaid Trim; and ſome diſmal winter's evening, when your honour is in the humour, they ſhall be told you with the reſt of Tom's ſtory, for it makes a part of it——

Then do not forget, Trim, ſaid my uncle Toby.

A negro has a ſoul? an' pleaſe your honour, ſaid the corporal (doubtingly)

I am not much verſed, corporal, quoth my uncle Toby, in things of that kind; but I ſuppoſe God would not leave him without one, any more than thee or me——

——It would be putting one ſadly over the head of another, quoth the corporal.

It would ſo; ſaid my uncle Toby. Why then, an' pleaſe your honour, is a black wench to be uſed worſe than a white one?

I can give you no reaſon, ſaid my uncle Toby——

——Only, cried the corporal, ſhaking his head, becauſe ſhe has no one to ſtand up for her——

——'Tis that very thing, Trim, quoth my uncle Toby, which recommends her to protection, and her brethren with her;——'tis the fortune of war which has put the whip into our hands now——

where:

where it may be hereafter, Heaven knows!—but be it where it will, the brave, Trim, will not use it unkindly.

——God forbid, said the corporal.

Amen, responded my uncle Toby, laying his hand upon his heart.

STERNE.

C H A P.　V.

RIVERS and Sir HARRY.

Sir Har. COLONEL, your most obedient: I am come upon the old business; for unless I am allowed to entertain hope of Miss Rivers, I shall be the most miserable of all human beings.

Riv. Sir Harry, I have already told you by letter, and now I tell you personally, I cannot listen to your proposals.

Sir Har. No, Sir?

Riv. No, Sir, I have promised my daughter to Mr. Sidney; do you know that, Sir?

Sir Har. I do; but what then? Engagements of this kind, you know——

Riv. So then, you do know I have promised her to Mr. Sidney?

Sir Har. I do; but I also know that matters are not finally settled between Mr. Sidney and you, and I moreover know, that his fortune is by no means equal to mine, therefore——

Riv. Sir Harry, let me ask you one question before you make your consequence.

Sir Har. A thousand if you please, Sir.

Riv. Why then, Sir, let me ask you, what you have ever observed in me or my conduct, that you desire me so familiarly to break my word? I thought, Sir, you considered me as a man of honour.

Sir

Sir Har. And so I do, Sir, a man of the nicest honour.

Riv. And yet, Sir, you ask me to violate the sanctity of my word; and tell me directly, that it is my interest to be a rascal.——

Sir Har. I really don't understand you, Colonel: I thought when I was talking to you, I was talking to a man who knew the world: and as you have not yet signed——

Riv. Why, this is mending matters with a witness! And so you think because I am not legally bound, I am under no necessity, of keeping my word! Sir Harry, laws were never made for men of honour; they want no bond but the rectitude of their own sentiments, and laws are of no use but to bind the villains of society.

Sir Har. Well! but my dear Colonel, if you have no regard for me, shew some little regard for your daughter.

Riv. I shew the greatest regard for my daughter by giving her to a man of honour; and I must not be insulted with any further repetition of your proposals.

Sir Har. Insult you, Colonel! is the offer of my alliance an insult? is my readiness to make what settlements you think proper——

Riv. Sir Harry, I should consider the offer of a kingdom an insult, if it was to be purchased by the violation of my word: Besides, though my daughter shall never go a beggar to the arms of her husband, I would rather see her happy than rich; and if she has enough to provide handsomely for a young family, and something to spare for the exigencies of a worthy friend, I shall think her as affluent as if she was mistress of Mexico.

Sir Har. Well, Colonel, I have done; but I believe——

Riv. Well, Sir Harry, and as our conference is done, we will, if you please, retire to the ladies: I shall always be glad of your acquaintance, though I cannot receive you as a son-in-law, for a union of

I 5

interest

intereft I look upon as a union of diſhonour, and confider a marriage for money, at beſt, but a legal proſtitution.

F ALSE DELICACY.

S ir JOHN MELVIL and STERLING.

STERL. WHAT are your commands with me, Sir John?

SIR JOHN. After having carried the negociation between our families to ſo great a length, after having aſſented ſo readily to all our propoſals, as well as received ſo many inſtances of your chearful compliance with the demands made on our part, I am extremely concerned, Mr. Sterling, to be the involuntary cauſe of any uneaſineſs.

STERL. Uneaſineſs! what uneaſineſs? Where buſineſs is tranſacted as it ought to be, and the parties underſtand one another, there can be no uneaſineſs. You agree, on ſuch and ſuch conditions to receive my daughter for a wife; on the ſame conditions I agree to receive you as a ſon-in-law; and as to all the reſt, it follows of courſe, you know, as regularly as the payment of a bill after acceptance.

SIR JOHN. Pardon me, Sir; more uneaſineſs has ariſen than you are aware of. I am myſelf, at this inſtant, in a ſtate of inexpreſſible embarraſſment; Miſs Sterling, I know, is extremely diſconcerted too; and unleſs you will oblige me with the aſſiſtance of your friendſhip I foreſee the ſpeedy progreſs of diſcontent and animoſity through the whole family.

STERL. What the deuce is all this? I do not underſtand a ſingle ſyllable.

SIR JOHN. In one word then, it will be abſolutely impoſſible for me to fulfil my engagements in regard to Miſs Sterling.

STERL.

STERL. How, Sir John? Do you mean to put an affront upon my family? What! refuse to——

SIR JOHN. Be affured, Sir, that I neither mean to affront, nor forfake your family. My only fear is, that you fhould defert me; for the whole happinefs of my life depends on being connected with your family by the neareft and tendereft ties in the world.

STERL. Why did not you tell me, but a moment ago, it was abfolutely impoffible for you to marry my daughter?

SIR JOHN. Tiue; But you have another daughter, Sir——

STERL. Well?

SIR JOHN. Who has obtained the moft abfolute dominion over my heart. I have already declared my paffion to her; nay Mifs Sterling herfelf is alfo apprifed of it, and if you will but give a fanction to my prefent addreffes, the uncommon merit of Mifs Sterling will no doubt recommend her to a perfon of equal, if not fuperior rank to myfelf, and our families may ftill be allied by my union with Mifs Fanny.

STERL. Mighty fine, truly! Why, what the plague do you make of us, Sir John? Do you come to market for my daughters, like fervants at a ftatute-fair? Do you think that I will fuffer you, or any man in the world, to come into my houfe, like the Grand Signior, and throw his handkerchief firft to one, and then to t'other, juft as he pleafes? Do you think I drive a kind of African flave-trade with them? and——

SIR JOHN. A moment's patience, Sir! Nothing but the excefs of my paffion for Mifs Fanny fhould have induced me to take any ftep that had the leaft appearance of difrefpect to any part of your family? and even now I am defirous to atone for my tranfgreffion, by making the moft adequate compenfation, that lies in my power.

STERL.

STERL. Compensation! what compensation can you possibly make in such a case as this, Sir John?

SIR JOHN. Come, come, Mr. Sterling; I know you to be a man of sense, and a man of business, a man of the world. I will deal frankly with you; and you shall see that I do not desire a change of measures for my own gratification, without endeavouring to make it advantageous to you.

STERL. What advantage can your inconstancy be to me, Sir John?

SIR JOHN. I will tell you, Sir. You know that by the articles at present subsisting between us, on the day of my marriage with Miss Sterling, you agree to pay down the gross sum of eighty thousand pounds——

STERL. Well!

SIR JOHN. Now if you will but consent to my waving that marriage——

STERL. I agree to your waving that marriage? Impossible, Sir John!

SIR JOHN. I hope not, Sir; as on my part, I will agree to wave my right to thirty thousand pounds of the fortune I was to receive with her.

STERL. Thirty thousand, do you say?

SIR JOHN. Yes, Sir; and accept of Miss Fanny with fifty thousand, instead of fourscore.

STERL. Fifty thousand——

SIR JOHN. Instead of fourscore.

STERL. Why, why, there may be something in that. Let me see; Fanny with fifty thousand instead of Betsey with fourscore. But how can this be, Sir John? For you know I am to pay this money into the hands of my Lord Ogleby; who, I believe, betwixt you and me, Sir John, is not overstocked with ready money at present; and threescore thousand of it, you know is to go to pay off the present incumbrances on the estate, Sir John.

SIR JOHN. That objection is easily obviated. Ten of the twenty thousand, which would remain

as a surplus of the fourscore, after paying off the
mortgage, was intended by his Lordship for my use,
that we might set off with some little eclat on our
marriage; and the other ten for his own. Ten
thousand pounds therefore I shall be able to pay
you immediately; and for the remaining twenty
thousand you shall have a mortgage on that part
of the estate which is to be made over to me, with
whatever security you shall require for the regular
payment of the interest, till the principal is duly
discharged.

STERL. Why, to do you justice, Sir John, there
is something fair and open in your proposal; and
since I find you do not mean to put an affront upon
the family —

SIR JOHN. Nothing was ever further from my
thoughts, Mr. Sterling. And after all, the whole
affair is nothing extraordinary; such things happen every day; and as the world has only heard
generally of a treaty between the families, when
this marriage takes place, no body will be the wiser,
if we have but discretion enough to keep our own
counsel.

STERL. True, true; and since you only transfer
from one girl to the other, it is no more than trans-
ferring so much stock, you know.

SIR JOHN. The very thing.

STERL. Odso! I had quite forgot. We are
reckoning without our host here. There is another
difficulty—

SIR JOHN. You alarm me. What can that
be?

STERL. I cannot stir a step in this business without consulting my sister Heidelberg. The family has
very great expectations from her, and we must not
give her any offence.

SIR JOHN. But if you come into this measure,
surely she will be so kind as to consent—

STERL. I do not know that. Betsey is her darling, and I cannot tell how far she may resent any
slight that seems to be offered to her favourite niece.
However,

However, I will do the beſt I can for you. You
ſhall go and break the matter to her firſt, and by the
time that I may ſuppoſe that your rhetoric has prevailed on her to liſten to reaſon, I will ſtep in to re-
inforce your arguments.

Sir John. I will fly to her immediately : you
promiſe me your aſſiſtance?

Sterl. I do.

Sir John, Ten thouſand thanks for it! and now
ſucceſs attend me!

Sterl. Harkee, Sir John!——Not a word of
the thirty thouſand to my ſiſter, Sir John.

Sir John. Oh, I am dumb, I am dumb, Sir.

Sterl You remember it is thirty thouſand.

Sir John. To be ſure I do.

Sterl. But Sir John! one thing more. My
Lord muſt know nothing of this ſtroke of friendſhip
between us.

. Sir John. Not for the world. Let me alone!
let me alone.

Sterl. And when every thing is agreed, we
muſt give each other a bond to be held faſt to the
bargain.

Sir John. To be ſure. A bond by all means!
a bond, or whatever you pleaſe.

Sterl. I ſhould have thought of more conditions, he is in a humour to give me every thing. Why,
what mere children are your fellows of quality ;
that cry for a plaything one minute, and throw it by
the next ! as changeable as the weather, and as uncertain as the ſtocks. Special fellows to drive a
bargain ! and yet they are to take care of the intereſt of the nation truly ! Here does this whirligig
man of faſhion offer to give up thirty thouſand
pounds in hard money, with as much indifference as
if it was a China orange. By this mortgage, I ſhall
have a hold on his Terra Firma ; and if he wants
more money, as he certainly will, let him have children by my daughter or no, I ſhall have his whole
eſtate in a net for the benefit of my family. Well ;
thus it is, that the children of citizens, who hav

acquired

acquired fortunes, prove perfons of fafhion; and thus it is, that perfons of fafhion, who have ruined their fortunes, reduce the next generation to cits.

CLANDESTINE MARRIAGE.

C H A P. VII.

BELCOUR AND STOCKWELL.

STOCK. MR. Belcour, I am rejoiced to fee you; you are welcome to England.

BEL. I thank you heartily, good Mr. Stockwell; you and I have long converfed at a diftance; now we are met, and the pleafure this meeting gives me, amply compenfates for the perils I have run through in accomplifhing it.

STOCK. What perils, Mr. Belcour? I could not have thought you would have met a bad paffage at this time o'year.

BEL. Nor did we: courier like, we came pofting to your fhores, upon the pinions of the fwifteft gales that ever blew; it is upon Englifh ground all my difficulties have arifen; it is the paffage from the river-fide I complain of.

STOCK. Ay, indeed! What obftructions can you have met between this and the river-fide?

BEL. Innumerable! Your town's as full of defiles as the ifland of Corfica; and, I believe, they are as obftinately defended; fo much hurry, buftle, and confufion, on your quays; fo many fugar-cafks, porter-butts, and common council-men, in your ftreets; that unlefs a man marched with artillery in his front, it is more than the labour of a Hercules can effect to make any tolerable way through your town.

STOCK. I am forry you have been fo incommoded.

BELL. Why, faith, it was all my own fault; accuftomed to a land of flaves, and, out of patience with the whole tribe of cuftom-houfe extortioners,

boat-men,

boat-men, tide-waiters, and water-bailiffs, that be-
fet me on all fides, worfe than a fwarm of mufque-
toes, I proceeded a little too roughly to brufh them
away with my rattan; the fturdy rogues took this in
dudgeon, and beginning to rebel, the mob chofe
different fides, and a furious fcuffle enfued; in the
courfe of which, my perfon and apparel fuffered fo
much, that I was obliged to ftep into the firft tavern
to refit, before I could make my approaches in any
decent trim.

STOCK. Well, Mr. Belcour, it is a rough fample
you have had of my countrymen's fpirit; but, I truft,
you will not think the worfe of them for it.

BEL. Not at all, not at all; I like them the better; was I only a vifitor, I might, perhaps, wifh them
a little more tractable; but as a fellow fubject, and
a fharer in their freedom, I applaud their fpirit,
though I feel the effects of it in every bone in my
fkin.—Well, Mr. Stockwell, for the firft time in
my life, here am I in England; at the fountain head
of pleafure, in the land of beauty, of arts and ele-
gancies. My happy ftars have given me a good e-
ftate, and the confpiring winds have blown me hither to fpend it.

STOCK. To ufe it, not to wafte it, I fhould hope;
to treat it, Mr. Belcour, not as a vaffal, over whom
you have a wanton defpotic power, but as a fubject,
which you are bound to govern with a temperate and
reftrained authority.

BEL. True Sir; moft truly faid; mine's a com-
miffion, not a right: I am the offspring of diftrefs,
and every child of forrow is my brother; while I
have hands to hold, therefore, I will hold them o-
pen to mankind: but, Sir, my Paffions are my mafters: they take me where they will; and oftentimes
they leave to reafon and virtue nothing but my wifhes and my fighs.

STOCK. Come, come, the man who can accufe
corrects himfelf.

BEL. Ah! that is an office I am weary of; I
wifh a friend would take it up: I would to Heaven
you

you had leifure for the employ; but, did you drive a trade to the four corners of the world, you would not find the tafk fo toilfome as to keep me free from faults.

STOCK. Well, I am not difcouraged; this candour tells me I fhould not have the fault of felf-conceit to combat; that, at leaft, is not amongft the number.

BEL. No; if I knew that man on earth who thought more humbly of me than I do of myfelf, I would take up his opinion and forego my own.

STOCK. And, was I to chufe a pupil, it fhould be one of your complexion; fo if you will come along with me, we will agree upon your admiffion, and enter upon a courfe of lectures directly.

BEL. With all my heart.

WEST INDIAN.

C H A P.   VIII.

LORD EUSTACE AND FRAMPTON.

LD. EUST. WELL, my dear Frampton, have you fecured the letters?

FRAM. Yes, my lord, for their rightful owners.

LD. EUST. As to the matter of property, Frampton, we will not difpute much about that. Neceffity, you know, may fometimes render a trefpafs excufable.

FRAM. I am not cafuift fufficient to anfwer you, upon that fubject; but this I know, that you have already trefpaffed againft the laws of hofpitality and honour, in your conduct towards Sir William Evans, and his daughter—And as your friend and counfellor, both, I would advife you to think ferioufly, of repairing the injuries you have committed, and not increafe your offence, by a farther violation.

LD. EUST. It is actually a pity you were not bred to the bar, Ned; but I have only a moment to
ftay,

stay, and am all impatience to know if there be a letter from Langwood, and what he says.

FRAM. I shall never be able to afford you the least information upon that subject, my lord.

LD. EUST. Surely, I do not understand you. You said you had secured the letters—Have you not read them?

FRAM. You have a right, and none but you, to ask me such a question. My weak compliance with your first proposal relative to these letters, warrants your thinking so meanly of me. But know, my lord, that though my personal affection for you, joined to my unhappy circumstances, may have betrayed me to actions unworthy of myself, I never can forget, that there is a barrier fixed before the extreme of baseness, which honour will not let me pass.

LD. EUST. You will give me leave to tell you, Mr. Frampton, that where I lead, I think you need not halt.

FRAM. You will pardon me, my lord; the consciousness of another man's errors, can never be a justification for our own; and poor, indeed, must that wretch be, who can be satisfied with the negative merit of not being the worst man he knows.

LD. EUST. If this discourse were uttered in a conventicle, it might have its effect; by setting the congregation to sleep.

FRAM. It is rather meant to rouse, than lull your lordship.

LD. EUST. No matter what it is meant for; give me the letters, Mr. Frampton.

FRAM. Yet, excuse me. I could as soon think of arming a madman's hand, against my own life, as suffer you to be guilty of a crime that will, for ever, wound your honour.

LD. EUST. I shall not come to you, to heal the wound: your medicines are too rough and coarse, for me.

FRAM. The soft poison of flattery, might perhaps please you better.

Ld. Eust. Your confcience may, probably, have as much need of palliatives, as mine, Mr. Frampton, as I am pretty well convinced, that your courfe of life, has not been more regular, than my own.

Fram. With true contrition, my lord, I confefs part of your farcafm to be juft. Pleafure was the objeƈt of my purfuit, and pleafure I obtained, at the expence, both of health, and fortune : but yet, my lord, I broke not in upon the peace of others ; the laws of hofpitality, I never violated ; nor did I ever feek to injure or feduce, the wife, or daughter, of my friend.

Ld. Eust. I care not what you did ; give me the letters.

Fram. I have no right to keep, and therefore fhall furrender them, though with the utmoft reluctance ; but, by our former friendfhip, I intreat you not to open them.

Ld. Eust. That you have forfeited.

Fram. Since it is not in my power to prevent your committing an error, which you ought, for ever, to repent of, I will not be a witnefs of it. There are the letters.

Ld. Eust. You may perhaps, have caufe to repent your prefent conduƈt, Mr. Frampton, as much as I do our paft attachment.

Fram. Rather than hold your friendfhip upon fuch terms I refign it for ever. Farewell, my lord.

Re-enter Frampton.

Fram. Ill treated as I have been, my lord, I find it impoffible to leave you furrounded by difficulties.

Ld. Eust. That fentiment fhould have operated fooner, Mr. Frampton. Recolleƈtion is feldom of ufe to our friends, though it may fometimes be ferviceable to ourfelves.

Fram. Take advantage of your own expreffion, my lord, and recolleƈt yourfelf. Born and educated as I have been, a gentleman, how have you injured both yourfelf and me, by admitting and uniting in the fame confidence, your rafcally fervant !

Ld. Eust.

Ld. Eust. The exigency of my situation is a sufficient excuse to myself, and ought to have been so to the man who called himself my friend.

Fram. Have a care, my lord, of uttering the least doubt upon that subject; for could I think you once mean enough to suspect the sincerity of my attachment to you, it must vanish at that instant.

Ld. Eust. The proofs of your regard have been rather painful of late, Mr. Frampton.

Fram. When I see my friend upon the verge of a precipice, is that a time for compliment? Shall I not rudely rush forward, and drag him from it? Just in that state you are at present, and I will strive to save you. Virtue may languish in a noble heart, and suffer her rival, vice, to usurp her power; but baseness must not enter, or she flies for ever. The man who has forfeited his own esteem, thinks all the world has the same consciousness, and therefore is what he deserves to be, a wretch.

Ld. Eust. Oh, Frampton! you have lodged a dagger in my heart.

Fram. No, my dear Eustace, I have saved you from one, from your own reproaches, by preventing your being guilty of a meanness, which you could never have forgiven yourself.

Ld. Eust. Can you forgive me, and be still my friend?

Fram. As firmly as I have been, my lord.——— But let us, at present, hasten to get rid of the mean business we are engaged in, and forward the letters we have no right to detain.

School for Rakes.

C H A P. IX.

DUKE and LORD.

Duke. NOW, my co-mates, and brothers in exile,
Hath not old custom made this life more sweet
Than

Than that of painted pomp? are not thefe woods
More free from peril, than the envious court?
Here feel we but the penalty of Adam,
The feafon's difference; as the icy fang,
And churlifh chiding of the winter's wind;
Which, when it bites and blows upon my body,
Even till I fhrink with cold, I fmile, and fay,
This is no flattery; thefe are counfellors,
That feelingly perfuade me what I am.
Sweet are the ufes of adverfity,
Which like the toad, ugly and venemous,
Wears yet a precious jewel in his head:
And this our life, exempt from public haunt,
Finds tongues in trees, books in the running brooks,
Sermons in ftones, and good in every thing.
——Come, fhall we go, and kill us venifon?
And yet it irks me, the poor dappled fools,
Being native burghers of this defart city,
Should, in their own confines, with forked heads
Have their round haunches goar'd.
    Lord. Indeed, my Lord,
The melancholy Jaques grieves at that:
And in that kind fwears you do more ufurp
Than doth your brother, that hath banifhed you.
To-day my Lord of Amiens, and myfelf,
Did fteal behind him, as he lay along
Under an oak, whofe antique roots peep out
Upon the brook that brawls along this wood;
To the which place a poor fequeftred ftag,
That from the hunter's aim had ta'en a hurt,
Did come to languifh; and, indeed, my Lord,
The wretched animal heav'd forth fuch groans
That their difcharge did ftretch his leathern coat
Almoft to burfting; and the big round tears
Cours'd one another down his innocent nofe
In piteous chafe; and thus the hairy fool,
Much marked of the melancholy Jaques,
Stood on th' extremeft verge of the fwift-brook,
Augmenting it with tears.
    Duke. But what faid Jaques?
Did he not moralize the fpectacle?

Lord.

LORD. O yes, into a thousand similes,
First, for his weeping in the needless stream ;
Poor deer, quoth he, thou mak'st a testament
As worldlings do, giving thy sum of more
To that which had too much. Then being alone,
Left and abandon'd of his velvet friends ;
'Tis right, quoth he, thus misery doth part
The flux of company. Anon a careless herd,
Full of the pasture, jumps along by him,
And never stays to greet him : Ay, quoth Jaques,
Sweep on, you fat and greasy citizens,
'Tis just the fashion : wherefore do you look
Upon that poor and broken bankrupt there ?
Thus most invectively he pierced through
The body of the country, city, court,
Yea, and of this our life ; swearing, that we
Are mere usurpers, tyrants, and what's worse,
To fright the animals, and to kill them up
In their assign'd and native dwelling-place.
 DUKE. And did you leave him in this contem-
  plation ?
 LORD. We did, my Lord, weeping and com-
  menting
Upon the sobbing deer.
 DUKE. Shew me the place ;
I love to cope him in these sullen fits,
For then he's full of matter.
 LORD. I'll bring you to him straight.
SHAKESPEAR.

C H A P.   X.

DUKE AND JAQUES.

DUKE. WHY, how now, Monsieur, what a
   life is this,
That your poor friend must woo your company ?
What ? you look merrily.
 JAQ. A fool, a fool ;——I met a fool i' th' forest,
A motley fool ; a miserable varlet !

As

As I do live by food, I met a fool,
Who laid him down and bafk'd him in the fun,
And rail'd on Lady Fortune in good terms,
In good fet terms, and yet a motley fool.
Good morrow, fool, quoth I ; No, Sir, quoth he,
Call me not fool, till Heaven hath fent me fortune ;
And then he drew a dial from his poak,
And looking on it with lack-luftre eye,
Says very wifely, It is ten o'clock :
Thus may we fee, quoth he, how the world wags :
'Tis but an hour ago fince it was nine,
And after one hour more 'twill be eleven ;
And fo from hour to hour we ripe and ripe,
And then from hour to hour we rot and rot,
And thereby hangs a tale.   When I did hear
The motley fool thus moral on the time,
My lungs began to crow like chanticleer,
That fools fhould be fo deep contemplative :
And I did laugh, fans intermiffion,
An hour by his dial.   O noble fool,
A worthy fool ! motley's the only wear.
   D u k e.   What fool is this ?
   J a q. O worthy fool ! one that hath been a courtier,
And fays, if ladies be but young and fair,
They have the gift to know it : and in his brain,
Which is as dry as the remainder bifket
After a voyage, he hath ftrange places cramm'd
With obfervations, the which he vents
In mangled forms.   O that I were a fool !
I am ambitious for a motley coat.
   D u k e.   Thou fhalt have one.
   J a q. It is my only fuit ;
Provided that you weed your better judgments
Of all opinion, that grows rank in them,
That I am wife.   I muft have liberty
Withal, as large a charter as the wind,
To blow on whom I pleafe ; for fo fools have,
And they that are moft galled with my folly,
They moft muft laugh. And why, Sir, muft they
        fo ?
The why is plain, as way to parifh-church ;
                                        He

He whom a fool does very wifely hit,
Doth very foolifhly, although he fmart,
Not to feem fenfelefs of the bob. If not,
The wife man's folly is anatomiz'd
Even by the fquand'ring glances of a fool.
Inveft me in my motley, give me leave
To fpeak my mind, and I will through and through
Cleanfe the foul body of th' infeted world,
If they will patiently receive my medicine.
    Duke. Fie on thee! I can tell what thou
        would'ft do.
    Jaq. What, for a counter, would I do but
        good?
    Duke. Moft mifchievous foul fin, in chiding
        fin,
For thou thyfelf haft been a libertine,
And all th' embolfed fores and headed evils,
That thou with licenfe of free foot haft caught,
Wouldft thou difgorge into the general world.
    Jaq. Why, who cries out on pride,
That can therein tax any private party?
Doth it not flow as hugely as the fea,
Till that the very, very means do ebb?
What woman in the city do I name,
When that I fay, the city-woman bears
The coft of princes on unworthy fhoulders?
Who can come in, and fay, that I mean her;
When fuch a one as fhe, fuch is her neighbour?
Or what is he of bafeft function,
That fays, his bravery is not on my coft;
Thinking, that I mean him, but therein fuits
His folly to the metal of my fpeech?
There then; how then? what then? let me fee
        wherein
My tongue hath wrong'd him; if it do him right,
Then he hath wrong'd himfelf; if he be free,
Why, then my taxing, like a wild goofe, flies
Unclaim'd of any man.
                    Shakespear.

CHAP.

C H A P. XI.

HENRY AND LORD CHIEF JUSTICE.

Сн. Just.   I AM affur'd, if I be meafur'd rightly,
      Your Majefty hath no juft caufe to
    hate me.
   P. Henry.   No! might a prince of my great
      hopes forget
So great indignities you laid upon me?
What! rate, rebuke, and roughly fend to prifon
Th' immediate heir of England! was this eafy?
May this be wafh'd in Lethe, and forgotten?
   Сн. Just.   I then did ufe the perfon of your
      father;
The image of his power lay then in me:
And in th' adminiftration of his law,
While I was bufy for the commonwealth,
Your Highnefs pleafed to forget my place,
The majefty and pow'r of law and juftice,
The image of the King whom I prefented;
And ftruck me in my very feat of judgment:
Whereon, as an offender to your father,
I gave bold way to my authority,
And did commit you. If the deed were ill,
Be you contented, wearing now the garland,
To have a fon fet your decrees at nought:
To pluck down juftice from your awful bench,
To trip the courfe of law, and blunt the fword
That guards the peace and fafety of your perfon:
Nay more, to fpurn at your moft Royal image,
And mock your working in a fecond body.
Queftion your Royal thoughts, make the cafe
      yours;
Be now the father and propofe a fon;
Hear your own dignity fo much profan'd;
See your moft dreadful laws fo loofely flighted;
Behold yourfelf fo by a fon difdain'd:
K

And

And then imagine me taking your part,
And in your pow'r so silencing your son.
After this cold confid'rance, sentence me;
And, as you are a King, speak in your state,
What I have done that misbecame my place,
My person, or my Liege's sovereignty.
      P. Henry. You are right, Justice, and you
            weigh this well;
Therefore still bear the balance and the sword:
And I do wish your honours may increase,
Till you do live to see a son of mine
Offend you, and obey you, as I did:
So shall I live to speak my father's words·
Happy am I, that have a man so bold
That dares do justice on my proper son;
And no less happy having such a son,
That would deliver up his greatness so
Into the hand of justice.——You committed me;
For which I do commit into your hand
Th' unstained sword that you have us'd to bear;
With this remembrance, that you use the same
With a like bold, just, and impartial spirit,
As you have done 'gainst me. There is my hand,
You shall be as a father to my youth:
My voice shall sound as you do prompt mine ear; ·
And I will stoop and humble my intents,
To your well practis'd wise directions.
And, Princes all, believe me, I beseech you;
My father is gone wild into his grave;
For in his tomb lie my affections;
And with his spirit sadly I survive,
To mock the expectations of the world;
To frustrate prophecies, and to raze out
Rotten opinion, which hath writ me down
After my seeming. Though my tide of blood
Hath proudly flow'd in vanity till now;
Now doth it turn and ebb back to the sea,
Where it shall mingle with the state of floods,
And flow henceforth in formal majesty.
Now call we our high court of parliament;

And

And let us chufe fuch limbs of noble counfel,
That the great body of our ftate may go
In equal rank with the beft govern'd nation;
That war or peace, or both at once, may be
As things acquainted and familiar to us,
In which you, father, fhall have foremoft hand.
Our coronation done, we will accite
(As I before remember'd) all our ftate,
And (Heaven configning to my good intents)
No prince, nor peer, fhall have juft caufe to fay,
Heav'n fhorten Harry's happy life one day.

SHAKESPEAR.

C H A P.   XII.

ARCHBISHOP of CANTERBURY and BISHOP of ELY.

CANT.   MY Lord, I'll tell you; that felf bill
            is urg'd,
Which, in th' eleventh year o' th' laft King's
        reign,
Was like, and had indeed againft us pafs'd,
But that the fcambling and unquiet time
Did pufh it out of further queftion.
    ELY.   But how, my Lord, fhall we refift it
        now?
    CANT.   It muft be thought on.   If it pafs
        againft us,
We lofe the better half of our poffeffion:
For all the temporal lands, which men devout
By teftament have given to the church,
Would they ftrip from us; being valu'd thus:
As much as would maintain, to the King's honour,
Full fifteen earls, and fifteen hundred Knights,
Six thoufand and two hundred good efquires;
And to relief of lazars, and weak age
Of indigent faint fouls, paft corporal toil,
A hundred alms-houfes, right well fupply'd;
And to the coffers of the King, befide,

K 2   A thou-

A thoufand pounds by th' year. Thus runs the
    bill.
  ELY.   This would drink deep.
  CANT.   'Twould drink the cup and all.
  ELY.   But what prevention?
  CANT.   The King is full of grace and fair re-
    gard.
  ELY.   And a true lover of the holy church.
  CANT.   The courfes of his youth promis'd it
    not;
The breath no fooner left his father's body,
But that his wildnefs, mortify'd in him,
Seem'd to die too; yea, at that very moment,
Confideration, like an angel, came,
And whipp'd th' offending Adam out of him;
Leaving his body as a paradife,
T' invelope and contain celeftial fpirits.
Never came reformation in a flood
With fuch a heady current, fcow'ring faults:
Nor ever Hydra-headed wilfulnefs
So foon did lofe his feat, and all at once,
As in this King.
  ELY.   We're bleffed in the change.
  CANT.   Hear him but reafon in divinity,
And, all-admiring, with an inward wifh
You would defire, the King were made a Prelate.
Hear him debate of commonwealth affairs,
You'd fay, it had been all in all his ftudy.
Lift his difcourfe of war, and you fhall hear
A fearful battle render'd you in mufic.
Turn him to any caufe of policy,
The Gordian knot of it he will unloofe,
Familiar as his garter. When he fpeaks,
The air, a charter'd libertine, is ftill;
And the mute wonder lurketh in men's ears,
To fteal his fweet and honeyed fentences :
So that the act, and practice part of life,
Muft be the miftrefs to this theorique.
Which is a wonder how his Grace fhould glean it,
Since his addiction was to courfes vain;

His

His companies unletter'd, rude, and shallow;
His hours fill'd up with riots, banquets, sports;
And never noted in him any study,
Any retirement, and sequestration,
From open haunts and popularity.
   ELY. The strawberry grows underneath the
       nettle,
And wholesome berries thrive, and ripen best,
Neighbour'd by fruit of baser quality :
And so the Prince obscur'd his contemplation
Under the veil of wildness; which no doubt,
Grew like the summer-grass, fastest by night,
Unseen, yet crescive in his faculty.
   CANT. It must be so : for miracles are ceas'd :
And therefore we must needs-admit the means,
How things are perfected.
SHAKESPEAR.

C H A P. - XIII.

H A M L E T AND H O R A T I O.

HOR. HAIL to your Lordship!
      HAM. I am glad to see you well;
Horatio,——or I do forget myself.
   HOR. The same, my Lord, and your poor ser-
     vant ever.
   HAM. Sir, my good friend; I'll change that
     name with you :
And what makes you from Wittenberg, Horatio?
   HOR. A truant disposition, good my Lord.
   HAM. I would not hear your enemy say so;
Nor shall you do mine ear that violence,
To make it truster of your own report
Against yourself. I know you are no truant;
But what is your affair in Elsinoor?
We'll teach you to drink deep ere you depart.
   HOR. My Lord, I came to see your father's fu-
     neral.
K 3 HAM.

 Ham. I pr'ythee, do not mock me, fellow-
    ftudent;
I think it was to fee my mother's wedding.
 Hor. Indeed, my Lord, it follow'd hard upon.
 Ham. Thrift, thrift, Horatio; the funeral bak'd
    meats
Did coldly furnifh forth the marriage-table.
Would I had met my deareft foe in heav'n,
Or ever I had feen that day, Horatio!
My father——methinks I fee my father.
 Hor. Oh where, my Lord?
 Ham. In my mind's eye, Horatio.
 Hor. I faw him once, he was a goodly king.
 Ham. He was a man, take him for all in all,
fhall not look upon his like again.
 Hor. My Lord, I think I faw him yefternight.
 Ham. Saw! who?——
 Hor. My Lord, the King your father.
 Ham. The King my father!
 Hor. Seafon your admiration but a while,
With an attentive ear; till I deliver,
Upon the witnefs of thefe gentlemen,
This marvel to you.
 Ham. For Heaven's love, let me hear.
 Hor. Two nights together had thefe gentle-
    men,
Marcellus and Bernardo, on their watch,
In the dead wafte and middle of the night,
Been thus encountered: A figure like your father,
Arm'd at all points exactly, cap a pie,
Appears before them, and with folemn march
Goes flow and ftately by them; thrice he walk'd
By their opprefs'd and fear-furprized eyes,
Within his truncheon's length; whilft they (diftill'd
Almoft to jelly with th' effect of fear)
Stand dumb, and fpeak not to him. This to me
In dreadful fecrecy they did impart,
And I with them the third night kept the watch;
Where, as they had deliver'd both in time,
Form of the thing, each word made true and
    good,
             The

The apparition comes.   I knew your father:
Thefe hands are not more like.
   Ham. But where was this?
   Hor. My Lord, upon the platform where we
     watch'd.
   Ham.   Did you not fpeak to it?
   Hor. My Lord,   did;
But anfwer made it none.   Yet once methought
It lifted up its head, and did addrefs
Itfelf to motion; like as it would fpeak,
But even then the morning-cock crew loud;
And at the found it fhrunk in hafte away,
And vanifh'd from our fight.
   Ham.   Tis very ftrange.
   Hor. As I do live, my honour'd Lord, 'tis
     true;
And we do think it writ down in our duty
To let you know of it.
   Ham. Indeed, indeed, Sir; but this troubles me.
Hold you the watch to-night?
   Hor. We do, my Lord.
   Ham.   Arm'd, fay you?
   Hor.   Arm'd, my Lord.
   Ham.   From top to toe?
   Hor.   My Lord, from head to foot.
   Ham.   Then faw you not his face?
   Hor.   Oh, yes, my Lord; he wore his bea-
     ver up.
   Ham.   What, look'd he frowningly?
   Hor.   A count'nance more in forrow than in
     anger.
   Ham.   Pale, or red?
   Hor.   Nay, very pale.
   Ham.   And fix'd his eyes upon you?
   Hor.   Moft conftantly.
   Ham.   I would I had been there!
   Hor.   It would have much amaz'd you.
   Ham.   Very like. Staid it long?
   Hor.   While one with moderate hafte might tell
     a hundred.
   Ham.   His beard was grifl'd?—no.—

K 4

Hor.

HOR. It was, as I have feen it in his life,
A fable filver'd.
HAM. I'll watch to-night; perchance 'twill
    walk again.
HOR. I warrant you, it will
HAM. If it affume my noble father's perfon,
I'll fpeak to it, tho' hell itfelf fhould gape,
And bid me hold my peace. I pray you,
If you have hitherto conceal'd this fight,
Let it be ten'ble in your filence ftill:
And whatfoever fhall befal to-night,
Give it an underftanding, but no tongue;
I will requite your love: fo fare ye well.
Upon the platform 'twixt eleven and twelve
I'll vifit you.

SHAKESPEAR.

C H A P. XIV.

B R U T U S AND C A S S I U S.

CAS. WILL you go fee the order of the courfe?
        BRU. Not I.
CAS. I pray you, do.
BRU. I am not gamefome; I do lack fome part
Of that quick fpirit that is in Antony,
Let me not hinder, Caffius, your defires;
I'll leave you.
CAS. Brutus, I do obferve you now of late;
I have not from your eyes that gentlenefs
And fhew of love as I was wont to have;
You bear too ftubborn and too ftrange a hand,
Over your friend that loves you.
BRU. Caffius,
Be not deceived: if I have veil'd my look,
I turn the trouble of my countenance
Merely upon myfelf. Vexed I am
Of late with paffions of fome difference,
Conceptions only proper to myfelf;
Which give fome foil perhaps to my behaviour:

But

But let not therefore my good friends be griev'd,
Among which number, Caſſius, be you one;
Nor conſtrue any farther my neglect,
Than that poor Brutus, with himſelf at war,
Forgets the ſhews of love to other men.
   Cas.   Then, Brutus, I have much miſtook your
        paſſion;
By means whereof, this breaſt of mine hath buried
Thought of great value, worthy cogitations.
Tell me, good Brutus, can you ſee your face?
   Bru.   No, Caſſius; for the eye ſees not itſelf,
But by reflection from ſome other thing.
   Cas.   'Tis juſt.
And it is very much lamented, Brutus,
That you have no ſuch mirror as will turn
Your hidden worthineſs into your eye,
That you might ſee your ſhadow.   I have heard,
Where many of the beſt reſpect in Rome,
(Except immortal Cæſar) ſpeaking of Brutus,
And groaning underneath this age's yoke,
Have wiſh'd that noble Brutus had his eyes.
   Bru.   Into what dangers would you lead me,
        Caſſius,
That you would have me ſeek into myſelf
For that which is not in me?
   Cas.   Therefore, good Brutus, be prepar'd to hear;
And ſince you know you cannot ſee yourſelf
So well as by reflection, I, your glaſs,
Will modeſtly diſcover to yourſelf
That of yourſelf which yet you know not of.
And be not jealous of me, gentle Brutus:
Were I a common laugher, or did uſe
To ſtale with ordinary oaths my love
To every new proteſtor; if you know,
That I do fawn on men, and hug them hard,
And after ſcandal them; or if you know,
That I profeſs myſelf in banqueting.
To all the rout; then hold me dangerous.
   Bru.   What means this ſhouting? I do fear the
        people
Chuſe Cæſar for their King.
           K 5   Cas.

CAS.   Ay, do you fear it?
Then muft I think you would not have it fo.
    BRU.   I would not, Caffius; yet I love him well.
But wherefore do you hold me here fo long?
What is it that you would impart to me?
If it be aught toward the general good,
Set Honour in one eye, and Death i' th' other,
And I will look on Death indifferently:
For let the gods fo fpeed me, as I love
The name of honour more than I fear death.
    CAS.   I know that virtue to be in you, Brutus,
As well as I do know your outward favour.
Well, honour is the fubject of my ftory.——
I cannot tell what you and other men
Think of this life; but for my fingle felf,
I had as lief not be, as live to be
In awe of fuch a thing as I myfelf.
I was born free as Cæfar, fo were you;
We both have fed as well; and we can both
Endure the winter's cold as well as he.
For once, upon a raw and gufty day,
The troubled Tyber chafing with his fhores,
Cæfar fays to me, Dar'ft thou, Caffius, now
Leap in with me into this angry flood,
And fwim to yonder point?—Upon the word,
Accoutred as I was, I plunged in,
And bid him follow, fo indeed he did.
The torrent roar'd, and we did buffet it
With lufty finews; throwing it afide,
And ftemming it with hearts of controverfy.
But ere we could arrive the point propos'd,
Cæfar cry'd, help me, Caffius, or I fink.
I, as Æneas, our great anceftor,
Did from the flames of Troy upon his fhoulder
The old Anchifes bear; fo from the waves of Tyber
Did I the tired Cæfar: and this man
Is now become a god, and Caffius is
A wretched creature; and muft bend his body,
If Cæfar carelefsly but nod on him:
He had a fever when he was in Spain,
And when the fit was on him, I did mark

                                                      How

How he did shake. 'Tis true, this god did shake ;
His coward lips did from their colour fly,
And that same eye whose bend does awe the world,
Did lose its lustre ; I did hear him groan :
Ay, and that tongue of his, that bade the Romans
Mark him, and write his speeches in their books,
Alas ! it cry'd—Give me some drink, Titinius——
As a sick girl. Ye gods, it doth amaze me,
A man of such a temper should
So get the start of the majestic world,
And bear the palm alone.

 Bru. Another general shout !
I do believe, that these applauses are
For some new honours that are heap'd on Cæsar,
 Cas. Why man, he doth bestride the narrow
   world
Like a Colossus ; and we petty men
Walk under his huge legs, and peep about
To find ourselves dishonourable graves.
Men at sometimes are masters of their fates :
The fault, dear Brutus, is not in our stars,
But in ourselves, that we are underlings.
Brutus—and Cæsar—what should be in that Cæsar ?
Why should that name be sounded, more than your's ?
Write them together ; your's is as fair a name :
Sound them, it doth become the mouth as well ;
Weigh them, it is as heavy ; conjure with 'em,
Brutus will start a spirit as soon as Cæsar.
Now, in the names of all the gods at once,
Upon what meats does this our Cæsar feed,
That he is grown so great ? Age, thou art sham'd ;
Rome, thou hast lost the breed of noble bloods.
When went there by an age, since the great flood,
But it was fam'd with more than with one man ?
When could they say, till now, that talk'd of Rome,
That her wide walls incompass'd but one man ?
Oh ! you and I have heard our fathers say,
There was a Brutus once that would have brook'd
Th' eternal devil to keep his state in Rome
As easily as a king.
          Bru.

Bru. That you do love me, I am nothing jealous;
What you would work me to, I have some aim:
How I have thought of this, and of these times,
I shall recount hereafter: for this present,
I would not (so with love I might intreat you)
Be any further mov'd. What you have said,
I will confider; what you have to say,
I will with patience hear; and find a time
Both meet to hear, and answer such high things.
Till then, my noble friend, chew upon this;
Brutus had rather be a villager,
Than to repute himself a son of Rome
Under such hard conditions as this time
Is like to lay upon us
    Cas. I am glad that my weak words
Have struck but thus much shew of fire from Brutus.
Shakespear.

C H A P. XV.

BELLARIUS, GUIDERIUS and ARVIRAGUS.

Bel. A GOODLY day! not to keep house
        with such
Whose roofs as low as ours: see, boys! this gate
Instructs you howt' adore the heav'ns; and bows to
     you
The morning's holy office. Gates of monarchs
Are arch'd so high, that giants may jet through,
And keep their impious turbands on, without
Good morrow to the sun. Hail, thou fair heav'n!
We house i' th' rock, yet use thee not so hardly
As prouder livers do.
    Guid. Hail, heav'n!
    Arv. Hail, heav'n!
    Bel. Now for our mountain-sport, up to yond
        hill
Your legs are young. I'll tread these flats. Consider,
When you, above, perceive me like a crow,
That

That it is place which leffens and fets off:
And you may then revolve what tales I told you,
Of courts, of princes, of the tricks in war;
That fervice is not fervice, fo being done,
But being fo allow'd. To apprehend thus,
Draws us a profit from all things we fee;
And often, to our comfort, fhall we find
The fharded beetle in a fafer hold,
Than is the full-wing'd eagle. Oh, this life
Is nobler than attending for a check;
Richer than doing nothing for a bauble;
Prouder, than ruftling in unpaid-for filk.
Such gain the cap of him, that makes them fine,
Yet keeps his books uncrofs'd—no life to ours,
 Guid. Out of your proof you fpeak; we, poor,
  unfledg'd,
Have never wing'd from view o' the neft? nor know
What air's from home. Haply this life is beft,
If quiet life is beft; fweeter to you,
That have a fharper known; well correfponding
With your ftiff age: but unto us it is
A cell of ign'rance; travelling a bed;
A prifon, for a debtor that not dares
To ftride a limit.
 Arv. What fhould we fpeak of,
When we are old as you? when we fhall hear
The rain and wind beat dark December? how,
In this our pinching cave, fhall we difcourfe
The freezing hours away? We have feen nothing;
We're beaftly; fubtle as the fox for prey,
Like warlike as a wolf, for what we eat.
Our valour is to chafe what flies; our cage
We make a choir, as doth the prifon'd bird,
And fing our bondage freely.
 Bel. How you fpeak!
Did you but know the city's ufuries,
And felt them knowingly; the art o' the court,
As hard to leave, as keep; whofe top to climb,
Is certain falling; or fo flipp'ry, that
The fear's as bad as falling; the toil of war;
A pain, that only feems to feek out danger
          I' th'

I' th' name of fame and honour; which dies i' th'
　　　　search,
And hath as often a fland'rous epitaph,
As record of fair act ; nay, many time,
Doth ill-deferve, by doing well : what's worfe,
Muft curt'fy at the cenfure.—Oh, boys this ftory
The world may read in me : my body's mark'd
With Roman fwords ; and my report was once
Firft with the beft of note. Cymbeline lov'd me ;
And when a foldier was the theme, my name
Was not far off : then was I as a tree,
Whofe boughs did bend with fruit. But in one night,
A ftorm, or robbery, call it what you will,
Shook down my mellow hangings, nay, my leaves;
And left me bare to weather.
　　Guid. Uncertain favour!
　　Bel. My fault being nothing, as I have told you
　　　　oft,
But that two villains (whofe falfe oaths prevail'd
Before my perfect honour) fwore to Cymbeline,
I was a confed'rate with the Romans : fo
Follow'd my banifhment ; and, this twenty years,
This rock and thefe demefnes have been my world ;
Where I have liv'd at honeft freedom ; paid
More pious debts to heaven, than in all
The fore-end of my time —But, up to the mountains!
This is not hunter's language ; he that ftrikes
The venifon firft, fhall be the lord o' th' feaft ;
To him the other two fhall minifter
And we will fear no poifon, which attends
In place of greater ftate.
I'll meet you in the valleys.

Shakespear.

BOOK

CHAP. I.

SENSIBILITY.

DEAR Senfibility! fource inexhaufted of all that's precious in our joys, or coftly in our forrows! thou chaineft thy martyr down upon his bed of ftraw, and it is thou who lifts him up to Heaven. Eternal Fountain of our feelings! It is here I trace thee, and this is thy divinity which ftirs within me: not that in fome fad and fickening moments, ' my foul fhrinks back upon herfelf, and ftartles at deftruction'—mere pomp of words!—but that I feel fome generous joys and generous cares beyond myfelf—all comes from thee, great, great Senforium of the world! which vibrates, if a hair of our head but falls upon the ground, in the remoteft defart of thy creation. Touched with thee, Eugenius draws my curtain when I languifh ; hears my tale of fymptoms, and blames the weather for the diforder of his nerves. Thou giveft a portion of it fometimes to the rougheft peafant who traverfes the bleakeft mountains.— He finds the lacerated lamb of another's flock. This moment I behold him leaning with his head againft his crook, with piteous inclination looking down upon it.—Oh ! had I come one moment fooner !—it bleeds to death—his gentle heart bleeds with it.

PEACE

Peace to thee, generous fwain! I fee thou walk eft off with anguifh——but thy joys fhall balance it; for happy is thy cottage, and happy is the fharer of it, and happy are the lambs which fport about you.

Sterne.

CHAP. II.

LIBERTY and SLAVERY.

DISGUISE thyfelf as thou wilt, ftill, Slavery! ftill thou art a bitter draught; and though thoufands in all ages have been made to drink of thee, thou art no lefs bitter on that account. It is thou, Liberty, thrice fweet and gracious goddefs, whom all in public and private worfhip, whofe tafte is grateful, and ever will be fo, till nature herfelf fhall change——no tint of words can fpot thy fnowy mantle, or chymic power turn thy fceptre into iron ——with thee to fmile upon him as he eats his cruft, the fwain is happier than his monarch, from whofe court thou art exiled Gracious heaven! grant me but health, thou great Beftower of it, and give me but this fair goddefs as my companion; and fhower down thy mitres, if it feems good unto thy divine providence, upon thofe heads which are aching for them.——

Pursuing thefe ideas, I fat down clofe by my table, and leaning my head upon my hand, I began to figure to myfelf the miferies of confinement. I was in a right frame for it, and fo I gave full fcope to my imagination.

I was going to begin with the millions of my fellow-creatures born to no inheritance but flavery; but finding, however affecting the picture was, that I could not bring it near me, and that the multitude of fad groups in it did but diftract me——

—I took.

—I took a single captive, and having first shut him up in his dungeon, I then looked through the twilight of his grated door to take his picture.

I beheld his body half wasted away with long expectation and confinement, and felt what kind of sickness of the heart it was which arises from hope deferred. Upon looking nearer I saw him pale and feverish: in thirty years the western breeze had not once fanned his blood—he had seen no sun, no moon in all that time—nor had the voice of friend or kinsman breathed through his lattice. His children——

—But here my heart began to bleed——and I was forced to go on with another part of the portrait.

He was sitting upon the ground upon a little straw, in the furthest corner of his dungeon, which was alternately his chair and bed: a little calendar of small sticks were laid at the head, notched all over with the dismal days and nights he had passed there——he had one of these little sticks in his hand, and with a rusty nail he was etching another day of misery to add to the heap. As I darkened the little light he had, he lifted up a hopeless eye towards the door, then cast it down—shook his head, and went on with his work of affliction. I heard his chains upon his legs, as he turned his body to lay his little stick upon the bundle—He gave a deep sigh—I saw the iron enter into his soul—I burst into tears—I could not sustain the picture of confinement which my fancy had drawn.

STERNE.

CHAP.

C H A P.   III.

Corporal TRIM's ELOQUENCE.

——MY young master in London is dead, said
Obadiah——

—Here is sad news, Trim, cried Susannah, wiping her eyes as Trim stepped into the kitchen,— master Bobby is dead.

I lament for him from my heart and my soul,
said Trim, fetching a sigh——Poor creature!—poor
boy! poor gentleman!

He was alive last Whitsuntide, said the coachman.
Whitsuntide! alas! cried Trim, extending his
right arm, and falling instantly into the same attitude
in which he read the sermon,—what is Whitsuntide,
Jonathan, (for that was the coachman's name) or
Shrovetide, or any tide or time past, to this? Are we
not here now, continued the corporal, (striking the
end of his stick perpendicularly upon the floor so as
to give an idea of health and stability) and are we not
(dropping his hat upon the ground) gone! in a moment!—It was infinitely striking! Susannah burst into a flood of tears.—We are not stocks and stones.—
Jonathan, Obadiah, the cook-maid, all melted.
—The foolish fat scullion herself, who was scour-
ing a fish-kettle upon her knees, was roused
with it.—The whole kitchen crouded about the
corporal.

" Are we not here now,—and gone in a moment?"—There was nothing in the sentence—it was
one of your self-evident truths we have the advantage
of hearing every day ; and if Trim had not trusted
more to his hat than his head, he had made nothing
at all of it.

" Are we not here now ;" continued the corpo-
" ral, and are we not" (dropping his hat plumb upon
the ground—and pausing, before he pronounced the
word) " gone! in a moment? The descent of the
hat

hat was as if a heavy lump of clay had been knead-
ed into the crown of it.——Nothing could have expreſſed the ſentiment of mortality, of which it was
the type and forerunner, like it, his hand ſeemed to
vaniſh from under it, it fell dead, the corporal's eye
fixed upon it, as upon a corps,——and Suſannah
burſt into a flood of tears.

STERNE.

C H A P.   IV.

THE MAN OF ROSS.

——ALL our praiſes why ſhould Lords engroſs?
　　Riſe, honeſt Muſe! and ſing the MAN of
　　　　Ross:
Pleas'd Vaga echoes through her winding bounds,
And rapid Severn hoarſe applauſe reſounds.
Who hung with woods yon mountain's ſultry brow?
From the dry rock who bade the waters flow?
Not to the ſkies in uſeful columns toſt,
Or in proud falls magnificently loſt.
But clear and artleſs, pouring through the plain
Health to the ſick, and ſolace to the ſwain.
Whoſe cauſe-way parts the vale with ſhady rows?
Whoſe ſeats the weary traveller repoſe?
Who taught that heav'n-directed ſpire to riſe?
" The MAN of Ross," each liſping babe replies.
Behold the market-place with poor o'erſpread!
The MAN of Ross divides the weekly bread:
He feeds yon alms-houſe, neat, but void of ſtate,
Where age and want ſit ſmiling at the gate:
Him portion'd maids, apprentic'd orphans bleſt,
The young who labour, and the old who reſt.
Is any ſick? The MAN of Ross relieves,
Preſcribes, attends, the med'cine makes, and gives.
Is there a variance? Enter but his door,
Balk'd are the courts, and conteſt is no more.
Deſpairing quacks with curſes fled the place,
And vile attorneys, now a uſeleſs race.

Thrice

Thrice happy man! enabled to purfue
What all fo wifh, but want the pow'r to do!
Oh fay, what fums that gen'rous hand fupply?
What mines, to fwell that boundlefs charity?
    Of debts and taxes, wife and children clear,
This man poffeft—five hundred pounds a year.
Blufh, Grandeur, blufh! proud Courts, withdraw
            your blaze!
Ye little Stars! hide your diminifh'd rays.
    And what! no monument, infcription, ftone!
His race, his form, his name almoft unknown!
    Who builds a Church to God, and not to fame.
Will never mark the marble with his Name:
Go, fearch it there, where to be born and die,
Of rich and poor makes all the hiftory;
Enough, that Virtue fill'd the fpace between;
Prov'd, by the ends of being, to have been.
                                POPE.

C H A P. V.

THE COUNTRY CLERGYMAN.

NEAR yonder copfe, where once the garden
            fmil'd,
And ftill where many a garden flower grows wild;
There, where a few torn fhrubs the place difclofe,
The village preacher's modeft manfion rofe.
A man he was, to all the country dear,
And paffing rich with forty pounds a year;
Remote from towns he ran his godly race,
Nor e'er had chang'd, nor wifh'd to change his place;
Unpractis'd he to fawn, or feek for power,
By doctrines fafhion'd to the varying hour;
Far other aims his heart had learn'd to prize,
More fkill'd to raife the wretched than to rife.
His houfe was known to all the vagrant train,
He chid their wandrings, but reliev'd their pain;
The long remember'd beggar was his gueft,
Whofe beard defcending fwept his aged breaft;
                                The

The ruin'd fpendthrift, now no longer proud.
Claim'd kindred there, and had his claim allow'd;
The broken foldier, kindly bade to ftay.
Sate by his fire, and talk'd the night away;
Wept o'er his wounds, or tales of forrow done,
Shoulder'd his crutch, and fhew'd how fields were won.
Pleas'd with his guefts, the good man learn'd to glow,
And quite forgot their vices in their woe:
Carelefs their merits, or their faults to fcan,
His pitty gave ere charity began.
    Thus to relieve the wretched was his pride,
And even his failings lean'd to Virtue's fide;
But in his duty prompt at every call,
He watch'd and wept, he pray'd, and felt, for all.
And, as a bird each fond endearment tries,
To tempt its new fledg'd offspring to the fkies;
He tried each art, reprov'd each dull delay,
Allur'd to brighter worlds, and led the way.
    Befide the bed where parting life was laid,
And forrow, guilt, and pain, by turns difmay'd,
The reverend champion ftood.   At his controul,
Defpair and anguifh fled the ftruggling foul;
Comfort came down the trembling wretch to raife,
And his laft faultering accents whifper'd praife.
    At church, with meek and unaffected grace,
His looks adorn'd the venerable place;
Truth from his lips prevail'd with double fway,
And fools, who came to fcoff, remain'd to pray.
The fervice paft, around the pious man,
With ready zeal each honeft ruftic ran;
Even children follow'd with endearing wile
And pluck'd his gown, to fhare the good man's fmile.
His ready fmile a parent's warmth expreft,
Their welfare pleas'd him, and their cares diftreft;
To them his heart, his love, his griefs were given,
But all his ferious thoughts had reft in Heaven.
As fome tall cliff that lifts its awful form,
Swells from the vale, and midway leaves the ftorm,
Tho' round its breaft the rolling clouds are fpread,
Eternal funfhine fettles on its head.

GOLDSMITH.

C H A P

CHAP. VI.

The WISH.

CONTENTMENT, parent of delight,
So much a ftranger to our fight,
Say, goddefs, in what happy place,
Mortals behold thy blooming face;
Thy gracious aufpices impart,
And for thy temple choofe my heart.
They, whom thou deigneft to infpire,
Thy fcience learn, to bound defire;
By happy alchymy of mind
They turn to pleafure all they find;
They both difdain in outward mein
The grave and folemn garb of Spleen,
And meretricious arts of drefs,
To feign a joy and hide diftrefs:
Unmov'd when the rude tempeft blows;
Without an opiate they repofe;
And cover'd by your fhield, defy
The whizzing fhafts, that round them fly;
Nor meddling with the gods' affairs,
Concern themfelves with diftant cares;
But place their blifs in mental reft,
And feaft upon the good poffefs'd.
  Forc'd by foft violence of pray'r,
The blithfome goddefs fooths my care,
I feel the deity infpire,
And thus fhe models my defire.
Two hundred pounds half-yearly paid,
Annuity fecurely made,
A farm fome twenty miles from town,
Small, tight, falubrious, and my own;
Two maids, that never faw the town,
A ferving man not quite a clown,
A boy to help to tread the mow,
And drive while t'other holds the plough;
A chief of temper form'd to pleafe,
Fit to converfe, and keep the keys;

And

And better to preserve the peace,
Commiſſion'd by the name of niece;
With underſtandings of a ſize
To think their maſter very wiſe.
May heav'n (it's all I wiſh for) ſend
One genial room to treat a friend,
Where decent cup-board, little plate,
Diſplay benevolence, not ſtate.
And may my humble dwelling ſtand
Upon ſome choſen ſpot of land:
A pond before full to the brim,
Where cows may cool, and geeſe may ſwim:
Behind a green like velvet neat,
Soft to the eye, and to the feet;
Where od'rous plants in evening fair
Breathe all around ambroſial air.
From Eurus, foe to kitchen ground,
Fenc'd by a ſlope with buſhes crown'd.
Fit dwelling for the feather'd throng,
Who pay their quit-rents with a ſong:
With op'ning views of hill and dale,
Which ſenſe and fancy too regale,
Where the half-cirque, which viſion bounds,
Like amphitheatre ſurrounds;
And woods impervious to the breeze,
Thick phalanx of embodied trees,
From hills through plains in duſk array
Extended far, repel the day.
Here ſtillneſs, height, and ſolemn ſhade
Invite, and contemplation aid:
Here nymphs from hollow oaks relate
The dark decrees and will of fate,
And dreams beneath the ſpreading beech
Inſpire and docile fancy teach,
While ſoft as breezy breath of wind,
Impulſes ruſtle through the mind:
Here Dryads, ſcorning Phœbus' ray,
While Pan melodious pipes away,
In meaſur'd motions friſk about,
'Till old Silenus puts them out.

There

There fee the clover, pea, and bean,
Vie in variety of green;
Fresh paftures speckled o'er with sheep,
Brown fields their fallow fabbaths keep,
Plump Ceres golden treffes wear,
And poppy-top-knots deck her hair,
And filver-ftreams through meadows ftray,
And Naiads on the margin play,
And leffer nymphs on fide of hills
From play-thing urns pour down the rills.
  Thus shelter'd, free from care and ftrife,
May I enjoy a calm through life;
See faction fafe in low degree,
As men at land fee ftorms at fea,
And laugh at miferable elves,
Not kind, fo nruch as to themfelves,
Curs'd with fuch fouls of bafe alloy,
As can poffefs, but not enjoy;
Debarr'd the pleafure to impart
By av'rice, fphincter of the heart,
Who wealth, hard earn'd by guilty cares,
Bequeath untouch'd to thanklefs heirs.
May I, with look ungloom'd by guile,
And wearing Virtue's liv'ry fmile,
Prone the diftreffed to relieve,
And little trefpaffes forgive,
With income not in fortune's pow'r,
And fkill to make a bufy hour,
With trips to town life to amufe,
To purchafe books, and hear the news,
To fee old friends, brufh off the clown,
And quicken tafte at coming down,
Unhurt by ficknefs' blafted rage,
And flowly mellowing in age,
When Fate extends its gathering gripe,
Fall off like fruit grown fully ripe,
Quit a worn being without pain;
In hope to bloffom foon again.

GREEN.

C H A P.

C H A P.   VII.

G R O N G A R   H I L L.

SILENT nymph, with curious eye !
Who, the purple ev'ning lie
On the mountain's lonely van,
Beyond the noife of bufy man,
Painting fair the form of things,
While the yellow linnet fings ;
Or the tuneful nightingale
Charms the foreft with her tale ;
Come with all thy various hues,
Come and aid thy fifter Mufe :
Now while Phœbus riding high
Gives luftre to the land and fky !
Grongar Hill invites my fong,
Draw the landfkip bright and ftrong;
Grongar, in whofe moffy cells
Sweetly mufing Quiet dwells ;
Grongar, in whofe filent fhade,
For the modeft Mufes made, .
So oft I have, the evening ftill,
At the fountain of a rill.
Sate upon a flow'ry bed,
With my hand beneath my head ;
While ftray'd my eyes o'er Towy's flood,
Over mead, and over wood,
From houfe to houfe, from hill to hill,
'Till contemplation had her fill.
   About his chequer'd fides I wind,
And leave his brooks and meads behind,
And groves and grottoes where I lay,
And viftoes fhooting beams of day :
Wide and wider fpreads the vale ;
As circles on a fmooth canal ;
The mountains round, unhappy fate !
Sooner or later, of all height,

L

Withdraw

Withdraw their fummits from the fkies,
And leffen as the others rife ;
Still the profpect wider fpreads,
Adds a thoufand woods and meads,
Still it widens, widens ftill,
And finks the newly-rifen hill. —
    Now, I gain the mountains brow ;
What a landfkip lies below !
No clouds, no vapours intevene,
But the gay, the open fcene
Does the face of nature fhow,
In all the hues of heaven's bow !
And, fwelling to embrace the light,
Spreads around beneath the fight.
Old caftles on the cliffs arife,
Proudly tow'ring in the fkies !
Rufhing from the woods, the fpires
Seem from hence afcending fires !
Half his beams Apollo fheds
On the yellow mountain-heads !
Gilds the fleeces of the flocks,
And glitters on the broken rocks !
    Below me trees unnumber'd rife,
Beautiful in various dyes :
The gloomy pine, the poplar blue,
The yellow beech, the fable yew,
The flender fir, that taper grows,
The fturdy oak, with broad-fpread boughs,
And beyond, the purple grove,
Haunt of Phillis, queen of love !
Gaudy as the opening dawn,
Lies a long and level lawn,
On which a dark hill, fteep and high,
Holds and charms the wand'ring eye ;
Deep are his feet in Towy's flood,
His fides are cloth'd with waving wood,
And ancient towers crown his brow,
That caft an awful look below ;
Whofe ragged walls the ivy creeps,
And with her arms from falling keeps ;

So

So both a fafety from the wind
On mutual dependence find.
   'Tis now the raven's bleak abode ;
'Tis now th' apartment of the toad ;
And there the fox fecurely feeds ;
And there the pois'nous adder breeds,
Conceal'd in ruins, mofs and weeds :
While, ever and anon, there falls
Huge heaps of hoary moulder'd walls.
Yet time has been, that lifts the low,
And level lays the lofty brow,
Has feen this broken pile compleat,
Big with the vanity of ftate ;
But tranfient is the fmile of fate !
A little rule, a little fway,
A funbeam in a winter's day,
Is all the proud and mighty have
Between the cradle and the grave.
   And fee the rivers how they run,
Through woods and meads, in fhade and fun,
Sometimes fwift, and fometimes flow,
Wave fucceeding wave, they go
A various journey to the deep,
Like human life to endlefs fleep !
Thus is nature's vefture wrought,
To inftruct our wand'ring thought ;
Thus fhe dreffes green and gay,
To difperfe our cares away.
   Ever charming, ever new,
When will the landfkip tire the view !
The fountain's fall, the river's flow,
The woody vallies, warm and low ;
The windy fummit, wild and high,
Roughly rufhing on the fky ;
The pleafant feat, the ruin'd tow'r,
The naked rock, the fhady bow'r ;
The town and village, dome and farm,
Each give each a double charm,
As pearls upon an Æthiop's arm.

L 2

See

See on the mountain's fouthern fide,
Where the profpect opens wide,
Where the evening gilds the tide ;
How clofe and fmall the hedges lie ;
What ftreaks of meadows crofs the eye !
A ftep methinks may pafs the ftream ;
So little diftant dangers feem ;
So we miftake the future's face,
Ey'd through hope's deluding glafs ;
As yon fummit foft and fair,
Clad in colours of the air,
Which to thofe who journey near,
Barren, brown, and rough appear,
Still we tread the fame coarfe way,
The prefent's ftill a cloudy day,

  O may I with myfelf agree,
And never covet what I fee !
Content me with an humble fhade,
My paffions tam'd, my wifhes laid ;
For while our wifhes wildly roll,
We banifh quiet from the foul :
'Tis thus the bufy beat the air ;
And mifers gather wealth and care.

  Now, ev'n now, my joy runs high,
As on the mountain-turf I lie ;
While the wanton Zephyr fings,
And in the vale perfumes his wings ;
While the waters murmur deep ;
While the fhepherd charms his fheep ;
While the birds unbounded fly,
And with mufic fill the fky,
Now' ev'n now, my joys run high.

  Be full, ye courts, be great who will,
Search for Peace with all your fkill :
Open wide the lofty door,
Seek her on the marble floor,
In vain you fearch, fhe is not there ;
In vain ye fearch the domes of care !
Grafs and flowers Quiet treads,
On the meads and mountain-heads,

Along

Along with Pleasure, close ally'd,
Ever by each other's side :
And often by the murmuring rill,
Hears the thrush, while all is still,
Within the groves of Grongar Hill.

DYER.

C H A P.   VIII.

HYMN TO ADVERSITY.

DAUGHTER of JOVE, relentless power,
  Thou Tamer of the human breast,
Whose iron scourge and tott'ring hour,
The bad affright, afflict the best !
Bound in thy adamantine chain,
The proud are taught to taste of pain,
And purple tyrants vainly groan
With pangs unfelt before, unpitied and alone.

When first thy fire to send on earth
Virtue, his darling child, design'd,
To thee he gave the heavenly birth,
And bade to form her infant mind.
Stern rugged nurse ! thy rigid lore
With patience many a year she bore :
What sorrow was, thou bad'st her know,
And from her own she learn'd to melt at other's woe.

Scared at thy frown terrific, fly
Self-pleasing Folly's idle brood,
Wild Laughter, Noise, and thoughtless Joy,
And leave us leisure to be good.
Light they disperse, and with them go
The summer Friend, the flattring Foe ;
By vain Prosperity receiv'd,
To her they vow their truth, and are again believ'd.

Wisdom in sable garb array'd
Immers'd in rapt'rous thought profound,

L 3

And

And Melancholy, filent maid,
With leaden eye, that loves the ground,
Still on thy folemn fteps attend :
Warm Charity, the gen'ral friend,
With Juftice to herfelf fevere,
And Pity, dropping foft the fadly-pleafing tear.

Oh, gently on thy fuppliant's head,
Dread goddefs, lay thy chaft'ning hand !
Not in thy Gorgon terrors clad,
Nor circled with the vengeful band,
(As by the impious thou art feen)
With thund'ring voice, and threat'ning mien,
With fcreaming Horror's funeral cry,
Defpair and fell Difeafe, and ghaftly Poverty.

Thy form benign, oh Goddefs, wear,
Thy milder influence impart,
Thy philofophic train be there
To foften, not to wound my heart.
The gen'rous fpark extinct revive,
Teach me to love and to forgive,
Exact my own defects to fcan,
What others are, to feel, and know myfelf a man.
GRAY.

CHAP.   IX.

ODE on a distant prospect of ETON COLLEGE

YE diftant fpires, ye antique towers,
  That crown the watery glade,
Where grateful Science ftill adores
Her HENRY's holy fhade :
And ye, that from the ftately brow
Of WINDSOR's heights th' expanfe below
Of grove, of lawn, of mead furvey,
Whofe turf, whofe fhade, whofe flowers among
Wanders the hoary Thames along
His filver-winding way.

Ah

Ah happy hills, ah pleafing fhade,
Ah fields belov'd in vain,
Where once my carelefs childhood ftray'd,
A ftranger yet to pain !
I feel the gales, that from ye blow,
A momentary blifs beftow,
As waving frefh their gladfome wing,
My weary foul they feem to footh,
And, redolent of joy and youth,
To breathe a fecond fpring.

Say, Father THAMES (for thou haft feen
Full many a fprightly race,
Difporting on thy margent green,
The paths of pleafure trace)
Who foremoft now delight to cleave
With pliant arm thy glaffy wave ?
The captive linnet to enthrall ?
What idle progeny fucceed
To chafe the rolling circle's fpeed,
Or urge the flying ball ?

While fome on earneft bufinefs bent
'Their murm'ring labours ply
'Gainft graver hours, that bring conftraint
To fweeten liberty :
Some bold adventurers difdain
The limits of their little reign,
And unknown regions dare defcry :
Still as they run they look behind,
They hear a voice in every wind,
And fnatch a fearful joy.

Gay hope is theirs by fancy fed,
Lefs pleafing when poffeft ;
The tear forgot as foon as fhed,
The funfhine of the breaft :
Theirs buxom health of rofy hue,
Wild wit, invention ever-new,

L 4.

And.

And lively chear of vigour born ;
The thoughtlefs day, the eafy night,
The fpirits pure, the flumbers light,
That fly th' approach of morn.

Alas, regardlefs of their doom,
The little victims play !
No fenfe have they of ills to come,
No care beyond to-day :
Yet fee how all around them wait
The minifters to human fate,
And black misfortune's baleful train !
Ah, fhew them where in ambufh ftand
To feize their prey the murth'rous band !
Ah, tell them, they are men !

Thefe fhall the fury Paffions tear,
The vultures of the mind,
Difdainful Anger, pallid Fear,
And Shame that fkulks behind ;
Or pining Love fhall wafte their youth,
Or Jealoufy with rankling tooth,
That inly gnaws the fecret heart,
And Envy wan, and faded Care,
Grim-vifag'd comfortlefs Defpair,
And Sorrow's piercing dart.

Ambition this fhall tempt to rife,
Then whirl the wretch from high,
To bitter Scorn a facrifice,
And grinning Infamy.
The ftings of Falfhood thofe fhall try,
And hard Unkindnefs' alter'd eye,
That mocks the tear it forc'd to flow ;
And keen Remorfe with blood defil'd,
And moody Madnefs laughing wild
Amid fevereft woe.

Lo, in the vale of years beneath
A griefly troop are feen,
The painly family of Death,
More hideous than their queen.

This

This racks the joints, this fires the veins,
That every labouring finew ftrains,
Thofe in the deeper vitals rage:
Lo, Poverty, to fill the band
That numbs the foul with icy hand,
And flow-confuming Age.

 To each his fuff'rings: all are men,
Condemn'd alike to groan;
The tender for another's pain,
Th' unfeeling for his own.
Yet ah! why fhould they know their fate?
Since forrow never comes too late,
And happinefs too fwiftly flies.
Thought would deftroy their paradife.
No more; where ignorance is blifs,
'Tis folly to be wife.

GRAY.

C H A P. X.

ELEGY WRITTEN IN A COUNTRY CHURCH-YARD.

THE curfew tolls the knell of parting day,
 The lowing herd wind flowly o'er the lea,
The ploughman homeward plods his weary way,
And leaves the world to darknefs and to me.

Now fades the glimmering landfcape on the fight,
And all the air a folemn ftillnefs holds,
Save where the beetle wheels his droning flight,
And drowfy tinklings lull the diftant folds;

Save that from yonder ivy-mantled tow'r,
The mopeing owl does to the moon complain.
Of fuch, as wand'ring near her fecret bow'r,
Moleft her ancient folitary reign.

L 5 Beneath

Beneath thofe rugged elms, that yew-tree's fhade,
Where heaves the turf in many a mould'ring heap,
Each in his narrow cell for ever laid,
The rude forefathers of the hamlet fleep.

The breezy call of incenfe-breathing Morn,
The fwallow twittering from the ftraw-built fhed,
The cock's fhrill clarion, or the echoing horn,
No more fhall roufe them from their lowly bed.

For them no more the blazing hearth fhall burn,
Or bufy houfe-wife ply her evening care
No children run to lifp their fire's return,
Or climb his knees the envied kifs to fhare.

Oft did the harveft to their fickle yield,
Their furrow oft the ftubborn glebe has broke;
How jocund did they drive their team afield!
How bow'd the woods beneath their fturdy ftroke!

Let not Ambition mock their ufeful toil,
Their homely joys, and deftiny obfcure;
Nor Grandeur hear with a difdainful fmile,
The fhort and fimple annals of the poor.

The boaft of heraldry, the pomp of pow'r,
And all that beauty, all that wealth e'er gave,
Await alike th' inevitable hour,
The paths of glory lead but to the grave.

Nor you, ye proud, impute to thefe the fault,
If Mem'ry o'er their tomb no trophies raife,
Where thro' the long-drawn ayle and fretted vault,
The pealing anthem fwells the note of praife.

Can ftoried urn or animated buft
Back to its manfion call the fleeting breath?
Can Honour's voice provoke the filent duft,
Or Flatt'ry footh the dull cold ear of Death?

Perhaps

Perhaps in this neglected fpot is laid
Some heart once pregnant with celeftial fire;
Hands, that the rod of empire might have fway'd,
Or wak'd to extafy the living lyre.

But Knowledge to their eyes her ample page
Rich with the fpoils of time did ne'er unroll;
Chill-Penury reprefs'd their noble rage,
And froze the genial current of the foul.

Full many a gem of pureft ray ferene,
The dark unfathom'd caves of ocean bear:
Full many a flower is born to blufh unfeen,
And wafte its fweetnefs on the defert air.

Some village-Hampden, that with dauntlefs breaft
The little Tyrant of his fields withftood;
Some mute inglorious Milton here may reft,
Some Cromwell guiltlefs of his country's blood.

Th' applaufe of lift'ning fenates to command,
The threats of pain and ruin to defpife,
To fcatter plenty o'er a fmiling land,
And read their hift'ry in a nation's eyes,

Their lot forbade: nor circumfcrib'd alone
Their growing virtues, but their crimes confin'd;
Forbade to wade through flaughter to a throne,
And fhut the gates of mercy on mankind.

The ftruggling pangs of confcious truth to hide,
To quench the blufhes of ingenuous fhame,
Or heap the fhrine of Luxury and Pride
With incenfe kindled at the Mufe's flame.

Far from the madding crowd's ignoble ftrife,
Their fober wifhes never learn'd to ftray;
Along the cool fequefter'd vale of life
They kept the noifelefs tenor of their lay.

Yet

Yet ev'n thefe bones from infult to protect
Some frail memorial ftill erected nigh,
With uncouth rhimes and fhapelefs fculpture deck'd,
Implores the paffing tribute of a figh.

Their name, their years, fpelt by th' unletter'd mufe,
The place of fame and elegy fupply:
And many a holy text around fhe ftrews,
That teach the ruftic moralift to die.

For who to dumb Forgetfulnefs a prey,
This pleafing anxious being e'er refign'd,
Left the warm precincts of the chearful day,
Nor caft one longing ling'ring look behind?

On fome fond breaft the parting foul relies,
Some pious drops the clofing eye requires,
Ev'n from the tomb the voice of Nature cries,
Ev'n in our afhes live their wonted fires.

For thee, who mindful of th' unhonoured dead
Doft in thefe lines their artlefs tale relate;
If chance, by lonely contemplation led,
Some kindred Spirit fhall inquire thy fate,

Haply fome hoary-headed Swain may fay,
' Oft have we feen him at the peep of dawn
' Brufhing with hafty fteps the dews away
' To meet the fun upon the upland lawn.

' There at the foot of yonder nodding beech
' That wreathes its old fantaftic roots fo high,
' His liftlefs length at noontide would he ftretch,
' And pore upon the brook that babbles by.

' Hard by yon wood, now fmiling as in fcorn,
' Mutt'ring his wayward fancies he would rove,
' Now drooping, woful wan, like one forlorn,
' Or craz'd with care, or crofs'd in hopelefs love.

' One

‘ One morn I mifs’d him on the cuftom’d hill,
‘ Along the heath, and near his fav’rite tree;
‘ Another came; not yet befide the rill,
‘ Nor up the lawn, nor at the wood was he;

‘ The next with dirges due in fad array
‘ Slow thro’ the church-way path we faw him
            borne.
‘ Approach and read (for thou can’ft read) the
            lay,
‘ ’Grav’d on the ftone beneath yon aged thorn.

The E P I T A P H.

HERE refts his head upon the lap of Earth
    A Youth to Fortune and to Fame unknown;
Fair Science frown’d not on his humble birth,
And Melancholy mark’d him for her own.

Large was his bounty, and his foul fincere,
Heav’n did a recompence as largely fend:
He gave to Mis’ry all he had, a tear,
He gain’d from Heav’n (’twas all he wifh’d) a friend.

No farther feek his merits to difclofe,
Or draw his frailties from their dread abode,
(There they alike in trembling hope repofe)
The bofom of his Father and his God.

                                    GRAY.

                                    C H A P.

C H A P. XI.

WARRINGTON ACADEMY.

MARK where its simple front yon mansion rears,
The nursery of men for future years!
Here callow chiefs and embryo statesmen lie,
And unfledg'd poets short excursions try:
While Mersey's gentle current, which too long
By fame neglected, and unknown to song,
Between the rushy banks, (no poet's theme)
Had crept inglorious, like a vulgar stream,
Reflects th' ascending seats with conscious pride,
And dares to emulate a classic tide,
Soft music breathes along each opening shade,
And sooths the dashing of his rough cascade,
With mystic lines his sands are figur'd o'er,
And circles trac'd upon the letter'd shore.
Beneath his willows rove th' inquiring youth,
And court the fair majestic form of Truth.
Here nature opens all her secrets springs,
And heav'n born Science plumes her eagle-wings:
Too long had bigot rage, with malice swell'd,
Crush'd her strong pinions, and her flight witheld;
Too long to check her ardent progress strove:
So writhes the serpent round the bird of Jove;
Hangs on her flight, restrains her tow'ring wing,
Twists its dark folds, and points its venom'd sting.
Yet still (if aught aright the Muse divine)
Her rising pride shall mock the vain design;
On sounding pinions yet aloft shall soar,
And thro' the azure deep untravell'd paths explore.
Where science smiles, the Muses join the train;
And gentlest arts and purest manners reign.

    Ye generous youth, who love this studious shade,
How rich a field is to your hopes display'd!
Knowledge to you unlocks the classic page;
And virtue blossoms for a better age.
Oh golden days! oh bright unvalued hours!
What bliss (did ye but know that bliss) were yours!

With

With richeſt ſtores your glowing boſoms fraught,
Perception quick, and luxury of thought;
The high deſigns that heave the labouring ſoul,
Panting for fame, impatient of controul;
And fond enthuſiaſtic thought, that feeds
On pictur'd tales of vaſt heroic deeds;
And quick affections, kindling into flame
At virtue's or their country's honour'd name;
And ſpirits light, to every joy in tune;
And friendſhip, ardent as a ſummer's noon;
And generous ſcorn of vice's venal tribe;
And proud diſdain of intereſt's ſordid bribe;
And conſcious honour's quick inſtinctive ſenſe;
And ſmiles unforc'd; and eaſy confidence;
And vivid fancy; and clear ſimple truth;
And all the mental bloom of vernal youth.

   How bright the ſcene to fancy's eye appears,
Thro' the perſpective of long diſtant years,
When this, this little group their country calls
From academic ſhades and learned halls,
To fix her laws, her ſpirit to ſuſtain,
And light up glory thro' her wide domain!
Their various taſtes in different arts, diſplay'd,
Like temper'd harmony of light and ſhade,
With friendly union in one maſs ſhall blend;
And this adorn the ſtate, and that defend.
Theſe the ſequeſter'd ſhade ſhall cheaply pleaſe,
With learned labour, and inglorious eaſe:
While thoſe, impell'd by ſome reſiſtleſs force,
O'er ſeas and rocks ſhall urge their vent'rous courſe;
Rich fruits matur'd by glowing ſuns behold,
And China's groves of vegetable gold;
From every land the various harveſt ſpoil,
And bear the tribute to their native ſoil:
But tell each land (while every toil they ſhare,
Firm to ſuſtain, and reſolute to dare,)
MAN is the nobler growth our realms ſupply,
And SOULS are ripen'd in our northern ſky,
   Some penſive creep along the ſhelly ſhore;
Unfold the ſilky texture of a flower;

With

With sharpen'd eyes inspect an hornet's sting,
And all the wonders of an insect's wing.
Some trace with curious search the hidden cause,
Of nature's changes, and her various laws;
Untwist her beauteous web, disrobe her charms,
And hunt her to her elemental forms:
Or prove what hidden powers in herbs are found
To quench disease and cool the burning wound;
With cordial drops the fainting head sustain,
Call back the flitting soul, and still the throbs of pain.
  The patriot passion this shall strongly feel,
Ardent, and glowing with undaunted zeal;
With lips of fire shall plead his country's cause,
And vindicate the majesty of laws.
This, cloath'd with Britain's thunder, spread alarms
Thro' the wide earth, and shake the pole with arms.
That, to the sounding lyre his deeds rehearse,
Enshrine his name in some immortal verse,
To long posterity his praise consign,
And pay a life of hardships by a line:
While others, consecrate to higher aims,
Whose hallow'd bosoms glow with purer flames,
Love in their heart, persuasion in their tongue,
With words of peace shall charm the list'ning throng,
Draw the dread veil that wraps th' eternal throne,
And launch our souls into the bright unknown.

Mrs. BARBAULD.

CHAP. XII.

ODE TO CONTENT.

O THOU, the nymph with placid eye!
O seldom found, yet ever nigh!
  Receive my temperate vow.
Not all the storms that shake the pole
Can e'er disturb thy halcyon soul,
  And smooth unalter'd brow.

O come

O come in fimpleft veft array'd,
With all thy fober cheer difplayed
      To blefs my longing fight;
Thy mein compos'd, thy even pace,
Thy meek regard, thy matron grace,
      And chafte fubdued delight.

No more by varying paffions beat,
O gently guide my pilgrim feet
      To find thy hermit cell;
Where in fome pure and equal fky
Beneath thy foft indulgent eye
      The modeft virtues dwell.

Simplicity in attic veft,
And Innocence with candid breaft,
      And clear undaunted eye;
And Hope, who points to diftant years,
Fair opening thro' this vale of tears
      A vifta to the fky.

There Health, thro' whofe calm bofom glide
The temperate joys in even tide,
      That rarely ebb or flow;
And Patience there, thy fifter meek,
Prefents her mild, unvarying cheek
      To meet the offered blow.

Her influence taught the Phrygian fage
A tyrant mafter's wanton rage
      With fettled fmiles to meet:
Inur'd to toil and bitter bread
He bow'd his meek fubmitted head,
      And kifs'd thy fainted feet.

But thou, oh Nymph retir'd and coy!
In what brown hamlet doft thou joy
      To tell thy tender tale?
The lowlieft children of the ground,
Mofs-rofe and violet bloffom round,
      And lily of the vale.

O fay

O fay what foft propitious hour
I beft may chufe to hail thy power,
    And court thy gentle fway?
When Autumn, friendly to the Mufe,
Shall thy own modeft tints diffufe,
    And fhed thy milder day:

When Eve, her dewy ftar beneath
Thy balmy fpirit loves to breathe,
    And every ftorm is laid;
If fuch an hour was e'er thy choice;
Oft left me hear thy foothing voice
    Low whifpering thro' the fhade.

MRS. BARBAULD.

C H A P. XIII.

O D E TO F E A R.

THOU, to whom the world unknown
    With all its fhadowy fhapes is fhewn;
Who feeft appall'd th' unreal fcene
While Fancy lifts the veil between:
    Ah Fear! ah frantic Fear!
    I fee, I fee thee near.
I know thy hurried ftep, thy haggard eye!
Like thee I ftart, like thee diforder'd fly;
For, lo what monfters in thy train appear!
Danger, whofe limbs of giant mould
What mortal eye can fix'd behold?
Who ftalks his round, an hideous form,
Howling amidft the midnight ftorm,
Or throws him on the ridgy fteep:
Of fome loofe hanging rock to fleep:
And with him thoufand phantoms join'd,
Who prompt to deeds accurs'd the mind:
And thofe, the fiends, who near allied,
O'er Nature's wounds and wrecks prefide;

While

While Vengeance, in the lurid air,
Lifts her red arm, expos'd and bare:
On whom that ravening Brood of fate,
Who lap the blood of Sorrow, wait:
Who, Fear, this ghaftly train can fee,
And look not madly wild, like thee?

   Thou who fuch weary lengths haft paft,
Where wilt thou reft, mad Nymph, at laft?
Say wilt thou fhroud in haunted cell,
Where gloomy Rape and Murder dwell?
Or in fome hollow'd feat,
'Gainft which the big waves beat,
Hear drowning feamen's cries in tempefts brought?
Dark power, with fhuddering meek fubmitted
      thought,
Be mine to read the vifions old,
Which thy awakening bards have told:
And, left thou meet my blafted view,
Hold each ftrange tale devoutly true;
Ne'er be I found, by thee o'er-aw'd,
In that thrice-hallow'd eve abroad,
When ghofts, as cottage-maids believe,
Their pebbled beds permitted leave,
And goblins haunt from fire or fen,
Or mine, or flood, the walks of men!

   O thou whofe fpirit moft poffeft
The facred feat of Shakefpear's breaft!
By all that from thy prophet broke,
In the divine emotions fpoke;
Hither again thy fury deal,
Teach me but once like him to feel:
His cyprefs wreath my meed decree,
And I, O Fear! will dwell with thee!

COLLINS.

CHAP.

CHAP. XIV.

ODE to TRUTH.

SAY, will no white-rob'd Son of Light,
Swift-darting from his heav'nly height,
  Here deign to take his hallow'd ftand;
Here wave his amber locks; unfold
  His pinions cloth'd with downy gold;
Here fmiling ftretch his tutelary wand?
  And you, ye hoft of Saints, for ye have known
Each dreary path in Life's perplexing maze,
  Tho' now ye circle yon external throne
With harpings high of inexpreffive praife,
  Will not your train defcend in radiant ftate,
To break with Mercy's beam this gathering cloud
      of Fate?

  'Tis filence all. No fon of Light
Darts fwiftly from his heav'nly height;
  No train of radiant Saints defcend.
" Mortals, in vain ye hope to find,
" If guilt, if fraud has ftain'd your mind,
  " Or Saint to hear, or angel to defend."
So TRUTH proclaims. I hear the facred found
Burft from the centre of her burning throne:
  Where aye fhe fits with ftar-wreath'd luftre
        crown'd
A bright Sun clafps her adamantine zone.
  So TRUTH proclaims: her awful voice I hear:
With many a folemn paufe it flowly meets my ear.

  " Attend, ye Sons of Men; attend, and fay,
Does not enough of my refulgent ray
  Break thro' the veil of your mortality?
  Say, does not reafon in this form defcry
                    Unnum-

Unnumber'd namelefs glories, that furpafs
The Angel's floating pomp, the Seraph's glowing
   grace ?
 Shall then your earth-born daughters vie
 With me ? Shall fhe, whofe brighteft eye
  But emulates the diamond's blaze,
 Whofe cheek but mocks the peaches bloom,
 Whofe breath the hyacinth's perfume,
Whofe melting voice the warbling wood-lark's lays,
 Shall fhe be deem'd my rival ? Shall a form
Of elemental drofs, of mould'ring clay,
 Vie with thefe charms imperial ? The poor worm
Shall prove her conteft vain. Life's little day
 Shall pafs, and fhe is gone : while I appear
Flufh'd with the bloom of youth thro' Heav'ns
   eternal year.

  Know, Mortals, know, ere firft ye fprung,
  Ere firft thefe orbs in æther hung,
   I fhone amid the heav'nly throng.
  Thefe eyes beheld Creation's day,
  This voice began the choral lay,
 And taught Archangels their triumphant fong.
  Pleas'd I furvey'd bright Nature's gradual birth,
 Saw infant Light with kindling luftre fpread,
  Soft vernal fragrance clothe the flow'ring earth,
 And Ocean heave on his extended bed ;
  Saw the tall pine afpiring pierce the fky,
The tawny lion ftalk, the rapid eagle fly.

  Laft, Man arofe, erect in youthful grace,
  Heav'n's hallow'd image ftamp'd upon his face,
   And, as he rofe, the high bequeft was giv'n,
   " That I alone of all the hoft of heav'n,
  " Should reign Protectrefs of the godlike
   Youth."
Thus the Almighty fpake : he fpake and call'd me
  Truth.
         Mason.

      C H A P.

C H A P.   XV.

O D E to F A N C Y.

O PARENT of each lovely Mufe,
  Thy fpirit o'er my foul diffufe,
O'er all my artlefs fongs prefide,
My footfteps to thy temple guide,
To offer at thy turf-built fhrine,
In golden cups no coftly wine,
No murder'd fatling of the flock,
But flowers and honey from the rock.
    O Nymph with loofely-flowing hair,
With bufkin'd leg, and bofom bare,
Thy waift with myrtle-girdle bound
Thy brows with Indian feathers crown'd,
Waving in thy fnowy hand
An all-commanding magic wand,
Of pow'r to bid frefh gardens grow
'Mid carelefs Lapland's barren fnow,
Whofe rapid wings thy flight convey
Thro' air, and over earth and fea,
While the various landfkip lies
Confpicuous to thy piercing eyes!
O lover of the defert, hail!
Say, in what deep and pathlefs vale,
Or on what hoary mountain's fide,
'Midft falls of water you refide,
'Midft broken rocks, a rugged fcene,
With green and graffy dales between,
'Midft foreft dark of aged oak,
Ne'er echoing with the woodman's ftroke
Where never human art appear'd,
Nor e'en one ftraw-roof'd cot was rear'd,
Where Nature feems to fit alone,
Majeftic on a craggy throne;
Tell me the path, fweet wand'rer, tell,
To thy unknown fequefter'd cell,

Where

Where woodbines cluster round the door,
Where shells and mofs o'erlay the floor,
And on whofe top an hawthorn blows,
Amid whofe thickly-woven boughs
Some nightingale still builds her nest,
Each evening warbling thee to reft :
Then lay me by the haunted ftream,
Rapt in fome wild poetic dream,
In converfe while methinks I rove
With Spenfer thro' a fairy grove ;
Till fuddenly awak'd, I hear
Strange whifper'd mufic in my ear,
And my glad foul in blifs is drown'd,
By the fweetly-foothing found !
   Me, Goddefs, by the right-hand lead,
Sometimes thro' the yellow mead,
Where Joy and white rob'd Peace refort,
And Venus keeps her feftive court,
Where Mirth and Youth each evening meet,
And lightly trip with nimble feet.
Nodding their lilly-crowned heads ;
Where Laughter rofe-lip'd Hebe leads ;
Where Echo walks fteep hills among,
Lift'ning to the fhepherd's fong.
   Yet not thofe flow'ry fields of joy
Can long my penfive mind employ :
Hafte, Fancy, from thefe fcenes of folly
To meet the matron Melancholy,
Goddefs of the tearful eye,
That loves to fold her arms and figh
Let us with filent footfteps go
To charnels and the houfe of woe,
To gothic churches, vaults and tombs,
Where each fad night fome Virgin comes,
With throbbing breaft, and faded cheek,
Her promis'd bridegroom's urn to feek :
Or to fome Abbey's mould'ring tow'rs,
Where to avoid cold winter's fhow'rs,
The naked beggar fhiv'ring lies,
While whiftling tempefts round her rife,

And trembles left the tottering wall
Should on her fleeping infants fall.
  Now let us louder ftrike the lyre,
For my heart glows with martial fire,
I feel, I feel, with fudden heat,
My big tumultuous bofom beat,
The trumpets' clangors pierce mine ear,
A thoufand widows' fhrieks I hear,
Give me another horfe, I cry,
Lo! the bafe Gallic fquadrons fly;
Whence is this rage?——What fpirit, fay,
To battle hurries me away?
'Tis Fancy, in her fiery car,
Tranfports me to the thickeft war,
There whirls me o'er the hills of flain,
Where Tumult and Deftruction reign;
Where mad with pain, the wounded fteed
Tramples the dying and the dead:
Where giant Terror ftalks around,
With fullen joy furveys the ground,
And pointing to th' enfanguin'd field
Shakes his dreadful Gorgon-fhield!
  O guide me from this horrid fcene
To high-arch'd walks and alleys green,
Which lovely Laura feeks to fhun
The fervours of the mid-day fun;
The pangs of abfence, O remove,
For thou canft place me near my love,
Canft fold in vifionary blifs,
And let me think I fteal a kifs.
  When young-ey'd Spring profufely throws
From her green lap the pink and rofe;
When the foft turtle of the dale
To Summer tells her tender tale,
When Autumn cooling caverns feeks
And ftains with wine his jolly cheeks,
When Winter like poor pilgrim old,
Shakes his filver beard with cold,
At ev'ry feafon let my ear
Thy folemn whifpers, Fancy, hear.

O warm,

O warm, enthufiaftic maid,
Without thy pow'rful, vital aid,
That breathes an energy divine,
That gives a foul to ev'ry line ;
Ne'er may I ftrive with lips profane
To utter an unhallow'd ftrain,
Nor dare to touch the facred ftring
Save when with fmiles thou bid'ft me fing.
O hear our prayer, O hither come
From thy lamented Shakefpear's tomb,
On which thou lov'ft to fit at eve,
Mufing o'er thy darling grave ;
O queen of numbers, once again
Animate fome chofen fwain,
Who fill'd with unexhaufted fire,
May boldly ftrike the founding lyre,
May rife above the rhyming throng,
And with fome new unequall'd fong
O'er all our lift'ning paffions reign,
O'erwhelm our fouls with joy and pain :
With terror fhake, with pity move,
Roufe with revenge, or melt with love.
O deign t' attend his evening walk,
With him in groves and grottos talk :
Teach him to fcorn with frigid art
Feebly to touch th' unraptur'd heart ;
Like lightning, let his mighty verfe
The bofom's inmoft foldings pierce :
With native beauties win applaufe,
Beyond cold critics ftudied laws :
O let each Mufe's fame increafe,
O bid Britannia rival Greece !

WARTON.

M

CHAP.

C H A P.   XVI.

L' A L L E G R O.

HENCE, loathed Melancholy,
 Of Cerberus, and blackeſt midnight born,
In Stygian cave forlorn
'Mongſt horrid ſhapes, and ſhrieks, and ſights unholy
Find out ſome uncouth cell,
 Where brooding darkneſs ſpreads his jealous wings,
And the night raven ſings ;
There under ebon ſhades, and low-brow'd rocks,
As ragged as thy locks,
 In dark Cimmerian deſart ever dwell.
 But come, thou Goddeſs fair and free,
In heav'n 'yclep'd Euphroſyne,
And by men heart-eaſing Mirth,
Whom lovely Venus at a birth
With two ſiſter Graces more
To ivy-crowned Bacchus bore ;
Or whether (as ſome ſages ſing)
The frolic wind that breathes the ſpring,
Zephyr with Aurora playing
As he met her once a maying,
There on beds of violets blue,
And freſh blown roſes waſh'd in dew,
Fill'd her with thee a daughter fair,
So buckſome, blithe, and debonair.
 Haſte thee, nymph, and bring with thee
Jeſt and youthful jollity,
Quips and cranks, and wanton wiles,
Nods, and becks, and wreathed ſmiles,
Such as hang on Hebe's cheek,
And love to live in dimple ſleek ;
Sport that wrinkled care derides,
And laughter holding both his ſides.
Come and trip it as you go
On the light fantaſtic toe ;

And

And in thy right hand lead with thee
The mountain nymph, sweet Liberty ;
And if I give thee honour due,
Mirth, admit me of thy crew,
To live with her, and live with thee,
In unreproved pleasures free :
To hear the lark begin his flight,
And singing startle the dull night,
From his watch-tower in the skies,
Till the dappled dawn doth rise ;
Then to come in spite of sorrow,
And at my window bid good-morrow,
Through the sweet briar or the vine,
Or the twisted eglantine :
While the cock with lively din
Scatters the rear of darkness thin,
And to the stack, or the barn door,
Stoutly struts his dames before :
Oft list'ning how the hounds and horn
Clearly rouse the slumb'ring morn,
From the side of some hoar hill,
Through the high wood echoing shrill :
Some time walking not unseen
By hedge-row elms, on hillocks green,
Right against the eastern gate,
Where the great sun begins his state,
Rob'd in flames, and amber light,
The clouds in thousand liveries dight :
While the plow-man near at hand,
Whistles o'er the furrow'd land,
And the milkmaid singeth blithe,
And the mower whets his scythe,
And every shepherd tells his tale
Under the hawthorn in the dale.
 Straight mine eye hath caught new pleasures,
Whilst the landskip round it measures ;
Russet lawns, and fallows gray,
Where the nibbling flocks do stray :
Mountains on whose barren breast
The labouring clouds do often rest ;

M 2

Meadows

Meadows trim with daisies pied ;
Shallow brooks, and rivers wide :
Towers and battlements it sees
Bosom'd high in tufted trees,
Where perhaps some beauty lies,
The Cynosure of neighbouring eyes.
Hard by a cottage chimney smokes,
From betwixt two aged oaks,
Where Corydon and Thyrsis met,
Are at their savoury dinner set
Of herbs, and other country messes,
Which the neat-handed Phillis dresses ;
And then in haste her bower she leaves,
With Thestylis to bind his sheaves ;
Or if the earlier season lead
To the tann'd haycock in the mead.
   Sometimes with secure delight
The upland hamlet will invite,
When the merry bells ring round,
And the jocund rebecks sound
To many a youth and many a maid,
Dancing in the chequer'd shade ;
And young and old come forth to play
On a sunshine holiday,
Till the live-long day-light fail ;
Then to the spicy nut brown ale,
With stories told of many a feat,
How Fairy-Mab the junkets eat ;
She was pincht, and pull'd, she said,
And he by friars lanthorn led ;
Tells how the drudging Goblin swet
To earn his cream-bowl duly set,
When in one night, ere glimpse of morn
His shadowy flail hath thresh'd the corn
That ten day-labourers could not end,
Then lies him down the lubbar fiend,
And stretch'd out all the chimney's length,
Basks at the fire his hairy strength ;
And crop-full out of doors he flings
Ere the first cock his mattin rings.

Thus

Thus done the tales, to bed they creep,
By whifpering winds foon lull'd afleep.
  Tow'red cities pleafe us then,
And the bufy hum of men,
Where throngs of knights and barons bold,
In weeds of peace high triumphs hold,
With ftores of ladies, whofe bright eyes
Rain influence, and judge the prize
Of wit or arms, while both contend
To win her grace, whom all commend.
There let Hymen oft appear
In faffron robe with taper clear,
And pomp, and feaft, and revelry,
With mafk, and antique pageantry.
Such fights as youthful poets dream
On fummer eves by haunted ftream.
Then to the well-trod ftage anon,
If Johnfon's learned fock be on,
Or fweeteft Shakefpear, fancy's child,
Warble his native wood-notes wild.
  And ever againft eating cares,
Lap me in foft Lydian airs,
Married to immortal verfe,
Such as the meeting foul may pierce,
In notes with many a winding bout
Of linked fweetnefs long drawn out,
With wanton heed, and giddy cunning ;
The melting voice thro' mazes running ;
Untwifting all the chains that tie
The hidden foul of Harmony :
That Orpheus' felf may heave his head
From golden flumber on a bed
Of heap'd Elyfian flowers, and hear
Such ftrains as would have won the ear
Of Pluto, to have quite fet free
His half-regain'd Eurydice.
  Thefe delights if thou canft give,
Mirth, with thee I mean to live.

MILTON.

M 3 C H A P.

C H A P. XVII.

Il. PENSEROSO.

HENCE, vain deluding joys,
    The brood of folly without father bred !
How little you befted.
      Or fill the fixed mind with all your toys!
Dwell in fome idle brain,
And fancies fond with gaudy fhapes poffefs,
As thick and numberlefs
      As the gay motes that people the fun-beams,
Or likeft hovering dreams,
      The fickle penfioners of Morpheus train.
  But hail, thou Goddefs, fage and holy,
Hail, divineft Melancholy,
Whofe faintly vifage is too bright
To hit the fenfe of human fight ;
And therefore to our weaker view,
O'erlaid with black, ftaid wifdom's hue,
Black, but fuch as in efteem,
Prince Memnon's fifter might befeem,
Or that ftarr'd Ethiope queen that ftrove
To fet her beauties praife above
The fea nymphs, and their powers offended :
Yet thou art higher far defcended,
Thee bright-hair'd Vefta long of yore
To folitary Saturn bore ;
His daughter fhe (in Saturn's reign
Such mixture was not held a ftrain)
Oft in glimmering bowers, and glades
He met her, and in fecret fhades
Of woody Ida's inmoft grove,
While yet there was no fear of Jove.
  Come, penfive nun, devout and pure,
Sober, ftedfaft, and demure,
All in a robe of darkeft grain,
Flowing with majeftic train,

And

And fable ftole of cyprefs lawn,
Over thy decent fhoulders drawn,
Come, but keep thy wonted ftate,
With even ftep, and mufing gait,
And looks commercing with the fkies,
Thy rapt foul fitting in thine eyes :
There held in holy paffion ftill,
Forget thyfelf to marble, till
With a fad leaden downward caft,
Thou fix them on the earth as faft.
And join with thee calm Peace, and Quiet,
Spare Faft, that oft with gods doth diet,
And hear the Mufes in a ring,
Ay round about Jove's altar fing.
And add to thefe retired Leifure,
That in trim gardens takes his pleafure ;
But firft, and chiefeft, with thee bring,
Him that yon foars on golden wing,
Guiding the fiery wheeled throne,
The Cherub Contemplation :
And the mute filence hift along,
'Lefs Philomel will deign a fong,
In her fweeteft, faddeft plight
Smoothing the rugged-brow of night,
While Cynthia checks her dragon yoke,
Gently o'er the accuftom'd oak ;
Sweet bird, that fhunn'ft the noife of folly,
Moft mufical, moft melancholy ?
Thee, chauntrefs, oft the woods among,
I woo to hear thy ev'ning fong :
And miffing thee, I walk unfeen
On the dry fmooth-fhaven green,
To behold the wandering moon,
Riding near her higheft noon,
Like one that had been led aftray
Through the heav'n's wide pathlefs way ;
And oft as if her head fhe bow'd,
Stooping through a fleecy cloud.
Oft on a plat of rifing ground,
I hear the far-off Curfeu found,

M 4

Over

Over fome wide-water'd fhore,
Swinging flow with fullen roar.
  Or if the air will not permit,
Some ftill removed place will fit,
Where glowing embers through the room
Teach light to counterfeit a gloom,
Far from all refort of mirth
Save the cricket on the hearth,
Or the belman's drowfy charm,
To blefs the doors from nightly harm.
  Or let my lamp at midnight hour,
Be feen in fome high lonely tow'r
Where I may oft out-watch the Bear,
With thrice great Hermes, or unfphere
The fpirit of Plato, to unfold
What worlds, or what vaft regions hold
The immortal mind that hath forfook
Her manfion in this flefhly nook :
And of thofe Dæmons that are found
In fire, air, flood, or under ground,
Whofe power hath a true confent
With planet, or with element.
  Sometime let gorgeous Tragedy
In fcepter'd pall come fweeping by,
Prefenting Thebes, or Pelops line,
Or the tale of Troy divine,
Or what (though rare) of later age,
Ennobl'd hath the bufkin'd ftage.
  But, O fad virgin, that thy power
Might raife Mufæus from his bower,
Or bid the foul of Orpheus fing
Such notes as warbled to the ftring,
Drew iron tears down Pluto's cheek,
And made hell grant what love did feek,
Or call up him that left half-told
The ftory of Cambufcan bold,
Of Camball, and of Algarfife,
And who had Canace to wife,
That own'd the virtuous ring and glafs,
And of the wondrous horfe of brafs,

On

On which the Tartar king did ride ;
And if aught elfe, great bards befide,
In fage and folemn tunes have fung,
Of tourneys and of trophies hung ;
Of forefts, and inchantments drear,
Where more is meant than meets the ear.
   Thus night oft fee me in thy pale career,
Till civil-fuited morn appear,
Not trick'd and flounc'd as fhe was wont,
With the Attic boy to hunt,
But kerchef'd in a comely cloud,
While rocking winds are piping loud,
Or ufher'd with a fhower ftill,
When the guft hath blown his fill,
Ending on the ruftling leaves,
With minute drops from off the eaves.
   And when the fun begins to fling
His flaring beams, me, Goddefs, bring
To arched walks of twilight groves,
And fhadows brown that Sylvan loves
Of pine or monumental oak,
Where the rude ax with heaved ftroke,
Was never heard the nymphs to daunt,
Or fright them from their hallow'd haunt.
There in clofe covert by fome brook,
Where no profaner eye may look,
Hide me from day's garifh eye,
While the bee with honied thigh,
That at her flow'ry work doth fing,
And the waters murmuring,
With fuch concert as they keep,
Entice the dewy-feather'd fleep :
And let fome ftrange myfterious dream,
Wave at his wings in airy ftream
Of lively portraiture difplay'd,
Softly on my eye-lids laid :
And as I wake fweet mufic breathe
Above, about, or underneath,
Sent by fome fpirit to mortals good,
Or th' unfeen Genius of the wood.
M 5

But

But let my due feet never fail
To walk the ftudious cloyfters pale,
And love the high embowed roof,
With antique pillars maffy proof,
And ftoried windows richly dight,
Cafting a dim religious light.
There let the pealing organ blow,
To the full voiced quire below,
In fervice high, and anthems clear,
As may with fweetnefs, through mine ear
Diffolv me into extafies,
And bring all heav'n before mine eyes.
    And may at laft my weary age
Find out the peaceful hermitage,
The hairy gown and moffy cell,
Where I may fit and rightly fpell,
Of every ftar that heav'n doth fhew,
And ev'ry herb that fips the dew :
Till old experience do attain
To fomething like prophetic ftrain.
    Thefe pleafures, Melancholy, give,
And I with thee will choofe to live.

MILTON.

C H A P.   XVIII.

THE PROGRESS OF LIFE.

ALL the world's a ftage,
    And all the men and women merely players;
They have their exits and their entrances,
And one man in his time plays many parts :
His acts being feven ages. At firft the infant,
Mewling and puking in the nurfe's arms.
And then the whining fchool-boy, with his fatchel,
And fhining morning face, creeping like fnail
Unwillingly to fchool. And then the lover,
Sighing like furnace, with a woful ballad
Made to his miftrefs' eye-brow. Then the foldier
Full of ftrange oaths, and bearded like the pard,

Jealous

Jealous in honour, fudden and quick in quarrel;
Seeking the bubble reputation.
Even in the cannon's mouth.   And then the juftice,
In fair round belly, with good capon lin'd,
With eyes fevere, and beard of formal cut,
Full of wife faws and modern inftances,
And fo he plays his part.   The fixth age fhifts
Into the lean and flipper'd pantaloon,
With fpectacles on nofe, and pouch on fide;
His youthful hofe well faved; a world too wide
For his fhrunk fhank; and his big manly voice,
Turning again toward childifh treble, pipes,
And whiftles in his found.   Laft fcene of all,
That ends this ftrange eventful hiftory,
Is fecond childifhnefs, and mere oblivion,
Sans teeth, fans eyes, fans tafte, fans every thing.
Shakespear.

C H A P.   XIX.

The ENTRY of BOLINGBROKE and RICHARD into LONDON.

Duch. **M**Y Lord, you told me, you would tell
the reft,
When weeping made you break the ftory off,
Of our two coufins coming into London.
    York.   Where did I leave?
    Duch.   At that fad ftop, my Lord,
Where rude mifgovern'd hands, from window-tops,
Threw duft and rubbifh on King Richard's head.
    York.   Then, as I faid, the Duke, great Bo-
lingbroke,
Mounted upon a hot and fiery fteed,
Which his afpiring rider feem'd to know,
With flow, but ftately pace, kept on his courfe;
While all tongues cry'd, God fave thee, Bolingbroke!
You would have thought the very windows fpake,
So many greedy looks of young and old
Through cafements darted their defiring eyes

Upon

Upon his vifage; and that all the walls
With painted imag'ry had faid at once,
Jefus preferve thee! welcome, Bolingbroke!
Whilft he, from one fide to the other turning,
Bare-headed, lower than his proud fteed's neck,
Befpoke them thus: I thank you, countrymen;
And thus ftill doing, thus he pafs'd along.
    Duch. Alas! poor Richard, where rides he the
        while?
    York. As in a theatre, the eyes of men,
After a well-grac'd actor leaves the ftage,
Are idly bent on him that enters next,
Thinking his prattle to be tedious:
Even fo, or with much more contempt, men's eyes
Did fcowl on Richard; no man cry'd, God fave him!
No joyful tongue gave him his welcome home:
But duft was thrown upon his facred head;
Which with fuch gentle forrow he fhook off,
(His face ftill combating with tears and fmiles
The badges of his grief and patience)
That had not God, for fome ftrong purpofe, fteel'd
The hearts of men, they muft perforce have melted,
And barbarifm itfelf have pitied him.
But Heaven hath a hand in thefe events,
To whofe high will we bound our calm contents.
                    Shakespear.

C H A P. XX.

L I F E.

——REASON thus with life:
    If I do lofe thee, I do lofe a thing
That none but fools would reck; a breath thou art,
Servile to all the fkiey influences,
That do this habitation, where thou keep'ft,
Hourly afflict: merely thou art death's fool;
For him thou labour'ft by thy flight to fhun,
And yet runn'ft tow'rd him ftill. Thou art noble;
For all th' accommodations, that thou bear'ft,

                        Are

Are nurs'd by bafenefs : thou'rt by no means valiant;
For thou doft fear the foft and tender fork
Of a poor worm. Thy beft of reft is fleep,
And that thou oft provok'ft; yet grofsly fear'ft
Thy death, which is no more. Thou'rt not thyfelf;
For thou exift'ft on many a thoufand grains,
That iffue out of duft. Happy thou art not;
For what thou haft not, ftill thou ftriv'ft to get;.
And what thou haft, forget'ft. Thou art not certain;
For thy complexion fhifts to ftrange effects,
After the moon. If thou art rich, thou'rt poor;
For, like an afs, whofe back with ingots bows,
Thou bear'ft thy heavy riches but a-journey,
And death unloadeth thee. Friend thou haft none;
For thy own bowels, which do call thee fire,
The mere effufion of thy proper loins,
Do curfe the Gout, Serpigo, and the Rheum,
For ending thee no fooner. Thou haft nor youth
            nor age;
But as it were an after dinner's fleep,
Dreaming on both; for pall'd, thy blazed youth
Becomes affuaged, and both beg the alms
Of palfied Eld; and when thou'rt old and rich,
Thou haft neither heat, affection, limb, nor bounty,
To make thy riches pleafant. What's yet in this
That bears the name of life? yet in this life
Lie hid more thoufand deaths; yet death we fear,
That makes thefe odds all even.

SHAKESPEAR.

C H A P.   XXI.

HOTSPUR's DESCRIPTION of a FOP.

I REMEMBER, when the fight was done,
   When I was dry with rage, and extreme toil,
Breathlefs and faint, leaning upon my fword;
Came there a certain Lord, neat, trimly drefs'd;
Frefh as a bridegroom, and his chin, new reap'd,
Shew'd like a ftubble-land at harveft home.

He

He was perfumed like a milliner;
And 'twixt his finger and his thumb he held
A pouncet-box, which ever and anon
He gave his nofe; and took't away again;
Who, therewith angry, when it next came there,
Took it in fnuff.——And ftill he fmil'd and talk'd;
And as the foldiers bare dead bodies by,
He call'd them untaught knaves, unmannerly,
To bring a flovenly, unhandfome corfe
Betwixt the wind, and his nobility.
With many holiday and lady terms.
He queftion'd me : amongft the reft demanded
My prifoners, in your majefty's behalf.
I then, all fmarting with my wounds, being gall'd
To be fo pefter'd with a popinjay,
Out of my grief, and my impatience,
Anfwer'd neglectingly, I know not what :
He fhould, or fhould not; for he made me mad;
To fee him fhine fo brifk, and fmell fo fweet,
And talk fo like a waiting gentle-woman,
Of guns, and drums, and wounds; (God fave the
       mark !)
And telling me the fovereign'ft thing on earth
Was parmacity, for an inward bruife;
And that it was great pity, fo it was,
This villainous fali-petre fhould be digg'd
Out of the bowels of the harmlefs earth
Which many a good tall fellow had deftroy'd:
So cowardly : and but for thefe vile guns,
He would himfelf have been a foldier.

SHAKESPEAR.

C H A P. XXII.

CLARENCE's DREAM.

Clarence and Brakenbury.

Brak. WHY looks your grace so heavily to-
day?
  Clar. O, I have pass'd a miserable night,.
So full of ugly sights, of ghastly dreams,
That, as I am a Christian faithful man,
I would not spend another such a night,
Though 'twere to buy a world of happy days;.
So full of dismal terror was the time.
    Brak. What was your dream, my lord? I
pray you tell me.
  Clar. Methought that I had broken from the
Tower,
And was imbark'd to cross to Burgundy,
And in my company my brother Glo'ster;
Who from my cabin tempted me to walk
Upon the hatches.   Thence we look'd tow'rd Eng-
land,
And cited up a thousand heavy times,
During the wars of York and Lancaster,
That had befall'n us.   As we pass'd along
Upon the giddy footing of the hatches,
Methought that Glo'ster stumbled, and in falling
Struck me (that sought to stay him) over-board,
Into the tumbling billows of the main.
    Lord, Lord, methought, what pain it was to
drown!
What dreadful noise of water in my ears!
What sights of ugly death within mine eyes!
I thought I saw a thousand fearful wrecks;
A thousand men, that fishes gnaw'd upon;
Wedges of gold, great anchors, heaps of pearl,
Inestimable stones, unvalued jewels.
Some lay in dead men's sculls; and in those holes
Where eyes did once inhabit, there were crept,

As

As 'twere in fcorn of eyes, reflecting gems;
That woo'd the flimy bottom of the deep,
And mock'd the dead bones that lay fcatter'd by.
    Brak. Had you fuch leifure in the time of death,
To gaze upon the fecrets of the deep?
    Clar. Methought I had; and often did I ftrive.
To yield the ghoft;. but ftill the envious flood
Kept in my foul, and would not let it forth
To find the empty, vaft, and wandering air;
But fmother'd it within my panting bulk,
Which almoft burft to belch it in the fea.
    Brak. Awak'd you not with this fore agony?
    Clar. No, no; my dream was lengthen'd after
        life.
O then began the tempeft to my foul:
I pafs'd, methought, the melancholy flood,
With that grim ferryman which poets write of,
Unto the kingdom of perpetual night.
The firft that there did greet my ftranger-foul,
Was my great father-in-law, renowned Warwick,
Who cry'd aloud—What fcourge for perjury
Can this dark monarchy afford falfe Clarence?
And fo he vanifh'd.. Then came wand'ring by
A fhadow like an angel, with bright hair
Dabbled in blood, and he fhriek'd out aloud——
Clarence is come, falfe, fleeting, perjur'd Clarence,
That ftabb'd me in the field of Tewkfbury;
Seize on him, furies, take him to your torments!——
With that, methought, a legion of foul fiends
Inviron'd me, and howled in mine ears
Such hideous cries, that with the very noife
I trembling waked; and for a feafon after
Could not believe but what I was in hell:
Such terrible impreffion made my dream.
    Brak. No marvel, Lord, that it affrighted
        you;
I am afraid, methinks, to hear you tell it.
    Clar. Ah! Brakenbury, I have done thofe
        things
That now give evidence againft my foul,
For Edward's fake; and fee how he requites me!
                 O God!

O God! if my deep prayers cannot appeafe thee,
But thou wilt be aveng'd on my mifdeeds,
Yet execute thy wrath on me alone;
O fpare my guiltlefs wife, and my poor children!
I pr'ythee, Brakenbury, ftay by me?
My foul is heavy, and I fain would fleep.

SHAKESPEAR.

CHAP. XXIII.

QUEEN MAB.

O THEN I fee Queen Mab hath been with you.
She is the fairies' midwife, and fhe comes
In fhape no bigger than an agate-ftone
On the fore-finger of an alderman;
Drawn with a team of little atomies,
Athwart men's nofes as they lie afleep:
Her waggon-fpokes made of long fpinners' legs;
The cover of the wings of grafhoppers;
The traces of the fmalleft fpider's web;
The collars of the moonfhine's watery beams;
Her whip of cricket's bone; the lafh of film;
Her waggoner a fmall gray-coated gnat.
Not half fo big as a round little worm,
Prick'd from the lazy finger of a maid.
Her chariot is an empty hazel-nut,
Made by the joiner fquirrel, or old grub,
Time out of mind the fairies' coach-makers,
And in this ftate fhe gallops; night by night,
Through lovers' brains, and then they dream of
      love:
On courtiers' knees, that dream on courtfies ftrait:
O'er lawyers' fingers, who ftrait dream on fees:
O'er ladies' lips, who ftrait on kiffes dream;
Sometimes fhe gallops o'er a courtier's nofe,
And then dreams he of fmelling out a fuit:
And fometimes comes fhe with a tithe-pig's tail,
Tickling the parfon as he lies afleep;
Then dreams he of another benefice.

Some

Sometimes she driveth o'er a soldier's neck,
And then he dreams of cutting foreign throats,
Of breaches, ambuscadoes, Spanish blades,
Of healths five fathom deep; and then anon
Drums in his ears, at which he starts and wakes;
And being thus frighted, swears a prayer or two,
And sleeps again.

SHAKESPEAR.

CHAP. XXIV.

APOTHECARY.

I DO remember an apothecary,
  And hereabouts he dwells, whom late I noted
In tatter'd weeds, with overwhelming brows,
Culling of simples; meagre were his looks;
Sharp Misery had worn him to the bones:
And in his needy shop a tortoise hung,
An alligator stuff'd, and other skins
Of ill-shap'd fishes; and about his shelves
A beggarly account of empty boxes;
Green earthen pots, bladders, and musty seeds,
Remnants of pack-thread, and old cakes of roses
Were thinly scatter'd to make up a show.
Noting his penury, to myself I said,
An' if a man did need a poison now,
Whose sale is present death in Mantua,
Here lives a caitiff wretch would sell it him.
Oh, this same thought did but fore-run my need,
And this same needy man must sell it me.
As I remember, this should be the house.
Being holiday, the beggar's shop is shut.

SHAKESPEAR.

CHAP.

C H A P.   XXV.

ODE to EVENING.

IF aught of oaten ftop, or paftoral fong,
  May hope, chafte Eve, to footh thy modeft ear,
      Like thy own folemn fprings,
      Thy fprings, and dying gales,
O Nymph referv'd, while now the bright-hair'd fun
Sits on yon weftern tent, whofe cloudy fkirts
      With brede ethereal wove,
      O'erhang his wavy bed :
Now air is hufh'd, fave where the weak-ey'd bat,
With fhort fhrill fhrieks flits on by leathern wing,
      Or where the beetle winds
      His fmall but fullen horn,
As oft he rifes 'midft the twilight path,
Againft the pilgrim borne in heedlefs hum.
      Now teach me, maid compos'd,
      To breathe fome foften'd ftrain,
Whofe numbers ftealing through thy dark'ning vale,
May not unfeemly with its ftillnefs fuit,
      As mufing flow, I hail
      Thy genial lov'd return !
For when thy folding ftar arifing fhews
His paly circlet, at his warning lamp
      The fragrant Hours, and Elves
      Who flept in flow'rs the day,
And many a Nymph who wreathes her brows with
        fedge,
And fheds the frefh'ning dew, and lovelier ftill,
      The penfive Pleafures fweet
      Prepare thy fhadowy car.
Then lead, calm Vot'refs, where fome fheety lake
Cheers the lone heath, or fome time-hallow'd pile,
      Or up-land fallows grey
      Reflect its laft cool gleam.
But when chill bluft'ring winds, or driving rain,
Forbid my willing feet, be mine the hut,
                    That

That from the mountain's fide,
Views wilds, and fwelling floods,
And hamlets brown, and dim-difcover'd fpires,
And hears their fimple bell, and marks o'er all
Thy dewy fingers draw
The gradual dufky veil.
While Spring fhall pour his fhow'rs, as oft he wont,
And bathe thy breathing treffes, meekeft Eve!
While Summer loves to fport
Beneath thy ling'ring light;
While fallow Autumn fills thy lap with leaves;
Or Winter yelling through the troublous air,
Affrights thy fhrinking train,
And rudely rends thy robes;
So long, fure-found beneath the Sylvan fhed,
Shall Fancy, Friendfhip, Science, rofe-lip'd Health,
Thy gentleft influence own,
And hymn thy fav'rite name!

Collins.

C H A P.   XXVI.

ODE to SPRING.

SWEET daughter of a rough and ftormy fire,
Hoar Winter's blooming child; delightful
Spring!
Whofe unfhorn locks with leaves
And fwelling buds are crown'd;

From the green iflands of eternal youth,
(Crown'd with frefh blooms, and ever fpringing
fhade)
Turn, hither turn thy ftep,
O thou, whofe powerful voice:

More fweet than fofteft touch of Doric reed,
Or Lydian flute, can footh the madding winds,
And thro' the ftormy deep
Breathe thy own tender calm.

Thee,

Thee, beft belov'd! the virgin train await
With fongs and feftal rites, and joy to rove
      Thy blooming wilds among,
      And vales and dewy lawns,

With untir'd feet; and cull thy earlieft fweets
To weave frefh garlands for the glowing brow
      Of him, the favour'd youth
      That prompts their whifper'd figh.

Unlock thy copious ftores; thofe tender fhowers
That drop their fweetnefs on the infant buds,
      And filent dews that fwell
      The milky ear's green ftem,

And feed the flowering ofier's early fhoots;
And call thofe winds which thro' the whifpering
          boughs
      With warm and pleafant breath
      Salute the blowing flowers.

Now let me fit beneath the whitening thorn,
And mark thy fpreading tints fteal o'er the dale;
      And watch with patient eye
      Thy fair unfolding charms.

O Nymph, approach! while yet the temperate fun
With bafhful forehead, thro' the cool moift air
      Throws his young maiden beams,
      And with chafte kiffes wooes

The earth's fair bofom; while the ftreaming veil
Of lucid clouds with kind and frequent fhade
      Protects thy modeft blooms
      From his feverer blaze.

Sweet is thy reign, but fhort; the red dog-ftar
Shall fcorch thy treffes, and the mower's fcythe
      Thy greens, the flow'rets all,
      Remorfelefs fhall deftroy.

Reluctant

Reluctant ſhall I bid thee then farewel ;
For O, not all that Autumn's lap contains,
    Nor Summer's ruddieſt fruits,
    Can aught for thee atone,
Fair Spring ! whoſe ſimpleſt promiſe more delights
Than all their largeſt wealth, and thro' the heart
    Each joy and new-born hope
    With ſofteſt influence breathes.
               MRS. BARBAULD.

C H A P. XXVII.

DOMESTIC LOVE AND HAPPINESS.

O HAPPY they ! the happieſt of their kind !
   Whom gentler ſtars unite, and in one fate
Their hearts, their fortunes and their beings blend.
'Tis not the coarſer tie of human laws,
Unnatural oft, and foreign to the mind,
That binds their peace, but harmony itſelf,
Attuning all their paſſions into love ;
Where friendſhip full-exerts her ſofteſt power,
Perfect eſteem enliven'd by deſire
Ineffable, and ſympathy of ſoul ;
Thought meting thought, and will preventing will,
With boundleſs confidence : for nought but love
Can anſwer love, and render bliſs ſecure.
Let him, ungenerous, who, alone intent
To bleſs himſelf, from ſordid parents buys
The loathing virgin, in eternal care,
Well-merited, conſume his nights and days ·
Let barbarous nations, whoſe inhuman love
Is wild deſire, fierce as the ſuns they feel ;
Let eaſtern tyrants from the light of Heaven
Seclude their boſom-ſlaves, meanly poſſeſs'd
Of a mere lifeleſs, violated form :
While thoſe whom love cements in holy faith,
And equal tranſport, free as nature live,
Diſdaining fear. What is the world to them,

                      Its

Its pomp, its pleasure, and its nonsense all ?
Who in each other clasp whatever fair
High fancy forms, and lavish hearts can wish ;
Something than beauty dearer, should they look
Or on the mind, or mind-illumin'd face ;
Truth, goodness, honour, harmony and love,
The richest bounty of indulgent Heaven.
Mean-time a smiling offspring rises round,
And mingles both their graces.   By degrees,
The human blossom blows ; and every day,
Soft as it rolls along, shews some new charm,
The father's lustre, and the mother's bloom.
Then infant reason grows apace, and calls
For the kind hand of an assiduous care.
Delightful task ! to rear the tender thought,
To teach the young idea how to shoot,
To pour the fresh instruction o'er the mind,
To breathe th' enlivening spirit, and to fix
The generous purpose in the glowing breast.
Oh speak the joy ! ye, whom the sudden tear
Surprises often, while you look around,
And nothing strikes your eye but sights of bliss ;
All various Nature pressing on the heart ;
An elegant sufficiency, content,
Retirement, rural quiet, friendship, books,
Ease and alternate labour, useful life,
Progressive virtue, and approving Heaven.
These are the matchless joys of virtuous love ;
And thus their moments fly.   The Seasons thus,
As ceaseless round a jarring world they roll,
Still find them happy ; and consenting Spring
Sheds her own rosy garland on their heads :
Till evening comes at last, serene and mild ;
When after the long vernal day of life,
Enamour'd more, as more remembrance swells
With many a proof of recollected love,
Together down they sink in social sleep ;
Together freed, their gentle spirits fly
To scenes where love and bliss immortal reign.
Thomson.

C H A P.

C H A P. XXVIII.

The PLEASURES of RETIREMENT.

O KNEW he but his happiness, of men
The happiest he ! who far from public rage,
Deep in the vale, with a choice few retir'd,
Drinks the pure pleasures of the rural life.
What tho' the dome be wanting, whose proud gate,
Each morning, vomits out the sneaking croud
Of flatterers false, and in their turn abus'd ?
Vile intercourse ! What tho' the glittering robe,
Of every hue reflected light can give,
Or floating loose, or stiff with mazy gold,
The pride and gaze of fools ! oppress him not ?
What tho', from utmost land and sea purvey'd,
For him each rarer tributary life
Bleeds not, and his insatiate table heaps
With luxury, and death ? What tho' his bowl
Flames not with costly juice ; nor sunk in beds,
Oft of gay care, he tosses out the night,
Or melts the thoughtless hours in idle state ?
What tho' he knows not those fantastic joys,
That still amuse the wanton, still deceive ;
A face of pleasure, but a heart of pain :
Their hollow moments undelighted all ?
Sure peace is his ; a solid life, enstrang'd
To disappointment, and fallacious hope ;
Rich in content, in Nature's bounty rich,
In herbs and fruits ; whatever greens the Spring,
When heaven descends in showers ; or bends the bough
When Summer reddens. and when Autumn beams ;
Or in the wintry glebe whatever lies
Conceal'd, and fattens with the richest sap :
These are not wanting ; nor the milky drove,
Luxuriant, spread o'er all the lowing vale ;
Nor bleating mountains ; nor the chide of streams,
And hum of bees, inviting sleep sincere
Into the guiltless breast, beneath the shade,

Or

Or thrown at large amid the fragrant hay;
Nor aught befides of profpect, grove, or fong,
Dim grottoes, gleaming lakes, and fountain clear.
Here too dwells fimple truth; plain innocence;
Unfullied beauty; found unbroken youth,
Patient of labour, with a little pleas'd;
Health ever blooming; unambitious toil;
Calm contemplation, and poetic eafe.
    The rage of nations, and the crufh of ftates,
Move not the man, who, from the world efcap'd,
In ftill retreats, and flowery folitudes,
To Nature's voice attends, from month to month,
And day to day, thro' the revolving year,
Admiring, fees her in her every fhape;
Feels all her fweet emotions at his heart;
Takes what fhe liberal gives, nor thinks of more.
He, when young Spring protrudes the burfting gems,
Marks the firft bud, and fucks the healthful gale
Into his frefhened foul; her genial hours
He full enjoys; and not a beauty blows,
And not an opening bloffom breathes in vain.
In Summer he, beneath the living fhade,
Such as o'er frigid Tempe wont to wave,
Or Hemus cool, reads what the Mufe, of thefe
Perhaps, has in immortal numbers fung;
Or what fhe dictates writes; and oft an eye
Shot round, rejoices in the vigorous year.
When Autumn's yellow luftre gilds the world,
And tempts the fickled fwain into the field,
Seiz'd by the general joy, his heart diftends
With gentle throws; and, thro' the tepid gleams
Deep mufing, then he beft exerts his fong.
Even Winter wild to him is full of blifs.
The mighty tempeft, and the hoary wafte,
Abrupt, and deep, ftretch'd o'er the buried earth,
Awake to folemn thought. At night the fkies,
Difclos'd, and kindled, by refining froft,
Pour every luftre on th' exalted eye.
A friend, a book, the ftealing hours fecure,
And mark them down for wifdom. With fwift wing,

O'er land and fea th' imagination roams;
Or truth, divinely breaking on his mind,
Elates his being, and unfolds his powers;
Or in his breaft heroic virtue burns.
The touch of kindred too and love he feels;
The modeft eye, whofe beams on his alone
Extatic fhine; the little ftrong embrace
Of prattling children, twin'd around his neck,
And emulous to pleafe him, calling forth
The fond parental foul.   Nor purpofe gay,
Amufement, dance, or fong, he fternly fcorns;
For happinefs and true philofophy
Are of the focial ftill, and fmiling kind.
This is the life which thofe who fret in guilt,
And guilty cities, never knew; the life,
Led by primeval ages, uncorrupt,
When Angels dwelt, and God himfelf, with Man!

Thomson.

C H A P.   XXIX.

G E N I U S.

FROM heav'n my ftrains begin; from heav'n defcends
The flame of genius to the human breaft,
And love and beauty, and poetic joy
And infpiration.   Erè the radiant fun
Sprang from the eaft, or 'mid the vault of night
The moon fufpended her ferener lamp;
Ere mountains, woods, or ftreams adorn'd the globe,
Or wifdom taught the fons of men her lore;
Then liv'd th' almighty One: then deep retir'd,
In his unfathom'd effence, view'd the forms,
The forms eternal of created things;
The radiant fun, the moon's nocturnal lamp,
The mountains, woods and ftreams, the rolling globe,
And wifdom's mien celeftial.   From the firft
Of days, on them his love divine he fix'd,
His admiration: till in time compleat,
What he admir'd and lov'd, his vital fmile

Unfolded

Unfolded into being.   Hence the breath
Of life informing each organic frame,
Hence the green earth, and wild refounding waves;
Hence light and fhade alternate; warmth and cold;
And clear autumnal fkies and vernal fhow'rs,
And all the fair variety of things.
    But not alike to every mortal eye
Is this great fcene unveil'd.   For fince the claims
Of focial life, to diff'rent labours urge
The active pow'rs of man; with wife intent
The hand of nature on peculiar minds
Imprints a diff'rent bias, and to each
Decrees its province in the common toil.
To fome fhe taught the fabric of the fphere,
The changeful moon, the circuit of the ftars,
The golden zones of heav'n: to fome fhe gave
To weigh the moment of eternal things,
Of time, and fpace, and fate's unbroken chain,
And will's quick impulfe: others by the hand
She led o'er vales and mountains, to explore
What healing virtue fwells the tender veins
Of herbs and flow'rs; or what the beams of morn
Draw forth, diftilling from the clifted rind
In balmy tears.   But fome to higher hopes
Were deftin'd; fome within a finer mould
She wrought, and temper'd with a purer flame.
To thefe the fire omnipotent unfolds
The world's harmonious volume, there to read
The tranfcript of himfelf.   On every part
They trace the bright impreffions of his hand:
In earth or air, the meadow's purple ftores,
The moon's mild radiance, or the virgin's form
Blooming with rofy fmiles, they fee pourtray'd
That uncreated beauty, which delights
The Mind fupreme.   They alfo feel her charms,
Enamour'd; they partake th' eternal joy.

Akenside.

N 2 C H A P.

C H A P. XXX.

G R E A T N E S S.

SAY, why was man so eminently rais'd
Amid the vast creation; why ordain'd
Thro' life and death to dart his piercing eye,
With thoughts beyond the limit of his frame;
But that th' Omnipotent might send him forth
In sight of mortal and immortal powers,
As on a boundless theatre, to run
The great career of justice; to exalt
His gen'rous aim to all diviner deeds;
To chase each partial purpose from his breast;
And thro' the mists of passion and of sense,
And thro' the tossing tide of chance and pain,
To hold his course unfalt'ring, while the voice
Of truth and virtue, up the steep ascent
Of nature, calls him to his high reward,
Th' applauding smile of Heav'n? Else wherefore
     burns
In mortal bosoms this unquenched hope,
That breathes from day to day sublimer things,
And mocks possession? Wherefore darts the mind,
With such resistless ardour to embrace
Majestic forms: impatient to be free,
Spurning the gross controul of wilful might;
Proud of the strong contention of her toils;
Proud to be daring? Who but rather turns
To Heav'n's broad fire his unconstrained view,
Than to the glimmering of a waxen flame?
Who that, from Alpine heights, his lab'ring eye
Shoots round the wide horizon, to survey
Nilus or Ganges rolling his bright wave
Thro' mountains, plains, thro' empires black with
     shade,
And continents of sand; will turn his gaze
To mark the windings of a scanty rill
That murmurs at his feet? The high-born soul
                      Disdains

Difdains to reft her heav'n afpiring wing
Beneath its native quarry.   Tir'd of earth
And this diurnal fcene, fhe fprings aloft
Thro' fields of air; purfues the flying ftorm;
Rides on the volley'd lightning thro' the heav'ns;
Or yok'd with whirlwinds and the northern blaft,
Sweeps the long tract of day. Then high fhe foars
The blue profound, and hovering round the fun
Beholds him pouring the redundant ftream
Of light; beholds his unrelenting fway
Bend the reluctant planets to abfolve
The fated rounds of time.   Thence far effus'd
She darts her fwiftnefs up the long career
Of devious comets; thro' its burning figns
Exulting meafures the perennial wheel
Of nature, and looks back on all the ftars,
Whofe blended light, as with a milky zone,
Invefts the orient.   Now amaz'd fhe views
Th' empyreal wafte, where happy fpirits hold,
Beyond this concave heav'n, their calm abode;
And fields of radiance, whofe unfading light
Has travell'd the profound fix thoufand years,
Nor yet arrives in fight of mortal things.
Ev'n on the barriers of the world untir'd
She meditates th' eternal depth below;
Till, half recoiling, down the headlong fteep
She plunges; foon o'erwhelm'd and fwallow'd up
In that immenfe of being.   There her hopes
Reft at the fated goal.   For from the birth
Of mortal man, the fovereign Maker faid,
That not in humble nor in brief delight,
Not in the fading echoes of renown,
Pow'r's purple robes, nor pleafure's flow'ry lap,
The foul fhould find enjoyment: but from thefe
Turning difdainful to an equal good,
Thro' all th' afcent of things enlarge her view,
Till every bound at length fhould difappear,
And infinite perfection clofe the fcene.

Akenside.

N 3 C H A P.

CHAP. XXXI.

NOVELTY.

CALL now to mind that high capacious pow'rs
Life folded up in man; how far beyond
The praise of mortals, may th' eternal growth
Of nature to perfection half divine,
Expand the blooming foul. What pity then
Should floth's unkindly fogs deprefs to earth
Her tender bloffom; choak the ftreams of life,
And blaft her fpring! Far otherwife defign'd
Almighty wifdom; nature's happy cares
'Th' obedient heart far otherwife incline.
Witnefs the fprightly joy when aught unknown
Strikes the quick fenfe, and wakes each active pow'r
To brifker meafures: witnefs the neglect
Of all familiar profpects, tho' beheld,
With tranfports once; the fond attentive gaze
Of young aftonifhment; the fober zeal
Of age, commenting on prodigious things.
For fuch the bounteous providence of Heav'n,
In every breaft implanting this defire
Of objects new and ftrange to urge us on
With unremitted labour to purfue
Thofe facred ftores that wait the ripening foul,
In truth's exhauftlefs bofom. What needs words
To paint its pow'r? For this, the daring youth
Breaks from his weeping mother's anxious arms,
In foreign climes to rove; the penfive fage
Heedlefs of fleep, or midnight's harmful damp,
Hangs o'er the fickly taper; and untir'd
The virgin follows, with inchanted ftep,
The mazes of fome wife and wondrous tale,
From morn to eve; unmindful of her form,
Unmindful of the happy drefs that ftole
The wifhes of the youth, when every maid
With envy pin'd. Hence finally by night

The

The village-matron, round the blazing hearth,
Sufpends the infant-audience with her tales,
Breathing aftonifhment! of witching rhimes,
And evil fpirits; of the death-bed call
Of him who robb'd the widow, and devour'd
The orphan's portion; of unquiet fouls
Ris'n from the grave to eafe the heavy guilt
Of deeds in life conceal'd; of fhapes that walk
At dead of night, and clank their chains, and wave
The torch of hell around the murd'rer's bed.
At every folemn paufe the croud recoil
Gazing each other fpeechlefs, and congeal'd
With fhiv'ring fighs: till eager for th'event,
Around the beldame all arreft they hang,
Each trembling heart with grateful terrors quell'd.

AKENSIDE.

 BOOK

B O O K   VIII.

P A T H E T I C   P I E C E S.

C H A P.   I.

Y O R I C K's   D E A T H.

A FEW hours before Yorick breathed his
laſt, Eugenius ſtept in with an intent to
take his laſt ſight and laſt farewel of him. Upon
his drawing Yorick's curtain, and aſking how he
felt himſelf, Yorick, looking up in his face, took
hold of his hand,———and, after thanking him for
the many tokens of his friendſhip to him, for which,
he ſaid, if it was their fate to meet hereafter, he
would thank him again and again; he told him, he
was within a few hours of giving his enemies the ſlip
for ever.—I hope not, anſwered Eugenius, with tears
trickling down his cheeks, and with the tendereſt
tone that ever man ſpoke,—I hope not, Yorick, ſaid
he.——Yorick replied, with a look up, and gentle
ſqueeze of Eugenius's hand,—and that was all,—but
it cut Eugenius to his heart.—Come, come, Yorick,
quoth Eugenius, wiping his eyes, and ſummoning up
the man within him,——my dear lad, be comforted,
—let not all thy ſpirits and fortitude forſake thee at
this criſis when thou moſt wanteſt them ;——who
knows what reſources are in ſtore. and what the
power of God may yet do for thee?—Yorick laid
his hand upon his heart, and gently ſhook his head;
—for my part, continued Eugenius, crying bitterly

as he uttered the words,—I declare I know not, Yorick, how to part with thee, and would gladly flatter my hopes, added Eugenius, chearing up his voice, that there is ſtill enough left of thee to make a biſhop,—and that I may live to ſee it.—I beſeech thee, Eugenius, quoth Yorick, taking off his night-cap as well as he could with his left hand.——his right being ſtill graſped cloſe in that of Eugenius,——I beſeech thee to take a view of my head.—— I ſee nothing that ails it, replied Eugenius.   Then, alas! my friend, ſaid Yorick, let me tell you, that it is ſo bruiſed and miſ-ſhapened with the blows which have been ſo unhandſomely given me in the dark, that I might ſay with Sancho Panca, that ſhould I recover, and " mitres thereupon be ſuffered " to rain down from heaven as thick as hail, not one " of them would fit it."——Yorick's laſt breath was hanging upon his trembling lips ready to depart as he uttered this;——yet ſtill it was uttered with ſomething of a Cervantic tone;——and as he ſpoke it, Eugenius could perceive a ſtream of lambent fire lighted up for a moment in his eyes;——faint pic-ture of thoſe flaſhes of his ſpirit which (as Shake-ſpear ſaid of his anceſtor) were wont to ſet the table in a roar.

Eugenius was convinced from this, that the heart of his friend was broke; he ſqueezed his hand ——and then walked ſoftly out of the room, weep-ing as he walked.   Yorick followed Eugenius with his eyes to the door,——he then cloſed them,—— and never opened them more.

He lies buried in a corner of his church-yard, un-der a plain marble ſlab, which his friend Eugenius, by leave of his executors, laid upon his grave, with no more than theſe three words of inſcription ſerving both for his epitaph, and elegy.

Alas,   poor Y O R I C K!

Ten times a day has Yorick's ghoſt the conſolati-
on to hear his monumental inſcription read over
with ſuch a variety of plaintive tones, as denote a
general pity and eſteem for him;——a footway croſ-
ſing the church yard cloſe by his grave,—not a paſ-
ſenger goes by without ſtopping to caſt a look upon
it——and ſighing as he walks on,

Alas, poor YORICK!

STERNE.

C H A P. II.

THE BEGGAR's PETITION.

PITY the ſorrows of a poor old man,
　　Whoſe trembling limbs have borne him to your
　　　　door,
Whoſe days are dwindled to the ſhorteſt ſpan,
Oh! give relief, and Heaven will bleſs your ſtore.

Theſe tatter'd cloaths my poverty beſpeak,
Theſe hoary locks proclaim my lengthen'd years;
And many a furrow in my grief-worn cheek
Has been the channel to a flood of tears.

Yon houſe, erected on the riſing ground,
With tempting aſpect drew me from my road;
For Plenty there a reſidence has found,
And Grandeur a magnificent above.

Hard is the fate of the infirm and poor!
Here, as I crav'd a morſel of their bread,
A pamper'd menial drove me from the door
To ſeek a ſhelter in an humbler ſhed.

Oh! take me to your hoſpitable dome;
Keen blows the wind, and piercing is the cold!
Short is my paſſage to the friendly tomb,
For I am poor and miſerably old.

Should

Should I reveal the fources of my grief,
If foft humanity e'er touch'd your breaft,
Your hands would not withhold the kind relief,
And tears of Pity would not be repreft.

Heaven fends misfortunes; why fhould we re-
            pine?
'Tis Heaven has brought me to the ftate you fee;
And your condition may be foon like mine,
The child of Sorrow, and of Mifery.

A little farm was my paternal lot,
Then like the lark I fprightly hail'd the morn;
But ah! oppreffion forc'd me from my cot,
My cattle dy'd, and blighted was my corn.

My daughter, once the comfort of my age,
Lur'd by a villain from her native home,
Is caft abandon'd on the world's wide ftage,
And doom'd in fcanty Poverty to roam.

My tender wife, fweet foother of my care!
Struck with fad anguifh at the ftern decree,
Fell, ling'ring fell, a victim to defpair,
And left the world to wretchednefs and me:

Pity the forrows of a poor old man,
Whofe trembling limbs have borne him to your
            door,
Whofe days are dwindled to the fhorteft fpan,
Oh! give relief, and Heaven will blefs your
            ftore.

C H A P

C H A P. III.

ELEGY on the DEATH of an unfortunate LADY.

WHAT beck'ning ghoſt, along the moon-light
        ſhade
Invites my ſteps, and points to yonder glade?
'Tis ſhe!—but why that bleeding boſom gor'd,
Why dimly gleams the viſionary ſword?
Oh ever beauteous, ever friendly! tell,
Is it, in heav'n, a crime to love too well?
To bear too tender, or too firm a heart,
To act a Lover's or a Roman's part?
Is there no bright reverſion in the ſky,
For thoſe who greatly think, or bravely die?
    Why bade ye elſe, ye pow'rs! her ſoul aſpire
Above the vulgar flight of low deſire?
Ambition firſt ſprang from your bleſt abodes;
The glorious fault of angels and of Gods:
Thence to their images on earth it flows,
And in the breaſts of Kings and Heroes glows.
Moſt ſouls, 'tis true, but peep out once an age,
Dull ſullen priſ'ners in the body's cage.
Dim lights of life, that burn a length of years
Uſeleſs, unſeen, as lamps in ſepulchres;
Like Eaſtern Kings a lazy ſtate they keep,
And cloſe confin'd to their own palace, ſleep.
    From theſe perhaps (ere nature bade her die)
Fate ſnatch'd her early to the pitying ſky.
As into air the purer ſpirits flow,
And ſep'rate from their kindred dregs below;
So flew the ſoul to its congenial place,
Nor left one virtue to redeem her race.
    But thou, falſe guardian of a charge too good,
Thou, mean deſerter of thy brother's blood!
See on theſe ruby lips the trembling breath,
Theſe cheeks, now fading at the blaſt of death;

Cold

Cold is that breaft which warm'd the world before,
And thofe love-darting eyes muft roll no more.
Thus, if eternal juftice rules the ball,
Thus, fhall your wives, and thus your children fall,
On all the line a fudden vengeance waits,
And frequent herfes fhall befiege your gates,
There paffengers fhall ftand, and pointing fay,
(While the long fun'rals blacken all the way)
Lo thefe were they, whofe fouls the Furies fteel'd,
And curs'd with hearts unknowing how to yield.
Thus unlamented pafs the proud away,
The gaze of fools, and pageants of a day !
So perifh all, whofe breaft ne'er learn'd to glow
For others good, or melt at others woe.
    What can atone (oh ever injur'd fhade !)
Thy fate unpity'd, and thy rites unpaid !
No friend's complaint, no kind domeftic tear
Pleas'd thy pale ghoft, or grac'd thy mournful bier :
By foreign hands thy dying eyes were clos'd,
By foreign hands thy decent limbs compos'd,
By foreign hands thy humble grave adorn'd,
By ftrangers honour'd, and by ftrangers mourn'd !
What tho' no friends in fable weeds appear,
Grieve for an hour, perhaps, then mourn a year,
And bear about the mockery of woe
To midnight dances, and the public fhow ?
What tho' no weeping Loves thy afhes grace,
Nor polifh'd marble emulate thy face ?
What tho' no facred earth allow thee room,
Nor hallow'd dirge be mutter'd o'er thy tomb ?
Yet fhall thy grave with humble flow'rs be dreft,
And the green turf lie lightly on thy breaft :
There fhall the morn her earlieft tears beftow,
There the firft rofes of the year fhall blow ;
While angels with their filver wings o'erfhade
The ground, now facred by thy reliques made.
    So peaceful refts, without a ftone, a name,
What once had beauty, titles, wealth, and fame,
How lov'd, how honour'd once, avails thee not,
To whom related, or by whom forgot ;
                                    A heap

A heap of duſt alone remains of thee,
'Tis all thou art, and all the proud ſhall be !
  Poets themſelves muſt fall, like thoſe they ſung,
Deaf the prais'd ear, and mute the tuneful tongue.
Ev'n he, whoſe ſoul now melts in mournful lays,
Shall ſhortly want the gen'rous tear he pays ;
Then from his cloſing eyes thy form ſhall part,
And the laſt pang ſhall tear thee from his heart,
Life's idle buſineſs at one gaſp be o'er,
The muſe forgot, and thou be lov'd no more !

POPE.

CHAP. IV.

MORNING HYMN.

THESE are thy glorious works, Parent of good !
   Almighty ! thine this univerſal frame.
Thus wondrous fair ; thyſelf how wondrous then !
Unſpeakable ! who ſitt'ſt above theſe heav'ns,
To us inviſible, or dimly ſeen
In theſe thy lowlieſt works ; yet theſe declare
Thy goodneſs beyond thought, and pow'r divine.
Speak ye who beſt can tell, ye ſons of light,
Angels ; for ye behold him, and with ſongs
And choral ſymphonies, day without night,
Circle his throne rejoicing ; ye in heav'n,
On earth join all ye creatures to extol
Him firſt, him laſt, him midſt, and without end.
Faireſt of ſtars, laſt in the train of night,
If better thou belong not to the dawn,
Sure pledge of day, that crown'ſt the ſmiling morn
With thy bright circlet, praiſe him in thy ſphere,
While day ariſes, that ſweet hour of prime.
Thou ſun, of this great world both eye and ſoul,
Acknowledge him thy greater ; ſound his praiſe
In thy eternal courſe, both when thou climb'ſt,
And when high noon haſt gain'd, and when thou
          fall'ſt.
Moon that now meet'ſt the orient ſun, now fly'ſt
                                   With

With the fix'd ftars, fix'd in their orb that flies;
And ye five other wand'ring fires that move
In myftic dance not without fong, refound
His praife, who out of darknefs call'd up light.
Air, and ye elements, the eldeft birth
Of Nature's womb, that in quaternion run
Perpetual circle, multiform, and mix,
And nourifh all things; let your ceafelefs change
Vary to our great Maker ftill new praife.
Ye mifts and exhalations, that now rife
From hill or ftreaming lake, dufky or gray,
Till the fun paint your fleecy fkirts with gold,
In honour to the world's great Author rife,
Whether to deck with clouds th'uncolour'd fky,
Or wet the thirfty earth with falling fhowers,
Rifing or falling, ftill advance his praife.
His praife, ye winds, that from four quarters blow,
Breathe foft or loud; and wave your tops, ye pines,
With every plant in fign of worfhip wave.
Fountains, and ye, that warble, as ye flow,
Melodious murmurs, warbling tune his praife.
Join voices, all ye living fouls; ye birds,
That finging up to heaven-gate afcend,
Bear on your wings and in your notes his praife.
Ye that in waters glide, and ye that walk
The earth, and ftately tread, or lowly creep;
Witnefs if I be filent, morn or even,
To hill or valley, fountain or frefh fhade,
Made vocal, by my fong, and taught his praife.
Hail, univerfal Lord, be bounteous ftill
To give us only good; and if the night
Have gather'd aught of evil, or conceal'd
Difperfe it, as now light difpels the dark.

MILTON.

C H A P. V.

S A T A N's S O L I L O Q U Y.

O THOU that, with furpaffing glory crown'd,
Look'it from thy fole dominion like the god
Of this new World; at whofe fight all the ftars
Hide their diminifh'd heads; to thee I call,
But with no friendly voice, and add thy name,
O Sun, to tell thee how I hate thy beams,
That bring to my remembrance from what ftate
I fell, how glorious once above thy fphere :
Till pride, and worfe ambition threw me down,
Warring in heav'n againft heaven's matchlefs King.
Ah wherefore ? he deferv'd no fuch return
From me, whom he created what I was,
In that bright eminence, and with his good
Upbraided none ; nor was his fervice hard.
What could be lefs than to afford him praife,
The eafieft recompence, and pay him thanks,
How due ! yet all his good prov'd ill in me,
And wrought but malice: lifted up fo high
I 'fdain'd fubjection, and thought one ftep higher
Would fet me high'ft, and in a moment quit
The debt immenfe of endlefs gratitude,
So burdenfome, ftill paying, ftill to owe :
Forgetful what from him I ftill receiv'd ;
And underftood not that a grateful mind
By owing owes not, but ftill pays, at once
Indebted and difcharged ; what burden then ?
O had his pow'rful deftiny ordain'd
Me fome inferior angel, I had ftood
Then happy ; no unbounded hope had rais'd
Ambition. Yet why not ? fome other power
As great might have afpir'd, and me though mean
Drawn to his part ; but other pow'rs as great
Fell not, but ftand unfhaken, from within
Or from without, to all temptations arm'd.
Hadft thou the fame free will and pow'r to ftand ?

Thou

'Thou hadſt. Whom haſt thou then, or what t' ac-
    cuſe,
But Heav'n's free love, dealt equally to all ?
Be then his love accurs'd, ſince love or hate,
To me alike, it deals eternal woe.
Nay curs'd be thou ; ſince againſt His thy will
Choſe freely what it now ſo juſtly rues,
Me miſerable ! which way ſhall I fly
Infinite wrath, and infinite deſpair ;
Which way I fly is hell ; myſelf am hell ;
And, in the loweſt deep, a lower deep
Still threat'ning to devour me opens wide,
To which the hell I ſuffer ſeems a heaven.
O then at laſt relent : is there no place,
Left for repentance, none for pardon left ?
None left but by ſubmiſſion ; and that word
Diſdain forbids me, and my dread of ſhame
Among the ſpirits beneath, whom I ſeduc'd
With other promiſes, and other vaunts,
Than to ſubmit, boaſting I could ſubdue
Th' omnipotent. Ah me, they little know
How dearly I abide that boaſt ſo vain,
Under what torments inwardly I groan,
While they adore me on the throne of hell :
With diadem and ſcepter high advance'd,
The lower ſtill I fall, only ſupreme
In miſery : ſuch joy ambition finds.
But ſay I could repent, and could obtain,
By act of grace, my former ſtate ; how ſoon
Would height recal high thoughts, how ſoon unſay
What feign'd ſubmiſſion ſwore ! eaſe would recant
Vows made in pain, as violent and void.
For never can true reconcilement grow
Where wounds of deadly hate have pierc'd ſo deep ·
Which would but lead us to a worſe relapſe,
And heavier fall : ſo ſhould I purchaſe dear
Short intermiſſion bought with double ſmart.
'This knows my puniſher : therefore as far
From granting he, as I from begging peace :
All hope excluded thus, behold in ſtead
Of us outcaſt, exil'd, his new delight,
Mankind

Mankind created, and for him this world.
So farewel hope, and with hope farewel fear,
Farewel remorse; all good to me is loft;
Evil be thou my good: by thee at leaft
Divided empire with heav'n's King I hold,
By thee and more perhaps fupreme will reign;
As man ere long, and this new world fhall know.

MILTON.

C H A P.   VI.

J U B A AND S Y P H A X.

JUB. SYPHAX, I joy to meet thee thus alone.
  I have obferv'd of late thy looks are fall'n.
O'ercaft with gloomy cares and difcontent;
Then tell me, Syphax, I conjure thee tell me,
What are the thoughts that knit thy brow in frowns,
And turn thine eye thus coldly on thy prince?

  SYPH. 'Tis not my talent to conceal my thoughts,
Or carry fmiles and fun-fhine in my face,
When difcontent fits heavy at my heart:
I have not yet fo much the Roman in me.

  JUB. Why doft thou caft out fuch ungen'rous
    terms
Againft the lords and fov'reigns of the world?
Doft thou not fee mankind fall down before them,
And own the force of their fuperior virtue?
Is there a nation in the wilds of Afric,
Amidft our barren rocks, and burning fands,
That does not tremble at the Roman name?

  SYPH. Gods! where's the worth that fets this
    people up
Above our own Numidia's tawny fons?
Do they with tougher finews bend the bow?
Or flies the javelin fwifter to its mark,
Launch'd from the vigour of a Roman arm?
Who like our active African inftructs
The fiery fteed, and trains him to his hand?
Or guides in troops th' embattled elephant,

Loaden

Loaden with war? Thefe, thefe are arts, my prince,
In which your Zama does not ftoop to Rome.
   Jub. Thefe all are virtues of a meaner rank,
Perfections that are plac'd in bones and nerves.
A Roman foul is bent on higher views :
To civilize the rude unpolifh'd world,
To lay it under the reftraint of laws ;
To make man mild, and fociable to man ;
To cultivate the wild licentious favage
With wifdom, difcipline, and lib'ral arts,
Th' embellifhments of life ; virtues like thefe,
Make human nature fhine, reform the foul,
And break our fierce barbarians into men.
   Syph. Patience, juft Heav'ns—Excufe an old
        man's warmth.
What are thefe wondrous civilizing arts,
This Roman polifh, and this fmooth behaviour,
That renders man thus tractable and tame ?
Are they not only to difguife our paffions,
To fet our looks at variance with our thoughts,
To check the ftarts and fallies of the foul,
And break off all its commerce with the tongue ?
In fhort, to change us into other creatures,
Than what our nature and the gods defign'd us ?
   Jub. To ftrike thee dumb : turn up thy eyes to
        Cato !
There may'ft thou fee to what a godlike height
The Roman virtues lift up mortal man.
While good, and juft, and anxious for his friends,
He's ftill feverely bent againft himfelf ;
Renouncing fleep, and reft, and food, and eafe,
He ftrives with thirft and hunger, toil and heat :
And when his fortune fets before him all
The pomps and pleafures that his foul can wifh,
His rigid virtue will accept of none.
   Syph. Believe me, prince, there's not an African
That traverfes our vaft Numidian defarts,
In queft of prey, and lives upon his bow,
But better practifes thefe boafted virtues.
Coarfe are his meals, the fortune of the chafe,
Amidft the running ftream he flakes his thirft,
Toils

Toils all the day, and at th' approach of night
On the firſt friendly bank he throws him down,
Or reſts his head upon a rock till morn :
Then riſes freſh, purſues his wonted game,
And if the following day he chance to find
A new repaſt, or an untaſted ſpring,
Bleſſes his ſtars, and thinks it luxury.

   Jub. Thy prejudices, Syphax, won't diſcern
What virtues grow from ignorance and choice,
Nor how the hero differs from the brute.
But grant that others could with equal glory
Look down on pleaſures, and the baits of ſenſe ;
Where ſhall we find the man that bears affliction,
Great and majeſtic in his griefs, like Cato ?
Heav'ns ! with what ſtrength, what ſteadineſs of
       mind,
He triumphs in the midſt of all his ſuff'rings !
How does he riſe againſt a load of woes,
And thank the gods that throw the weight upon him !
   Syph. 'Tis pride, rank pride, and haughtineſs
      of ſoul :
I think the Romans call it Stoiciſm.
Had not your royal father thought ſo highly
Of Roman virtue, and of Cato's cauſe, .
He had not fall'n by a ſlave's hand, inglorious :
Nor would his ſlaughter'd army now have lain
On Afric ſands disfigur'd with their wounds,
To gorge the wolves and vultures of Numidia.
   Jub. Why doſt thou call my ſorrows up afreſh ?
My father's name brings tears into mine eyes.
   Syph. Oh, that you'd profit by your father's ills !
   Jub. What would'ſt thou have me do !
   Syph. Abandon Cato.
   Jub. Syphax, I ſhould be more than twice an
      orphan
By ſuch a loſs.
   Syph. Ay, there's the tie that binds you !
You long to call him father. Marcia's charms
Work in your heart unſeen, and plead for Cato.
No wonder you are deaf to all I ſay.

                     Jub.

Jub. Syphax, your zeal becomes importunate ;
I've hitherto permitted it to rave,
And talk at large ; but learn to keep it in,
Left it fhould take more freedom than I'll give it.
   Syph. Sir, your great father never us'd me thus.
Alas, he's dead ! but can you e'er forget
The tender forrows and the pangs of nature,
The fond embraces and repeated bleffings,
Which you drew from him in your laft farewel ?
Still muft I cherifh the dear, fad remembrance,
At once to torture, and to pleafe my foul.
The good old King at parting wrung my hand,
(His eyes brim-full of tears) then fighing cry'd,
Pr'ythee be careful of my fon ! ——His grief
Swell'd up fo high, he could not utter more.
   Jub. Alas ! the ftory melts away my foul.
That beft of fathers! how fhall I difcharge
The gratitude and duty which I owe him ?
   Syph.   By laying up his counfels in your heart.
   Jub.   His counfels bade me yield to thy directi-
            ons :
Then, Syphax, chide me in fevereft terms,
Vent all thy paffion, and I'll ftand its fhock,
Calm and unruffled as a fummer fea,
When not a breath of wind flies o'er its furface.
   Syph.   Alas, my prince, I'd guide you to your
            fafety.
   Jub. I do believe thou wouldft ; but tell me how?
   Syph. Fly from the fate that follows Cæfar's foes.
   Jub. My father fcorn'd to do it.
   Syph. And therefore dy'd.
   Jub. Better to die ten thoufand deaths,
Than wound my honour.
   Syph. Rather fay your love.
   Jub. Syphax, I've promis'd to preferve my tem-
            per ;
Why wilt thou urge me to confefs a flame
I long have ftifled, and would fain conceal ?
   Syph. Believe me, prince, tho' hard to conquer
            love,

'Tis

'Tis eafy to divert and break its force :
Abfence might cure it, or a fecond miftrefs
Light up another flame, and put out this.
The glowing dames of Zama's royal court
Have faces flufh'd with more exalted charms ;
The fun that rolls his chariot o'er their heads,
Works up more fire and colour in their cheeks :
Were you with thefe, my prince, you'd foon forget
The pale, unripen'd beauties of the North.
  Jub. 'Tis not a fet of features, or complexion,
The tincture of the fkin that I admire.
Beauty foon grows familiar to the lover,
Fades in his eye, and palls upon the fenfe.
The virtuous Marcia tow'rs above her fex :
True, fhe is fair (Oh, how divinely fair !)
But ftill the lovely maid improves her charms,
With inward greatnefs, unaffected wifdom,
And fanctity of manners. Cato's foul
Shines out in ev'ry thing fhe acts or fpeaks,
While winning mildnefs and attractive fmiles
Dwell in her looks, and with becoming grace
Soften the rigour of her father's virtues.
  Syph.   How does your tongue grow wanton in
      her praife !

Cato.

C H A P.   VII.

C A T O's S O L I L O Q U Y.

IT muft be fo—Plato, thou reafon'ft well—
Elfe whence this pleafing hope, this fond defire,
This longing after immortality ?
Or whence this fecret dread and inward horror,
Of falling into nought ? Why fhrinks the foul
Back on herfelf, and ftartles at deftruction ?
'Tis the Divinity that ftirs within us ;
'Tis heav'n itfelf that points out an hereafter,
And intimates eternity to man.
Eternity ! thou pleafing, dreadful thought !

Thro'

Thro' what variety of untry'd being,
Thro' what new scenes and changes must we pass!
The wide, th' unbounded prospect lies before me ;
But shadows, clouds, and darkness rest upon it.
Here will I hold. If there's a Pow'r above us,
(And that there is, all Nature cries aloud
Thro' all her works) he must delight in virtue ;
And that which he delights in, must be happy.
But when ? or where ?—This world was made for
        Cæsar.
I'm weary of conjectures—this must end 'em.
  Thus am I doubly arm'd. My death and life,
My bane and antidote are both before me.
This in a moment brings me to an end ;
But this informs me I shall never die.
The soul, secur'd in her existence, smiles
At the drawn dagger, and defies its point :
The stars shall fade away, the sun himself
Grow dim with age, and nature sink in years :
But thou shalt flourish in immortal youth,
Unhurt amidst the war of elements,
The wreck of matter and the crush of worlds.
                      Cato.

C H A P.   VIII.

SOUTHAMPTON and ESSEX.

Officer. **M**Y Lord,
          We bring an order for your exe-
cution,
And hope you are prepar'd ; for you must die
This very hour.
  South. Indeed, the time is sudden !
  Ess. Is death th' event of all my flatter'd hope ?
False sex ! and Queen more perjur'd than them all ?
But die I will without the least complaint,
My soul shall vanish silent as the dew
Attracted by the sun from verdant fields,
And leaves of weeping flowers. Come, my dear friend,
                    Partner

Partner in fate, give me thy body in
Thefe faithful arms, and O now let me tell thee,
And you, my Lords, and Heaven my witnefs too,
I have no weight, no heavinefs on my foul,
But that I've loft my deareft friend his life.

 Soutʜ. And I proteft by the fame powers divine,
And to the world ; 'tis all my happinefs,
The greateft blifs my mind yet e'er enjoy'd
Since we muft die, my Lord, to die together.

 Officer. The Queen, my Lord Southampton,
   has been pleas'd
To grant particular mercy to your perfon ;
And has by us fent a reprieve from death,
With pardon of your treafons, and commands
You to depart immediately from hence.

 Soutʜ. O my unguarded foul ! Sure never was
A man with mercy wounded fo before !

 Ess. Then I am loofe to fteer my wand'ring voy-
   age ;
Like a bad veffel that has long been croft,
And bound by adverfe winds, at laft gets liberty,
And joyfully makes all the fail fhe can,
To reach its wifh'd for port——Angels protect
The Queen, for her my chiefeft prayers fhall be,
That as in time fhe has ſpar'd my noble friend,
And owns his crimes worth mercy, may fhe ne'er
Think fo of me too late when I am dead————
Again, Southampton, let me hold thee faft,
For 'tis my laft embrance

 Soutʜ. O be lefs kind, my friend, or move lefs pity,
Or I fhall fink beneath the weight of fadnefs !
I weep that I am doom'd to live without you,
And fhould have fmil'd to fhare the death of Effex.

 Ess. O fpare this tendernefs for one that needs it,
For her that I commit to thee, 'tis all that I
Can claim of Southampton————O my wife !
Methinks that very name fhould ftop thy pity,
And make thee covetous of all as loft
That is not meant to her——be a kind friend
To her, as we have been to one another ;
        Name

Name not the dying Eſſex to thy queen,
Leſt it ſhould coſt a tear, nor e'er offend her.
   South. O ſtay, my Lord, let me have one
        word more,
One laſt farewel, before the greedy axe
Shall part my friend, my only friend from me,
And Eſſex from himſelf—I know not what
Are call'd the pangs of death, but ſure I am
I feel an agony that's worſe than death——
Farewel.
   Ess. Why that's well ſaid——Farewel to
        thee——
Then let us part, juſt like two travellers,
Take diſtant paths, only this difference is,
Thine is the longeſt, mine the ſhorteſt way——
Now let me go——if there's a throne in heaven
For the moſt brave of men and beſt of friends,
I will beſpeak it for Southampton.
   South. And I, while I have life, will hoard thy
       memory:
When I am dead, we then ſhall meet again.
   Ess. Till then, Farewel.
   South. Till then, Farewel.
                Earl of Essex,

C H A P. IX.

J A F F I E R and P I E R R E.

Jaff. **B**Y Heav'n, you ſtir not,
      I muſt be heard, I muſt have leave to
        ſpeak :
Thou haſt diſgrac'd me, Pierre, by a vile blow :
Had not a dagger done thee nobler juſtice?
But uſe me as thou wilt, thou can'ſt not wrong me,
For I am fallen beneath the baſeſt injuries :
Yet look upon me with the eye of mercy,
With pity and with charity behold me;
Shut not thy heart againſt a friend's repentance;
          O ·
                         But

But as there dwells a godlike nature in thee,
Liften with mildnefs to my fupplications.
   Pier. What whining monk art thou? what holy
      cheat,
That wouldft incroach upon my credulous ears,
And cant'ft thus vilely? hence! I know thee not.
   Jaff. Not know me, Pierre!
   Pier. No, know thee not; what art thou?
   Jaff. Jaffier, thy friend, thy once lov'd, valu'd
      friend!
Tho' now defervedly fcorn'd, and us'd moft hardly.
   Pier. Thou Jaffier! thou my once lov'd, valu'd
      friend!
By heav'ns! thou ly'ft; the man fo call'd my friend,
Was generous, honeft, faithful, juft, and valiant,
Noble in mind, and in his perfon lovely,
Dear to my eyes, and tender to my heart:
But thou a wretched, bafe, falfe, worthlefs coward,
Poor even in foul, and loathfome in thy afpect:
All eyes muft fhun thee, and all hearts deteft thee.
Prithee avoid, no longer cling thus round me,
Like fomething baneful, that my nature's chill'd at.
   Jaff. I have not wrong'd thee, by thefe tears I
      have not,
But ftill am honeft, true, and hope too, valiant;
My mind ftill full of thee, therefore ftill noble.
Let not thy eyes then fhun me, nor thy heart
Deteft me utterly: Oh! look upon me,
Look back and fee my fad, fincere fubmiffion!
How my hearts fwells, as e'en 'twould burft my
      bofom;
Fond of its goal, and labouring to be at thee;
What fhall I do? what fay to make thee hear me?
   Pier. Haft thou not wrong'd me? dar'ft thou
      call thyfelf
That once lov'd, valu'd friend of mine,
And fwear thou haft not wrong'd me? Whence
      thefe chains?
Whence the vile death, which I may meet this mo-
     ment?
                  Whence

Whence this dishonour, but from thee, thou false
     one?
  Jaff. —All's true; yet grant one thing, and
     I've done asking.
  Pier. What's that?
  Jaff. To take thy life on such conditions
The council have propos'd: thou and thy friend
May yet live long, and to be better treated.
  Pier. Life! ask my life! confess! record my-
     self
A villain for the privilege to breathe,
And carry up and down this cursed city
A discontented and repining spirit,
Burdensome to itself, a few years longer,
To lose it, may be; at last, in a lewd quarrel
For some new friend; treacherous and false as thou
     art!
No, this vile world and I have long been jangling,
And cannot part on better terms than now,
When only men like thee are fit to live in't.
  Jaff. By all that's just——
  Pier. Swear by some other powers,
For thou hast broke that sacred oath too lately.
  Jaff. Then by that hell I merit, I'll not leave
     thee,
Till to thyself at last thou'rt reconcil'd,
However thy resentment may deal with me.
  Pier. Not leave me!
  Jaff. No; thou shalt not force me from thee;
Use me reproachfully, and like a slave;
Tread on me, buffet me, heap wrongs on wrongs
On my poor head; I'll bear it all with patience;
I'll weary out thy most friendly cruelty;
Lie at thy feet and kiss 'em, tho' they spurn me,
Till wounded by my sufferings thou relent,
And raise me to thy arms with dear forgiveness.
  Pier. Art thou not——
  Jaff. What?
  Pier. A traytor?
  Jaff. Yes.
  Pier. A villain?

Jaff. Granted.

Pier. A coward, a moſt ſcandalous coward,
Spiritleſs, void of honour, one who has ſold
Thy everlaſting fame for ſhameleſs life?

Jaff. All, all, and more, much more: my
    faults are numberleſs.

Pier. And would'ſt thou have me live on terms
    like thine?
'Baſe as thou'rt falſe——

Jaff. No; 'tis to me that's granted:
The ſafety of thy life was all I aim'd at,
In recompence for faith and truſt ſo broken.

Pier. I ſcorn it more, becauſe preſerv'd by
    thee;
And as when firſt my fooliſh heart took pity
On thy misfortunes, ſought thee in thy miſeries,
Reliev'd thy wants, and rais'd thee from thy ſtate
Of wretchedneſs, in which thy fate had plung'd
    thee,
To rank thee in my liſt of noble friends;
All I receiv'd, in ſurety for thy truth,
Were unregarded oaths, and this, this dagger,
Given with a worthleſs pledge thou ſince haſt ſtol'n:
So I reſtore it back to thee again:
Swearing by all thoſe powers which thou haſt vio-
    lated,
Never from this curs'd hour to hold communion,
Friendſhip or intereſt with thee, tho' our years
Were to exceed thoſe limited the world.
Take it——Farewel, for now I owe thee nothing.

Jaff. Say thou wilt live then.

Pier. For my life, diſpoſe of it
Juſt as thou wilt, becauſe 'tis what I'm tir'd with.

Jaff. Oh Pierre!

Pier. No more.

Jaff. My eyes won't loſe the ſight of thee,
But languiſh after thine, and ake with gazing.

Pier. Leave me—Nay, then thus, thus I throw
    thee from me;
And curſes great as is thy falſehood catch thee.

Venice Preserved.
C H A P.

C H A P. X.

E D W A R D and W A R W I C K.

Edw.　　L ET me have no intruders; above all
　　　　　 Keep Warwick from my fight——
　　　　　　　Enter Warwick.

　　War. Behold him here;
No welcome gueft, it feems, unlefs I afk
My lord of Suffolk's leave—there was a time
When Warwick wanted not his aid to gain
Admiffion here.
　　Edw. There was a time perhaps,
When Warwick more defir'd and more—deferv'd it.
　　War. Never; I've been a foolifh faithful flave;
All my beft years, the morning of my life,
Hath been devoted to your fervice : what
Are now the fruits ? Difgrace and infamy;
My fpotlefs name, which never yet the breath
Of calumny had tainted, made the mock
For foreign fools to carp at : but 'tis fit
Who truft in princes, fhould be thus rewarded.
　　Edw. I thought, my lord, I had full well
　　　　　 repay'd
Your fervices with honours, wealth, and pow'r
Unlimited : thy all-directing hand
Guided in fecret ev'ry latent wheel
Of government, and mov'd the whole machine :
Warwick was all in all; and pow'rlefs Edward
Stood like a cypher in the great account.
　　War. Who gave that cypher worth, and feated
　　　　　 thee.
On England's throne ? Thy undiftinguifh'd name
Had rotted in the duft from whence it fprang,
And moulder'd in Oblivion, had not Warwick
Dug from its fordid mine the ufelefs ore,
And ftamp'd it with a diadem. Thou know'ft,
This wretched country, doom'd, perhaps, like Rome,
To fall by its own felf-deftroying hand,

Tost for so many years in the rough sea
Of civil discord, but for me had perished.
In that distressful hour I seiz'd the helm,
Bade the rough waves subside in peace, and steer'd
Your shatter'd vessel safe into the harbour.

You may despise perhaps that useless aid
Which you no longer want ; but know, proud
       youth,
He who forgets a friend, deserves a foe.

Edw. Know too, reproach for benefits receiv'd
Pays ev'ry debt, and cancels obligation.

War. Why, that indeed is frugal honesty,
A thrifty saving knowledge, when the debt
Grows burthensome, and cannot be discharg'd,
A spunge will wipe out all, and cost you nothing.

Edw. When you have counted o'er the numer-
      ous train
Of mighty gifts your bounty lavish'd on me,
You may remember next the injuries
Which I have done you ; let me know them all,
And I will make you ample satisfaction.

War. Thou can'st not ; thou hast robb'd me of
      a jewel
It is not in thy power to restore :
I was the first, shall future annals say,
That broke the sacred bond of public tru
And mutual confidence ; ambassadors,
In after times, mere instruments perhaps,
Of venial statesmen, shall recal my name
To witness, that they want not an example,
And plead my guilt to sanctify their own.

Amidst the herd of mercenary slaves
That haunt your court, cou'd none be found but
      Warwick,
To be the shameless herald of a lie ?

Edw. And would'st thou turn the vile reproach
      on me ?
If I have broke my faith, and stain'd the name
Of England, thank thy own pernicious counsels,
That urg'd me to it, and extorted from me
A cold consent to what my heart abhorr'd.

                  War.

War. I've been abus'd, infulted, and betray'd;
My injur'd honour cries aloud for vengeance,
Her wounds will never clofe!

Edw. Thefe gufts of paffion,
Will but inflame them: if I have been right
Inform'd, my lord, befides thefe dang'rous fears
Of bleeding honour, you have other wounds
As deep, tho' not fo fatal: fuch perhaps
As none but fair Elizabeth can cure.

War. Elizabeth!

Edw. Nay, ftart not, I have caufe
To wonder moft: I little thought indeed
When Warwick told me I might learn to love,
He was himfelf fo able to inftruct me:
But I've difcover'd all.——

War. And fo have I!
Too well I know thy breach of friendfhip there,
Thy fruitlefs bafe endeavours to fupplant me.

Edw. I fcorn it, fir,—Elizabeth hath charms,
And I have equal right with you to admire them;
Nor fee I aught fo godlike in the form;
So all-commanding in the name of Warwick,
That he alone fhould revel in the charms
Of beauty, and monopolize perfection,
I knew not of your love.

War. By Heav'n, 'tis falfe!
You knew it well, and meanly took occafion,
Whilft I was bufy'd in the noble office,
Your grace thought fit to honour me withal,
To tamper with a weak unguarded woman,
To bribe her paffions high, and bafely fteal
A treafure which your kingdom could not purchafe.

Edw. How know you that? But be it as it may,
I had a right, nor will I tamely yield
My claim to happinefs; the privilege,
To chofe the partner of my throne and bed:
It is a branch of my prerogative.

War. Prerogative!—what's that? the boaft of
    tyrants:
A borrow'd jewel, glitt'ring in the crown,

O 4.   With

With specious lustre, lent but to betray,
You had it, sir, and hold it—from the people.
    Edw.   And therefore do I prize it; I wou'd
            guard
Their liberties, and they shall strengthen mine :
But when proud faction and her rebel crew
Insult their sov'reign, trample on his laws,
And bid defiance to his pow'r, the people
In justice to themselves, will then defend
His cause, and vindicate the rights they gave.
    War.   Go to your darling people then; for soon,
If I mistake not, 'twill be needful; try
Their boasted zeal, and see if one of them
Will dare to lift his arm up in your cause,
If I forbid them.
    Edw.   Is it so, my lord ?
Then mark my words : I've been your slave too
            long,
And you have rul'd me with a rod of iron,
But henceforth know, proud peer, I am thy master,
And will be so : the king, who delegates
His pow'r to other's hands, but ill deserves
The crown he wears.
    War.   Look well then to your own ;
It sits but loosely on your head, for know,
The man who injur'd Warwick never pass'd
Unpunish'd yet.
    Edw.   Nor he who threaten'd Edward—
You may repent it, Sir,—my guards there—
            seize
This traitor, and convey him to the tow'r,
There let him learn obedience.
                    EARL OF WARWICK.

C H A P. XI.

O R L A N D O and A D A M.

Orla. WHO's there?
    Adam. What! my young master?
      Oh, gentle master,
Oh my sweet master, O you memory
Of old Sir Rowland! Why, what makes you here?
Why are you virtuous? Why do people love you?
And wherefore are you gentle, strong, and valiant?
Why would you be so fond to overcome
The bony prifer of the humorous Duke?
Your praife is come too swiftly home before you.
Know you not, master, to some kind of men
Their graces ferve them but as enemies?
No more do yours; your virtues, gentle master,
Are fanctified and holy traytors to you.
Oh, what a world is this, when what is comely
Invenoms him that bears it!
  Orla. Why, what's the matter?
  Adam. O unhappy youth,
Come not within thefe doors; within this roof
The enemy of all your graces lives:
Your brother——(no; no brother; yet the fon,——
Yet not the fon; I will not call him fon
Of him I was about to call his father),
Hath heard your praifes, and this night he means
To burn the lodging where you us'd to lie,
And you within it; if he fail of that,
He will have other means to cut you off;
I overheard him, and his practices:
This is no place, this houfe is a butchery;
Abhor it, fear it, do not enter it.
  Orla. Why, whither, Adam, would'ft thou
    have me go?
  Adam. No matter whither, fo you come not
    here.

ORLA. What would'ſt thou have me go and
    beg my food?
Or with a baſe and boiſterous ſword enforce
A thieviſh living on the common road?
This I muſt do, or know not what to do:
Yet this will not do, do how I can;
I rather will ſubject me to the malice
Of a diverted blood, and bloody brother.

ADAM. But do not ſo; I have five hundred crowns,
The thrifty hire I ſav'd under your father,
Which I did ſtore, to be my foſter-nurſe
When ſervice ſhould in my old limbs lie lame,
And unregarded age in corners thrown:
Take that; and he that doth the ravens feed,
Yea, providently caters for the ſparrow,
Be comfort to my age! here is the gold,
All this I give you, let me be your ſervant;
Though I look old, yet I am ſtrong and luſty;
For in my youth I never did apply
Hot and rebellious liquors in my blood;
Nor did I with unbaſhful forehead woo
The means of weakneſs and debility;
Therefore my age is as a luſty winter,
Froſty, but kindly; let me go with you;
I'll do the ſervice of a younger man
In all your buſineſs and neceſſities.

ORLA. Oh! good old man, how well in thee
    appears
The conſtant ſervice of the antique world;
When ſervice ſweat for duty, not for meed!
Thou art not for the faſhion of theſe times,
Where none will ſweat, but for promotion;
And having that, do choak their ſervice up,
Even with the having; it is not ſo with thee;
But, poor old man, thou prun'ſt a rotten tree,
That cannot ſo much as a bloſſom yield,
In lieu of all thy pains and huſbandry.
But come thy ways, we'll go along together;
And ere we have thy youthful wages ſpent,
We'll light upon ſome ſettled low content.

ADAM,

Adam. Mafter, go on; and I will follow thee
To the laft gafp, with truth and loyalty.
From feventeen years till now, almoft fourfcore,
Here lived I, but now live here no more.
Ah feventeen years, many their fortunes feek;
But at fourfcore, it is too late a week;
Yet fortune cannot recompenfe me better
Than to die well, and not my mafter's debtor.

Shakespear.

C H A P.   XII.

SCROOP and RICHARD.

Scroop. MORE health, and happinefs betide
my Liege,
Than can my care-tun'd tongue deliver him!
K. Rich. Mine ear is open, and my heart pre-
par'd;
The worft is worldly lofs thou canft unfold.
Say is my kingdom loft? Why, 'twas my care;
And what lofs is it, to be rid of care?
Strives Bolingbrooke to be as great as we?
Greater he fhall not be, if he ferve God,
We'll ferve him too, and be his fellow fo.
Revolt our fubjects? That we cannot mend;
They break their faith to God, as well as us.
Cry, woe, deftruction, ruin, lofs, decay;
The worft is death, and death will have his day.
Scroop. Glad am I that your Highnefs is fo
arm'd
To bear the tidings of calamity.
Like an unfeafonable ftormy day,
Which makes the filver rivers drown their fhores,
As if the world were all diffolv'd to tears;
So high above his limits fwells the rage
Of Bolingbrooke, cov'ring your fearful land
With hard bright fteel, and hearts more hard than
fteel.
White beards have arm'd their thin and hairlefs fcalps
Againft

Againſt thy Majeſty ; boys with women's voices
Strive to ſpeak big, and claſp their female joints
In ſtiff unwieldly arms, againſt thy crown :
Thy very beadſmen learn to bend their bows
Of double-fatal yew, againſt thy ſtate :
Yea, diſtaff-women manage ruſty bills.
Againſt thy ſeat both young and old rebel,
And all goes worſe than I have pow'r to tell.
   K. Rich.   Too well, too well thou tell'ſt a
       tale ſo ill.
Where is the Earl of Wiltſhire ? where is he got?
What is become of Buſhy ? Where is Green ?
—No matter where; of comfort no man ſpeak.
Let's talk of graves, of worms, and epitaphs,
Make duſt our paper, and with rainy eyes
Write ſorrow on the boſom of the earth !
Let's chuſe executors, and talk of wills;
And yet not ſo——for what can we bequeath,.
Save our depoſed bodies to the ground ?
Our lands, our lives, and all, are Bolingbrooke's,
And nothing can we call our own, but death;
And that ſmall model of the barren earth,
Which ſerves as paſte and cover to our bones.
For heav'n's ſake, let us ſit upon the ground,
And tell ſad ſtories of the death of Kings;
How ſome have been depos'd, ſome ſlain in war;
Some haunted by the ghoſts they diſpoſſeſs'd;
Some poiſon'd by their wives, ſome ſleeping kill'd;
All murder'd.——For within the hollow crown,
That rounds the mortal temples of a King,
Keeps Death his court; and there the antic ſits,
Scoffing his ſtate, and grinning at his pomp;
Allowing him a breath, a little ſcene
To monarchize, be fear'd, and kill with looks;
Infuſing him with ſelf and vain conceit,
As if this fleſh which walls about our life
Were braſs impregnable; and, humour'd thus,
Comes at the laſt, and with a little pin
Bores through his caſtle walls, and farewel King!
Cover your heads, and mock not fleſh and blood
With ſolemn rev'rence : throw away reſpect,
               Tradition,

Tradition, form, and ceremonious duty,
For you have but miftook me all-this while.
I live on bread like you, feel want like you;
Tafte grief, need friends, like you: fubjected thus,
How can you fay to me I am a King?

SHAKESPEAR.

CHAP.   XIII.

HOTSPUR and GLENDOWER.

GLEND. SIT, coufin Percy; fit, good coufin
Hotfpur;
For, by that name, as oft as Lancafter
Doth fpeak of you, his cheek looks pale; and with
A rifing figh, he wifheth you in heav'n.
HOT. And you in hell, as often as he hears
Owen Glendower fpoke of.
GLEND. I blame him not: at my nativity,
The front of heaven was full of fiery fhapes,
Of burning creffets: know that, at my birth,
The frame and the foundation of the earth
Shook like a coward.
HOT. So it would have done
At the fame feafon if your mother's cat
Had kitten'd, though yourfelf had ne'er been born.
GLEND. I fay, the earth did fhake when I was
born.
HOT. I fay, the earth then was not of my mind;
If you fuppofe, as fearing you, it fhook.
GLEND. The heav'ns were all on fire, the earth
did tremble.
HOT. O, then the earth fhook to fee the heav'ns
on fire,
And not in fear of your nativity.
Difeafed nature oftentimes breaks forth
In ftrange eruptions; and the teeming earth
Is with a kind of colic pinch'd and vex'd,
By the imprifoning of unruly wind
Within her womb; which for enlargement ftriving,

Shakes

Shakes the old beldame earth, and topples down
High tow'rs and mofs-grown fteeples. At your birth,
Our grandam earth, with this diftemperature,
In paffion fhook.

  GLEND. Coufin, of many men
I do not bear thefe croffings:—give me leave
To tell you once again, that at my birth
The front of heav'n was full of fiery fhapes;
The goats ran from the mountains, and the herds
Were ftrangely clam'rous in the frighted fields;
Thefe figns have mark'd me extraordinary,
And all the courfes of my life do fhew;
I am not in the roll of common men.
Where is he living, clipt in with the fea
That chides the banks of England, Wales, or Scot-
   land,
Who calls me pupil, or hath read to me?
And bring him out, that is but woman's fon,
Can trace me in the tedious ways of art,
Or hold me pace in deep experiments.

  HOT. I think there is no man fpeaks better Welch.
  GLEND. I can fpeak Englifh, Lord, as well as you,
For I was train'd up in the Englifh court:
Where, being young, I framed to the harp,
Many an Englifh ditty, lovely well,
And gave the tongue a helpful ornament;
A virtue that was never feen in you.

  HOT. Marry, and I'm glad of it with all my
   heart,
I had rather been a kitten, and cry Mew!
Than one of thefe fame metre-ballad mongers;
I'd rather hear a brazen candleftick tun'd,
Or a dry wheel grate on the axle-tree,
And that would nothing fet my teeth on edge,
Nothing fo much as mincing poetry;
'Tis like the forc'd gait of a fhuffling nag.——

  GLEND. I can call fpirits from the vafty deep.
  HOT. Why, fo can I, or fo can any man:
But will they come when you do call them?
  GLEND. Why, I can teach thee to command
   the devil.

           HOT.

HOT.   And I can teach thee, coz. to fhame the
       devil,
By telling truth; *Tell truth and fhame the devil.——*
   If thou haft pow'r to raife him, bring him hither;
And I'll be fworn, I've pow'r to fhame him hence.
Oh, while you live, *Tell truth and fhame the devil.*

SHAKESPEAR.

CHAP. XIV.

HOTSPUR READING A LETTER.

" BUT for mine own part, my Lord, I could be
"   well contented to be there, in refpect of the
" love I bear your houfe."   He could be contented
to be there; why is he not then? " In refpect of the
" love he bears our houfe!"   He fhews in this, he
loves his own barn better than he loves our houfe.
Let me fee fome more.   " The purpofe you undertake is dangerous."   Why, that is certain: it is dangerous to take a cold, to fleep, to drink: but I tell
you, Lord fool, out of this nettle danger, we pluck
this flower fafety.   " The purpofe you undertake
" is dangerous, the friends you have named uncer-
" tain, the time itfelf unforted, and your whole plot
" too light, for the counterpoife of fo great an op-
" pofition."   Say you fo, fay you fo? I fay unto
you again, you are a fhallow cowardly hind, and you
lie.   What a lack-brain is this? By the Lord, our
plot is a good plot as ever was laid; our friends true,
and conftant: a good plot, good friends, and full
of expectation; an excellent plot, very good friends.
What a frofty-fpirited rogue this is? Why, my
Lord of York commends the plot, and the general
courfe of the action. By this hand, if I were now,
by this rafcal, I could brain him with his Lady's fan.
Is there not my father, my uncle, and myfelf, Lord
Edmund Mortimer, my Lord of York, and Owen
Glendower? Is there not, befides, the Douglas?
Have I not all their letters, to meet me in arms by
the

the ninth of the next month? and are there not some
of them set forward already? What a Pagan rascal
is this? an infidel.   Ha! you shall see now, in very
sincerity of fear and cold heart, will he to the King,
and lay open all our proceedings. O, I could divide
myself, and go to buffets, for moving such a dish of
skimmed milk with so honourable an action. Hang
him, let him tell the King. We are prepared, I will
set forward to-night.

SHAKESPEAR.

C H A P.   XV.

HENRY IV.'s SOLILOQUY on SLEEP.

HOW many thousands of my poorest subjects
    Are at this hour asleep! O gentle Sleep,
Nature's soft nurse, how have I frighted thee,
That thou no more will weigh my eye-lids down,
And steep my senses in forgetfulness?
Why rather, Sleep, ly'st thou in smoky cribs,
Upon uneasy pallets stretching thee,
And hush'd with buzzing night-flies to thy slumber;
Than in the perfum'd chambers of the great,
Under the canopies of costly state,
And lull'd with sounds of sweetest melody?
O thou dull god, why ly'st thou with the vile
In loathsome beds, and leav'st the kingly couch,
A watch-case to a common larum-bell?
Wilt thou upon the high and giddy mast,
Seal up the ship-boys eyes, and rocks his brains,
In cradle of the rude imperious surge;
And in the visitation of the winds,
Who take the ruffian billows by the top,
Curling their monstrous heads, and hanging them
With deaf'ning clamours in the slipp'ry shrouds,
That, with the hurly, death itself awakes:
Can't thou, O partial Sleep, give thy repose
To the wet sea-boy in an hour so rude;
And, in the calmest and the stillest night,

With

With all appliances and means to boot,
Deny it to a king? Then, happy low! lie down;
Uneasy lies the head that wears a crown.

SHAKESPEAR.

C H A P.   XVI.

HENRY IV. AND PRINCE HENRY.

P. Henry. **I** NEVER thought to hear you speak
                again.
K. Henry.   Thy wish was rather, Harry, to that
       .   thought.
I stay too long by thee, I weary thee.
Doft thou so hunger for my empty chair,
That thou wilt needs inveft thee with my honours,
Before thy hour be ripe! O foolish youth!
Thou feek'ft the greatnefs that will o'erwhelm thee.
Stay but a little; for my cloud of dignity
Is held from falling with fo weak a wind,
That it will quickly drop; my day is dim.
Thou haft ftol'n that, which after fome few hours,
Were thine without offence; and at my death,
Thou haft feal'd up my expectation;
Thy life did manifeft, thou lov'dft me not; -
And thou wilt have me die affur'd of it.
Thou hid'ft a thoufand daggers in thy thoughts,
Which thou haft whetted on thy ftony heart,
To ftab at half an hour of my frail life.
What! canft thou not forbear me half an hour?
Then get thee gone, and dig my grave thyfelf,
And bid the merry bells ring to thy ear,
That thou art crowned, not that I am dead.
Let all the tears that fhould bedew my hearfe,
Be drops of balm to fanctify thy head;
Only compound me with forgotten duft,
Give that which gave thee life unto the worms.
Pluck down my officers, break my decrees;
For now a time is come to mock at form;
Henry the Fifth is crown'd: up, Vanity!

Down,

Down, Royal ftate! All you fage counfellors, hence!
And to the Englifh court affemble now,
From ev'ry region apes of idlenefs:
Now, neighbour confines, purge you of your fcum;
Have you a ruffian that will fwear? drink? dance?
Revel the night? rob? murder? and commit
The oldeft fins the neweft kind of ways?
Be happy, he will trouble you no more:
England fhall give him office, honour, might:
For the Fifth Harry from curb'd licence plucks
The muzzle of reftraint, and the wild dog
Shall flefh his tooth on every innocent.
O my poor kingdom, fick with civil blows!
When that my care could not with-hold thy riots,
What wilt thou do when riot is thy care?
O, thou wilt be a wildernefs again,
Peopled with wolves, thy old inhabitants.
    P. Henry.   O pardon me, my Liege! but for
        my tears,
(The moift impediments unto my fpeech)
I had foreftall'd this dear and deep rebuke,
Ere you with grief had fpoke, and I had heard
The courfe of it fo far.   There is your crown;
And he that wears the crown immortally,
Long guard it yours! If I affect it more,
Than as your honour, and as your renown,
Let me no more from this obedience rife,
Which my moft true and inward-duteous fpirit
Teacheth this proftrate and exterior bending.
Heav'n witnefs with me, when I here came in,
And found no courfe of breath within your Majefty,
How cold it ftruck my heart! If I do feign,
O let me in my prefent wildnefs die,
And never live to fhew th' incredulous world
The noble change that I have purpofed.
Coming to look on you, thinking you dead,
(And dead almoft, my Liege, to think you were)
I fpake unto the crown, as having fenfe,
And thus upbraided it. The care on thee depend-
        ing
Hath fed upon the body of my father,
                      Therefore

Therefore thou beſt of gold art worſt of gold ;
Other, leſs fine in carrat, is more precious,
Preſerving life in med'cine potable :
But thou, moſt fine, moſt honour'd, moſt renewn'd,
Haſt eat thy bearer up. Thus, royal Liege,
Accuſing it, I put it on my head,
To try with it (as with an enemy,
That had before my face murder'd my father)
The quarrel of a-true inheritor.
But if it did infeƈt my blood with joy,
Or ſwell my thoughts to any ſtrain of pride,
If any rebel or vain ſpirit of mine
Did with the leaſt affeƈtion of a welcome
Give entertainment to the might of it ;
Let Heav'n for ever keep it from my head,
And make me as the pooreſt vaſſal is,
That doth with awe and terror kneel to it !
    K. Henry. O my ſon !
Heav'n put it in thy mind to take it hence,
That thou might'ſt win the more thy father's love,
Pleading ſo wiſely in excuſe of it,
Come hither, Harry, ſit thou by my bed ;
And hear, I think, the very lateſt counſel
That ever I ſhall breathe. Heav'n knows, my ſon,
By what by-paths, and indireƈt crook'd ways
I met this crown ; and I myſelf knew well,
How troubleſome it ſat upon my head.
To thee it ſhall deſcend with better quiet,
Better opinion, better confirmation ;
For all the toil of the atchievement goes
With me into the earth. It ſeem'd in me
But as an honour ſnatch'd with boiſt'rous hand,
And I had many living to upbraid
My gain of it by their aſſiſtances ;
Which daily grew to quarrel and to bloodſhed,
Wounding ſuppoſed peace. All their bold feats,
Thou ſee'ſt, with peril I have anſwered.
For all my reign hath been but as a ſcene
Aƈting that argument : and now my death
Changes the mode ; for what in me was purchas'd,
Falls upon thee in a much fairer ſort ;
                                                    For

For thou the garland wear'ſt ſucceſſively.
Yet tho' thou ſtand'ſt more ſure than I could do,
Thou art not firm enough, ſince griefs are green ;
And all thy friends, which thou muſt make thy
            friends,
Have but their ſtings and teeth newly ta'en out ;
By whoſe fell working I was firſt advanced,
And by whoſe pow'r I well might lodge a fear,
To be again diſplac'd ; which to avoid
I cut them off, and had a purpoſe now
To lead out many to the holy land ;
Leſt reſt and lying ſtill might make them look
Too near into my ſtate. Therefore, my Harry,
Be it thy courſe to buſy giddy minds
With foreign quarrels ; that action, hence, borne
            out
May waſte the memory of former days.
More would I, but my lungs are waſted ſo,
That ſtrength of ſpeech is utterly deny'd me.
How I came to the Crown, O God, forgive !
And grant it may with thee in true peace live !
    P. Henry. My gracious Liege,
You won it, wore it, kept it, gave it me ;
Then plain and right muſt my poſſeſſion be ;
Which I with more than with a common pain,
'Gainſt all the world, will rightfully maintain.
                        Shakespear.

C H A P.   XVII.

HENRY V. to his SOLDIERS.

WHAT's he that wiſhes for more men from
            England ?
My couſin Weſtmoreland ? No, my fair couſin,
If we are mark'd to die, we are enow
To do our country loſs ; and if to live,
The fewer men, the greater ſhare of honour.
God's will ! I pray thee wiſh not one man more.
By Jove, I am not covetous of gold ;
                        Nor

Nor care I who doth feed upon my coft ;
It yearns me not if men my garments wear ;
Such outward things dwell not in my defires :
But if it be a fin to covet honour,
I am the moft offending foul alive.
No, 'faith my Lord, wifh not a man from England :
God's peace, I would not lofe fo great an honour,
As one man more, methinks, would fhare from me,
For the beft hopes I have. Don't wifh one more :
Rather proclaim it (Weftmoreland) through my hoft,
That he which hath no ftomach to this fight,
Let him depart ; his paffport fhall be made,
And crowns for convoy put into his purfe :
We would not die in that man's company,
That fears his fellowfhip to die with us.
This day is call'd the feaft of Crifpian :
He that outlives this day, and comes fafe home,
Will ftand a tip-toe when this day is nam'd,
And roufe him at the name of Crifpian :
He that outlives this day, and fees old age,
Will yearly on the vigil feaft his neighbours,
And fay, To morrow is Saint Crifpian :
Then will he ftrip his fleeves and fhew his fcars.
Old men forget : yet fhall not all forget,
But they'll remember, with advantages,
The feats they did that day. Then fhall our names,
Familiar in their mouths as houfhold-words,
Harry the King, Bedford, and Exeter,
Warwick and Talbot, Salifbury and Glo'fter,
Be in their flowing cups frefhly remember'd.
This ftory fhall the good man teach his fon ;
And Crifpin Crifpian fhall ne'er go by,
From this day to the ending of the world,
But we in it fhall be remembered ;
We few, we happy few, we band of brothers :
For he to-day that fheds his blood with me,
Shall be my brother ; be he e'er fo vile,
This day fhall gentle his condition.
And gentlemen in England, now a-bed,
Shall think themfelves accurs'd they were not here ;

And

And hold their manhoods cheap, while any speaks,
That fought with us upon St. Crispian's day.
SHAKESPEAR.

C H A P.   XVIII.

HENRY VI. AND CARDINAL BEAUFORT.

K. HENRY. HOW fares my lord? Speak, Beau-
              fort, to thy Sovereign.
    CAR. If thou be'st Death, I'll give thee Eng-
              land's treasure,
Enough to purchase such another island,
So thou wilt let me live and feel no pain.
    K. HENRY. Ah, what a sign it is of evil life,
Where death's approach is seen so terrible!
    CAR. Bring me unto my trial when you will.
Dy'd he not in his bed? Where should he die?
Can I make men live whether they will or no?
Oh! torture me no more, I will confess———
Alive again? Then shew me where he is:
I'll give a thousand pounds to look upon him———
He hath no eyes, the dust hath blinded them:
Comb down his hair; look! look! it stands up-
              right
Like lime-twigs set to catch my winged soul.
Give me some drink, and bid th' apothecary
Bring the strong poison that I bought of him.
    K. HENRY. O thou eternal Mover of the
              heav'ns,
Look with a gentle eye upon this wretch;
Oh, beat away the busy, meddling fiend,
That lays strong siege unto this wretch's soul,
And from his bosom purge this black despair.
——Peace to his soul, if God's good pleasure be!
Lord Cardinal, if thou think'st on heaven's bliss,
Hold up thy hand, make signal of thy hope.
He dies, and makes no sign? O God, forgive him.
SHAKESPEAR.
C H A P.

WOLSEY and CROMWELL.

Wol. SO farewel to the little good you bear me
      Farewel, a long farewel to all my great-
         nefs !
This is the ftate of man : To-day he puts forth
The tender leaves of hopes ; to morrow bloffoms,
And bears his blufhing honours thick upon him :
The third day comes a froft, a killing froft
And when he thinks, good eafy man, full furely
His greatnefs is a-ripening, nips his fhoot ;
And then he falls, as I do. I have ventur'd,
Like little wanton boys, that fwim on bladders,
Thefe many fummers in a fea of glory ;
But far beyond my depth ; my high-blown pride
At length broke under me ; and now has left me,
Weary and old with fervice, to the mercy
Of a rude ftream, that muft for ever hide me.
Vain pomp and glory of the world, I hate ye !
I feel my heart new open'd. Oh, how wretched
Is that poor man that hangs on-princes' favours !
There is, betwixt that fmile he would afpire to,
That fweet afpect of princes, and his ruin,
More pangs and fears than war or women have ;
And when he falls, he falls like Lucifer,
Never to hope again.
Why, how now, Cromwell ?
    Crom. I have no power to fpeak, Sir.
    Wol. What, amaz'd
At my misfortunes ? Can thy fpirit wonder
A great man fhould decline ? Nay, if you weep,
I'm fallen indeed.
    Crom. How does your Grace ?
    Wol. Why, well ;
Never fo truly happy, my good Cromwell.
I know myfelf now, and I feel within me
A peace above all earthly dignities.;

A ftill

A ftill and quiet confcience. The King has cur'd me,
I humbly thank his Grace ; and, from thefe fhoulders,
Thefe ruin'd pillars, out of pity taken
A load would fink a navy, too much honour.
O, 'tis a burden, Cromwell, 'tis a burden,
Too heavy for a man that hopes for heav'n !
    Crom. I'm glad your Grace has made that right ufe of it,
    Wol. I hope I have : I'm able now methinks,
Out of a fortitude of foul I feel,
T' endure more miferies, and greater far,
Than my weak-hearted enemies dare offer.
What news abroad ?
    Crom. The heavieft and the worft,
Is your difpleafure with the King.
    Wol. God blefs him !
    Crom. The next is, that Sir Thomas More is chofen
Lord Chancellor in your place.
    Wol. That's fomewhat fudden———
But he's a learned man. May he continue
Long in his Highnefs' favour, and do juftice
For truth's fake and his confcience ; that his bones,
When he has run his courfe, and fleeps in bleffings,
May have a tomb of orphans' tears wept on him !
What more !
    Crom. That Cranmer is return'd with wel-come ;
Inftall'd Lord Archbifhop of Canterbury.
    Wol. That's news indeed.
    Crom. Laft, that the lady Anne,
Whom the King hath in fecrefy long married,
This day was view'd in open as his Queen,
Going to chapel ; and the voice is now
Only about her coronation.
    Wol. There was the weight that pull'd me down. O Cromwell,
The king has gone beyond me ; all my glories
In that one woman I have loft for ever.

No

No fun fhall ever ufher forth my honours,
Or gild again the noble troops that waited
Upon my fmiles. Go, get thee from me, Crom-
       well;
I am a poor fall'n man, unworthy now
To be thy lord and mafter. Seek the King,
(That fun I pray may never fet) I've told him
What and how true thou art; he will advance thee;
Some little memory of me will ftir him,
(I know his noble nature) not to let
Thy hopeful fervice perifh too. Good Cromwell,
Neglect him not; make ufe now and provide
For thine own future fafety.
    Crom. O my Lord,
Muft I then leave you? Muft I needs forego
So good, fo noble, and fo true a mafter?
Bear witnefs, all that have not hearts of iron,
With what a forrow Cromwell leaves his Lord.
The King fhall have my fervice; but my prayers
For ever, and for ever, fhall be yours.
    Wol. Cromwell, I did not think to fhed a tear
In all my miferies, but thou haft forc'd me,
Out of thy honeft truth, to play the woman——
Let's dry our eyes: and thus far hear me, Crom-
       well,
And when I am forgotten, as I fhall be,
And fleep in dull cold marble, where no mention
Of me muft more be heard, fay then I taught thee:
Say, Wolfey, that once rode the waves of glory,
And founded all the depth and fhoels of honour,
Found thee a way, out of his wreck, to rife in:
A fure and fafe one, though thy mafter mifs'd it.
Mark but my fall, and that which ruin'd me:
Cromwell, I charge thee, fling away ambition;
By that fin fell the angels; how can man then
(Tho' th' image of his Maker) hope to win by't?
Love thyfelf laft; cherifh thofe hearts that wait
      thee!
Corruption wins not more than honefty.
Still in thy right hand carry gentle peace,
To filence envious tongues. Be juft, and fear not.

P

Let

Let all the ends thou aim'ſt at, be thy Country's,
Thy God's and Truth's; then if thou fall'ſt, O
      Cromwell,
Thou fall'ſt a bleſſed martyr. Serve the King——
And pr'ythee lead me in——
There take an inventory of all I have,
To the laſt penny, 'tis the King's. My robe,
And my integrity to Heav'n, is all
I dare now call mine own. O Cromwell, Cromwell,
Had I but ſerv'd my God with half the zeal
I ſerv'd my King, he would not in mine age
Have left me naked to mine enemies.
  Crom. Good Sir, have patience.
  Wol. So I have. Farewel
The hopes of court! My hopes in heaven do dwell.
Shakespear.

C H A P. XIX.

L E A R.

B L O W winds, and crack your cheeks; rage,
      blow!
You cataracts, and hurricanes, ſpout
Till you have drench'd our ſteeples, drown'd the
      cocks!
You ſulph'rous and thought-executing fires,
Singe my white head. And thou, all-ſhaking thun-
      der,
Strike flat the thick rotundity o' th' world;
Crack nature's mould, all germins ſpill at once
That make ungrateful man!
  Rumble thy belly full, ſpit fire, ſpout rain!
Nor rain, wind, thunder, fire, are my daughters,
I tax not you, you elements, with unkindneſs;
I never gave you kingdoms, call'd you children;
You owe me no ſubſcription. Then let fall
Your horrible pleaſure.——Here I ſtand your
      brave;
A poor, infirm, weak, and deſpis'd old man!
But

But yet I call you fervile miniſters,
That have with two pernicious daughters join'd
Your high-engender'd battles, 'gainſt a head
So old and white as this.   Oh! oh! 'tis foul.
   Let the great gods,
That keep this dreadful pudder o'er our heads,
Find out their enemies now.   Tremble, thou
         wretch,
That haſt within thee undivulged crimes,
Unwhipp'd of juſtice! Hide thee, thou bloody
         hand;
Thou perjure, and thou ſimular of virtue,
That art inceſtuous! caitiff, ſhake to pieces,
That, under cover of convivial ſeeming,
Haſt practis'd on man's life!——Cloſe-pent up
      guilts,
Rive your concealing continents, and aſk
Thoſe dreadful ſummoners grace!——I am a
         man,
More ſinn'd againſt, than ſinning.
                              SHAKESPEAR.

CHAP. XX.

MACBETH's SOLILOQUY.

IS this a dagger which I ſee before me,
   The handle tow'rd my hand? come, let me clutch
         thee.——
I have thee not, and yet I ſee thee ſtill.
Art thou not, fatal viſion, ſenſible
To feeling, as to ſight? or art thou but
A dagger of the mind; a falſe creation
Proceeding from the heat-oppreſſed brain?
I ſee thee yet, in form as palpable
As this which now I draw.——
Thou marſhal'ſt me the way that I was going;
And ſuch an inſtrument I was to uſe.
Mine eyes are made the fools o' th' other ſenſes,
Or elſe worth all the reſt—I ſee thee ſtill;

P 2

And

And on the blade of th' dudgeon, gouts of blood,
Which was not fo before. There's no fuch thing.—
It is the bloody bufinefs, which informs
Thus to mine eyes.—Now o'er one half the world
Nature feems dead, and wicked dreams abufe
The curtain'd fleep; now witchcraft celebrates
Pale Hecate's offerings: and wither'd Murther,
(Alarum'd by his centinel, the wolf,
Whofe howl's his watch) thus with his ftealthy pace,
With Tarquin's ravifhing ftrides, tow'rds his defign
Moves like a ghoft.——Thou found and firm-fet
      earth,
Hear not my fteps, which way they walk, for fear
The very ftones prate of my where-about;
And take the prefent horror from the time,
Which now fuits with it.—Whilft I threat, he
      lives——
Words to the heat of deeds too cold breath gives.—
I go, and it is done; the bell invites me.
Hear it not, Duncan; for it is a knell
That fummons thee to heaven, or to hell.

Shakespear.

C H A P.   XXI.

MACDUFF, MALCOLM, and ROSSE.

Macd. SEE who comes here!
    Mal. My countryman; but yet I
    know him not.
  Macd.   My ever-gentle coufin, welcome hither.
  Mal. I know him now. Good God, betimes
    remove
The means that makes us ftrangers!
  Rosse.   Sir, Amen.
  Macd.   Stands Scotland where it did?
  Rosse.   Alas, poor country,
Almoft afraid to know itfelf. It cannot
Be call'd our mother, but our grave; where
    nothing

But

But who knows nothing, is once feen to fmile;
Where fighs and groans, and fhrieks that rend the
          air,
Are made, not mark'd; where violent forrow feems
A modern ecftafy; the dead man's knell
Is there fcarce afk'd, for whom: and good mens'
    —   lives
Expire before the flowers in their caps;
Dying or e'er they ficken.
    MACD.   Oh, relation
Too nice, and yet too true!
    MAL. What's the neweft grief?
    ROSSE.   That of an hour's age doth : fs the
          fpeaker,
Each minute teems a new one.
    MACD.. How does my wife? .
    ROSSE. Why, well.——
    MACD. And all my children?
    ROSSE. Well too.——
    MACD. The tyrant has not batter'd at their
          peace?
    ROSSE. No; they were at peace when I did
          leave 'em.
    MACD. Be not a niggard of your fpeech: how
          goes it?
    ROSSE. When I came hither to tranfport the
          tidings,
Which I have heavily borne, there ran a rumour
Of many worthy fellows that were out,
Which was to my belief witnefs'd the rather,
For that I faw the tyrant's power a-foot.
Now is the time of help; your eye in Scotland
Would create foldiers, and make woman fight,
To doff their dire diftreffes.
    MAL.   Be't their comfort
We're coming thither: gracious England hath
Lent us good Siward and ten thoufand men;
An older and a better foldier, none
That Chriftendom gives out.
    ROSSE. Would I could anfwer
This comfort with the like: But I have words

That would be howl'd out in the defart air,
Where hearing fhould not catch them.
  MACD. What concern they?
The gen'ral caufe? or is it a free-grief
Due to fome fingle breaft?
  ROSSE. No mind that's honeft,
But in it fhares fome woe; though the main part
Pertains to you alone.
  MACD. If it be mine,
Keep it not from me, quickly let me have it.
  ROSSE. Let not your ears defpife my tongue for
     ever,
Which fhall poffefs them with the heavieft found,
That ever yet they heard.
  MACD. Hum! I guefs at it.
  ROSSE. Your caftle is furpris'd, your wife and
     babes
Savagely flaughter'd; to relate the manner,
Were on the quarry of thefe murther'd deer
To add the death of you.
  MAL. Merciful Heav'n!
What, man! ne'er pull your hat upon your brows,
Give forrow words; the grief that does not fpeak,
Whifpers the o'er-fraught heart, and bids it break.
  MACD. My children too!——
  ROSSE. Wife, children, fervants, all that could
     be found.
  MACD. And I muft be from thence! my wife
     kill'd too!
  ROSSE. I've faid.
  MAL. Be comforted.
Let's make us med'cines of our great revenge,
To cure this deadly grief.
  MACD. He has no children.—All my pretty ones?
Did you fay, all? what, all! oh, hell-kite! all?
  MAL. Endure it like a man.
  MACD. I fhall do fo;
But I muft alfo feel it as a man.
I cannot but remember fuch things were,
That were moft precious to me. Did Heav'n look on,
And would not take their part? finful Macduff,
They

They were all ftruck for thee! naught that I am,
Not for their own demerits, but for mine,
Fell flaughter on their fouls. Heav'n reft them now!
   Mal. Be this the whet-ftone of your fword, let grief
Convert to wrath: blunt not the heart, enrage it.
   Macd. O, I could play the woman with mine eyes,
And baggart with my tongue. But, gentle Heav'n!
Cut fhort all intermiffion: front to front,
Bring thou this fiend of Scotland and myfelf;
Within my fword's length fet him, if he 'fcape,
Then heav'n forgive him too!
   Mal. This tune goes manly.
Come, go we to the King, our pow'r is ready;
Our lack is nothing but our leave. Macbeth :
Is ripe for fhaking, and the powers above
Put on their inftruments. Receive what cheer you may;
The night is long that never finds the day.
Shakespear.

C H A P. XXII.

ANTONY's SOLILOQUY over CÆSAR's BODY.

O PARDON me, thou bleeding piece of earth!
That I am meek and gentle with thefe but-
   chers.
Thou art the ruins of the nobleft man
That ever lived in the tide of times.
Woe to the hand that fhed this coftly blood!
Over thy wounds now do I prophefy,
(Which like dumb mouths, do ope their ruby lips,
To beg the voice and utterance of my tongue,)
A curfe fhall light upon the line of men;
Domeftic fury, and fierce civil ftrife,
Shall cumber all the parts of Italy;
Blood and deftruction fhall be fo in ufe,

P 4

And

And dreadful objects fo familiar,
That mothers fhall but fmile, when they behold
Their infants quarter'd by the hands of war :
All pity chok'd with cuftom of fell deeds ; .
And Cæfar's fpirit, raging for revenge,
With Até by his fide, come hot from hell,
Shall in thefe confines, with a monarch's voice,
Cry *Havock*, and let flip the dogs of war.

SHAKESPEAR.

C H A P.   XXIII.

ANTONY's FUNERAL ORATION over CÆSAR's BODY.

FRIENDS, Romans, countrymen, lend me your
               ears.
I come to bury Cæfar, not to praife him.
The evil that men do lives after them;
The good is oft interred with their bones;
So let it be with Cæfar! Noble Brutus
Hath told you, Cæfar was ambitious;
If it were fo, it was a grievous fault;
And grievoufly hath Cæfar anfwer'd it.
Here, under leave of Brutus, and the reft,
(For Brutus is an honourable man,
So are they all, all honourable men)
Come I to fpeak in Cæfar's funeral.
He was my friend, faithful and juft to me;
But Brutus fays, he was ambitious;
And Brutus is an honourable man,
He hath brought many captives home to Rome,
Whofe ranfoms did the general coffers fill;
Did this in Cæfar feem ambitious?
When that the poor hath cry'd, Cæfar hath wept;
Ambition fhould be made of fterner ftuff.
Yet Brutus fays he was ambitious;
And Brutus is an honourable man.
You all did fee, that on the Lupercal,
I thrice prefented him a kingly crown;

Which

Which he did thrice refuse. Was this ambition?
Yet Brutus fays he was ambitious;
And, fure, he is an honourable man.
I fpeak not to difprove what Brutus fpoke,
But here I am to fpeak what I do know.
You all did love him once, not without caufe.
What caufe with-holds you then to mourn for him?
O judgment! thou art fled to brutifh beafts,
And men have loft their reafon—Bear with me.——
My heart is in the coffin there with Cæfar,
And I muft paufe till it come back to me.

If you have tears prepare to fhed them now.
You all do know this mantle; I remember,
The firft time ever Cæfar put it on,
'Twas on a fummer's evening in his tent,
That day he overcame the Nervii————
Look! in this place ran Caffius' dagger through;—
See what a rent the envious Cafca made.——
Through this the well-beloved Brutus ftabb'd:
And as he pluck'd his curfed fteel away,
Mark how the blood of Cæfar follow'd it!
As rufhing out of doors, to be refolv'd,
If Brutus fo unkindly knock'd, or no:
For Brutus, as you know, was Cæfar's angel.
Judge, oh you gods! how dearly Cæfar lov'd him;
This, this was the unkindeft cut of all;
For when the noble Cæfar faw him ftab,
Ingratitude more ftrong than traitor's arms,
Quite vanquifh'd him; then burft his mighty heart:
And, in his mantle muffling up his face,
Which all the while ran blood, great Cæfar fell,
Even at the bafe of Pompey's ftatue.
O what a fall was there, my countrymen!
Then I and you, and all of us fell down,
Whilft bloody treafon flourifh'd over us.
O, now you weep; and I perceive you feel
The dint of pity; thefe are gracious drops.
Kind fouls! what, weep you when you but behold
Our Cæfar's vefture wounded? look you here!
Here is himfelf, marr'd as you fee by traitors.——

                    Good

Good friends, sweet friends, let me not ftir you up
To any fudden flood of mutiny.
They that have done this deed are honourable;
What private griefs they have, alas, I know not,
That made them do it; they are wife and honourable;
And will, no doubt, with reafon anfwer you:
I come not, friends, to fteal away your hearts;
I am no orator, as Brutus is:
But, as you know me all, a plain blunt man,
That love my friend; and that they know full well
That give me public leave to fpeak of him :
For I have neither wit, nor words, nor worth,
Action nor utt'rance, nor the power of fpeech,
To ftir men's blood; I only fpeak right on.
I tell you that which you yourfelves do know;
Shew you fweet Cæfar's wounds, poor poor dumb
         mouths:
And bid them fpeak for me.   But were I Brutus,
And Brutus Antony, there were an Antony
Would ruffle up your fpirits, and put a tongue
In every wound of Cæfar, that fhould move
The ftones of Rome to rife and mutiny.

SHAKESPEAR.

C H A P.   XXIV.

THE QUARREL OF BRUTUS
AND CASSIUS.

Cas. THAT you have wrong'd me, doth ap-
         pear in this,
You have condemn'd and noted Lucius Pella,
For taking bribes here of the Sardians;
Wherein my letter (praying on his fide,
Becaufe I knew the man) was flighted of.
  Bru. You wrong'd yourfelf to write in fuch a
      cafe.
  Cas. In fuch a time as this, it is not meet
That ev'ry nice offence fhould bear its comment.

BRU.

Bru.   Yet let me tell you, Caffius, you yourfelf
Are much condemned to have an itching palm,
'To fell and mart your offices for gold,   .
To undefervers.

Cas.   I an itching palm?
You know, that you are Brutus that fpeak this,
Or, by the gods, this fpeech were elfe your laft.

Bru.   The name of Caffius honours this cor-
        ruption,
And chaftifement doth therefore hide its head.

Cas.   Chaftifement!——

Bru.   Remember March, the ides of March re-
        member!
Did not great Julius bleed for juftice fake?
What villain touch'd his body, that did ftab,
And not for juftice? What, fhall one of us,
That ftruck the foremoft man of all this world,
But for fupporting robbers; fhall we now
Contaminate our fingers with bafe bribes?
And fell the mighty meed of our large honours
For fo much trafh, as may be grafped thus?
I had rather be a dog, and bay the moon,
Than fuch a Roman.

Cas.   Brutus, bay not me,
I'll not endure it; you forget yourfelf,
To hedge me in; I am a foldier, I,
Older in practice, abler than yourfelf
To make conditions.

Bru.   Go to; you are not, Caffius.

Cas.   I am.

Bru.   I fay, you are not.

Cas.   Urge me no more, I fhall forget my-
        felf——
Have mind upon your health—tempt me no further.

Bru.   Away, flight man!

Cas.   Is't poffible?

Bru.   Hear me, for I will fpeak.
Muft I give way and room to your rafh choler?
Shall I be frighted when a madman ftares?

Cas.   O gods! ye gods! muft I endure all this?
                                        Bru.

.Bru.   All this? ay more.   Fret till your proud
          heart break;
And make your bondmen tremble.   Muſt I budge!
Muſt I obſerve you? muſt I ſtand and crouch
Under your teſty humour?   By the gods,
You ſhall digeſt the venom of your ſpleen,
Tho' it do ſplit you: for, from this day forth,
I'll uſe you for my mirth, yea, for my laughter,
When you are waſpiſh.
     Cas.   Is it come to this?
     Bru.   You ſay, you are a better ſoldier;
Let it appear ſo; make your vaunting true,
And it ſhall pleaſe me well.   For mine own part,
I ſhall be glad to learn of noble men.
     Cas.   You wrong me every way——you wrong
          me, Brutus;
I ſaid, an older ſoldier; not a better.
Did I ſay better?
     Bru.   I' you did, I care not.
     Cas.   When Cæſar liv'd, he durſt not thus have
          mov'd me.
     Bru.   Peace, peace you durſt not ſo have tempt-
          ed him.
     Cas.   I durſt not!
     Bru.   No.
     Cas.   What? durſt not tempt him?
     Bru.   For your life you durſt not.
     Cas.   Do not preſume too much upon my love;
I may do what I ſhall be ſorry for.
     Bru.   You have done that you ſhould be ſorry for.
There is no terror, Caſſius, in your threats;
For I am arm'd ſo ſtrong in honeſty,
That they paſs by me as the idle wind,
Which I reſpect not.   I did ſend to you
For certain ſums of gold, which you deny'd me;
For I can raiſe no money by vile means:
By heaven, I had rather coin my heart,
And drop my blood for drachmas, than to wring
From the hard hands of peaſants their vile traſh,
By any indirection.   I did ſend
To you for gold to pay my legions,

Which

Which you denied me; was that done like Caffius?
Should I have anfwer'd Caius Caffius fo?
When Marcus Brutus grows fo covetous,
To lock fuch rafcal counters from his friends,
Be ready, gods, with all your thunderbolts,
Dafh him to pieces!
    Cas.   I deny'd you not.
    Bru.   You did.
    Cas.   I did not—he was but a fool
That brought my anfwer back.—Brutus hath riv'd
        my heart.
A friend fhould bear a friend's infirmities.
But Brutus makes mine greater than they are.
    Bru.   I do not.   Still you practife them on me.
    Cas.   You love me not.
    Bru.   I do not like your faults.
    Cas.   A friendly eye could never fee fuch faults.
    Bru.   A flatt'rer's would not, tho' they do appear
As huge as high Olympus.
    Cas. Come, Antony, and young Octavius, come!
Revenge yourfelf alone on Caffius,
For Caffius is a-weary of the world;
Hated by one he loves; brav'd by his brother?
Check'd by a bondman; all his faults obferv'd,
Set in a note-book, learn'd, and conn'd by rote,
To caft into my teeth. O I could weep
My fpirit from mine eyes!—There is my dagger,
And here my naked breaft—within a heart
Dearer than Plutus' mine, richer than gold;
If that thou needft a Roman's, take it forth.
I, that deny'd thee gold, will give my heart;
Strike as thou didft at Cæfar : for I know,
When thou didft hate him worfe thou lov'dft him
        better
Than ever thou lov'dft Caffius.
    Bru.   Sheathe your dagger;
Be angry when you will, it fhall have fcope;
Do what you will, difhonour fhall be humour.
O Caffius, you are yoked with a lamb,
That carries anger, as a flint bears fire;
Who much inforced, fhews a hafty fpark,
And ftraight is cold again.
                            Cas.

C̄ᴀs. Hath Caſſius liv'd
To be but mirth and laughter to his Brutus,
When grief and blood ill-temper'd vexeth him?
  Bʀᴜ. When I ſpoke that, I was ill-temper'd too.
  Cᴀs. Do you confeſs ſo much? give me your
    hand.
  Bʀᴜ. And my heart too.
  Cᴀs. O Brutus!
  Bʀᴜ. What's the matter?
  Cᴀs. Have you not love enough to bear with me,
When that raſh humour which my mother gave me,
Makes me forgetful?
  Bʀᴜ. Yes, Caſſius, and from henceforth
When you are over earneſt with your Brutus,
He'll think your mother chides, and leave you ſo.
Sʜᴀᴋᴇsᴘᴇᴀʀ.

C H A P. XXV.

OᴛHELLO ᴀɴᴅ IAGO.

Iᴀɢᴏ. MY noble Lord,——
  Oᴛʜ. What doſt thou ſay, Iago?
  Iᴀɢᴏ. Did Michael Caſſio, when you woo'd
    my Lady,
Know of your love?
  Oᴛʜ. He did from firſt to laſt; why doſt thou
    aſk?
  Iᴀɢᴏ. But for a ſatisfaction of my thought,
No farther harm.
  Oᴛʜ. Why of thy thought, Iago?
  Iᴀɢᴏ. I did not think he'd been acquainted with it.
  Oʜ. Oh, yes, and went between us very oft.
  Iᴀɢᴏ. Indeed?
  Oᴛʜ. Indeed! ay, indeed. Diſcern'ſt thou
    aught in that?
Is he not honeſt?
  Iᴀɢᴏ. Honeſt, my Lord?
  Oᴛʜ. Honeſt? ay, honeſt.
  Iᴀɢᴏ. My Lord, for aught I know.
Oᴛʜ.

OTH. What doft thou think?

IAGO. Think, my Lord!

OTH. Think, my Lord! Why, by Heav'n, thou
         – echo'ft me ;

As if there were fome monfter in thy thought,

Too hideous to be fhewn. Thou doft mean fome-
         thing ;

I heard thee fay but now, " thou lik'dft not that,"—

When Caffio left my wife. What didft not like ?

And when I told thee, he was of my counfel,

In my whole courfe of wooing ; thou cry'dft, " In-
         deed !"

And didft contract and purfe thy brow together,

As if thou then hadft fhut up in thy brain

Some horrible conceit. If thou doft love me,

Shew me thy thought.

IAGO. My lord, you know I love you.

OTH. I think thou doft :

And for I know thou art full of love and honefty,

And weigh'ft thy words before thou giv'ft them breath,

Therefore thefe ftops of thine fright me the more :

For fuch things in a falfe difloyal knave,

Are tricks of cuftom ; but in a man that's juft,

They're cold dilations working from the heart,

That paffion cannot rule.

IAGO. For Michael Caffio,

I dare be fworn, I think, that he is honeft.

OTH. I think fo too.

IAGO. Men fhould be what they feem ;

Or, thofe that be not, 'would they might feem knaves!

OTH. Certain ! men fhould be what they feem,

IAGO. Why then I think Caffio's an honeft man.

OTH. Nay, yet there's more in this ;

I pray thee fpeak to me as to thy thinkings,

As thou doft ruminate; and give thy worft of thoughts

The worft of words.

IAGO. Good my Lord, pardon me,

Though I am bound to every act of duty,

I am not bound to that all flaves are free to ;

Utter my thoughts !—Why, fay, they're vile and
         falfe ;

As

As where's that palace, whereinto foul things
Sometimes intrude not ? Who has a breaft fo pure,
But fome uncleanly apprehenfions
Keep leets and law-days, and in feffions fit
With meditations lawful ?

OTH. Thou doft confpire againft thy friend, Iago,
If thou but think'ft him wrong'd, and mak'ft his ear
A ftranger to thy thoughts.

IAGO. I do befeech you,
Think I, perchance, am vicious in my guefs,
(As, I confefs, it is my nature's plague
To 'fpy into abufe ; and oft my jealoufy
Shapes faults that are not) I intreat you then,
From one that fo imperfectly conjects,
Your wifdom would not build yourfelf a trouble
Out of my fcattering and unfure obfervance :
It were not for your quiet, nor your good,
Nor for my manhood, honefty, and wifdom,
To let you know my thoughts.

OTH. What doft thou mean ?

IAGO. Good name in man and woman, dear my
    Lord,
Is the immediate jewel of their fouls.
Who fteals my purfe, fteals trafh ; 'tis fomething,
   nothing ;
'Twas mine, 'tis his ; and has been flave to thoufands:
But he that filches from me my good name,
Robs me of that which not enriches him,
And makes me poor indeed.

OTH, I'll know thy thoughts——

IAGO. You cannot, if my heart were in your
    hand ;
Nor fhall not whilft 'tis in my cuftody,

OTH. Ha !

IAGO. Oh, beware,, my Lord, of jealoufy ;
It is a green-ey'd monfter, which doth mock
The meat it feeds on. That cuckold lives in blifs,
Who, certain of his fate, loves not his wronger ;
But, oh, what damned minutes tells he o'er,
Who doats, yet doubts ; fufpects, yet ftrongly loves!

OTH. O mifery !

IAGO.

Iago. Poor and content, is rich and rich enough;
But riches endlefs, is as poor as winter, .
To him that ever fears he fhall be poor.
Good Heaven ! the fouls of all my tribe defend
From jealoufy !
 Oth. Why ? why is this ?
Think'ft thou I'd make a life of jealoufy ?
To follow ftill the changes of the moon
With frefh fufpicions ?—Tis not to make me jealous
To fay, my wife is fair, feeds well, loves company,
Is free of fpeech, fings, plays, and dances well ;
Where virtue is, thefe make more virtuous.
Nor from mine own weak merits will I draw
The fmalleft fear, or doubt of her revolt,
For fhe had eyes, and chofe me. No, Iago,
I'll fee, before I doubt ; when I doubt, prove ;
And, on the proof, there is no more but this,
Away at once with love or jealoufy.
 Iago. I'm glad of this; for now I fhall have reafon
To fhew the love and duty that I bear you
With franker fpirit. Therefore as I'm bound,
Receive it from me. I fpeak not yet of proof,
Look to your wife, obferve her well with Caffio;
Wear your eye, thus ; not jealous, nor fecure ;
I would not have your free and noble nature
Out of felf-bounty be abus'd ; look to't,
I know our country-difpofition well ;
In Venice they do let Heav'n fee the pranks
They dare not fhew their hufbands.
 Oth. Doft thou fay fo ?
 Iago. She did deceive her father, marrying you ;
And when fhe feem'd to fhake, and fear your looks,
She lov'd them moft.
 Oth. And fo fhe did.
 Iago. Go to then ;
She, that, fo young, could give out fuch a feeming
To feal her father's eyes up, clofe as oak——
He thought it witchcraft—but I'm much to blame :
I humbly do befeech you of your pardon,
For too much loving you.
 Oth. I am bound to you for ever.
Iago.

Iago. I fee this hath a little dafh'd your fpirits.

Oth. Not a jot, not a jot,

Iago. Truft me, I fear it has ,
I hope you will confider, what is fpoke
Comes from my love. But I do fee you're mov'd——
I am to pray you, not to ftrain my fpeech
To groffer iffues, nor to larger reach,
Than to fufpicion.

Oth. I will not.

Iago. Should you do fo, my Lord,
My fpeech would fall into fuch vile fuccefs,
Which my thoughts aim not at. Caffio's my worthy
    friend.
My Lord, I fee you're mov'd————

Oth. No, not much mov'd————
I do not think but Defdemona's honeft.

Iago. Long live fhe fo! and long live you to
    think fo!

Oth. And yet, how nature erring from itfelf—

Iago. Ay, there's the point ;—as (to be bold with
    you)
Not to affect many propofed matches
Of her own clime, complexion, and degree ;
Whereto we fee in all things nature tends :
Foh! one may fmell, in fuch, a will moft rank,
Foul difproportions, thoughts unnatural.
But, pardon me, I do not in pofition
Diftinctly fpeak of her ; tho' I may fear,
Her will, recoiling to her better judgment,
May fall to match you with her country-forms,
And, haply, fo repent.

Oth. Farewel, farewel ;
If more thou doft perceive, let me know more :
Set on thy wife t'obferve. Leave me, Iago.

Iago. My Lord, I take my leave.

Oth. Why did I marry ?
This honeft creature, doubtlefs,
Sees and knows more, much more, than he unfolds.

Iago. My Lord, I would I might intreat your
    honour
To fcan this thing no further ; leave it to time :
                                        Altho'

Altho' 'tis fit that Caffio have his place,
For, fure, he fills it up with great ability ;
Yet if you pleafe to hold him off a while,
You fhall by that perceive him and his means ;
Note, if your Lady ftrain his entertainment
With any ftrong or vehement importunity ;
Much will be feen in that.   In the mean time,
Let me be thought too bufy in my fears,
(As worthy caufe I have to fear I am)
And hold her free, I do befeech your Honour.
   Oth.   Fear not my government.
   Iago.   I once more take my leave.
Shakespear.

C H A P.   XXVI.

HAMLET's SOLILOQUY on his MOTHER's MARRIAGE.

OH that this too too folid flefh would melt,
   Thaw, and refolve itfelf into a dew !
Or that the Everlafting had not fix'd
His canon 'gainft felf-flaughter !
How weary, ftale, flat, and unprofitable,
Seem to me all the ufes of this world !
Fie on't ! oh fie ! 'tis an unweeded garden,
That grows to feed; things rank, and grofs in nature,
Poffefs it merely. That it fhould come to this !
But two months dead ! nay, not fo much; not two:——
So excellent a king, that was, to this !
Hyperion to a fatyr : fo loving to my mother,
That he permitted not the winds of heav'n
Vifit her face too roughly.   Heaven and earth !
Muft I remember——why, fhe would hang on him,
As if increafe of appetite had grown
By what it fed on ; yet, yet within a month,——
Let me not think——Frailty, thy name is Woman !
A little month ! or ere thofe fhoes were old,
With which fhe follow'd my poor father's body,
Like Niobe, all tears——Why, fhe, ev'n fhe——
(O heav'n !

(O heav'n ! a beaft that wants difcourfe of reafon,
Would have mourn'd longer———)married with mine
          uncle,
My father's brother ; but no more like my father,
Than I to Hercules. Within a month !———
Ere yet the falt of moft unrighteous tears
Had left the flufhing in her gauled eyes,
She married———Oh, moft wicked fpeed, to poft
With fuch dexterity to inceftuous fheets !
It is not, nor it cannot come to good.
But break, my heart, for I muft hold my tongue.

SHAKESPEAR.

C H A P. XXVII,

HAMLET AND GHOST.

HAM. **A**NGELS and minifters of grace defend us!
          Be thou a fpirit of health, or goblin
          damn'd,
Bring with thee airs from heav'n, or blafts from hell,
Be thy intent wicked or charitable,
Thou com'ft in fuch a queftionable fhape,
That I will fpeak to thee. I'll call thee Hamlet,
King, father, Royal Dane : oh ! anfwer me ;
Let me not burft in ignorance ; but tell,
Why thy canoniz'd bones, hearfed in earth,
Have burft their cearments ? why the fepulchre,
Wherein we faw thee quietly inurn'd,
Hath op'd his ponderous and marble jaws,
To caft thee up again ? What may this mean ?
That thou, dead corfe, again in compleat fteel,
Revifit'ft thus the glimpfes of the moon,
Making night hideous, and us fools of nature
So horridly to fhake our difpofition
With thoughts beyond the reaches of our fouls ?
Say, why is this ? wherefore ? what fhould we do ?
  GHOST. Mark me.
  HAM. I will.

GHOST.

Ghost. My hour is almoft come,
When I to fulphurous and tormenting flames
Muft render up myfelf.

    Ham. Alas, poor ghoft!

    Ghost. Pity me not, but lend thy ferious hearing
To what I fhall unfold.

    Ham. Speak, I am bound to hear.

    Ghost. So art thou to revenge, when thou fhalt
        hear.

    Ham. What?

    Ghost. I am thy father's fpirit;
Doom'd for a certain term to walk the night,
And for the day, confin'd to faft in fire;
Till the foul crimes done in my days of nature,
Are burnt and purg'd away. But that I am forbid
To tell the fecrets of my prifon houfe
I could a tale unfold, whofe lighteft word
Would harrow up thy foul, freeze thy young blood,
Make thy two eyes, like ftars, ftart from their
        fpheres,
Thy knotty and combined locks to part,
And each particular hair to ftand an end
Like quills upon the fretful porcupine;
But this eternal blazon muft not be
To ears of flefh and blood; lift; oh lift!
If thou did'ft ever thy dear father love———

    Ham. O heav'n!

    Ghost. Revenge his foul and moft unnatural
        murther.

    Ham. Murther?

    Ghost. Murther moft foul, as in the beft it is;
But this moft foul, ftrange and unnatural.

    Ham. Hafte me to know it, that I, with wings
        as fwift
As meditation or the thoughts of love,
May fly to my revenge:

    Ghost. I find thee apt;
And duller fhouldft thou be, than the fat weed
That roots itfelf in eafe on Lethe's wharf,
Wouldft thou not ftir in this. Now, Hamlet, hear:
'Tis given out, that, fleeping in my orchard,
A ferpent

'A ferpent ftung me. So the whole ear of Denmark
Is by a forged procefs of my death
Rankly abus'd : but know, thou noble youth,
The ferpent that did fting thy father's life,
Now wears his crown.

    Ham. Oh, my prophetic foul ! my uncle !

    Ghost. Ay, that inceftuous, that adulterate
        beaft,
With witchcraft of his wit, with trait'rous gifts,
(O wicked wit, and gifts, that have the power
So to feduce !) won to his fhameful luft
The will of my moft feeming-virtuous Queen.
Oh Hamlet, what a falling off was there !
But foft ! methinks I fcent the morning air————
Brief let me be : Sleeping within mine orchard,
My cuftom always of the afternoon,
Upon my fecure hour thy uncle ftole
With juice of curfed hebenon in a phial,
And in the porches of mine ear did pour
The leperous diftilment.
Thus was I, fleeping, by a brother's hand,
Of life, of crown, of Queen, at once bereft ;
Cut off even in the bloffoms of my fin ;
No reck'ning made ! but fent to my account
With all my imperfections on my head !

    Ham. Oh horrible ! oh horrible ! moft horrible !

    Ghost. If thou haft nature in thee, bear it not ;
But howfoever thou purfu'ft this act,
Taint not thy mind, nor let thy foul contrive
Againft thy mother aught ; leave her to heav'n,
And to thofe thorns that in her bofom lodge,
To prick and fting her. Fare thee well at once !
The glow worm fhews the matin to be near,
And 'gins to pale his uneffectual fire.
Adieu, adieu, adieu : remember me.

    Ham. Oh, all you hoft of heav'n ! oh earth !
        what elfe ?
And fhall I couple hell ? oh fie ! hold, my heart ?
And you, my finews, grow not inftant old ;
But bear me ftiffly up. Remember thee !
Ay, thou poor ghoft, while memory holds a feat

In

In this diſtracted globe ; remember thee !
Yea, from the table of my memory
I'll wipe away all trivial fond records,
All ſaws of books, all forms, all preſſures paſt,
That youth and obſervation copied there ;
And thy commandment all alone ſhall live
Within the book and volume of my brain,
Unmix'd with baſer matter.

SHAKESPEAR.

C H A P.   XXVIII.

HAMLET's SOLILOQUY ON DEATH.

TO be, or not to be ?—that is the queſtion.—
   Whether it is nobler in the mind to ſuffer
The ſlings and arrows of outrageous fortune ;
Or to take up arms againſt a ſea of troubles,
And by oppoſing end them ?—To die,—to ſleep—
No more ; and by a ſleep, to ſay, we end
The heart ache, and a thouſand natural ſhocks
That fleſh is heir to ;—'tis a confummation
Devoutly to be wiſh'd. To die—to ſleep—
To ſleep ? perchance to dream ; —— ay, there's the
    rub.
For in that ſleep of death what dreams may come,
When we have ſhuffled off this mortal coil,
Muſt give us pauſe.—There's the reſpect
 That makes calamity of ſo long life :
For who would bear the whips and ſcorns of th' time,
Th' oppreſſor's wrong, the proud man's contumely,
The pang of deſpis'd love, the law's delay,
The inſolence of office, and the ſpurns
That patient merit of th' unworthy takes ;
When he himſelf might his *quietus* make
With a bare-bodkin ? Who would fardels bear,
To groan and ſweat under a weary life ;
But that the dread of ſomething after death
(That undiſcover'd country, from whoſe bourne
No traveller returns) puzzles the will ;

And

And makes us rather bear thofe ills we have,
Than fly to others that we know not of ?
Thus confcience does make cowards of us all :
And thus the native hue of refolution
Is ficklied o'er with the pale caft of thought ;
And enterprifes of great pith and moment,
With this regard their currents turn awry,
And lofe the name of action.

SHAKESPEAR.

C H A P.   XXIX.

SOLILOQUY of the KING in HAMLET.

OH ! my offence is rank, it fmells to heav'n,
It hath the primal, eldeft curfe upon't ;
A brother's murder—Pray I cannot :
Though inclination be as fharp as 'twill,
My ftronger guilt defeats my ftrong intent ;
And, like a man to double bufinefs bound,
I ftand in paufe where I fhall firft begin,
And both negleft.   What if this curfed hand
Were thicker than itfelf with brother's blood ?
Is there not rain enough in the fweet heav'ns
To wafh it white as fnow ? whereto ferves mercy,
But to cohfront the vifage of offence ?
And what's in prayer, but this twofold force,
To be foreftalled ere we come to fall,
Or pardon'd being down ?—Then I'll look up ;
My fault is paft.—But oh, what form of prayer
Can ferve my turn ? Forgive me my foul murder!—
That cannot be, fince I am ftill poffefs'd
Of thofe effects for which I did the murder,
My crown, mine own ambition, and my Queen.
May one be pardon'd and retain th' offence ?
In the corrupted currents of this world,
Offence's gilded hand may fhove by juftice ;
And oft 'tis feen, the wicked prize itfelf
Buys out the laws. But 'tis not fo above.
There is no fhuffling ; there the action lies

In

In his true nature, and we ourselves compell'd,
Ev'n to the teeth and forehead of our faults,
To give in evidence.   What then ? what rests ?
Try what repentance can ; what can it not ?
Yet what can it, when one cannot repent ?
Oh wretched state ! oh bosom black as death !
Oh limed soul, that, struggling to be free,
Art more engag'd ! Help, angels ! make assay !
Bow, stubborn knees ; and, heart, with strings of
 steel,
Be soft as sinews of the new-born babe!
All may be well.

Shakespear.

C H A P.   XXX.

ODE on St. CECILIA's DAY.

DESCEND, ye Nine ! descend and sing ;
 The breathing instruments inspire,
Wake into voice each silent string,
And sweep the founding lyre !
 In a sadly-pleasing strain
 Let the warbling lute complain :
  Let the loud trumpets sound,
  'Till the roofs all around
  The shrill echoes rebound.

While in more lengthen'd notes and slow,
The deep, majestic, solemn organs blow.
 Hark ! the numbers soft and clear,
 Gently steal upon the ear ;
 Now louder, and yet louder rise,
 And fill with spreading sounds the skies ;
Exulting in triumph now swell the bold notes,
In broken air, trembling, the wild music floats ;
 'Till, by degrees, remote and small,
  The strains decay,
  And melt away,
 In a dying, dying fall.

Q
By

By Mufic, minds an equal temper know,
    Nor fwell too high, nor fink too low.
If in the breaft tumultuous joys arife,
Mufic her foft, affuafive voice applies ;
    Or, when the foul is prefs'd with cares,
    Exalts her in enlivening airs.
Warriors fhe fires with animated founds ;
Pours balm into the bleeding lovers wounds:
    Melancholy lifts her head,
    Morpheus rouzes from his bed,
    Sloth unfolds her arms and wakes,
    Lift'ning Envy drops her fnakes ;
Inteftine war no more our Paffions wage,
And giddy Factions hear away their rage.

But when our country's caufe provokes to Arms,
How martial mufic every bofom warms !
So when the firft bold veffel dar'd the feas,
High on the ftern the Thracian rais'd his ftrain,
    While Argo faw her kindred trees
    Defcend from Pelion to the main.
    Tranfported demi-gods ftood round,
And men grew heroes at the found,
    Enflam'd with glory's charms ;
Each chief his fev'nfold fhield difplay'd,
And half unfheath'd the fhining blade ;
And feas, and rocks, and fkies rebound
To arms, to arms, to arms !

But when thro' all th' infernal bounds,
Which flaming Phlegeton, furrounds,
    Love, ftrong as Death, the Poet led
    To the pale nations of the dead,
What founds were heard,
What fcenes appear'd,
    O'er all the dreary coafts !
    Dreadful gleams,
    Difmal fcreams,
    Fires that glow,
    Shrieks of woe,

Sullen

   Sullen moans,
   Hollow groans,
  And cries of tortur'd ghofts !
But hark ! he ftrikes the golden lyre ;
And fee ! the tortur'd ghofts refpire,
   See, fhady forms advance !
  Thy ftone, O Syfiphus, ftands ftill,
 Ixion refts upon his wheel,
   And the pale fpectres dance !
The furies fink upon their iron beds,
And fnakes uncurl'd hang lift'ning round their heads.

  By the ftreams that ever flow,
  By the fragrant winds that blow
   O'er th' Elyfian flow'rs ;
  By thofe happy fouls who dwell
  In yellow meads of Afphodel,
   Or Amaranthine bow'rs ;
  By the hero's armed fhades,
  Glitt'ring thro' the gloomy glades ;
  By the youths that dy'd for love,
  Wand'ring in the myrtle grove,
Reftore, reftore Eurydice to life :
Oh take the hufband, or return the wife !
 He fung, and hell confented
  To hear the Poet's prayer :
 Stern Proferpine relented,
  And gave him back the fair.
   Thus fong could prevail
   O'er death, and o'er hell,
A conqueft how hard, and how glorious !
  Tho' fate had faft bound her
  With Styx nine times round her,
Yet mufic and love were victorious.

But foon, too foon, the lover turns his eyes :
Again fhe falls, again fhe dies, fhe dies!
How wilt thou now the fatal fifters move ?
No crime was thine, if 'tis no crime to love.
 Now under hanging mountains,
 Befide the falls of fountains,
    Q 2   Or

Or where Hebrus wanders,
Rolling in mæanders,
   All alone,
   Unheard, unknown,
   He makes his moan;
   And calls her ghoſt,
For ever, ever, ever loſt!
Now with furies ſurrounded,
Deſpairing, confounded,
He trembles, he glows,
Amidſt Rhodope's ſnows;
See, wild as the winds, o'er the deſart he flies;
Hark! Hæmus reſounds with the Bacchanals cries—
             Ah ſee, he dies!
Yet ev'n in death Eurydice he ſung,
Eurydice ſtill trembled on his tongue,
   Eurydice the woods,
   Eurydice the floods,
Eurydice the rocks, and hollow mountains rung.

   Muſic the fierceſt grief can charm,
   And fate's ſevereſt rage diſarm:
   Muſic can ſoften pain to eaſe,
   And make deſpair and madneſs pleaſe:
   Our joys below it can improve,
   And antedate the bliſs above.
This the divine Cecilia found,
And to her Maker's praiſe confin'd the ſound.
When the full organ joins the tuneful quire,
  Th' immortal pow'rs incline their ear:
Borne on the ſwelling notes our ſouls aſpire,
While ſolemn airs improve the ſacred fire;
  And Angels lean from heav'n to hear.
Of Orpheus now no more let poets tell,
'To bright Cecilia greater power is giv'n;
  His numbers rais'd a ſhade from hell,
   Hers lift the ſoul to heav'n.

POPE.

CHAP.

CHAP. XXXI.

ALEXANDER's FEAST.

'TWAS at the royal feaſt, for Perſia won,
    By Philip's warlike ſon:
  Aloft in awful ſtate
  The god-like hero ſate
    On his imperial throne:
    His valiant peers were plac'd around;
Their brows with roſes and with myrtle bound:
    So ſhould deſert in arms be crown'd.
The lovely Thais by his ſide
Sat, like a blooming eaſtern bride,
In flow'r of youth and beauty's pride.
    Happy, happy, happy pair!
    None but the brave,
    None but the brave deſerve the fair.

Timotheus plac'd on high
    Amid the tuneful quire,
    With flying fingers touch'd the lyre:
    The trembling notes aſcend the ſky,
        And heavenly joys inſpire.
The ſong began from Jove;
Who left his bliſsful ſeats above,
Such is the pow'r of mighty love!
A dragon's fiery form bely'd the God:
Sublime on radiant ſpheres he rode,
    When he the fair Olympia preſs'd,
    And while he ſought her ſnowy breaſt:
Then, round her ſlender waiſt he curl'd,
And ſtamp'd an image of himſelf, a ſov'reign of the
    world.—
  The liſtning crowd admire the lofty ſound;
A preſent deity, they ſhout around:
A preſent deity, the vaulted roofs rebound:
    With raviſh'd ears
    The monarch hears,

                      Aſſumes

Assumes the god,
Affects to nod,
And seems to shake the spheres.

The praise of Bacchus then, the sweet musician
            sung;
Of Bacchus ever fair, and ever young:
The jolly god in triumph comes;
Sound the trumpets, beat the drums;
Flush'd with a purple grace
He shews his honest face.
Now give the hautboys breath; he comes, he comes!
Bacchus, ever fair and young,
Drinking joys did first ordain:
Bacchus' blessings are a treasure,
Drinking is the soldiers' pleasure;
Rich the treasure,
Sweet the pleasure;
Sweet is pleasure after pain.

Sooth'd with the sound the king grew vain;
Fought all his battles o'er again;
And thrice he routed all his foes; and thrice he slew
            the slain.—
The master saw the madness rise;
His glowing cheeks, his ardent eyes;
And while he heav'n and earth defy'd,
Chang'd his hand and check'd his pride.
He chose a mournful muse
Soft pity to infuse:
He sung Darius great and good,
By too severe a fate,
Fall'n, fall'n, fall'n, fall'n,
Fall'n from his high estate,
And weltring in his blood:
Deserted at his utmost need,
By those his former bounty fed,
On the bare earth expos'd he lies,
With not a friend to close his eyes.
With down-cast look the joyless victor sate,
Revolving in his alter'd soul

The various turns of fate below;
And now and then a figh he ftole;
And tears began to flow.
The mighty mafter fmil'd, to fee
That love was in the next degree:
'Twas but a kindred found to move;
For pity melts the mind to love.
Softly fweet in Lydian meafures,
Soon he footh'd his foul to pleafures.
War he fung is toil and trouble;
Honour but an empty bubble;
    Never ending, ftill beginning,
Fighting ftill, and ftill deftroying:
    If the world be worth thy winning,
Think; O, think it worth enjoying!
    Lovely Thais fits befide thee,
    Take the good the gods provide thee.—
The many rend the fkies with loud applaufe;
So love was crown'd, but mufic won the caufe.
The prince, unable to conceal his pain,
    Gaz'd on the fair
    Who caus'd his care,
And figh'd and look'd, figh'd and look'd,
Sigh'd and look'd, and figh'd again:
At length, with love and wine at once opprefs'd,
The vanquifh'd victor funk upon her breaft.

Now ftrike the golden lyre again;
A louder yet, and yet, a louder ftrain.
Break his bands of fleep afunder,
And roufe him like a rattling peal of thunder.
    Haik, hark, the horrid found
    Has rais'd up his head;
    As awak'd from the dead,
And amaz'd, he ftares around.
Revenge, revenge, Timotheus cries,
    See the Furies arife,
    See the fnakes that they rear,
    How they hifs in their hair,
And the fparkles that flafh from their eyes!
                                        Behold

Behold a ghaſtly band,
Each a torch in his hand !
Theſe are Grecian ghoſts, that in battle were ſlain,
    And unbury'd remain
    Inglorious on the plain :
    Give the vengeance due
    To the valiant crew :
Behold how they toſs their torches on high,
    How they point to the Perſian abodes,
And glitt'ring temples of their hoſtile gods !—
    The Princes applaud, with a furious joy;
And the King ſeiz'd a flambeau, with zeal to deſtroy;
    Thais led the way,
    To light him to his prey,
And, like another Helen, fir'd another Troy.

    Thus, long ago
    Ere heaving bellows learn'd to blow,
    While organs yet were mute;
    Timotheus to his breathing flute
    And ſounding lyre,
Could ſwell the ſoul to rage, or kindle ſoft deſire.
    At laſt divine Cecilia came,
    Inventreſs of the vocal frame;
The ſweet enthuſiaſt, from her ſacred ſtore,
    Enlarg'd the former narrow bounds,
    And added length to ſolemn ſounds,
With nature's mother-wit, and arts unknown before
    Let old Timotheus yield the prize,
    Or both divide the crown;
    He rais'd a mortal to the ſkies;
    She drew an angel down.

                    DRYDEN.